IN THE SHADOW OF THE GATHERING STORM

ERL WILKIE

No part of this publication may be reproduced in a retrieval system, or transmitted, in any form or by any means, without the prior permission in writing of the author.

First published 2017
Cartvalepress * Fiction
cartvalepress@btconnect.com
ISBN 978-0-9576590-4-9

ALSO BY ERL WILKIE:

Fiction
Overture

Non-Fiction
Glasgow's Pathways
Walking the Central Scottish Way
25 Cycle Routes in and around Glasgow
25 Cycle Routes – Stirling and the Trossachs
25 Cycle Routes – The Kingdom of Fife
25 Cycle Routes – Argyll and Bute

This book is dedicated to my three wonderful girls
Anne, Kirsten and Maisy.

ABOUT THE AUTHOR

 Erl Wilkie was born and brought up in Glasgow. During a career in Civil Engineering, he worked in Canada, South Africa, the Middle East and Ecuador, as well as Scotland. In the nineties he began writing a series of books about walking and cycling but in the last few years, has turned to fiction with the gripping, political thriller, Overture.

In the shadow of the gathering storm is his second novel. He now divides his time between Glasgow and a small village in the Vienne in Central France.

This book is a work of fiction set in the turbulent period at the end of the First World War and the story is embedded within four great historical events.

- The German Revolution of 1918 – 21.
- The internment and scuttling of the German Fleet at Scapa Flow, in 1918 –19.
- The Battle of George Square in January 1919 (Part of Red Clydeside).
- The Irish Declaration of Independence also in January 1919 and the struggle that followed it.

When these events occurred, the people listed at the end of the book were involved. However, any interaction between them and the characters contained within the story is purely fictitious.

For a greater understanding of the events which took place when the ringleaders of the mutiny at Schillig Roads were languishing in the Naval Guard House in Kiel, you can go to the author's website www.erlwilkie.com where you can read an account of this and the circumstances that motivated the armed forces and the German people to take power away from the ruling dynasty.

This website also contains other historical snapshots of events contained in this book.

PROLOGUE

Glasgow, August 1914

It was the first Sunday after war had been declared between Britain and Germany. Had an observer given the two, young men standing outside the Grand Hotel more than a cursory glance, they may have thought they looked odd together.

Gerry O'Brien, as his name suggested, was of Irish lineage and had come to Glasgow in 1911 from the Mull of Galloway to find work. He was short and thickset and wore a tweed jacket, a shirt with no collar and a kerchief around his neck. A Kilmarnock bonnet covered a head of auburn hair and the sweat was running freely from his brow. The second man, Charlie Tennant, a third generation Glaswegian from Govanhill, was at least a foot taller, thin with fine features and dapperly dressed in a dark suit, white shirt, starched collar and tie and a bowler hat which covered mousy blond hair. They were platers in Fairfield's shipyard in Govan, working on new ships for the Royal Navy.

The two were so engrossed in conversation that they didn't notice a Black Maria draw up on the other side of Sauchiehall Street. Six policemen spilled out onto the pavement and walked towards them. It was only when this high barrier of helmeted navy blue completely encircled them, that they realised the drink they had anticipated was unlikely to be forthcoming.

They were taken to the van quietly so as not to disturb the peace of a Scottish Sunday and made to sit on benches accompanied by four of the policemen. And outside the door was slammed shut.

Dublin, April 1916

"For God's sake run for your lives, girls. The bastards have seen us."

The four women had just emerged from a small, side door of the GPO onto Henry Street, having delivered eight, heavy boxes of ammunition to Pearse and Connolly's garrison inside. They could see three armed British soldiers two blocks away, running across Sackville Street towards them and they took to their heels, running past the rubble caused by the incessant shelling of the buildings occupied by the rebel forces. Reaching Moore Street, the girls separated and Kate A'Herne and Sally Traynor continued along Moore Street. As they ran, they could hear the sound of rifle fire behind them. A'Herne was suddenly thrust into a doorway by Traynor, who started pounding on the door which was quickly opened. Traynor pushed A'Herne inside and followed. As the man closed the door behind them, he put a finger to his lips. Within thirty seconds they could hear the sound of army boots clattering down the cobbled street as a soldier ran past the door.

Without a word, the two women were taken down to the basement and shown into a small, dark room. The man pointed down the hall to a door at the end. "Right, Sally, when you think it's safe, that door leads out to the yard and the lane beyond. I don't want you here long. You should never have come. If that soldier had seen you, we would have been in real trouble," he said angrily before he abruptly closed the door behind them.

The room was dusty and smelt overwhelmingly of damp and mothballs. It was sparsely furnished with old and broken furniture and there were piles of old newspapers dumped in one corner.

A'Herne was still breathless from the chase. She sat down on an old chaise longue, its springs protruding from the worn and torn fabric. "Bejesus, that was feckin' close. I thought our goose was well and truly cooked this time. I wonder if the other two got away. Did you hear? They were firing at them. It's just as well you knew about this place. What is it anyway, Sally?"

"It's a safe house."

"That fellah wasn't exactly friendly, was he?"

"The less anyone knows about this place or the people inside, the less likely the Brits are to get wind of its existence. We'll stay here for about half an hour and by that time it should be dark enough to leave."

"Me brother Liam says things aren't going well."

"He's right. That's the first time since the Rising began that the British could access these streets. We probably wasted our time delivering that ammo."

"Liam says James Connelly's been shot in the thigh and Pearse is thinkin' about surrenderin' tomorrow."

Traynor nodded. "I heard they've brought Connelly here for medical attention, so it's little wonder they weren't happy about us turnin' up with the army on our heels. I just did it in the spur of the moment."

"Just as well you did. That soldier wasn't far behind us," Kate said with a nod, before continuing, "Liam says I should get out of Ireland for a while. He's given me money to get the ferry to Glasgow, although he's going to stick it out till the end. Oh God, I hope he doesn't get shot."

"Do you have family in Glasgow?"

"No, but he says I stand the best chance of getting a job there. There's work for seamstresses and a lot more support for our cause than in English cities." After half an hour, the women emerged separately from the safe house and melted into the night.

Two days later, the young Kate A'Herne, originally from County Offaly, walked down the gangway of the steamer from Dublin onto the quay in Glasgow, carrying a small, brown suitcase that contained all her worldly possessions.

Kiel, June 1916

The Light Cruiser, München, had been badly damaged at the battle of Jutland and had taken several days to limp back to Kiel where it would undergo major repairs at the Germania Naval Dockyard. When it docked, the dead and wounded were taken off and the ship's crew were marched away to the naval barracks at the Wik destroyer base. On the stipulation that they remain billeted at the barracks, they were given leave until they were transferred to other ships of the High Seas Fleet.

As they marched, Johann Schettler, a fresh faced, young Unteroffizier noticed groups of people standing around silently watching the sailors as they passed by. They were mostly women and children and were poorly dressed, thin and emaciated. Some were begging.

Aboard ship, conditions were tolerable, but the sailors had heard the British naval blockade, stopping food and supplies getting to German ports, was biting hard. Now Schettler could see the proof with his own eyes and it shocked him. Jutland was supposed to alleviate this, but the battle had ended in stalemate and the blockade would continue.

When they arrived at the barracks, they were met by disgruntled sailors who told them that the conditions were becoming intolerable and the food being served up to them was disgusting, compared to the officers who seemed to live in the lap of luxury.

When Schettler and six of his compatriots went to the dining hall that evening, they experienced this for themselves. They were served with tiny portions of food not fit for pigs. Schettler was so incensed that he threw the contents of his plate back at the catering orderly and shouted at the top of his voice, "We've just returned from fighting the British at Jutland and you expect us to eat this shit? Surely, if we're giving our lives for the Kaiser, we have a right to expect him to feed us properly." His comment was met by cheers.

When the cheering stopped, another voice boomed out. "Our comrades from the München have just seen what we have to contend with day in and day out and they sound like they're not going to accept it." There, framed in the door, was a stocky sailor with a large brown moustache. "Take my advice and strike for better food and conditions. Let's join with civilian workers whose families are starving and refuse to fight this bloody war to preserve the Kaiser and his ruling class. They're not only having our men killed in battle but their families here at home are dying through malnutrition, while the rich want for nothing."

As he finished, two armed marines appeared and tried to detain him. He was having none of it and a struggle began. Schettler was surprised when no one in the room went to his aid. After a few seconds he ran forward, shouting, "Come on, boys from the München, we can't let this man be arrested for speaking the truth." He and his comrades set upon the guards. It only took a few seconds for the man to be released from their grasp and soon they were running out of the building.

"I suppose we've just caused a major incident here on our first night ashore," Schettler said to the sailor, once they were outside.

But the sailor shook his head. "No, the marines feel as we do. If they had arrested me, they would have released me after half-an-hour. They only go through the motions to satisfy orders. It happens almost every week with either me or some other militant around here."

Schettler extended his hand to introduce himself. "We're just off the Cruiser München, but of course you already know that. We're on leave and on our way to town. Why don't you join us? If you can, that is?"

"I'd be delighted to join you. My name is Karl Artelt."

"Are you an engineer?" Schettler said, having noticed the flash on his tunic.

"I'm a pump specialist. There aren't many of us, so I've been assigned to the Germania shipyard to work with the civilians. That's how I knew you were off the München. After work, I have a pass to more or less come and go as I please."

The others were hell bent on getting very drunk and headed off for a tour of the bars. This left Schettler and Artelt to find somewhere which could supply some decent food.

Both men were confirmed socialists so they talked well into the night. At the end of it, Schettler knew he had made a long-lasting friend.

A week later Schettler was assigned to the battleship König, but over the remainder of the war it and other ships of the fleet, spent most of the time confined to port. This allowed Schettler to become involved in the struggle against the barbarism being meted out by the Kaiser's regime against the German people.

PART 1

Chapter 1

Johann Schettler lay alone on the filthy cot, cold and frightened, in the bleak prison cell. He knew, if found guilty, he was likely to be imprisoned or even executed. He shivered. Looking for solace, his thoughts turned to his family.

The silence in the cell was suddenly interrupted by loud shouting in the corridor and guffaws of hysterical laughter, bringing his present situation sharply back into focus. This was followed by the key turning in the lock and the iron door burst open with such force that it hit the side wall of the cell with a heavy clatter, causing the floor to shake. Peter Kalb stood there framed in the door, naked from the waist up, with a coil of rope slung over his left shoulder. He was holding an almost full bottle of Schnapps in his right hand and two glasses in his left. Judging from the noise behind him there were other people with him.

Kalb snarled: "Well, Schettler, I've decided to save the Navy the time and effort of a trial, so we're going to hang you right here and now, you piece of shit."

Schettler sprang to his feet and pressed his back hard against the wall, staring at Kalb wide eyed, while two young naval ratings ran into the cell and grabbed him by his arms.

Kalb went on. "But before you die, Schettler, you'll toast the Kaiser and the Reich," and he poured some Schnapps

1

into a glass, handing it to the rating holding Schettler's right arm. He filled the other glass and held it up, straightened and clicked his heels. "The Kaiser and the Reich." Then he snapped at the rating, "Give the pig the glass so he can drink to the Kaiser's health."

But when the rating released his grip, Schettler swiped the glass out of his hand and it smashed against the wall.

"You fucking, disrespectful bastard," Kalb snarled. "Hold him down, boys. He will drink to the Kaiser." After a scuffle, he was held firmly on the cot while Kalb forced the alcoholic liquid down his throat, carefully making sure he didn't choke. After half the Schnapps was administered, Kalb asked him again to toast Kaiser and country and he was dragged back to his feet. Schettler just stared at the half-naked man in insolent silence, until Kalb hit him hard across the side of the face with his clenched fist and indicated to his men to force him back on the cot. After two more blows to his head, Kalb roughly administered the rest of the Schnapps, making him choke and splutter.

In Schettler's confused state, he was only vaguely aware of another person entering the cell. He seemed to be telling Kalb something which caused the chief petty officer to shout out, "We'll see to this bastard later." In an instant Schettler was alone again.

The large amount of alcohol and his injuries took immediate effect and he passed in and out of consciousness. In his delirium, the thoughts that flashed into his mind continued to be about his family. His father, Heinrich, who had forced him to join the navy as a young and naive eighteen-year-old in September 1912, as a protest at having to join the family business when he left school and not being allowed to apply to the Hochschule für bildende Künste in Hamburg to further his aptitude and love for art.

Marion, his wonderful, Scottish mother, had met and married his father in America, when he himself had escaped from joining the same family business, thirty two years earlier. She was from a poor, Glasgow family and had fled to America herself to avoid the sexual advances of her brother-in-law when her sister Nell was pregnant. Marion had found work as a maid in the home of the McLanahan's in Hollidaysburg in Pennsylvania, where Heinrich Schettler was also employed by this Irish-American family business – developing washing and crushing equipment for the mining and phosphate industries.

A year after the couple were married, Heinrich received a letter from his mother, explaining that his father had died and he must return to Bremen to take over the family business. It was a tough decision, for life in America was good and with a Scottish wife who could speak no German, it was not likely to be easy. However, they decided to go and in July 1887, arrived in Bremen.

Despite their fears, the young couple thrived and thanks to Heinrich's experience in business in the USA, his shipping company prospered. Marion soon learned German and Frau Schettler took her into her heart, calling her Marianne.

They had three sons, the youngest of whom was Johann, born in March 1894. The older boys, Heinrich and Andreas, took after their father with fair hair but Johann was different, having almost black hair and brown eyes just like his mother. Marion was a proud Scot and had her own names for her sons, calling them Henry, Andrew and Ian. She ensured they all learned English which they spoke with a pronounced Scottish accent.

When Schettler eventually regained consciousness, lying in a cold sweat, he tried to make sense of what had happened. He knew Kalb was very drunk and it was clear enough what his intensions were, but he didn't know if the person he saw coming into the cell was real or just a hallucination. If he was real, what had been said to Kalb to stop him carrying out the execution and when would he be back to finish him off? At this thought, panic welled up inside him. Head pounding, he vomited.

*

Two days earlier, Schettler had opened the bulkhead door to the main deck of the battleship, König, and was confronted by a heavily armed second lieutenant and two ratings. "Bootsmann Schettler, I am arresting you for incitement to mutiny..." The officer's forceful words were almost drowned out by heckling from a group of sailors working close by. The second lieutenant continued angrily, "Take this man to the stockade. And you men get on with your work immediately, or you'll be next."

The third squadron of the High Seas Fleet had just been ordered back to its home port of Kiel, after the crews of twenty seven ships of the German High Seas Fleet had been involved in a failed mutiny rather than go into battle against the British Navy, when the war was already lost.

As Schettler was led away, he shouted towards the seamen, "Don't worry, Comrades, they'll not hold us for long."

One of his escorts punched him hard between the shoulder blades causing him to stumble.

On the König, eight other ringleaders of the mutiny were arrested with Schettler and imprisoned in the ship's stockade in the bowels of the ship, between the ratings aft Scheißhaus and oil distribution room. The smell was unbearable.

When the flotilla docked at the Reichs Kreigshafen on that cold, dank morning, the prisoners from the König were led away to join the detainees from the other ships. Schettler had shivered as he tried to edge down the gang plank in only the thin tunic he had been wearing since his arrest, perhaps partly through fear, as he thought of what was likely to lie ahead of him. He had to adopt a sideways gait as it was difficult to walk in his thick sea-boots while his ankles were manacled, and he cursed. Mist billowed around the trucks waiting on the quay to take them to the military prison. Continuing his slow descent, Schettler could see that the ships' crews had stopped work and were watching the pitiful procession in silence.

As the small group reached the truck, Leading Seaman Karl Brand turned towards the ships and raised his clenched fist in the air. Pockets of cheering answered the gesture, low and eerie in the cold morning mist. But as Brand turned back, a punch met him full in the face, making him cry out in pain and surprise as the blood flowed freely from his nose. The punch came from Oberstabsbootsmann Peter Kalb, the most senior Unteroffizier on the Markgraf and known to be a sadistic bastard. Many a sailor regretted having contact with Kalb and today, more than ever, would be no exception.

"Get on the fucking truck, you commie pig."

His words to Schettler were no less venomous. "I'm going to make sure you suffer every minute before they hang you, which they will, sooner or later. You'd better pray it's sooner. As a senior petty officer, you're guiltier than the rest of this mutinous…"

A shot rang out from the Markgraf. All eyes turned to see a sailor slide helplessly down the aft flagpole where a red flag hung as limp and lifeless as the man who had put it there. An officer ran up, smoking pistol in hand and snatched the flag from the pole. Voices began to chant, "Murderer, shame!"

The shouts grew ever louder, taking over first the Markgraf and continuing along the line of ships. Amidst this clamour, Kalb turned back to the group and repeated the order to get on board. The sailors took little notice, so he grabbed a rifle from one of the armed guards and heaved the butt into Seaman Hans Meyer's groin causing him to double over, fall to his knees, and bring up the meagre, undigested contents of his stomach. Kalb pointed the rifle towards the group and they began to climb onto the truck as fast as their manacled ankles would allow. The guards manhandled Meyer on board before climbing on and the truck moved off to the Naval Guard House.

Chapter 2

When Kalb had arrived at the military guard house with his prisoners, he found it in the hands of disgruntled petty officers and ratings. He took command, immediately restored discipline and began the reign of terror he had promised would be meted out to the political prisoners. True to his word, the worst befell Schettler, who was subjected to harrowing threats of execution and frequent beatings over his four-day incarceration.

Through the brutal interrogation of another prisoner, Kalb discovered Schettler had family ties in the UK and, fired with even more loathing, arrived again at Schettler's cell, this time to accuse him of being a British agent. He was accompanied by two junior ratings, who grabbed Schettler as he lay on top of his cot, dragged him to his feet and held him tight as Kalb drove his clenched fist into his stomach several times, causing him to cry out in agony.

"Now I've got to the truth of your game. Spreading discontent throughout our service to make it easier for the British to force us to end the war, that's it eh? You're not just a commie thug – you're a fucking English spy, you bastard. I should have hanged you when I had the chance."

He snapped at the ratings. "We'll finish him off in the yard. We can't allow this pig to live any longer."

As the ratings dragged him through the dark, acrid corridor, Schettler saw the large outer door of the prison being opened and a stream of revolutionary sailors flooded into the yard. The two men let Schettler fall and bolted for safety. Behind them, the enraged Kalb drew his pistol. As he ran past Schettler, he discharged a bullet in his direction, but it ricocheted off the cobbled yard a few inches from his head.

Kalb continued sprinting towards the approaching hoard, shouting, "I'll get the bastard who's in control here." And as he drew level, the men seemed to part, allowing him to run between their ranks, through the outer gate into Feldstraße straight towards the leaders of the revolutionaries and the military band that accompanied them. A shot rang out and Kalb, still propelling himself forward and holding his pistol over his head, fell to the ground, sliding along the road until his head, spurting with blood, came to rest at the edge of the pavement.

Silence descended as the band stopped in mid tune and the men watched the life draining out of the convulsing body.

Seeing the game was up, the other prison guards appeared at the door of the west wing with their hands in the air in capitulation. The prison was now in the hands of the revolutionaries.

In the commotion, Schettler managed to drag himself to his feet and stagger to the outer door, where he leant holding his distended stomach. He was in considerable pain and although it was a cold day, his hair was soaked with sweat. Seeing him emerge from the prison, Karl Artelt, the chairman of the newly appointed Workers' and Soldiers' Council and Erich Schmidt, another council member, walked forward to join him.

Schettler spoke through gritted teeth. "Am I glad to see you, Karl. God, you took your bloody time getting here."

Artelt took hold of Schettler's arm. "You're safe now, Johann. We didn't want to force our way in earlier, in case they decided to make an example of some of you."

Schettler smiled. The irony amused him. "Believe me, Karl, as far as I'm concerned you arrived just in time. Kalb was having me taken to the yard to be shot. Five minutes later I'd be dead."

Schmidt said, "You're in a lot of pain. What else did he do?"

"I think I'll survive. He accused me of being a British spy and gave my stomach a good pounding. He was going to hang me the other day and I can't understand what stopped him. I'm lucky to be alive."

Artelt addressed Schmidt. "This could be difficult. A chief petty officer was shot while trying to fight a single-handed action in defence of the prison. I'll have to find out who did it. The council can't be seen to condone killing someone for disagreeing with us. Who is this Kalb anyway?"

"The chief petty officer on board the Markgraf. He was an evil bastard." Schmidt spat.

Artelt shook his head. "Evil or not, he deserved a fair trial." Then he brightened as he looked back at Schettler. "As long-standing activists and heroes of the mutiny, in your absence, you and Karl Brand were voted onto the executive of the Workers' and Soldiers' Council, with me as chairman. If you wait while I have the other political prisoners released, we'll have you taken to hospital then we can talk later."

He turned to a young rating standing close by. "Comrade Hoelz, will you fetch Karl Müller?"

When the stocky Petty Officer Müller appeared, Artelt made it clear that after the political prisoners were released, thirty sailors were to be billeted with Müller in charge, and an armed guard posted at the gates at all times. The rest of the prisoners would remain until their circumstances were assessed, but until then they should be looked after with compassion.

Artelt went off to oversee the release of the political prisoners, leaving Schmidt to take care of Schettler.

Schmidt explained that the city, the naval bases, the docks and factories were now in the control of the WSC. In other areas, although fighting was still going on, many army units had joined the side of the revolution and it was expected they would soon have the final victory.

Schettler was astounded. In prison, there had been rumours of fighting and people being killed but he had no idea that Kiel was now under revolutionary control. The tears flowed down his cheeks.

Schmidt looked bewildered. "Does my news not please you?"

"Of course it does but I could never have expected the city to fall so quickly."

Schmidt held his clenched fist aloft and punched the air. "Yes, Comrade, and we did it with a minimum of bloodshed. Karl was glorious. He and Lothar Popp organised and addressed many demonstrations and we got mass support from the bases and factories throughout the city."

Schmidt beamed with enthusiasm. "On Sunday, the sailors and the workers with their wives and children marched to insist that all of you in prison be released. They were shouting slogans calling for an immediate end to the war, down with the Kaiser and all hail a socialist republic. It was wonderful!"

Then he bowed his head. "But during the march a unit loyal to High Command fired on the demonstration killing eight of our comrades and wounding twenty nine of us. We quickly attacked them, and they fled for their lives, but not before we managed to kill the officer in charge. So, including the sailor on the Markgraf, they killed nine of us. And even with that bastard Kalb today, only two of them were killed."

He brightened once again. "Yesterday we formed the WSC, armed ourselves and took the city. Karl went to see Rear Admiral Souchon, the Military Governor, and gave him the ultimatum that the WSC were now in control, which the bastard had to accept. And today, here we are, with our military band, to release you!"

Schettler smiled through his pain. "To have achieved such a goal so quickly and with such little bloodshed is incredible."

"Yes, it is, but we couldn't have done it without Artelt and Popp."

"Who is Popp?"

"He's the local secretary of the USPD. All the socialist organisations were involved, except the SPD of course. And surprise, surprise, Gustav Noske of the SPD and State Secretary Haußman are being sent from Berlin to try to resolve the current situation, as they put it, and address the people."

Schettler frowned. "You know the SPD are not to be trusted. They have consistently sided with the Kaiser's Government throughout this war. It was even their support that carried the vote to start the war in 1914. We shouldn't have anything to do with them now."

The conversation was cut short as Artelt returned with over two hundred jubilant, if rather ragtag and clearly battered and bruised, political prisoners. Two of them, Brand and Meyer, also needed medical attention. In Meyer's case, urgently.

Artelt addressed the gathered group of sailors. "The time for saluting pompous officers is over. We ought to salute these brave men for their work in shortening this terrible war." The men began cheering. The group got into formation, with the prisoners behind the band, followed by their liberators. They marched back to the Wik barracks while the band played the International.

Schmidt escorted Brand, Meyer and Schettler to hospital while Artelt went off to the Staatsbahnhof to join other members of the council to prepare for Haußman and Noske's arrival from Berlin.

Schettler's visit to hospital revealed that his repeated beatings hadn't left any lasting damage. His stomach, though very swollen, would soon recover. Brand, through painful manipulation, had his nose reset and a blood clot drained from his septum. Hans Meyer was not so lucky, for Kalb's rifle butt to his groin had caused internal bleeding which would mean an immediate operation. He was lucky to be alive but would be out of action for some time.

When Schettler arrived back at the hospital's dark vestibule where Schmidt had told them to await his return, Brand was already there.

Schettler couldn't contain his laughter when he saw him.

"What the fuck are you laughing at, you cheeky, young bastard?"

"Sorry, Karl, you just look a bit comical with that bandage over your nose and your two black eyes."

At forty two, Karl Brand was older than most of his compatriots in the navy, although his bearing and full head of brown hair made him look younger. Originally from Berlin, he joined the merchant navy where he became a union official. He was a member of the SPD, but when war broke out he joined the USPD because of his anti-war stance. For this, he was conscripted into the navy in December 1914, a method the Government used to control those suspected of being troublemakers.

As Schettler and Brand waited for Schmidt, they recounted their experiences at the hands of Kalb.

"Why did Kalb think you were an English spy, Johann?" Brand asked after the other had mentioned it.

"I have relatives in Glasgow."

Brand looked surprised. "That's a coincidence. I was born and brought up in Glasgower Straße in Wedding." He laughed. "All our streets were called after English cities."

Schettler shook his head. "Glasgow's not in England, Karl."

"Isn't it? Where is it then?"

"It's in Scotland."

"Ach, it's the same thing."

"You better not let my mother hear you say that."

"Oh, your mother's English, is she?"

"No Karl, don't be so bloody stupid, she's Scottish."

Schmidt returned, and the argument was dropped. He handed them each a white arm band to denote membership of the WSC. "We've commandeered the Hotel Hansa opposite the Bahnhof as our HQ. There's a room waiting for you, though I'm afraid you'll have to share."

This concerned Schettler. "Doesn't Karl want us with him when he meets Noske?"

13

"No. He says that after what you two have been through, it's more important to get some food and rest. There's much to be done and you should start afresh tomorrow morning. Let's go."

Schettler awoke just before seven o'clock. Every sinew in his body ached and his stomach felt as if he had been gored by a bull. Even in his exhausted state, he had only slept fitfully. Brand's broken nose meant he had snored loudly all night long.

Schettler got up and began dressing. He hadn't spent much time in hotels but the room with its floral wallpaper, old fashioned furniture and pictures of seaside scenes, reminded him of the rooms in the hotel in Perth where his family had stayed while visiting his Scottish relatives. For an eleven year old, the trip had started badly. When his mother had met his aunt at Queen Street Station, there had been a lot of tears after so many years apart. At the Nairn's house in Glasgow, his Uncle Charles had acted in a very sullen manner when being introduced to the Schettlers. It was clear he was drunk. When Johann went to shake his hand, the man snarled something incomprehensible and when the boy asked him to repeat himself, he flew into a rage. Aunt Nell had to stop him striking the boy. This frightened Johann and caused his aunt great embarrassment.

It was not until the two families, minus Uncle Charles, who claimed he had to stay behind to look after the family's expanding grocery business, embarked on a tour around Perthshire that they began to enjoy themselves. It was amazing how much fun his four cousins became when they were away from their father. Heinrich and Andreas had enjoyed the company of Charles and Helen, who were of similar age. Schettler smiled as he remembered the younger two, Bob and Margaret, who had taught him how to say so many phrases in a broad, Glasgow accent. How they had laughed as he used his new talent to talk to the local children. They had also spent many hours drawing and painting with Margaret's little tin box of watercolours which both children had used to great effect.

Since the two countries had entered the war in 1914, he had heard very little from his relatives there. How was his Aunt Nell since Uncle Charles's death? What about his cousins? It was likely that Charlie and Bob were fighting for their country, as he was for his. If they were still alive what were they thinking, now that the war was so close to its end? Did they also want to change the political system to protect the people against another such outrage happening? What of the girls? Where were they now? An even louder snore from Brand brought him back to the present.

He shoved on his only tunic and went along the corridor to the bathroom. It was unoccupied, so he ran a bath and painfully climbed in. He hadn't had a proper bath since his last home-leave eighteen months ago. As he immersed himself, the heat of the water began to soothe away his aches and pains. It was blissful, and he soon fell into that relaxed trance, where time doesn't exist anymore. This time, his mother came to mind. He had been away from home when war broke out and therefore hadn't seen her reaction to her two beloved countries becoming embroiled in a war with one another. His brother had written to him saying that she had taken it very badly and spent much time trying to persuade the boys not to get involved, arguing that it was not a war of the people. How right she had been. However, she hadn't been able to dissuade them, and both had joined the army. His father also needed to persuade the authorities not to intern his mother. The thought had often crossed his mind that perhaps money had changed hands, although anytime he had been home on leave, it was never mentioned.

A loud knocking on the door startled him. He quickly washed taking care with his stomach, got out, dried himself and dressed again in his stinking clothes. Today, he thought, he would have to return to the ship to collect his belongings. When he opened the door, Brand was leaning against the wall, almost bent double. "Christ, you took your time. I'm dying for a piss here." At that he hurried past Schettler, slamming the door behind him.

Schettler returned to their room and glancing out of the window, he saw it was snowing – another reason to go back to the ship for heavier clothing – but for now, there was too much work to be done.

*

The revolution progressed at a fast pace and Schettler's prediction that Noske would cause problems was more than justified when, in a misjudged move, the WSC elected him as the new Governor of Kiel. Although his power was not to exceed that of the Revolutionary Council in the long term, the consequences of this would be catastrophic.

Chapter 3

Since the revolutionary takeover, there had been nothing to stop sailors leaving the barracks whenever they liked. Drunkenness, fighting and vandalism in some of the city's bars had been reported to the council.

This could not be tolerated, but it was clear that the navy's own shore patrol was seen as part of the old guard. Their discipline would not be accepted by the men, so a council member was assigned to the shore patrol to give it validity. This was time consuming but seen as necessary, until a new military order was established.

Schettler was to lead the shore patrol to apprehend sailors absent from duty. The group simply had to tour bars, cafés, brothels and clubs within the city centre and fish out those who had succumbed to their attractions.

He dreaded this assignment and had wakened very early after a fitful night. Since childhood, he had hated extreme drunkenness in others.

He'd only managed to collect his belongings the previous evening and he was looking forward to another bath before dressing himself in a clean and warm uniform. When he arrived at the bathroom however, he discovered that the water wasn't hot enough and had to make do with a tepid wash instead. Obviously, the boiler hadn't been lit. When he returned to the room, he didn't bother to keep the noise down, kicking the wardrobe closed and waking Brand.

Later, when the two went down to breakfast there was no sign of staff, confirming Schettler's theory that after five days the management had decided to withdraw the staff until they had been paid. This set him mumbling under his breath.

Brand looked askance at his room-mate.

"What the hell's wrong with you this morning?

"It's none of your dammed business."

In silence, they left the hotel and headed to the Bahnhof, in search of something to eat. As they crossed Sophienblatt, they noticed that many of the shops and cafés around this normally busy area were still bolted and shuttered. Thankfully, when they entered the station, they found the buffet open.

Later that morning, Schettler met up with the ten men of the shore patrol under the command of Chief Petty Officer Meier. On their way in the truck to the first bar, Meier brought Schettler up to date with what he was likely to encounter. The men they would be dealing with would be disillusioned. This could be for personal reasons such as just wanting to go home, but for some, it would be political. This could mean trouble if they were prepared to fight for the Kaiser's Reich. Together with a surfeit of booze, Schettler reckoned, it could be incendiary.

At the first two establishments, they found a few men who'd been on long term benders and were easy enough to deal with. However, when they reached the Kaiser Café, where the dead and wounded from the demonstration had been deposited the previous week, Schettler became aware that all was not well. The noise from inside was loud and intimidating and his heart began to race.

The shore patrol entered the long tap room with traditional harbour scenes painted in panels on the walls. The place was packed with sailors sitting at wooden tables which ran along its length of the large room. Others were standing in tightly packed groups next to the bar which took up the middle third of the opposite wall. Meier and Schettler were at the head of the group and with a shout that managed to pierce the din Schettler told the heaving mass of sailors that the shore patrol had arrived. Slowly the place became silent. All eyes turned towards the group at the door. The atmosphere became menacing.

Schettler decided to stand on a table near the door to tell the drunken occupants that this shore patrol was under the orders of the Revolutionary Council, but as he began to speak, a bottle came whizzing past him, narrowly missing his head and smashing on the wall beyond. It appeared that the crowd didn't care. Soon more bottles were thrown at the assembled group by the door and Meier gave the order for his men to draw their sticks and start removing the sailors by force. He told Schettler to stand well back, an instruction with which he was happy to comply, for his hands were shaking and he felt sick.

Before the mêlée began, another shout came from the crowd. A large, well-built seaman tried to climb onto one of the tables but he was so drunk that it took several men to help him up. When he finally found enough stability to allow him to stand comparatively unaided, he spoke out remarkably well for a man as drunk as he.

"Listen, you shower of misfits, I'm glad this stupid war is almost over and I can get back to work. I'm a blacksmith and if…" He stopped while he again adjusted his balance with the aid of his friends below. "…this revolution does really work, so much the better. Maybe we'll get some decent money for a change, enough even to feed our families. I'm going back to the Wik to gather up my things and go home. I say, let's all do that and have no trouble. What do you say, boys?"

As the seaman was helped from the table, there was the sound of agreement from the men around him and a large group fell in behind him as he staggered to the door.

While they were being helped onto the truck, Schettler noticed that another group of six sailors was still sitting at a table towards the back of the bar. They looked sullen and as a member of the shore patrol walked towards them, one of them stood up and hit him on the side of the head with what looked like an iron bar. The blow knocked his cap off, sending it across the room and, as he crumpled to the floor, blood oozed from the large open wound on his right temple. More members of the shore patrol came hurrying down the bar, sticks at the ready but as they closed in on the seamen, now on their feet, one drew an automatic Mauser from under his tunic.

"If you come closer, I'll fire." The group started towards the door with two more now brandishing automatic pistols. When they got outside, they moved fast and soon disappeared around the corner. The shore patrol gave chase but one fired his weapon stopping them in their tracks. The six men piled into a waiting car. When the last man was inside, it sped off heading out of town, while one fired indiscriminately out of the back window.

As the injured shore patrolman was being helped into the front of the truck with the last stragglers climbing unsteadily into the back, Meier returned to the café where Schettler was talking to the bar staff. They were glad to see the back of the sailors who had been drinking solidly since the previous evening, with more of them arriving throughout the night. The bar staff had lost control and some of the sailors had even been helping themselves to beer and Schnapps from behind the bar, which they hadn't paid for.

Schettler discovered the group of troublemakers with the guns were systematically going around the tables, buying drinks and talking to the others, but not drinking themselves. The barman added, "It looked to me like they were trying to incite the men with toasts of 'God bless His Majesty' and leading the singing of the old Reich songs. You know what we think of that in here."

Meier scratched his head. "I think they were officers impersonating enlisted men to try to incite a backlash to the revolution. They had weapons that aren't available to the rank and file."

Schettler nodded. "Yes, I agree, and they'll have to be found. Next time they might be successful."

After taking the injured patrolman to hospital, they drove to the Wik submarine base to decant the seething mass of drunken humanity to be sorted out and categorised by the overworked ombudsmen. At the gate they were met by two guards, who merrily waved the truck through without even a cursory inspection. Schettler ordered the vehicle to stop, but as he jumped down from the cab to challenge the guards' lack of security, one shouted, "Isn't this the most fantastic news, Comrade?"

"What news?"

"Haven't you heard?" cried the beaming man. "The Kaiser has just abdicated. The war must end now."

Unable to contain himself, Schettler jumped back onto the running board and bawled the news at those within, before opening the door to sit beside his grinning colleagues as they drove into the barracks. The more conscious occupants in the back also began cheering and singing.

Later that day, the council heard that Wilhelmshaven had been brought under revolutionary control. Armed uprisings had taken place in Hannover, Brunswick, Frankfurt, Stuttgart and Munich and soon the revolution was being consolidated with Workers' and Soldiers' Councils taking charge in most German cities.

As the Kaiser fled for his life to the Netherlands, in Berlin Germany was declared a republic and the Council for People's Delegates headed by the SPD, formed a provisional government. However, it had little effective power outside the capital.

Two days later, the draft Armistice between Germany and the Western Allies was signed in a railway carriage at Compiègne in Northern France and negotiations for peace began.

Chapter 4

As an early part of the negotiations for peace, the Allies demanded that seventy-four ships of the Imperial German Navy were to be disarmed and sent to the Firth of Forth, where they would be escorted to neutral ports for internment, until the final Armistice was sealed.

It would take officers and men to convey these ships to Scotland so Naval High Command and the Revolutionary Councils were forced to agree to work together to carry out this task. The two sides would have joint responsibilities during the time of internment.

As the British would not negotiate with the agents of the revolution, it was agreed Rear-Admiral Ludwig von Reuter would be in overall authority and solely responsible for negotiations. The responsibility for the navigation would be with the officers. The sailors would appoint an executive of six soldiers' councillors, four from Wilhelmshaven and two from Kiel. They would be in charge of all political matters and the welfare of the crews.

The WSC in Kiel chose Brand, who had many years of experience as a party and trade union negotiator, and Schettler, who as well as having political experience spoke fluent English, which could be an advantage, if he was kept as close as possible to any negotiations between Reuter and the British.

Schettler was to sail on the battleship, Friedrich der Grosse, Reuter's flag ship, with Brand on the battleship

Markgraf. The four councillors from Wilhelmshaven would be billeted on the following ships: Hoffman – Grosse Kurfürst, Schröder – Von der Tann, Grasse – Emden and Dittmann – Frankfurt. All ships would keep their own ombudsmen who would be answerable to the councillors.

When the toothless armada assembled at Schillig Roads, Admiral von Reuter requested a meeting with the six councillors on board the Dicke Fritz, the nickname given to the Friedrich der Grosse. When the men arrived, they were shown into the admiral's state room and received by Reuter in silence.

Without preliminaries or pleasantries, Reuter addressed the councillors. "I see the red flag is flying from each ship," he said, as he looked along the row of standing men.

"Yes, that's right," Schröder answered. "We're flying the flag of the authority that control the ships."

"This is not a flag recognised by any nation and even if it was previously agreed, I'm not prepared to take the chance that our fleet is taken for pirates and fired upon. I request that you fly the imperial flag. It's the only flag we have which is recognised by International Maritime Law," Reuter replied.

"We'll consider your request in the light of this information, Admiral Reuter, and let you know our decision before we're due to sail," Schettler said, and the six turned and walked out.

The officers in the room turned to each other. "These men are nothing but upstarts. How will we manage to endure them during this tragic voyage?" one of them said.

Reuter snapped, "You *will* endure them, and with as much good grace as you can muster, gentlemen, for if we rile them we will find ourselves in serious trouble. Do you understand?" The assembled group stayed silent as they studied the floor.

As the six councillors huddled in the corner of the deck, trying to avoid the cold wind howling in from the Baltic Sea, Schröder snarled, "We won't fly the flag of the principal enemy of our new-found freedom. Right, Comrades?" Grunts of agreement came from the group.

Schettler spoke up. "I agree with your sentiment, Axel, but it's better to stay within the law. I don't fancy being fired upon when we're completely helpless and you must admit the British have more than their fair share of arrogant bastards too. I wouldn't be surprised at anything they might do."

But Schröder countered, "It's fine you saying that, Johann, but how will we justify flying the imperial flag to the men?"

"Surely, it can be argued," Schettler said, "that as the war was fought by Imperial Germany, it's only fitting that it's *their* fleet being sent for internment? Anyway, it's better to have the discomfort of flying that repugnant flag, than lying dead at the bottom of the North Sea. After all, isn't it one of our principal duties to look after the welfare of the men? We can pacify them, by ordering the red flag to be flown on the fore masthead."

As his comrades prepared to be taken back to their ships, Schettler went to find the ombudsman on board the Dicke Fritz, a rating called Harald Herzmann. He had come across him in Kiel in 1917 and remembered he was a good man, with a keen sense of humour. He knew they would hit it off.

He finally found him in the canteen and reintroduced himself to the other's delight. Once he had imparted the news that the ensign of the Imperial German Navy was to be flown on all ships and agreed that a circular of explanation should be sent around the crew, they settled down for a chat. After fifteen minutes of light-hearted banter, Herzmann became serious.

"Listen, Johann, I don't know if you've heard but there are a few groups on board various ships, mostly a bunch of thugs but they're calling themselves the Red Guard. Basically, they're just out to create trouble. There's a small group here on board led by a leading seaman called Axel Penzberg, who was also stationed at Kiel in 1917. You may have come across him?"

Schettler thought for a minute. "Yes, I remember him but only by reputation. He was a trouble-maker and used most of his guile to try to avoid work of any kind."

"Yes," said Herzmann. "That paints a pretty accurate picture. How do you think we should handle them?"

"My first reaction is that we should try to separate the men from the leaders and bring them into line, but if that doesn't work, then we'll have to get control of them in some other way. Let's just see how things turn out. I'll let the councillors know about this if you handle the ombudsmen."

The other nodded and the two returned to reminiscing – a pleasure Schettler had not experienced in a long time.

*

The fleet finally got under way at 13.30 on the November 19th, twenty four hours late, with the capital ships in one long line headed by the battle-cruiser, Seydlitz, preceding forty nine destroyers in five lines.

The voyage to the Firth of Forth continued through the first night in calm seas for the earlier wind had dropped. Schettler had nothing to do. As a member of the fleet's

Soldiers' Council Executive he was not part of the ship's company, so he wandered the decks watching the long line of ships both in front and behind them. It was strange to see them lit up, unlike during the war, when they were kept darkened to prevent recognition and attack by the enemy. Around ten o'clock he began to feel very cold, so he decided to go to the bridge for warmth and get a better view of the ships ahead. When he arrived at the starboard door, he found a sailor on guard and, as he made to pass him, the sailor said, "What is your name, Bootsmann?"

"Schettler."

The sailor picked up a clip board by his side and slid his finger down a list of names, which he did twice before saying, "I'm sorry, Bootsmann, I'm instructed only to admit authorised personnel and your name's not on the list."

Schettler shook his head. "As the Soldiers' Council's representative, I have a right to go anywhere on this ship without hindrance. Go to the officer in charge of the bridge and tell him I'm waiting to enter."

"I'm sorry, Councillor. I've been instructed not to leave my post."

"Very well, I'll go for the moment." Since his reason for entering the bridge was entirely personal, Schettler decided he better just back off and take the matter up at his next meeting with the admiral's representatives. "It's cold tonight. Couldn't they have posted you on the other side of the door?"

"Yes, it is, but you know what they're like."

Schettler nodded in agreement and turned to walk down the aft ladder. He had been allocated a small cabin on the quarter deck, which would have belonged to a sub-lieutenant when the ship's company was at full strength. Under normal circumstances he wouldn't have accepted this privilege but since he would only be a target for moans, complaints and gossip, he decided it was better to take it.

As he headed down through the ship, he toyed with going to the petty officer's mess but then decided to go straight to his cabin. He would write to his cousin, Margaret, and as soon as the fleet arrived in Scotland he would try to post it.

He retrieved his treasured, green Parker fountain pen, bought by his parents for his eighteenth birthday and a cheap writing pad from his kit bag. He sat down on his bunk and, supporting the pad open on his knee, began to write.

My Dear Cousin Margaret,

I have been thinking a lot about my Scottish family, Aunt Nell and my cousins Charles and Helen, but you and Bob are the ones mostly on my mind. I remember with great fondness the fun we had all those years ago in Glasgow and Perthshire.

It's hard to come to terms with the family having to be separated by war and not being able to communicate with each other, although I know my mother took the opportunity to write to Aunt Nell when my father had a ship sailing to a neutral port where a letter could be posted, however inadequate that was. Now the war is over, I'm sure she will be making contact with you all again. She was heart broken when war was declared between her two beloved countries and always told my brothers and me that it was not a war of the people and she was right. All that we ever got out of it was death and poverty and I'm sure it was the same where you are. Most of the German people never wanted this war and even those who were deluded into thinking it was a good thing back in 1914, are now convinced that it was a great evil perpetrated by the ruling classes of both our countries and we must now crush their power and banish them to the annals of history.

I am very proud to tell you, that as a part of the new revolutionary naval force in North Germany, we have been instrumental in bringing about the end to the war and setting up Workers' Republics throughout Germany. I know that without our intervention the war could have dragged on indefinitely. This is another reason I am writing to you, because as part of the Armistice negotiations, some of our fleet is to be held in neutral ports to wait for the final Armistice agreement and at the moment I am one of the Soldiers' Council's Executive sailing on our flag ship, Friedrich der Grosse, to the Firth of Forth to liaise with the Allied Fleets under your Admiral Beatty. After that, I don't know where we will be sent but I hope where ever that is, it won't be for long and I can return to a socialist Germany and perhaps can go home to be with my family, for a while at least.

I don't know what your politics are, but I feel sure that if my mother is anything to go by, you will agree with me that we must strive for a socialist Europe where the rights of the people are respected. I have heard that Glasgow has many socialist activists, but I've only heard of one by name, John Maclean, who is held in great esteem throughout Europe.

As far as I know my mother and father are well. My brother, Heinrich, was badly wounded at the Second Battle of Ypres and as he lost a leg, had to be invalided out the army in 1915. He now works in the family business. Andreas spent the entire war being sent from battle to battle and is now a major and probably, not yet returned home. I joined the navy before the war, to avoid having to join the family business, therefore I am not an officer. I wanted to go to Art School, but father said no.

I was lucky because our great Imperial Navy spent most of the war in one port or another, although I saw action at Dogger Bank and at Jutland. Thankfully, I came through unscathed.

When we arrive in the Firth of Forth, I will try to have someone post this letter for me. I don't know how difficult this will be, but I hope it can be done. So, if you can, please write back to me using my ship as an address and tell me about yourself and all the family. I remember, when I was in Scotland all those years ago, you and I did lots of watercolours together. Do you still paint?

I will address the letter to you at Seton Terrace although I don't know whether you still stay with your mother, or if you are married.

I so much look forward to hearing from you.

Your loving cousin

Johann Schettler

It was after one in the morning when he finished by addressing the envelope to Miss Margaret Nairn, 7, Seton Terrace, Glasgow E.1. and stuffing the six, small sheets of writing paper into it. He removed his uniform, climbed into his bunk and lay there, feeling the familiar gentle motion of the ship. The thoughts of Scotland evaporated into sleep.

The next day, conditions at sea had worsened and he was awakened early by the pitching of the ship. It was some time since he had been at sea in these conditions and he felt decidedly bilious. He dressed quickly and went to the canteen, because experience told him that eating something would help settle his stomach. When he got there, he joined a significant queue of ratings just off the overnight watch. The atmosphere was subdued. When his turn came, the food, bread and bratwurst, was not the freshest. Commenting on this, he was told that many of the stores assigned to the ships hadn't appeared. This would have to be another matter to be discussed with the ship's command later that morning.

He sat down at a table beside an elderly mechanic's mate who, on seeing Schettler's white arm band, began to harangue him that it was the Soldiers' Councils fault that this miserable voyage was taking place. The man had been proud to wear the Kaiser's uniform, and this was an ignominious end to a naval fleet that had never been defeated. There were a few grunts of support from the men sitting close by. But when Schettler went on to defend the actions of the Councils and the establishment of a new Germany fit for its people, many of the men around the room voiced their agreement. One man jumped to his feet and shouted, "The old Germany's dead, thank God. It's time the people had a chance…" He was stopped in mid-sentence by the noise of an explosion. The men looked at each other in astonishment, but after a few seconds started towards the door and soon everyone was clambering up the port and starboard ladders towards the deck. The ship rolled in the rough sea. As Schettler reached the aft port deck, he could see smoke billowing in the grey light some distance behind them and some of the men around him were saying that one of the destroyers had been torpedoed by an English submarine. Schettler immediately headed to the bridge.

Climbing higher, he could see that the smoke was coming from a destroyer, but it was clearly on a different course from the others in the group. At the bridge, the door was still being guarded by a sailor. This time Schettler addressed him in a much more urgent tone. "My name is Councillor Schettler, and in the light of this explosion, it is imperative I speak to the officer of the watch immediately. Go and inform him of this."

The sailor looked perplexed. "I'm not supposed to leave my post."

"I don't care. Go now."

The sailor looked at him for a second then turned, opened the door and disappeared inside. He was gone for less than a minute and when he returned, he closed the door behind him. "A second lieutenant will be out to speak to you shortly. You're to stay where you are."

"That's unacceptable. I'm going in there and don't try to stop me." The sailor made no move to stop him, so Schettler brushed past and entered the bridge. The second lieutenant who had been assigned to speak to him ran up, took him by the arm and tried to turn him back towards the door. Schettler shrugged him off and continued towards the centre of the bridge, where a senior lieutenant and a lieutenant stood beside the helmsman, looking towards the smoke through binoculars. The senior lieutenant swung round. "Get out of here. How dare you come into this bridge without permission?" Schettler used the same tone. "What flag is this vessel flying at its fore masthead?"

"That red rag, but it could be the skull and crossbones for all I care, Bootsmann."

"You will address me as councillor as you've been instructed to do. You're only in command of this vessel as far as the navigation to the Firth of Forth is concerned. The Soldiers' Council, whom I represent, is in joint command here. So now tell me what has happened in the group of destroyers behind."

"I will not—"

A voice came from behind. "You better tell him, Mr Scharke. He has every right to know, as indeed I do too."

Schettler and the two officers turned to see Vice-Admiral von Reuter standing by the starboard door.

The two officers saluted smartly and Scharke said, "Certainly, sir. We have had radio messages from several destroyers in the area. While steaming into the Heligoland Bite towards Channel 400, the V30 strayed off course and struck a mine. The ship is sinking fast, but because of the mine field, no rescue mission can be attempted. We are waiting for the crew to steer their lifeboats out of it, before they can be picked up safely."

Reuter asked, "Have there been any casualties?"

"We won't know that until the rescue takes place, sir."

Schettler spoke up. "I recommend that all ships' companies are informed of this as soon as possible. The rumour is that the V30 was torpedoed by a British submarine and we don't want the men to demand that the fleet return to Wilhelmshaven." The admiral nodded. "That's very sensible, Councillor. Will you deal with this, Scharke?"

"Yes, sir, right away."

The admiral shook his head. "I know you're anxious to get the fleet to the Firth of Forth to comply with the terms of the Armistice negotiations, Councillor, as, of course, am I. However, you must understand that this is the saddest and most repugnant task I have ever had to carry out in my entire career as a German sailor. We had the finest and most modern fleet in the world which was never beaten in battle. And to see it reduced to a flotilla of unarmed hulks, some hardly sea worthy, being taken to England to satisfy the thirst of the English to have their final victory, which they could not achieve in battle, makes me sick."

Schettler pondered the admiral's statement. "This war was never going to end in victory for anyone. It would have dragged on, only ending when there were no more men to kill in the battlefields. Someone had to halt the madness and that was what we did and I am very proud of that. The world cannot go on being governed by people who play with the lives of millions to create death, poverty and untold misery just to satisfy their own thirst for power."

It was the admiral's turn to reflect. His response was measured and controlled. "Your sentiments are very laudable, Councillor, and I respect you for them. Now the Allies can record the final victory, do you think they'll change their attitude to the people and adopt communist states? I expect they will carry on in the same way as before, especially England. It's still an imperialist power. What they *will* be though, is the most vociferous enemy of communist Germany and Soviet Russia."

Schettler looked at the admiral. Although courteous, he stood for an out of date and repugnant ideology. He hated that.

"You're probably right," he said, watching the man's response, "but their revolution has yet to come. The British people have suffered as much as we have and they must be sick and tired of it."

The admiral sighed. "Well, Councillor, we'll just have to see, won't we?"

Reuter turned to the senior officer of the watch. "What speed are we doing, Mr Scharke?"

"Eight knots, sir."

Reuter grimaced. "Is that all we can muster? I was going to suggest that we order the fleet to stop until the crew of the V30 is picked up. At that speed, I doubt we really need to but we had better do it anyway. Carry on. I'm returning to my quarters. Please let me know if there are any casualties or any other developments. And make sure that a radio message is sent to Beatty telling him why there will be one less destroyer arriving in the Firth of Forth."

"Yes, sir."

Schettler spoke up once more. "Just before you go, Admiral Reuter, the rations on board, as I have experienced myself, are meagre. I'm led to believe many of the stores were not loaded on board. Is there enough food for the voyage and what will happen when we reach our destination?"

Reuter frowned. "I'm afraid it was your organisation, or the lack of it, that caused that problem, Councillor, but yes, there's enough for the voyage. The English have agreed to allow us to bring in supply ships to replenish our stocks as soon as we have reached our final destination, where ever that might be."

The officers saluted as he left the bridge.

Scharke turned to Schettler. "If you want to stay on the bridge, please do so and I will arrange for the men on guard duty to allow you access at any time."

"Thank you, Lieutenant, but now I've a communiqué about the V30 to prepare. Since the weather has deteriorated, I think the guard should be posted on the inside of the bridge door. Don't you?"

Schettler first went to seek out the Red Guard on board and found them playing cards in the canteen. He introduced himself to the eight ratings and, nodding to Penzberg, said, "I think we were at Kiel barracks together in 1917?"

Schettler apologised for the delay in introducing himself to them and explained the V30's situation. He received an indifferent response. The men didn't want to be side-tracked from their card game, so he went on, "I take it you accept this explanation." Receiving only a grunt from Penzberg, he turned and was about to go off to the radio room, when Penzberg snarled, "Listen, Schettler, what kind of arseholes are your so-called, executive? Letting these bastards fly the Kaiser's flag?"

Schettler turned. The other's expression was one of complete contempt as he stared back at him.

"Didn't you get the explanation? It was circulated amongst the crews of the entire fleet."

"Oh, we got it. We just think it's a load of bollocks. You better realise we're watching you and if we think the executive is stepping out of line and kowtowing to the bloody officers, there'll be trouble. Do you hear?"

Penzberg sounded like a man trying to impress his compatriots.

"Do you think so? We'll see about that," Schettler snapped over his shoulder as he walked away.

Chapter 5

When the V30's company was rescued, it turned out that two men had been killed in the explosion.

When this message was conveyed to the men, the feeling of despondency they had felt since the beginning of the voyage intensified. After the majority of men had volunteered to crew the ships, a rumour had circulated that Beatty wasn't going to allow the German ships to be berthed in neutral ports but somewhere in England. Artelt had challenged High Command about this but was told that they had no knowledge of such a plan. Even the most committed advocates of the new socialist order were beginning to look on the mission as an unlucky voyage which could only end in misery.

As Schettler sat eating bratwurst and stale bread in the canteen, a Bootsmann articulated those fears. "It's all right for you, Councillor, but as soon as the ships arrive in England, you'll go back to Germany while we'll be stuck there as prisoners till the Allies get their way."

It was something Schettler hadn't thought through. It was true he'd assumed he would return to Germany as soon as possible but he realised now, that wouldn't be fair to the men left behind in Britain. "I don't think we'll be prisoners, Comrade. Hostilities are over and we're unlikely to be there for long. The Armistice negotiation period is thirty six days and we're a few days into that already."

His words must have pacified the Bootsmann, who turned quietly to his table.

Schettler had taken no more than two mouthfuls, when a voice came from behind. "It's Johann – Johann Schettler. It is you, isn't it?"

He looked up, annoyed at yet another interruption but then saw a man standing with his hand outstretched, smiling. For a moment Schettler didn't recognise the young, blond haired man also in the uniform of a Bootsmann. "It's me, Axel Kegel."

Schettler smiled broadly. They had spent so much time together, during their early days in the navy. "Of course, how could I fail to recognise you, Axel! How are you, my old friend? I haven't seen you since we arrived back in Wilhelmshaven after the fighting at Jutland and they carried you off the old tub on a stretcher."

"Yes, the English blew the second funnel down with me underneath. I was lucky to come out alive. I ended up with both my legs broken and a very sore head. I spent almost six months in the naval hospital in Hamburg learning to walk again."

Just then a rating appeared at the door of the canteen and shouted, "Is Councillor Schettler here?" Schettler raised his hand.

"You are to go to the bridge at once, Councillor."

"Oh, have I? Very well, Comrade."

He turned back to Kegel. "Get some food, if you can call it that and I'll see you later. Say about seven in the petty officers' mess. We can talk then. It's really great to see you."

When he arrived on the bridge, the guard let him pass without comment. Inside, it was busy. As well as the three lieutenants and the boatswain who were there earlier, the

Kapitän zur See and the first officer were standing with Admiral von Reuter.

"Good evening, Schettler. Have you been introduced to the captain and first officer of this fine ship?" the admiral said, as Schettler approached.

"No, I've not met the captain, but Korvettenkapitän von Wachter and I met a couple of times before we sailed."

Who had told the admiral his name? There had been no reference to it during his last visit.

"Let me rectify that. After all, it's one commander to another, Kapitän zur See von Lessel, this is Councillor Schettler of the Soldiers' Council."

Schettler thought he could detect cynicism in von Reuter's voice, but he couldn't be sure. He seemed to be sincere enough when they last spoke.

The three senior officers looked immaculate in their command finery with a large array of medals between them. Reuter was the most striking, with his iron-grey hair cut short, his full moustache and little beard which only covered the middle third of his chin. Lessel and Wachter were younger, both clean shaven, and the latter bore a scar on his cheek, which identified him as a graduate of Heidelberg University.

Lessel made no attempt to shake Schettler's hand, but briefly nodded his head. Schettler returned the gesture.

"I believe we have you to thank for the Imperial Ensign being hoisted on most of the ships of the fleet, Schettler?"

"No, Captain. The decision was made by our council."

The captain nodded. "I see. Are you aware that two men were killed in the explosion on the Destroyer V30? This is regrettable. The ship was sailing in an erratic manner, no doubt due to its insubordinate crew."

Schettler grimaced. "Have you got proof of that, Captain?"

"Not yet, but it won't be hard to find."

"In that case, I recommend we appoint a court of enquiry at the earliest opportunity with an equal number of officers and Soldiers' Council representatives presiding. But when we reach the conclusion of who's to blame, we might not have the power to do anything about it."

"Yes, I'm sure you're right on that score, Schettler," Reuter interjected, "so I think we should defer this matter to a more appropriate time. Seeing as we're having a full and frank discussion, I must say that the slovenly conduct of the men is causing me concern. They're hanging about the decks swearing and smoking with their uniforms in a dirty and dishevelled state. Something will have to be done, otherwise it will create a terrible impression when contact is made with the English."

Schettler had already come to the same conclusion, albeit for different reasons. He had thought the councillors and ombudsmen should tell all personnel their slovenly and unkempt appearance was an insult to the revolution and they should smarten themselves up. But he hadn't got around to it.

"I have it in hand," he said.

Reuter nodded. "Very well."

Lessel made to make another comment but Reuter dismissed him with a wave of his hand. An awkward silence ensued, finally broken by Wachter. "I believe you have family ties with the Schettler Shipping Company in Bremen. Is that correct?" Here we go again, Schettler thought. I should know better than be a socialist. "Where did you get that information, Korvettenkapitän?"

"From a friend, Korvettenkapitän Angermann. He's had dealings with your family. Why, isn't it true?"

"It's perfectly true. My father owns the company."

The officers exchanged glances. Schettler could see they were surprised by his statement.

"I believe you speak very good English. Is that true?" Wachter added.

Schettler raised his eyes. "I speak English with a distinctly Scottish accent but yes, I'm pretty fluent, although I haven't had much cause to speak it in the last six years."

Reuter looked puzzled. "Why a Scottish accent?"

"My mother taught me to speak English and she's a Scot."

"We would like you to translate for us," Wachter continued. "One of our staff officers speaks English and I have a few words myself but I suspect neither of us is as fluent as you."

"I have no objection, but I believe the British Admiral Beatty has refused to have anything to do with the Soldiers' Council. If that's still the case, then I'd be useless."

Reuter butted in. "What he actually said, was he wouldn't negotiate. He can't object to you being an interpreter."

"Very well, I'd be happy to do it." This was better than Schettler could have hoped. It would give him the best possible chance of keeping tabs on what was going on.

"Very good, I think that is all for the moment," Reuter said in a dismissive tone.

Schettler continued, "Just one thing, gentlemen, I would appreciate if you send for me when we make contact with the British Fleet."

"They have been in constant contact with us by radio asking for our course, speed and position," Reuter said.

"They also told us that we will be met by, what Beatty calls, a 'sufficient force'."

Lessel added, "At this rate, I think we should make contact with them early tomorrow morning. If you want to return to the bridge then, I think that'll be time enough. But if something should occur before that, I'll see you are informed."

Schettler left the bridge and went to the radio room to send a message to the other councillors and ombudsmen about the men's behaviour. He sought out Herzmann and the two of them wrote out posters which they put up around the ship.

*

His alarm woke Schettler at six o' clock the following day. He had only got to bed after one and he felt decidedly groggy. He and Kegel had drunk too much whilst they discussed their rumbustious youth.

He put on his trousers and went to the toilet, but the smell was so foul that he made do with the briefest visit, giving himself only a cursory wash and cleaning his teeth with bicarbonate of soda and toothpaste to try to get rid of his stinking breath.

He returned and finished dressing, putting on his best uniform to look smart in case he had to meet the British later. Arriving at the canteen, he found the queue was too long for him to get to the bridge on time, so he decided to skip breakfast and go directly there.

The darkened bridge was peaceful with only four on duty; the pilot, the officer of the watch and two able seamen, one at the helm and one scouring the area with binoculars. Not recognising any of them, Schettler introduced himself.

The two officers, a lieutenant and a second lieutenant, returned his introduction and the bridge fell silent again. Schettler looked out of the window to the dark sea ahead and the calm and quiet atmosphere increased his feeling of tiredness. The quiet was broken by his stomach rumbling so loudly that everyone, except the rating with the binoculars, turned to look at him. The starboard door opened before he could make an excuse and the admiral, the captain and the first officer filed in. The lieutenant shouted at the top of his voice, "Atten-shun," and the two officers turned smartly towards them and saluted. The able seamen came smartly to attention and Schettler found himself in the same stiff and erect position before he had a chance to think and relax his posture. He hoped the three senior officers hadn't noticed his lapse into military discipline.

Another worry surfaced. Was cleaning his teeth earlier enough to get rid of the smell of last night's beer from his breath? He had better not take the chance. He would stay out of range, or if that wasn't possible, he would keep his mouth tightly shut. His head was beginning to pound, as was his heart, and he hoped that he wouldn't start feeling sick. He shouldn't have drunk so many beers.

The admiral looked in sombre mood. "Good morning, gentlemen. Let's see what the English have in store for us today. Have we made contact yet?"

"No, sir, not yet," answered the lieutenant.

"It's early yet, sir," Lessel said and asked the lieutenant for their course, speed and position. Then he asked when was the last time the British had requested a positional update and was told, half an hour ago. The lieutenant went on to say that the fleet was now in the formation ordered by the British with three nautical miles between the groups. The convoy was a total length of nineteen miles.

Lessel nodded, giving the lieutenant an order to move all clocks back an hour to Greenwich Mean Time.

The admiral looked at Schettler. "Good morning, Councillor. Are you ready for a long day?"

"Yes, Admiral."

"Good. Unless you have more pressing matters to deal with, I think you should stay here on the bridge."

Schettler nodded.

Having heard their current position was twenty miles east of St Abbs Head, where the mouth of the River Forth meets the North Sea, the senior officers went to the chart table and watched as the lieutenant pinpointed their position. Lessel stated that he thought they would encounter the British within half an hour. He invited Schettler to have a look and he wandered over to peer at the chart.

Wachter asked if he could see where they were. Schettler, still conscious of his beery breath, kept his answer to "Mmm" and nodded his head. Wachter looked questioningly at him but he said nothing. Schettler returned to where he'd been standing at the port end of the bridge.

The weather was dry with little wind, but the visibility was low, due to a slight haze. Just before eight o'clock, the watchman reported seeing a beam of a searchlight ten degrees to port, about two kilometres away.

Binoculars were passed around and all, but the helmsman looked for signs of the British Fleet.

Two minutes later, Schettler caught sight of the first ship, as it suddenly loomed out of the mist so fast it made him start. The lieutenant, who was standing at the starboard end of the bridge, reported a parallel sighting on that side. Soon, ship after ship passed down in two lines on either side of them. It looked like they were making between ten and fifteen knots. Each ship had her guns aligned towards them and their decks were cleared for action, an act against the agreement reached between the two commands. Reuter flew into a rage. There was no reason why the unarmed German Fleet, that was obeying the orders of their former enemy to the letter, should be intimidated in this way. It could only be to humiliate them. He paced back and forth across the bridge, muttering to himself. "Captain, will you see to it that each outrage we encounter in the remainder of this awful voyage is documented in full," he growled at Lessel, "so that we can bring them up when we meet Beatty."

Lessel nodded first to Reuter and then to the lieutenant, who picked up a pencil and paper and started writing.

The ships passed continuously for almost an hour, battleships, battle-cruisers, even two of the new aircraft carriers and many destroyers, mostly British, but US, French and Japanese flags could also be seen.

"Clearly, gentlemen, the British thought fit to involve such a large force, in case we have hidden means of retaliation," Reuter commented contemptuously.

Although Schettler was personally ambivalent towards the methods used by the Allies, he did think that such a blatant show of force was unnecessary and very arrogant. He found himself feeling a little sorry for Reuter. It seemed to be a charade.

Schettler could hear cheering coming from the decks and noticed that the officers were hearing it too. He left the bridge and went down to find out what it was about. As much as anything it would be an opportunity to clear his head.

The cheering was coming from the starboard deck where groups of sailors were standing. When he asked what was going on, a rating turned to him grinning, and said that the British sailors were flying the red flag as a token of respect for the revolution. Sure enough when Schettler looked, every ship that passed was flying a red banner from its mast. He turned and walked to the port deck. The ships on that side were flying blue flags. This was probably to identify which flotilla the Allied ships were in and had nothing to do with support for the revolution. He returned to the starboard side and imparted the bad news to the sailors, whereupon the cheering stopped, and they continued to watch the ships in silence. Having solved one problem, he decided to tackle another. "Comrades, I think you should smarten yourselves up. Appearing in such a slovenly manner is to insult the revolution."

One asked if he had put the notice up in the canteen.

"You know that, I signed it."

"It's a load of shit."

Another man piped up, "You can't say that. I think the councillor has a point."

A full debate started. Schettler left them to it and moved along the deck. He stood there for ten minutes, just watching the row of ships as they continued, till, in one beautifully choreographed manoeuvre, the lines slowed and turned 180 degrees, continuing in the same direction as the ships they would escort. Schettler made his way back to the bridge, feeling better for the fresh air.

Reuter, who had now regained his composure, was complementing the British seamanship.

The lookout reported that he could see an Allied ship manoeuvring into position ahead of the Seydlitz. Everyone trained their binoculars on her.

After five minutes, the British sent a radio message that the escort was now in place and HMS Cardiff would lead them into the Firth of Forth. They asked that the Germans make twelve knots. This was the final embarrassment. Reuter knew that this was impossible, but he ordered a message be sent back saying they would. As the ships were entering the Firth of Forth, it was clear that they were falling behind, and the Cardiff was radioed to request a reduction to ten knots.

HMS Queen Elizabeth, flying the flag of the Commander of the Fleet, Sir David Beatty, ran down between the Germans and the starboard Allied escort with a full complement of the ship's company cheering as they went. The Germans could only watch in stunned silence. As Schettler looked on at all this sea power, a flight of aircraft appeared overhead. He might find it difficult to identify with the old order, but he understood why Reuter was so mortified. Beattie had not allowed his opposite number to retain even his self-respect. Schettler was in no doubt that the same would have happened had the boot been on the other foot and for him, this only confirmed the barbarity and callous nature of this system that had to achieve total power regardless of the cost. He wondered if Reuter's earlier warning was right too. If British Naval Command could organise such a show of strength against an unarmed fleet, a preposterous act of self- gratification, they must still be in tight control of their rank and file.

*

As the 320 war ships, the largest fleet ever seen in naval history, steamed into the Firth of Forth that morning, the Allied ships manoeuvred from two columns on either side of the Germans to one long column. Then they took a course to the north of the Island of May, while the Germans continued to the south. The earlier mist had thickened considerably, and it was impossible, at least at the wide river mouth, to see the coast.

Soon the German's received a radio message saying a pinnace would come along side and six naval inspectors would board to check all armaments had been properly de-commissioned. They expected complete co-operation.

As they sailed further up the estuary, Schettler could just make out the coast through the mist. They were passing some small towns but one in particular interested him. It had three rocky islands close by its coast, so he went to the chart and identified the largest and most easterly was the Bass Rock, so the town must be North Berwick. He thought it must have been a centre for whaling, as he could see the jaw bone of a large whale protruding from the top of the conical hill above the town. His meticulous survey of the southern coast of the Firth of Forth came to an end when a rating arrived to say that the naval inspectors and a pilot had arrived, and they required to be shown around the ship's armaments. Lessel told the rating to bring the British pilot to the bridge and asked if Schettler would meet the gunnery officer, Lieutenant Retzlaw, and the six British inspectors, to act as interpreter. Schettler followed the rating to the main after deck to join the inspection team and collect the pilot. When he got there, Retzlaw was standing beside a senior rating with the gunnery flash on his arm, while the British, two lieutenants and four gunnery ratings, were standing close by.

"I'm Councillor Schettler. I'm here to translate," he said to Retzlaw.

Retzlaw, who looked to be in his mid-twenties, sounded nervous. "That's good. I don't speak English and I don't think Müller does either." The rating nodded.

"That's fine. Shall we go and ask them what they want to do?"

They approached the six and Schettler introduced himself and the lieutenant and asked them to identify themselves. The younger of the two British lieutenants looked him up and down. "You're a petty officer, I believe, so refer to myself and my colleague as sir, as is expected in the British Navy."

Schettler smiled pleasantly back at him. "I'm not *in* the British Navy. I'm a Councillor of the Soldiers' Council. We've a Vice-Admiral on our bridge and I don't call him, sir. Just identify yourselves for the record and tell us what you want of us, Lieutenant."

The older spoke. "My name is Gardner and my colleague here is Brown. These gunnery senior ratings are Gilbert, Gordon, Maclean and Winterbottom. We wish to inspect your armaments, although we'll have to be brief as there are only five teams to carry out the inspection of your ships. I suggest we start with your twelve-inch guns and work our way down. Is that acceptable?"

Schettler translated and Retzlaw answered affirmatively, and as they were aft they should start here and work forward. When Schettler translated, there was a lot of nodding. The inspection was brief as they only looked to see if the firing mechanisms had been dismantled. They didn't check if they were still capable of being refitted.

Soon the three lieutenants had identified a way of working and communicating without language and the work was divided into two groups, the first with the officers and the second with the gunnery ratings. Schettler found himself with little to do. As he stood there, the senior rating known as Gordon contrived to stand close by. He smiled at Schettler then spoke. "Aye, you fairly took Brown down a peg or two there." Schettler just grinned but said nothing. The other continued, "Has, what was it you called it? The Soldiers' Councils got control all over Germany?"

Schettler nodded. "Yes, more of less, Workers' and Soldiers' Councils have taken control in all the main towns and cities. The Soldiers' Council is in control within the fleet."

"Is it just like what happened in Russia?"

"Pretty much!"

"That's great. We'll need to do the same here. I come from Glasgow and there's a lot of unrest there. We'll need jobs when we get demobbed but there's not many to be had. We'll just have to take power just like you."

Gordon furrowed his brow. "How come you have a Scottish accent, my friend?"

"The person who taught me to speak English is Scottish."

They stopped their conversation as the group came together once again to walk to the next set of guns.

Towards the end of the inspection, Schettler and Gordon found themselves together again, and Schettler asked, "Look, Mr Gordon, could you do me a favour?"

"Yes, if a' can."

He pulled Margaret's letter from his pocket. "Could you post this for me please? I don't have any money, though."

Gordon took the envelope and read the address. "God, that's only ten minutes' walk from my house. Can you credit that? Aye of course, I'll post it for you. Who's Margaret Nairn anyway? A hope she's not a German spy." He laughed loudly.

"No, she's my cousin. My mother was a Glasgower."

"You mean a Glaswegian?"

"Ah, I forgot the proper term! See, my Scottish is rusty. I'll need to practice. It's a long time since I was there."

Gordon looked wistful. "Us, fightin' with each other for four years, and your mother was from Glasgow and you've even been there yourself." He shook his head and put the letter into his tunic pocket. "It's a small world right enough. Och, within a couple of weeks you'll be speaking like a native again."

"You better keep that to yourself or they'll confiscate the letter and you'll probably get in trouble for fraternising with the enemy," Schettler warned.

"You're right there, pal. I'll say nothing. Don't worry."

When the six inspectors left the ship, Schettler was about to return to the bridge when he realised that his hangover had gone, and he was ravenously hungry. He made for the canteen.

Reuter broadcast to all ships that afternoon that he'd received a message from Admiral Beatty. The German flag was to be hauled down at sunset and not hoisted again without permission. He added that he thought this was an outrage and would be taking the matter up with Admiral Beatty when they met. For the time being, though, the order was to be carried out.

Schettler watched through binoculars as the great ships slid, dead slow, past the city of Edinburgh, where he could see there were large pockets of sightseers watching this great spectacle from the docks and harbours. It was eerily quiet. Soon, despite the mist, he could see the three steel spans of the vast bridge ahead which took the railway across the River Forth. He remembered his excitement when he and his family rode across it on the train heading for Perthshire all those years ago and he hoped that Gordon would be able to post his letter to Margaret.

As the ship came parallel to an island Schettler identified on the chart as Inchkeith, the pilot gave the order to stop engines and drop anchor.

Just before sunset, Reuter asked Lessel and Wachter to accompany him to the deck to haul down the flag and await the deputation from the British. He asked Schettler to attend too. When he arrived on the main deck, Schettler went around the groups of ratings asking that they stay well back and not cause any disruption. His argument was that to show any form of dissent would be counter-revolutionary. The hauling down of the Imperial Ensign, would be the last act of banishment of the old order, but it should be allowed to be done with dignity. Most of them agreed. The man chosen to haul down the flag was an elderly chief petty officer, who was immaculately dressed in his uniform, but with 'His Majesties' removed from his cap badge. An order which had come from the WSC before the fleet had sailed. Now all was in place.

When sunset came at 3.57pm, Reuter addressed Lessel. "Have the flag hauled down, Captain." The chief petty officer stepped smartly forward and took down the flag precisely in accordance with military regulations, while the company of officers saluted.

Minutes later, a British motor vessel came alongside and four Royal Naval Officers, in full dress uniform and sword, boarded accompanied by six naval ratings armed with rifles and fixed bayonets. They all stood to attention and both sets of officers saluted. The senior staff officer, Commodore Michael Hodges, presented his party to Reuter, who invited them to join him in his stateroom. As the senior officers from both navies walked towards the stateroom door, Reuter indicated that Schettler should join them.

They sat along the length of the conference table, with the Germans on one side and the British on the other and formal introductions were made. When it came to Schettler, Commodore Hodges interrupted. "It has already been made clear that the Allied Authorities won't negotiate with any representative whom the British Government doesn't recognise."

Reuter shook his head. "Councillor Schettler is acting as an interpreter and won't be party to any negotiations." The British exchanged uncertain glances with one another and Hodges said, "We have an interpreter."

Reuter nodded. "Ja, das machen wir!" Schettler had taken the initiative, and began translating.

Hodges presented the Germans with a thick, unbound document of typewritten standing orders for their fleet during internment. It went into minute details, from boiler pressure to anchor chain lengths. The more important aspects were highlighted. There were to be no radio transmissions. Signal communications were to be made by light flashing Morse code and it was forbidden to lower boats.

Reuter brought up his points of complaint. Although they listened, the British refused to consider them. Reuter wasn't content with this outcome and said he would put them in writing to Admiral Beatty. "Why is the Admiral not here?" he asked.

The answer, that he had to attend to matters in Rosyth, sounded feeble, as did the answer to his next question, "Will you tell us where our ships are to be interned?"

Hodges said that he didn't know the final locations of internment but in the next three days, the fleet would be escorted to Scapa Flow in groups, after a detailed check that they were properly disarmed. He said this was the only location which could provide a safe anchorage for that number of ships, until the final destination was decided.

This caused further disquiet among the Germans. Looking Hodges in the eye, Reuter said, "This is a disgraceful way to treat a naval fleet which has never been defeated in battle and is now not actively in a state of war. Where is the English sense of fair-play, Commodore Hodges?"

Hodges replied that he wasn't in a position to discuss anything more and rose. It seemed the meeting was over.

It was now clear that any idea they would be treated in a way other than virtual prisoners of war, was erroneous.

Reuter did write a letter to Beatty, but it was ignored and by November 24th 1918, the German fleet had been escorted to Scapa Flow.

Chapter 6

"Please, Miss, Miss, please Miss."

"What is it, Walker?"

"I'm stuck, Miss."

"Well, have a think about it and if you're still unsure in the morning, I'll go over it with you."

Just then the bell rang for the end of day and Margaret Nairn shouted, "Right, boys and girls. Put your books away quickly and get into line at the door. Hurry now."

The class did as they were told as they always did at home time and soon they had vacated the room. Margaret quickly took her coat from the cupboard and put it on. She was in a hurry to get home for her evening meal before she had to travel back to town to meet her fiancé, Charlie Tennant, who had a twenty-four hour leave from his ship.

As she left the room and started down the corridor, she heard a shrill voice behind her. "Miss Nairn, can you spare a second?"

The voice was instantly recognisable – not one she could ignore, unfortunately. She turned, to find Miss Harkness, the head mistress, swishing down the corridor towards her. Damn, she thought.

Her tram was due in less than seven minutes and she needed to catch this one if she was to have any chance of getting home on time.

"I was wondering if your absentees are reducing in number?"

"Yes, they are. We have only six absent with influenza and I think most of them have had it now."

"That's good! I was very sorry to hear that the boy, Balfour, died."

"I'm afraid that family was rather decimated. His mother and grandfather died, and his father and older brother, Peter, are still on the danger list, I believe."

"It's tragic. The school has lost twelve children so far but I think things are beginning to get a little better. And how are you feeling yourself, Miss Nairn?"

"Much better, thank you. I felt quite tired last week. Trying to manage a class was an effort, but I'm back to normal now."

"Good. I also wanted to talk to you about the boy, Anderson. I've just had his mother up for the second time. She thinks two boys in Miss Cunningham's class are bullying him. Has he spoken to you about it?"

"No, he's said nothing."

"Well if he does, will you let me know."

"Yes, of course, I will." Margaret tried not to let her impatience show, but the clock was ticking and she had less time than ever to catch that tram.

"This bullying business is becoming an issue. I think it's because the boys are being namby-pambied by their mothers because the fathers are still not back from the war. What do think, Miss Nairn?"

"I really couldn't say, but I'm sure you're right."

"Things like this are getting out of hand—"

Desperation set in and Margaret forced herself to speak up. "I'm sorry, Miss Harkness, I have an appointment. I will have to go."

The head, who clearly wanted a long conversation, didn't look pleased but she said, "Very well, Miss Nairn. Remember to let me know if Anderson talks to you."

"I certainly will," said Margaret, and she once again began her flight from Glasgow's Hillhead Primary School.

As she reached Great Western Road, she could see the green tram coming over the brow of the hill and she was glad of her new, shorter skirt as she made a dash across the main road to the stop. This was behaviour thought unbecoming for a young lady and she hoped the head wasn't watching her from some convenient window.

She got there at the same time as the tram and was happy to see someone getting off; otherwise, it might have passed her by. She boarded and stood on the platform pondering whether to go upstairs, until the conductress shouted, "Hurry along now." She went inside. It was busy and the only seat she could find was beside a fat man who took up most of the seat and made no attempt to squeeze his bulk further in. She sat precariously on the edge, as the tram hurtled and jolted towards the city centre. As it turned from Cambridge Street into Sauchiehall Street, a dray that had shed two of its barrels was blocking the way and they were held up for twenty minutes while the mess was cleared up. When Margaret arrived at her stop beside Duke Street Hospital, she walked the short distance uphill to the house, feeling irritated.

To Margaret's annoyance, her mother, Nell, began fussing over her as soon as she entered the kitchen. Her mother was all too aware that Margaret was lucky to be alive. The flu epidemic had killed thousands throughout the city that year.

Margaret was the only one still living in the family home. Her father had died before the war, her brother, Charles, had been killed in the Gallipoli Campaign in 1915, her older sister, Helen, was married and widowed with two children, and her brother, Bob, was still in the army, although a few days earlier they had received a letter from Aldershot Barracks saying he thought he would be home before the New Year. Between Margaret's flu and Bob's imminent return, her mother was in a highly-charged state.

"When's tea, Mother?"

"It's mince and tatties. And I'll just have to boil the potatoes. What's the big hurry, anyway?"

"I'm meeting Charlie."

"Oh. Are you? When did *he* show up?"

"He phoned the school this morning. He has a twenty-four hour leave."

Her mother sniffed. She wasn't fond of Charlie Tennant, as she felt he was a bit common. She had hoped Margaret would have met another teacher or a doctor, perhaps. But Charlie had only worked in the shipyards before joining the Navy.

"I better get on with tea then. Oh, a letter came for you today. The handwriting looks like a man's and it has a Haddington postmark."

"How intriguing! Put it on the table and I'll look at it after I've changed."

When she returned to the kitchen, the letter was lying on top of the place mat and her mother was busy plating up the mince and tatties.

She studied the envelope and felt all around it with her fingers. Then she studied the writing.

"You're right! I've never seen an envelope like this before. The writing's strange and yes, I think it's been written by a man."

Her mother turned to see her still gazing at the envelope and said exasperatedly,

"Why don't you open it, then?"

Margaret slit the top with her knife, pulled the pages out and unfolded them. She began to read, but then turned to the last page to see the signature.

"Oh my God!" she said under her breath. As she read on, she fell silent and tears welled up inside her. Her mother stood beside her, holding the steaming plate of food until she could stand it no longer and shouted, "Well?"

"Well what?"

"Who's it from?"

"Your nephew!"

"*Who?*"

"Johann. And you'll never guess."

"*What?*"

"He's here!"

"*Where?*"

"In Scotland."

"How on earth can he be here?"

By this time Margaret had finished reading.

"Here, read it yourself."

Her mother put down the plate of food and took the letter.

As her mother read the letter, Margaret could see she too had tears in her eyes. Marion and she were very close and not being able to communicate with her sister had been irritating and intensely worrying. She had known about Heinrich being wounded because this news had been contained within one of the few letters that had arrived through a neutral port. She had resented the suffering this war had caused her family and her son Charles' death had polarised that into grief. Because she couldn't write back, Marion was still unaware of this and therefore not able to offer the comfort her sister had desperately needed. Johann's description of the suffering of the Germans and the futility of the war added a feeling of remorse to her resentfulness, tugging at her already threadbare emotions. Nell had always believed that someday, the family would be reunited and it was good to hear that this would soon come to pass.

Nell pulled herself together. "What do you think these Workers' Republics mean?"

"They've set up socialist states in the same way as the Russian people did last year and it's ended the war. I think it's wonderful! I'm so proud, one of our family is involved. We would be better off if it happened here."

Her mother changed the subject. "When you're out tonight, I'm going to write to my sister."

"I wouldn't advise that, Mother. Not until the Armistice is signed. The authorities don't know we have a German side to our family and it could still cause us trouble."

Her mother looked disappointed. "I suppose you're right."

"I'm sure it'll soon be over and you'll be able to write to Aunt Marion. Anyway, I have to go." She returned Johann's letter to the envelope, put it in her handbag and went to collect her coat and hat from the stand in the hall.

Margaret was ten minutes late when she arrived at the Willow Tearoom in Sauchiehall Street. Charlie was already waiting outside, looking immaculate in his best chief petty officer's uniform. He smiled and put his arms around her, squeezed her tightly and kissed her cheek. She struggled to breathe and told him to stop. "Not here, Charlie, not in the street." He loosened his grip but still held her close. "It's been months and I've missed you, my love."

"I've missed you too, Charlie, but let's get inside."

She loved the Willow Tearoom. It had such a pleasant and relaxed ambience with its Mackintosh art nouveau interior. It seemed to represent a civilised world where she could be happy.

"Let's have high tea," Charlie said, when they were shown to their table.

"No, let's not! It's too expensive and anyway I've already eaten. I told you to do the same when you phoned me," she scolded. "That's another thing. You shouldn't phone the school either. Harkness doesn't like it. I only got away with it because you're in the Navy. What's all the mystery about anyway? And why have you got a twenty-four hour leave?"

"One question at a time, my darling," he said teasing her, before becoming serious.

"The thing is, I've had my demob postponed for at least six months. They want the Emperor of India to be part of the escort of the German fleet to Scapa Flow and then guard them when they're up there. The rumour is we might have to escort them somewhere else later. Just my luck. It sounds a really bad posting. Scapa's a bleak place at the best of times, but in the winter it's miserable. We're all cheesed off about it. We've not to get any local shore leave which isn't really much of a sacrifice. There's not much to do in Stromness. But here's the good bit."

He brightened up. "We've to get five days a month home leave worked out on some sort of rota system. So I'll be back home very soon, maybe even for Christmas or New Year. I don't know yet."

He smiled and then went on, "I suppose there's some compensation. I'll still be paid as long as I'm in the Navy. If I was demobbed now, I'd be going straight on the dole."

Margaret nodded, taking his hand across the table. "That's right. Things are bad here. The Trades' Council's talking tough but the government's getting really repressive too. I think it's all going to explode soon. I suppose you've heard that John Maclean's back in prison again?"

"Aye, I did, a few months back, but only from the papers. You know what they're like, always trying to do him down."

"He got five years this time but there's a huge campaign to get him released, we've been demonstrating every week," Margaret said. "Oh Charlie, his final speech from the dock was a triumph! He talked for seventy-five minutes about how we must end the war and the working class must take power through revolution. He said the capitalists still need colonies to expand their markets, so before we know it there'll be another war. I can't bear the thought of another war!"

Charlie nodded fervently. "I've always supported Maclean. I'm sure my comrades in the Navy would join any bid for power. So many sailors died and the survivors are coming home to unemployment and hardship worse than before the war. Anyway, tell me what's worrying you about Scapa. I noticed your reaction when I spoke about it earlier."

"I'll tell you later. How is it you're only here for twenty-four hours?"

Just then the waitress came over to take their order. Margaret didn't bother to look at the menu, asking instead for a pot of tea for two, and some assorted cakes and tea bread.

"Very well, miss," the waitress said, her face dimpling as she looked at Charlie.

When she had gone, Margaret laughed. "She fancies you, Charlie. It must be that nice, new uniform. Anyway what were you saying?"

Charlie shook his head. "You're incorrigible! As the ship's in the Forth, local men could take short leave if they wanted, so first thing this morning I took a bus to Edinburgh and caught the train home, but I'll have to get the nine o'clock train back to Edinburgh tonight because we leave for Scapa with some of the German ships tomorrow morning. So tell me what's bothering you?"

"Nothing's bothering me, but I can't help being amazed at how fate comes into play sometimes."

His reply was interrupted as the waitress arrived back with the tea and a laden cake stand. As she set out the cups, she said, "Are you just home on leave, sir?"

Charlie nodded. "Yes, but not for long."

"That's a pity." Then she gave him a big smile, before walking off.

Margaret smirked. "Told you! Mind you, she's quite good looking."

"Oh, shut up! What's fate got to do with anything?"

"Read that, I just received it today." Margaret thrust the letter across the table.

Charlie pulled the pages from the envelope and began reading.

As he read, he ate several items from the cake stand and made muffled exclamations. When he'd finished, he looked at Margaret.

"That's a bolt from the blue, isn't it? They were right to mutiny and stop the war. I wish we'd done that."

Spotting two women at an adjacent table staring in their direction, Margaret put her hand up to his mouth. "Ssh, Charlie, keep your voice down when you say things like that. You don't know who's listening."

Charlie quietened down. "It's fine, don't worry. I wonder how he got the letter posted? These men aren't allowed off their ships." He looked at the envelope. "It's got a Haddington postmark."

"I was wondering about that too. And it's never been past the censor because he's written things that wouldn't have been tolerated."

"I see he's on Freddy the Grocer. That's their flag ship."

"The what?"

"I don't know how you pronounce it. But that's what we call it."

"That's the Friedrich der Grosse, Charlie."

"Aye. Whatever you say, teacher."

"I would like to write back to him about family things and what's happening here politically. I think it's a pot that'll soon boil over, don't you? But I know it wouldn't get through. We've never let on we have German relatives in case we got into trouble in some way. I'm certainly not going to let it be known now, not until the Armistice is signed anyway."

"Yes. I see what you mean. Oh well, if I come across him, I'll at least tell him you got the letter."

"Is that likely?"

"I shouldn't think so. But you never know. On my next leave, you could give me a letter to deliver, in the off-chance I can find a way of getting it to him."

Margaret looked thoughtful. "I might just do that."

After taking a bite of her Paris bun, she mused, "I felt so sorry for my mother when she read Johann's letter. It made her so unhappy. She and Aunt Marion are very close. She managed to hold her emotions together during the war and now it looks like they're all going to spill out."

*

Thomas Sinclair wasn't happy about being back in Glasgow. He found the city dank, cold and dirty and he hated it, but he hated Glaswegians most of all. They were aggressive. He didn't understand the way they talked or their sense of humour, and he certainly didn't like their preponderance towards socialism.

Sinclair was from Selby in Yorkshire and his father had started work at twelve in the pits. Right from the start, he had saved every penny and even after he married he kept doing so, to the point of keeping his family in a state of near destitution. Eventually, he had enough to buy his own hardware shop, which in time had blossomed into a company which provided machinery to the mining industry. It went from strength to strength and elevated the family's status in the town. This had brought with it a hatred for his humble background and those who still had to live like that and he saw to it that his three sons were privately educated.

He said to them, "Just remember, lads. If these people aren't wise enough, like me, to pull themselves from the mire they find themselves in, then they're only worth being ground down further by their betters. Whatever you do, don't waste your time sympathising with them." It was advice the three brothers took to heart.

A brilliant career in the army elevated Thomas to the rank of captain by the age of twenty eight, when he joined the intelligence service.

As he sat waiting to be served with high tea that Friday evening in the Willow Tearoom, a place he liked – an oasis of decorum – he spotted a man in naval uniform he recognised. He was with a pretty, young lady and they were heading for the door. The man seemed oblivious to anything around him, but Sinclair lifted his Evening Citizen a little higher to hide his face. As the couple left the tearoom, Sinclair tried to remember the man's name. Yes, it was Tennant – Charlie Tennant. He was one of the men he had interrogated back in 1914, a member of a small group of extremist trade unionists who had begun to arm themselves to fight against the authorities. These had been difficult times between 1913 and 14. Industrial unrest had taken the city to the brink of revolution. If war hadn't intervened, God knows what would have happened, he thought.

They had prosecuted three men in the organisation, the two ringleaders and another man – what was *his* name? He was a pal of Tennant's. Gerry something, that's right Gerry O'Brien, that was it. O'Brien and Tennant were small fry and they, like all the others, were invited to join up and shut up. They had accepted. O'Brien and Tennant were taken to join the navy but O'Brien failed the medical. That left the security services in a quandary. He couldn't be set free so he had to be prosecuted with the ringleaders. Sinclair grinned to himself. Four years for being unfit for duty. How ironic.

The guns had come from Ireland but because they were of German origin, the prosecution was able to prove treason. In consequence, the two ringleaders had been hanged. It was rubbish of course but they had to be treated harshly to deter others from doing the same, though it was only possible because the country was on a war footing with Germany. O'Brien must be due for release about now. Sinclair sighed.

In the last year, the fervour for revolution had been whipped up again by Glasgow's own socialist evangelists, John Maclean, Willie Gallacher and Harry McShane. Now matters were being made worse by men being demobilised from the forces and unable to find work. Sinclair and his small team of secret service operatives had been sent to Glasgow once more, to try to deal with the problem.

*

As Margaret sat down inside the almost empty tram and blew a kiss towards Charlie who stood waving on Sauchiehall Street, all sorts of thoughts were bombarding her mind. She was relieved that he had been kept on in the navy, as she knew when his demob did come, her excuse to defer their marriage was over. She had told him often enough that she wasn't prepared to give up her job as a teacher any time soon, which she would have to do as a married woman. She loved him and some day she would like to have children of her own. But right now, her career was the most important. It was extraordinary that women had to make these choices. She wanted a sexual relationship but even that was denied to her outside marriage in this so-called decent society. She felt it was important to be in the vanguard of the fight against the system that advocated this and yet also denied most women the right to vote. God, she thought, we're denied the basic rights as human beings!

She thought about Johann's letter. Like the German people, the Scots would have to be fighters too. Fighters like her friend, Kate A'Herne, who had managed to escape to Glasgow from Dublin after her part in the Easter Rising.

It had taken a long time and a lot of prompting to get Kate to talk about her experiences and when she finally did, it was in a very self-effacing way.

"Ach, I did very little really, Margaret. They thought I was too young, ye see. I was a member of Cumann na mBan and, along with the Irish Volunteers and the Irish Citizen Army, we were all drafted into the Army of the Irish Republic just before the rising. Mind you, some of my comrades were very courageous. Helena Molony fought beside the men who attacked Dublin Castle, Constance Markievicz shot a policeman near St Stephen's Green and my friend Margaret Skinnider – she came from Coatbridge, you know – was shot three times while an attack was being mounted against soldiers in the Russell Hotel, but she wasn't killed."

Kate sighed. The effort of recalling what had happened seemed to affect her.

"All they would allow me to do, was to act as a courier, or forage for rations for the men. Sometimes though, I was sent on scouting expeditions to gather intelligence on what the British Army was getting up to or carry dispatches between units. The best job was when I joined my comrades to transfer arms from the stores to where they were needed for the fighting. We nearly got caught doing that once. Four of us had just delivered eight boxes of ammunition to the GPO, when we were spotted by the army who fired on us but we managed to get away."

Margaret tried to imagine what it must have felt like to flee from bullets. "How did you get away after it was all over?"

"Padraig Pearse declared that we had to get out on the Friday, the day before he surrendered and I managed to speak to my brother, Liam, who was in the GPO at the time. He said I should get out of Ireland right away in case of recriminations, and here I am. Mind you some of the women stayed where they were and were arrested and jailed, just like the men."

What would happen here if the people rose up against British imperialism, Margaret wondered? She suspected there would be a similar, brutal response and she hoped, if and when the time came, she would have the guts to fight like Kate.

Chapter 7

Scapa Flow is surrounded by the eight large and small islands of the Orkneys. Some of them, especially the main island to the north, have a flat shoreline with rolling land behind, but Hoy, the most westerly island is mountainous – like a giant standing over his quarry, dark and menacing.

It was ten o'clock on the morning of November 26th when the last assemblage of capital ships, including the Friedrich der Grosse, sailed through the defensive boom. The ships dropped anchor in the northwest to await the British naval pilots who would manoeuvre them into their final anchorage.

In the winter light, the view was grey and bleak. As Schettler, Herzmann and Kegel joined many of the crew on deck surveying the scene, the wind penetrated their winter overcoats and seemed to bite into their very souls.

The silent vigil was eventually broken by Müller, an engineering officer. "You men have work to do. I suggest you stop staring into space and get on with it."

There were many groans, as the men began shuffling around despondently, although some began to move away. Not content with the slow and pondering response, Müller barked again. "If you don't get a move on, I'll see that you are disciplined."

"What, are you going to confine us to our quarters?" a stoker shouted, his remark making those within earshot laugh. Müller rushed forward and struck him on the side of the head, and the man fell backwards onto the deck. The men mobbed the officer, pushing him around the deck, until a voice boomed from the back, "Make way, Comrades!"

Axel Penzberg barged through the crowd and grabbed Müller by the lapels. With their faces only centimetres apart, he bellowed, "If you ever strike any man again, I'll have you strung up by the balls." Still holding the officer by one hand, he half turned to address the sailors. "The Red Guard says just stay where you are, Comrades, and ignore this prick's order."

Schettler was still standing, watching, by the bulwark. "I'm sure you'll agree with me, Councillor, won't you?" Penzberg challenged.

Schettler had dreaded this. Müller and Penzberg were both wrong. He would now have to sort it out and diffuse a very volatile situation. He nodded. "Yes, Comrade Penzberg, I agree that no man should be treated in that brutal way."

Herzmann went over to speak to the stoker who had been helped to his feet. "Are you all right, Comrade?" The stoker, who looked shaken, nodded.

Schettler addressed the men. "I'll be reporting this officer's conduct to Admiral Reuter and insist he is punished, but I must make it clear that when you volunteered for this assignment, it was on the basis that orders from the officers concerning the running of the ships would be carried out and this was accepted by the Soldiers' Council. So this officer does have the right to tell you to get back to work if, that is, you are on duty."

Penzberg laughed. "Listen to this, Comrades! Which side is our Councillor Schettler on? First he gave orders to strike down our red banners of revolution to put back the imperial flag of the Kaiser who had us killed in our millions, and now he tells us to obey the very officers who were there to aid his task."

Schettler shook his head. "This is no way to conduct ourselves, Comrades. We have to show solidarity. It was the whole council who took that decision and you all know the reason why. And it was the Workers' and Soldiers' Councils in Kiel and Wilhelmshaven who agreed to your working conditions aboard these vessels. But make no mistake, Comrade Herzmann and I, are, and always will be, on the side of the revolution."

Penzberg sneered. "I say you shouldn't trust your so-called Comrade Schettler. You can hear from the way he speaks – all lah de dah. He's not one of us."

But the men had already begun to disperse and Penzberg could do no more than unhand the officer and walk away.

Schettler walked over to the officer. "I *will* report your conduct to Admiral Reuter."

The officer turned on his heel. "Go to hell, Bootsmann."

Schettler walked back to join Kegel at the bulwark and shook his head. "I knew this would happen with Penzberg on board. He's a devious bastard but, like it or not, we can't do without the officers' expertise and the British won't negotiate with us, only with them."

Kegel muttered, "You really don't know who to believe these days, do you? To my mind, you're all working towards Germany's downfall."

Schettler gave him a sceptical look. "I've a lot of work to do, but we should talk about that sometime." He turned to Herzmann. "Let's go, we need to write a report about this."

The British naval pilot came aboard as darkness was

already beginning to engulf the surroundings. The ship weighed anchor and it was manoeuvred towards its final anchorage further west towards Cava. Because the pilot was unfamiliar with the ways of the ship, he had two abortive attempts to reach it, something that caused the crew great merriment.

*

As time passed, the crews settled into a life of inactivity and boredom in this isolated location. When they discovered this was their final place of internment, and therefore High Command had been deceived, this further polarised the rift between officers and men, and more joined the Red Guard.

The Soldiers' Council was caught up in the middle of a conflict between Reuter and the British, about the numbers of officers and men who were to be repatriated. The British wanted the crews to be reduced to that of care and maintenance, but Reuter, fearing that if this happened the Germans would lose control of the ships, requested that a greater number be kept on board.

As far as the council was concerned, the more sailors sent home the better, but the more important issue, was who was to be sent back. Trouble between the officers and men was seen by Reuter as the sole responsibility of the council, which was wrong, but in an endeavour to solve this, the council saw an opportunity to cut down the numbers of Red Guard. There was also the urgent question of food. If the stores weren't replenished soon, the men would starve.

If it was to have any chance of resolving these ever-growing problems, the council would need to meet more often. Communications between the ships was inadequate, and Schettler was sent to Reuter to make the case for all councillors to be billeted together aboard the Friedrich der Grosse, leaving the ships under the control of the ombudsmen. Reuter accepted the suggestion reluctantly, adding that if the arrangement didn't work, they would be sent back.

It was subsequently revealed that many of the senior officers were to be repatriated including Reuter himself, who was going back for health reasons, but would later return.

When the first two ships, the SS Sierra Ventana and SS Graf Waldsee arrived on December 3rd with space to repatriate 175 officers and 3,200 men between them, it was discovered that they were carrying insufficient stores to re-stock the fleet. To make matters worse, the British gave the ships only six hours to unload and then embark their human cargo. The result was pandemonium. So in the coming days, at the request of the council, Reuter negotiated that future incoming ships would be allowed to berth for twice the time.

Chapter 8

As the train pulled into Glasgow's Buchanan Street station at midday on Tuesday December 3rd, the cold and heavy rain didn't deter the thousands of people awaiting John Maclean's arrival from Aberdeen.

They packed the concourse, the forecourt and spilled out onto the street. The crowds were so thickly packed that the traffic was unable to pass for hours. The government had been forced to release Maclean from Peterhead Prison after a little over six months of a five year prison sentence, thanks to the constant demonstrations objecting to his trial and incarceration.

As the train neared the station, Gerry O'Brien, who had also been released that day and had shared the compartment with Maclean, his wife Agnes, and the prominent suffragette, Mrs Dora Montefiore, stood up and addressed the great man. "I'd just like to say cheerio because when we get into the station you'll be too busy to talk to me. I ken it was in jail and all, but meeting you and listening to what you were saying – they've been the happiest days of my life. I've learned such a lot from you. Thanks so much, John."

Maclean smiled. "I'm never too busy to talk to you, Gerry. It was a pleasure. Your understanding of Marxist economics must now be as good as mine. But remember what I told you. It's education that will do the most for the working class. I think you should attend night-school to get the qualifications to enter university. Take care, Gerry."

As the train stopped to the sound of cheering and the singing of the Red Flag, the two shook hands.

When the compartment door opened, the cheering seemed to reverberate from every surface of the station building. It echoed over and over as the crowds outside heard that their hero had arrived.

The group climbed down and was greeted by two local leaders of the British Socialist Party who conducted them through the cheering crowds to an open carriage, the horses having been replaced by ten muscular workers. In this seething mass of people, O'Brien lost ground to Maclean's party. When the carriage moved off, with Maclean waving a large red flag on a wooden pole, O'Brian was still walking twenty yards behind.

Charlie Tennant and Kaitlin A'Herne were among the jubilant crowd. When she arrived in Glasgow in 1916, she joined the BSP, as a way of finding out who of her gender was interested in revolutionary politics in Glasgow. It was at their meetings she met Margaret Nairn.

Kate had thick, rich, auburn hair that fell around her shoulders, fine features with pale skin and green eyes that marked thousands of years of Celtic blood. She had an effervescent personality and a keen wit. She was fun to be with but also very single minded and resourceful when necessary.

Not wishing to attract any undue police attention, Tennant chose to wear civvies. It was his last full day of a week's leave, that he had been compelled to take so soon after his ship had berthed in Scapa Flow, to comply with the rota. The time hadn't suited him because he couldn't see much of Margaret, who was working. However, the news that John Maclean would be in Glasgow, made it worthwhile. He had tried to persuade Margaret to take a day's sick leave to see him arrive but she refused, saying that depriving children a day's education was too high a price, even to witness such an historic occasion. However, when she suggested that, as Kate had just been laid off from her job as a seamstress, he should take her instead, Tennant readily agreed.

The crowd around them was happy – singing and cracking jokes. The two were having fun. As the carriage reached Jamaica Street, it was forced to halt by the surging mass of people. Tennant had to lift Kate up to see what was going on and was glad she was small and light. Her hair protruded from her bottle-green hat and kept blowing into his eyes and mouth, obscuring his vision. Maclean shouted, "Three hearty cheers for the German Socialist Revolution!" As the crowd responded enthusiastically, Maclean continued, "The shouts that rent the air today are bound to haunt the capitalists of the Clyde for many days to come."

It was a particularly poignant moment for Tennant, knowing he would carry Margaret's letter to a comrade who had been involved in the Kiel insurrection – as long as he could find him.

As the carriage moved on its way once again, Tennant caught sight of a scuffle breaking out about twenty yards behind it. He took Kate's arm and they edged their way through the crowd to get a better look.

"What's going on, Charlie?" Kate said as she strained on tiptoe.

"It's just a bit of trouble," he answered.

Drawing closer, Tennant told her two men were trying to hold onto one small man, who was carrying a suitcase, as if to apprehend him. As they grabbed hold of him, the crowd intervened and the men were pushed and jostled and voices were raised. Two uniformed police arrived on the scene, guided by another man. The small man was quickly overpowered by the policemen and dragged to the side of the road. Tennant was startled to see the little man looked like his old friend from Fairfield's, Gerry O'Brien. He shouted his name, but in the din his voice was lost.

"Do you know the man?" Kate shouted to Tennant. As he answered that he thought he did, O'Brien disappeared. By the time they had squeezed through the crowd, O'Brien was long gone.

Kate asked, "Who is he?"

"He was someone I used to know in Fairfields."

As he counted back in his mind, Tennant realised if it was O'Brien he must have just been released. But what had he done now to be dragged away?

He smiled at Kate. "Never mind, I'm sure I was mistaken, I only saw his face for a second. Let's follow the carriage," and they re-joined the moving crowd as it crossed Glasgow Bridge to the Trades' Council building in Carlton Place on the south side of the Clyde.

As the carriage arrived, some of the party addressed the crowd, but Maclean who looked tired and drawn, said nothing. He had to be assisted down and, despite the crowd shouting for him to speak he just smiled and waved before he was taken inside.

Tennant looked down at Kate. "I think the show's over."

Kate agreed. Waiting around in the damp and cold of the afternoon would probably only result in another quick glimpse of Maclean, before he and his wife were taken back to their home.

They wandered across the suspension footbridge and headed around St Enoch Square to Argyle Street, where Kate could catch a tram to the east end.

As they stood at the tram stop, she talked animatedly about how ill Maclean had looked and hoped he would be able carry on working for a socialist Scotland. Then she added, "I hope your friend's all right. I wonder why he was picked up?"

Not wanting to make too much of it, Tennant said, "He's not really a friend, just someone I used to know at work. If I remember right, he liked a good drink. He was probably drunk and disorderly. Anyway, it probably wasn't him."

"Perhaps, although from what you described, it didn't sound drink related to me, Charlie..."

Before he could reply, her tram arrived, last in a group of three and she had to run to get in front of the crowd of shoppers who surged towards it from all over the busy street.

"Thanks, Charlie, I had a great time. See you soon."

Tennant decided to go to the Scotia Bar in Stockwell Street for a quick pint. He was convinced it was Gerry O'Brien and he had to agree with Kate, it didn't look drink related. The memory of the incident made him think about his old friend – Gerry never had much luck and it looked like that hadn't changed. It made him feel very uneasy.

*

The two policemen frogmarched O'Brien along Howard Street to St Enoch Square with the other three men walking behind, one carrying his case. Experience told O'Brien that trying to struggle or even to reason with the police was pointless, so he made no effort to hinder their progress.

When they reached the subway station, the two policemen stopped and held him, while one of the men spoke to him. "Look here, O'Brien, you'll remember Mr Sinclair? He was the man who interviewed you at Oxford Street Police Station in 1914."

"I never knew either the man's name or the place I was being held but if you say so I'll believe it. He was a right bastard, I remember."

"Mr Sinclair wants a word with you, so the best thing you can do is co-operate with us and you'll be on your way home in an hour or so. All right with you?"

"Sure thing, pal, I just got out of jail this morning and I don't want any trouble."

"Very good, Gerry. We'll go into St Enoch Hotel here and see him." The man thanked the policemen, who nodded and walked off.

O'Brien was taken up the ramp to where the entrance of the large and imposing railway hotel stood, set on a level above St Enoch Square. They walked past the elegant entrance to the other corner and entered through a seedy, staff door and into a goods elevator which took them to the fifth floor. They continued along the plush, green carpeted corridor to room 513. The man knocked on the ornate door and they waited. When O'Brien looked around him, the other two men had disappeared. The door opened and the man who had beaten him up four years ago was standing looking at him.

"How are you, Gerry?" he asked, smiling. Behind him was a large bedroom with a high ceiling, chintz curtains and matching bedspread. O'Brien thought it looked posh. He and the other man entered. The man set the suitcase down.

O'Brien said, "I was all right till ah saw you."

"Come now, Gerry, let's not have any hard feelings. You've paid your debt to society. I want to do you a favour." He pointed to the other man. "This is Mr Bradshaw and of course, I'm Mr Sinclair. It's good to get properly acquainted, isn't it? Let's sit down, shall we." Sinclair gestured to an easy chair by the large, double window. O'Brien walked to it and sat down. "Which part o' society did I pay my debt to? And before you answer that, if you two have to be Misters then I'll be one to, so it's Mr O'Brien, all right? What favour is it you want to do me?"

"All right, Mr O'Brien. Would you like a drink?"

"Ah don't mind if I do. It's been a while since I've had one."

"Will Scotch do you?"

"Oh aye, that'll be fine, with a drop of water."

Sinclair ordered Bradshaw to give O'Brien a good measure of Scotch, and ordered a gin and tonic for himself.

O'Brien held up his hand. "Don't make it a big one for me. I don't want to be agreein' to something I might regret later."

When Bradshaw had poured three drinks and handed them round, Sinclair continued, "Now that you're out of jail, what are your plans?"

"I thought I'd try to get my old job in Fairfield's back."

"Do you really think they'd employ a jailbird, especially one that might have shot the management?"

O'Brien sipped his whisky. "Well, I suppose when you put it like that…"

"That's right, not a chance, eh? But I can help you. I can get you a job in Beardmore's Parkhead Forge, if you want it.

No questions asked. What do you think?"

"Ah don't suppose you're doing this out of the goodness of your heart. What have ah to do for you?"

"I just want you to keep an eye on things." Mr Sinclair smiled, as if what he asked was perfectly reasonable. "Get yourself onto the shop stewards' committee and join the British Socialist Party. Let me know what's happening and what they're up to – who the extremists are and so on – nothing too taxing."

"And if I say no?"

"I'll see to it that you never work again. And you might be surprised how often you're picked up by the police for any number of reasons. Believe me, Mr O'Brien, I can make your life a complete misery."

O'Brien finished his whisky and put the glass down. "What if the shop stewards ask me how I got a job, after being in jail?"

"Tell them you had demob papers forged and they passed without trouble. That'll do your street credit a lot of good and we'll give you the papers anyway. All right?"

"I suppose I've really got no choice."

Sinclair smiled. "Good, that's settled then. You'll be reporting to Mr Bradshaw from now on. What about another drink for our friend here, Mr Bradshaw?"

Bradshaw poured more whisky into O'Brien's glass. "Let's make it Dick, and Gerry, shall we?"

"Aye whatever you like." O'Brien sighed.

Sinclair walked across to the sideboard and leant against it. "Good. Now tell us how well you knew John Maclean in Peterhead?"

Chapter 9

The weather was foul, torrential rain and a vicious northerly wind was blowing, as Tennant and his new-found friend climbed down onto platform two at Inverness station.

The journey from Glasgow had taken four and a half hours and, with an hour to go, the two had met and shared out each other's stock of alcohol. After a forty-five minute wait, they would continue to Thurso and then walk two miles to Scrabster Harbour where a naval launch may, weather permitting, be waiting to take men coming off shore leave back to their ships.

Tennant wasn't drunk, although he had consumed a few, but his friend, a thin, wiry man with a shock of deep red hair was plastered.

"What's your name again, pal?" he asked.

"Sydney, eh – Sydney Cartwright and it's great to have met you, eh...?"

"Charlie."

"It's great to make your acquaintance, Charlie. You're a fine CPO. I can see that."

"You don't even know me, but I think we should get out of this rain," Tennant said, glancing upwards at the forbidding skies. "Let's see if the waiting room's open. Come on, and bring your kit bag."

"Oh right then, Jock."

"Don't fuckin' call me Jock, you English bugger. I hate that. Which country do you think you're in anyway?"

Cartwright giggled. "A bloody cold and wet one, anyway. Sorry, I didn't mean to offend."

As the two walked across the station concourse, it was already dark and the chilled wind howled across the grey, stone floor.

The waiting room was damp and sparsely furnished with a few wooden benches. The bottle green walls and the single gas mantle gave it a dark and dreary ambience. It was also very smoky, a combination of pipe smoke and the fire which blew smoke back into the room from time to time.

Finding a seat by the fire, Tennant rummaged in his kit and brought out a new half bottle of Bell's whisky, pulled out the cork and took a healthy swig before offering it to Cartwright.

"I better not, Charlie, I think I've had enough already," Cartwright slurred.

"You'll be fine, take a drink."

Cartwright took a swig and passed the bottle back to Tennant.

Tennant settled back in his seat and took another swig of whisky. "What ship are you on, Sid?"

"Don't call me Sid. My mother always said no one should shorten my name."

"All right. I don't call you Sid, and you don't call me Jock." said Tennant, smiling.

"I've just been transferred to HMS Revenge."

"Have you now!" Tennant sniffed. "I think someone's trying to get their revenge on you, pal."

"How's that?"

"Well, you're there to guard the Germans and if your mother will excuse the language, it's the most fucking boring job in His Majesty's Navy!"

The Englishman began to nod off but Tennant shook him awake. "You can get your head down on the Jellicoe Express, so we should get to the platform. It starts here, so it might already be in."

The two made to leave, but when Cartwright tried to lift his duffle bag, he fell back. Tennant, now realising how drunk he was, had to help him to his feet and support him out of the waiting room. When the cold air hit their faces, the young man seemed to revive slightly. Tennant checked the notice board and they wandered, Cartwright still unsteadily, to platform three where, to Tennant's relief, the train was waiting. He bundled Cartwright into an empty compartment on the two coach corridor-less train and sat him next to the window on the far side. He lifted their bags onto the luggage rack and stuck both their caps next to them, then loosened Cartwright's tie.

Suddenly Cartwright's eyes opened with a start. "I think I'm going to be sick."

Tennant made a dive for the window and slid it down, grabbed the lad by the shoulders and pushed his head out, just in time for him to vomit all over the adjacent track. At this, the door on the platform side opened revealing a well-dressed couple. The woman stepped up into the compartment. Having worked out what was going on, she backed out hastily and the man closed the door.

Tennant shook his head. "See what you've done now, Sydney, depriving some good Highland citizens of a place in this compartment. That'll not do at all."

Cartwright indicated with a backward wave of his arm and a few grunts, that he was finished being sick. Tennant dragged him inside and bundled him back into his seat where he instantly fell asleep. Just as Tennant settled down opposite, the guard's whistle blew but as the little train started, the door opened with a bang and an elderly man dressed in black was pushed through the door by a porter, knocking his top hat to one side. Tennant rushed over and offered him his hand, pulling him inside, while behind him the porter slammed the door shut. The man, sat down breathlessly, taking off his hat and putting his bag on the seat next to him.

Returning to his seat, Tennant was horrified to spot the dog collar and from the style, he knew he was a Protestant minister, probably from the Free Church of Scotland. As the minister settled into his surroundings, he noticed the disreputable bundle sleeping in the corner seat. He started to make those exaggerated, sniffing noises of someone who wanted to convey their displeasure.

He turned to Tennant. "Thank you for assisting me onto the train, young man. I didn't realise I had left it so late."

Tennant smiled and nodded, not wishing to continue the conversation. The minister continued to sniff what Tennant knew to be whisky, while Cartwright snored loudly.

"Have you come far?" the minister asked.

To disassociate himself from his drunken compatriot, Tennant said, "I've come from Glasgow but I think he's come from down south somewhere."

"Oh I see, Glasgow." It was clear from the way the minister said the city's name he didn't think much of it.

There was another long silence, before the minister spoke again. "And where might you be going?"

"Scrabster, then back to our ships which are stationed at Scapa Flow."

"Oh well." His sepulchral tone made him sound as though God's work was a burdensome task. "I'm not going as far as that, just to Helmsdale." And he went into his bag, retrieved a church magazine and started to read.

Tennant turned away and fell asleep.

The train stopped seven times before the minister got off and as he put on his hat he said, "I'll be glad to get some fresh air. There's a terrible smell of strong drink in here. Good day to you."

As the train reached the last leg of its ponderous journey north, Cartwright suddenly started raving in his sleep. "Help, help me." He shouted something that sounded like the sea's on fire and other unintelligible words.

Tennant shook him. "You're having a bad dream, Sydney. You need to wake up anyway. We'll soon arrive in Thurso."

Cartwright looked pale and Tennant wondered if he was going to be sick again, but he said he felt all right and seemed to become more compos mentis.

Tennant continued their conversation. "What were you dreaming about that caused you to rave so much?"

"Oh well, I'm not sure but it's usually about my ship being sunk at Jutland."

"What ship were you on?"

Cartwright tried to sit up straighter, but failed. "HMS Queen Mary," he slurred, proudly. "I was lucky, I got thrown clear when the magazines blew and when I landed in the water it was on fire."

Tennant nodded. "That sounds right. You were shouting something about the water being on fire."

"It was an oil slick but luckily I got picked up immediately or I'd have been badly burned. As it was I got these." He held out his hands. They were both white and disfigured by burn scars.

Tennant grimaced. "Do they still hurt you?"

"Not so much now but I was ten weeks in hospital."

"How many of you survived?"

"There were just eighteen of us, out of a crew of more than a thousand."

Tennant looked thoughtful. "Was the Queen Mary not sunk by the German battle-cruiser, Derfflinger?"

"Yes, I think so."

"Boy, are you lucky because it's here. It's in Scapa."

But Cartwright was too groggy to care. He succumbed to the alcohol again and slumped back into sleep.

Tennant shook his head. No wonder the man had bad dreams.

When the train pulled into Thurso Station, Tennant opened the door, lifted Cartwright to his feet and manhandled him onto the single platform. He tried to lean the man up against the side of the coach but his legs wouldn't hold his weight. As he tried to figure out what to do, an able seaman and two stokers rolled up from the other end of the train. "What have you done with our Mr Cartwright, Chiefy?" one said amiably.

"Good, I'm glad you're here," Tennant said, relieved he would no longer need to deal with the man on his own. "He's drunk, so just hold him there while I collect our kit."

The two stokers took hold of him while Tennant and the able seaman went to fetch the caps and kit bags. One of the stokers snorted. "That's rich! He told us he didn't drink."

Tennant shrugged. "He's got a half empty gin bottle in his kit and he's been demolishing my whisky as well."

Although the three had also been drinking, they managed to carry Cartwright's duffle bag and support him as the ragtag procession faced the bitterly cold, wet and windy walk to the harbour. They had all travelled together from London to Glasgow, but there, they got separated. Knowing they still had twenty-four hours to get back to their ship, the seamen had gone to explore some of Glasgow's pubs. They hadn't counted on the city's draconian licensing laws and they were closed, so they ended up travelling at different ends of the trains.

At the harbour, a printed notice stated that a naval launch would arrive at 19.30 hours. Noticing a pub opposite, Tennant invited the men to join him for a drink.

As they pressed Cartwright and their kit through the door, they found the public bar busy with local fisherman and some sailors. The place smelt musky and unpleasant. The men wanted beer so Tennant went to the bar, ducking under an oak beam which supported a fine array of ships' plaques and ordered three pints of heavy and a whisky for himself from the monosyllabic barman. They found a seat close to other sailors and deposited Cartwright in a corner on top of their duffle bags to continue to sleep it off.

Tennant's three companions had also been on a week's leave and, like himself, were not pleased to be going back. They had been looking forward to their first Christmas at home for years.

After finishing the first round, the able seaman went to get more drinks. He returned and put a large glass of golden spirit in front of each of them. "Try these. The barman said it's good stuff. Anyway, it's bloody cheap."

"What is it?" Tennant asked.

"It's called Asbach Uralt. It's German brandy. Everyone's drinking it."

"Where are they getting that from?" Tennant looked puzzled.

"From the Germans, who else?"

One of the group of sailors sitting alongside, butted in, "Where have you lot been? The Huns are trading it for stuff they don't have, like soap or cans of fruit. So we sell a few bottles to the pub."

Another piped up. "One of them was telling me the other night that they've got more brandy than they know what to do with but until more stores arrive, they haven't got a lot to eat."

"How do you talk to them?" said the able seaman.

"Oh, we get by. Most just speak a few words but some have quite good English. It seems to work. We're also learning a few words of German!"

Tennant thought of the letter in his pocket from Margaret to Johann Schettler. "I thought there was to be no contact at all."

The other man nodded. "That's right, but we go at night and anyway no one seems bothered. Even some of our officers are asking us for brandy and souvenirs."

"Yes, I do a good line in Iron Crosses," another added.

A sailor, who had been silent up till now, spoke in what Tennant thought was a broad Glasgow accent. "Ah don't go to do any barterin'. Ah go to find out how they managed to start a revolution. Some of them are what they call Soldiers' Councillors, and they've got more power than the officers. I want to find out how we can do that, and take power from our shower of bastards."

The sailor who had been doing most of the talking shouted, "Shut up Archie," and then addressed Tennant. "Don't pay any attention to him, he's a crackpot."

"Crackpot – that *will* be right!" Archie shouted back. "Ah'm just fed up with this fuckin' navy!"

Tennant rose and headed to the toilet. He could see rain was still pouring down outside, and the sight of it made him shiver.

When he returned he sat beside Archie. "How are you doing, Archie? Listen, do you ever go to their flag ship?"

"What, Freddy the Grocer? Aye, a few times."

"Could you take me there?"

"No, we canny go from ship to ship because we still have to avoid the armed trawlers patrolin' the bay. But what ship are you on?"

"The Emperor of India, pal."

"That's all right then. They'll have their own boats moored alongside. Everyone's at it. You'll get somebody to take you across."

"That's good, thanks."

Tennant returned to his seat and drank his brandy.

"That is good stuff," he said to one of the stokers. "I didn't know the Germans made brandy. You learn something new every day."

When it was time to catch the launch, they shook Cartwright awake. He seemed to have recovered enough to walk on his own. This was better, because as a new posting, he would have to report to the master-at-arms when he arrived on board the Revenge. The group gathered up their kit bags and headed towards the harbour.

Chapter 10

As December continued, an atmosphere of peace was restored to the ships because the numbers of men had been significantly reduced and with them, the Red Guard. Many of those still on board were busy preparing themselves for the journey home and demobilisation from the navy.

Reuter received a message from the British that two vessels, the SS Batavia and SS Norderney, would arrive on December 12th, to transport the remainder of the officers and men still to be repatriated. This information took Schettler aback. These ships belonged to his father.

Reuter had recently managed to negotiate an end to British censorship and Schettler had written a letter home saying where he was, that he was fit and well and in communication with his cousin, Margaret, in Glasgow. He hoped that the ships would bring a reply from his mother.

The current atmosphere on board ship allowed the executive some time away from their responsibilities and one evening they had arranged to have a drink together in the petty officers' mess. When it came to it, however, Schettler didn't feel like company. Thoughts of his family had made him feel a little homesick, so he put on his heavy jacket and went to the upper deck. He would meet the rest of them later. The moon was almost full and he leant on the bulwark, watching the other ships clearly silhouetted in its cold, white light.

Stress was pulling him in all directions. Firstly, his feelings about the revolution; it was right, without question.

But as well as having to deal with the officers who opposed it, there was also the Red Guard. Although presently under control, they would no doubt regain strength and their lack of any political judgement would play into the hands of the officers and ultimately the British. And what of the British? Seeing them operate, he realised a similar uprising could not take place. Reuter's prophesy was probably right.

Herzmann appeared with another rating for a smoke and saw Schettler standing there alone. They came up behind him and one slapped him on the shoulder making him jump, interrupting his train of thought. "How are you tonight, Johann?"

Schettler turned. "Hello, lads, I'm afraid I was miles away. It's a fine night."

"Do you think so? It's a bloody cold and lonely place this," Herzmann replied.

The other smiled. "If you had managed to get up here early enough, you might have seen the sun set. It was beautiful. Even if it was only five minutes after it rose."

Herzmann offered Schettler a cigarette.

"No thanks, Harald, I don't use them."

"Have you just stopped or have you never smoked?"

"I never got hooked. My father caught my brother and I drinking one New Year, I think I was about eleven. He didn't say anything at the time but the next morning he called us into his study and offered us a cigar and a large whisky. We said no thanks, but he said that if we were going to act like adults then we should do it right and he made us drink the whisky and smoke the cigar till we both turned green. For me it did the trick, with smoking anyway." The two enjoyed his story and Schettler started to feel in a better mood.

Herzmann then began another story, "My father caught..."

But at that moment they heard a voice shouting in English, "Hey, Heini, are you there?"

Looking out, they could see a large rowing boat with four men coming towards them. As it reached the ship's shadow it disappeared out of sight, then there was a loud bump as it struck the side.

The voice came again. "Hey, Heini, where are you? It's us, Tony and Mark."

Schettler looked at the others then he shouted back in English. "What is it you want, boys?"

The voice from below replied. "Who's that – who's there?"

"It's big Davie. Who are you?"

"Christ, boys, there's a fucking Scotsman up there. What ship are you off?"

"I'm big Davie Beatty," Schettler shouted. "Ah'm the Admiral of the Fleet. Ah asked you, who you are."

The voice from below was muted. "Jesus Christ, Tony, it's the fucking admiral."

"Don't be daft. It's somebody taking the piss."

Heini must have appeared as they could hear a heavily accented voice whisper, "Eets all right, boys, come on board."

The three on the upper deck began to hoot with laughter and a voice came from below, "Whoever you are you're nothing but a right bastard."

They heard the men scramble onto the quarter deck.

Herzmann guffawed. "Where did you learn to do that?"

"Remind me to tell you sometime," Schettler said. "But did you understand what was going on?"

Herzmann shook his head. "Not all of it, but I think we got the gist."

Heartened by the evening's entertainment, Schettler decided he would go for a drink and, after taking leave of his two companions, he headed for the petty officers' mess. As he reached the door, a rating approached him. "Councillor Schettler. Can I speak to you?"

It could only be another complaint. "Go ahead, but make it quick, Comrade. I'm busy."

"There's an English petty officer on the quarter deck and he's asking to speak to you urgently," the rating whispered.

Schettler looked puzzled. "Who is he? I don't know anyone in the British Navy. What does he want to speak to me about?"

"I don't know. I just came to look for you."

"Very well. Thanks, Comrade, you better lead me to him."

When they arrived on the quarter deck, there was a group of three British sailors light-heartedly bartering with some of the crew. This was obviously Tony and Mark with Heini and others. A tall man in the uniform of a chief petty officer stood apart from the group. When he saw Schettler arrive, he smiled and waved in greeting. When Schettler reached him, he offered his hand.

"You must be Johann Schettler. I'm Charlie Tennant – your cousin, Margaret Nairn, is my fiancée." Schettler was taken aback but managed to smile broadly. "That's wonderful. But how did you know how to find me, Charlie?"

"It's a long story. Is there somewhere we can talk?"

Schettler looked over to the other men. "We could go to my cabin, but we'll have to be careful you're not spotted by an officer. How long do you have?"

Tennant called over to the group. "Reilly, how long have I got?"

"About an hour."

"Fine, but don't go without me."

Schettler addressed the Germans. "We'll be in my cabin. Don't let these men leave without this petty officer. Do you know where I'm located?"

One young rating nodded. "I know where you are, Councillor. If something turns up, I'll let you know."

"Fine, thanks."

As the two men sat in the cabin talking animatedly about Margaret and her family, it was hard to think they had been, so recently, on opposing sides during the war. The hour passed quickly and Tennant had just begun to tell Schettler about John Maclean's triumphant arrival in Glasgow, when there was a knock on the cabin door. It was the rating to say that business had been completed and the British sailors were ready to leave.

On his way out, Tennant produced the letter Margaret had written and shaking hands with Schettler, said he would try to get over again soon.

When Tennant had gone, Schettler went to the mess but after one drink, excused himself and returned to his cabin to read his letter.

Dear Johann,

My mother and I cried when we received your letter. It was so wonderful to hear from you. I just hope Charlie is able to deliver this reply to you soon. I didn't want to trust it to the mail and risk falling foul of the censor. We have never let it be known that a part of our dearest family is German, in case it got us into trouble with the authorities.

This war has devastated us all and I doubt any of us will ever be the same again. I don't think we know anyone who has come through it unscathed and I'm sure it's the same for you. We did hear about Heinrich being wounded when Aunt Marion had a letter sent to my mother from a neutral port but we knew nothing else until we received your letter. Where our family is concerned my brother, Charles, was killed at Gallipoli in 1915 and my sister Helen's husband, James Jenkins, was killed at Ypres in 1915, two months after they were married. Helen was pregnant at the time and now has three-year-old twin sons, John and James, your second cousins! Helen's husband was a solicitor before the war and it was fortunate that she was left comfortably off as it can't be easy bringing up a family on your own. She manages very well with help from my mother and her mother- in- law, who is very kind. It's so strange to think that both our families had a tragic event in the same battle in Ypres.

Like you and Andreas, Bob has survived the war and for this we count ourselves very lucky. He is due to be demobbed in a week or two and we are keeping our fingers crossed he'll be home for Christmas.

I was very proud to hear about your active role in ending the war and setting up a socialist republic. I believe everything must change now. I do agree, 'we must all strive for a socialist Europe where the rights of the people are respected' as you put so well in your letter. This is precisely what John Maclean was telling us until the authorities sent him to jail for five years. There are others, too, who are determined to lead the people towards socialism, the great Willie Gallacher and Harry McShane to name but two. But we have to be careful who we trust. There are others who would sacrifice the people for their own ambitions and they are without exception within our social democratic party, the British Labour Party. From what I hear, it is the same in Germany, where the revolutionary movement is being undermined by your social democratic party, the SPD.

Here in Glasgow, unrest is reaching boiling point with many strikes and demonstrations every week. We are demanding the release of John Maclean. Every parliamentary candidate in the forthcoming general election is being asked if they support this demand and then he can lead us towards the formation of a socialist state. My sincere wish is that this can be done without bloodshed.

When you read this letter I hope you will have met, however fleetingly, my fiancé, Charlie. He shares my views in a socialist future, so I hope you can find a way to meet and strike up a friendship with each other. If you can do this, give him another letter to deliver to me. I so look forward to hearing from you again.

As far as I'm concerned, I still live with mother so you addressed your letter to me correctly. We were intrigued to know how you managed to post it. Do tell!

I am a primary school teacher in a large school in Glasgow's west end which I enjoy immensely. As you will have gathered, I am deeply interested in politics and of course, I am involved in the women's suffrage movement. The People Act of 1918 has just been passed allowing women over thirty, who meet certain property qualifications, to vote. So my mother will have the right to vote in the General Election on December 14th, but I won't. This is a ridiculous situation and we will go on fighting until we get equality with men.

My engagement to Charlie will have to be a long one. Once I'm married, I have to give up work and I'm not prepared to do that. I have contemplated living with him in what would be described as 'in sin' at some point, but if I do so my family would be ostracised by the community and I couldn't do that to them.

As far as painting is concerned, I do still dabble, but in truth I've little talent. I love the Art Nouveau movement and I'm particularly fond of the work of Gustav Klimt from Vienna and here in Glasgow, we have our own world famous exponent of the movement, Charles Rennie Mackintosh, who has designed the most beautiful buildings throughout the city.

I will finish for now but I know there is still much for us to talk about. I hope this letter finds you well and that your circumstances in Scapa Flow are not too terrible.

Your loving cousin,

Margaret

PS John Maclean has just been released from prison. Hoorah!

Schettler put down the letter and sat for a long time, thinking. What Margaret had written was a revelation. To be so candid about her circumstances and aspirations was indomitable and this made him proud. It was clear that he had been born into a family of strong and resourceful women. He was proud too, that one of the first acts of the Revolutionary Council was to grant all women over the age of twenty one the right to vote. Germany had gone to war without the approval of its women but this could never happen again.

Since movement between the two navies was so lax, perhaps with Charlie's help, they could devise a way of travelling to Glasgow to meet up with his family. He dismissed the idea as impossible, put it out of his mind and turned in for the night.

Chapter 11

The Council Executive met with Commander von Wachter and three other officers brought in from other ships on December 11th, to finalise the names of those being repatriated on the SS Batavia and SS Norderney due to arrive the next day.

For a change, it had been a quiet and generally amiable meeting and business had been concluded quickly. Commander von Wachter cleared his throat and said in a low voice, "Err... there's still a number of men to be dealt with." Hesitantly, he began to read out seven names of officers, a lieutenant commander, four lieutenants and two engineers, who had been charged with offences, with a recommendation they should all be repatriated.

Brand, who had been voted earlier by his comrades as chairman of the executive, asked what offences they had committed.

Again, in a low and embarrassed voice, Wachter explained, "They were involved in a drinking game on board Von der Tann."

"Is that all?" Brand cried. "Surely that's forgivable, Commander?"

"Well no, Chairman, it's not that simple. You see the object of this game was that anyone not conforming to the rules must remove an article of clothing."

"I see, Commander," Brand said. "Does that mean these men were naked?"

"When they were discovered running around the deck, they were all naked except the one being chased. It ended up in a drunken brawl to try to remove this officer's clothing."

"And how is this matter being viewed," Brand asked, "drunken and disorderly conduct or youthful over exuberance?"

"The former. Some of them were not youthful, Chairman."

Brand couldn't help laugh out loud, the other five members of the executive joining in. Even two of the officers couldn't resist a smile.

"Given the situation all the men are in at the moment, officers and other ranks alike, Commander, I think they should be treated leniently. Don't you?"

"No, I do not! If they are, it'll be a message to other ranks to behave in the same way."

"I think this is nonsense."

A second lieutenant had entered the ward room and came smartly to attention, saying, "If the Commander pleases, Admiral von Reuter wishes to see Councillor Schettler."

Schettler stood up. He didn't want to be involved in anymore of this charade. "I'll leave the matter in your capable hands, gentlemen, and abide by whatever conclusion is reached." He invited the lieutenant to escort him to the admiral.

When he entered Reuter's quarters, the admiral was sitting at his desk and invited Schettler to sit down opposite.

"Since you were next door, Schettler, I thought I might as well see you personally. I have just been informed by Wilhelmshaven, through the usual channels," he cleared his throat, "that when the SS Norderney arrives tomorrow, it will have a relative of yours on board."

Schettler couldn't hide his surprise. "A relative of mine?"

"Yes, I presume Heinrich Schettler is a family member?"

"Yes, Heinrich is either my father or my brother."

The admiral nodded. "Anyway, since I'm sure you'll want to meet him, I've taken the liberty of arranging with the English for you to be transferred to the Norderney, as soon as it drops anchor and returned here when it sails."

"Thank you, Admiral, I'm obliged to you."

Reuter waved his hand to show his thanks weren't necessary. "I, too, will be transferring to the Norderney tomorrow, but I'm sure our paths won't cross again until I return here from leave. I'll say goodbye for the time being." Schettler rose and made for the door.

He turned. "Goodbye and thank you again. I hope you enjoy your leave." Reuter nodded.

Why was either his father or his brother coming to see him, Schettler wondered. He felt rattled, sure that it meant bad news. He knew he would worry constantly till they met.

That night, he slept fitfully and woke with a headache. He needed some fresh air and headed for the deck which was still awash after the rain storm that had continued over the last twenty four hours. It had stopped momentarily and the wind had dropped a little. Had the two ships from home arrived? From where he stood, he couldn't see any sign of them. He still felt listless. Perhaps changing into a fresh tunic and best uniform might help because what he was wearing was dirty. He went back to his cabin to change. The present environment aboard ship had affected everyone. Even Reuter had looked a little dishevelled when he saw him yesterday.

It was approaching midday when the barge arrived to take Schettler and the first group of homeward bound officers to the SS Norderney. It crossed to the Hindenburg, Derfflinger and Von der Tann to pick up more officers, then turned and headed towards the German ships. As the barge drew near, the activity on the Norderney was manic with stores and material being unloaded from the port side while the barge navigated towards starboard. When it drew level with the stern, a commotion broke out as a large timber packing case broke free while being winched from the ship and fell into the sea, almost swamping one of the barges beneath. A man was struck by a loose rope from the winch, and was knocked overboard, striking his head on the corner of the case as he fell. Schettler rushed to the side of the barge, shouting to the others that their barge was the closest vessel free to manoeuvre and that they should pick the man up.

"No, no, Bootsmann, they'll handle it themselves. Anyway, after such a knock it looks like the blighter's already dead," a middle aged lieutenant commander shouted back.

His disregard for a man's life sickened Schettler. He walked up to the elderly British barge master and said in English, "Comrade, can you run alongside that packing case and see if we can rescue that man?"

The master nodded. "I don't know about bein' your comrade, ma friend, but you're right enough." He ordered the helmsman to turn the barge towards the fallen man.

The man, who was wearing a life jacket, was floating lifelessly in the water, a large gash on his temple. A seaman steered him to the side of the barge with a boat hook while another, helped by Schettler, hauled him on board as the crews of the Norderney and the surrounding barges watched in silence.

The barge master came across to look at the rescued German seaman. "Aye, ah'm afraid the poor man's dead all right." He shook his head then shouted to the helmsman, "Take her round now, Hamish."

Five minutes later, the barge tied up alongside the suspended accommodation ladder of the Norderney and the sailor's body was roped aboard before the officers, followed by Schettler, ascended to the main deck.

Schettler's father, who had been waiting on deck, walked towards him – his face downcast and set. As soon as Schettler saw him, his heart fell. This could only mean bad news.

As he watched his father's face, he could see no discernible change of expression. Has something happened to my mother, was his first thought and he immediately stiffened. A firm hand dragged his shoulder round and he found himself looking at the lieutenant commander from the barge.

"How dare you countermand my instructions, Bootsmann," he snarled. "I told you the ship's crew would handle that matter because the blighter was already dead and you carried on…"

This was too much for Schettler. "Take your hands off me, you bastard," he said giving the officer a push, sending him reeling backwards. His heel struck a deck cleat causing him to trip over and land ignominiously on his backside, less than a metre from the open hold. Father and son stared dumbfounded at the officer, in the realisation that this could easily have been another fatality.

Schettler rushed forward to help the man to his feet. "I'm sorry. I didn't mean to push you so hard. Are you all right?"

As the officer got to his feet, he hissed through gritted teeth, "I'm reporting this serious incident to Admiral von Reuter when he arrives on board and I'll be looking for you to receive a fitting punishment, Bootsmann."

Anger again took hold of Schettler, who prodded the officer in the chest. "You should know by now I'm addressed as councillor and your attitude towards a merchant seaman who has just been killed on duty – it's disgusting. I will be reporting you to the admiral."

His father took him by the forearm. "Leave this officer now, son. Come away. We'll go to my cabin."

"And who might you be?" the officer shouted.

"My name is Heinrich Schettler."

The officer kept up his questioning. "And what is your business on this ship?"

"I am the owner of this vessel, sir, and I'm here to see my son."

"You mean this communist pig is your son? You certainly failed in your duty as a father if you were responsible for bringing *that* up," he said, pointing at Schettler.

Johann made to step towards the officer but his father held him back. "Leave it Johann."

"Kindly tell me who I'm addressing," asked the senior Schettler.

"My name is Wolfgang Hesse and I'm an officer on the battle-cruiser SMS Von der Tann, sir."

Schettler realised that this must be one of the officers who had been removed from duty for the naked games the other day.

"I, too, will be making a serious complaint about your behaviour when Admiral von Reuter comes aboard this vessel," his father said, "but in the meantime, I don't want you here, so please hold yourself in readiness to be transferred to the SS Batavia as soon as I can make the necessary arrangements."

The officer turned and walked back to join the group of officers standing nearby. A furious conversation ensued between them.

Father and son walked silently to the cabin where Heinrich brought out a bottle of brandy from his locker and offered his son a drink.

After both men had taken a stiff drink from their glasses, Heinrich said, "You must be wondering why I'm here, Johann?" He didn't wait for an answer. "I'm afraid Heinrich died."

Although Johann had just been given terrible news, he was relieved that it was his brother who had died and not his mother. All he could say was, "When – How?"

His father looked devastated, but neither father nor son could embrace each other. "He died two weeks ago from influenza and we didn't know how to get in touch with you until your first letter arrived. Since we had received this contract from the navy in Wilhelmshaven, I thought it best to come to see you personally."

Johann's mind raced. "Was poor Heinrich the only one to get influenza?"

His father shook his head. "No, your mother got it too."

"Is she all right?" Johann gasped, battling a sudden feeling of dread.

"Yes, she's still very weak but she's over the worst. But she was devastated when she wasn't well enough to attend Heinrich's funeral."

Johann thought of his cousin. "Margaret was very ill with influenza too, Father."

His father looked puzzled. "Who's Margaret, Johann?"

"Your niece, Aunt Nell's daughter."

"Oh."

Johann could tell the news meant little to his father.

The two sat in silence until Johann could bear it no longer. He walked over to his father and put his hand on his shoulder. "I'm sorry about Heinrich, Father." Inside, he felt very little. Perhaps grief would hit home later.

His father patted his hand. "Yes, Heinrich was a good son. I miss him very much." Johann didn't know if this remark meant that he wasn't a good son but he said nothing. His father rose eventually, saying he would have to go to the bridge to ask Captain Schmidt to see to the arrangements for transferring the lieutenant commander to the Batavia.

As Johann sat alone, he wondered if there was still another reason for his father's visit.

Heinrich had been the oldest – some six years older than Johann with Andreas in the middle to act as a buffer between them. They had never been particularly close. Heinrich didn't seem to get into trouble either at school or with his parents which wasn't the case with Johann. He had always been the most volatile and outspoken of the three. By the time he reached school age, Heinrich was about to go to upper school, so any time Johann needed rescuing from trouble it was Andreas he called upon. Perhaps he should have taken more time to get to know his brother better but equally he could never remember a time when Heinrich had much to do with him.

He did remember one time when he was eight and Heinrich was fourteen. He was being looked after by his brothers and they weren't happy about it. It was the Christmas holidays and it had been very cold with snow lying deep on the ground. The short stretch of water between the north shore of the Werdersee and Vogeleiland was frozen and the boys decided to cross to explore this normally unreachable, small island. Johann couldn't keep up. It seemed that they were deliberately trying to get away from him. When he arrived on the island, he decided to play by himself among some protruding tree-stumps at the shore but he slipped and fell backwards hitting his head on the thick ice. He was knocked unconscious and, when he finally came to, he was in hospital. It turned out that if it hadn't been for Heinrich's quick thinking and an immense amount of luck, he would not have survived. Heinrich had eventually broken away from the rest of the boys to search for Johann and when he found him, he had loaded him onto his sledge and pulled him across the ice to a close-by house. A doctor was called and he had been whisked off to hospital. Given his quick thinking, Heinrich's initial inattention was ignored by his parents, who were overjoyed that Johann was none the worse for his ordeal. The memory now gave Johann a sense of loss.

When his father returned to the cabin, he replenished both their glasses with more brandy. It had been some time since he'd last eaten and the liquid went straight to Johann's head.

His father was first to speak. "What happened between you and that officer to make you both so angry, Johann?"

"He was arrogant and his attitude towards that poor man who died, was disgusting."

"Captain Schmidt has just informed me of the circumstances of the man's death. He was one of the Norderney's crew and I'm told he'd been with us for over ten years. It could cause the company a lot of trouble, particularly in this new political order."

Johann shook his head. "Oh Father, listen to yourself. We're mourning the death of my brother and yet you can only see this man's life in terms of trouble for the company. Surely he's more important than that?"

His father looked shocked. "How can you make that comparison? We don't know that man except that he worked for our company and it will cost a lot of money in compensation."

"It's not our company, Father. It's your company."

"As a matter of fact, that's why I came to see you. Now that the war's over, I want you home to join the company. I need you to take Heinrich's place."

"What about Andreas? He's the next in line."

"Andreas wants to finish his degree at university and I'm happy for him to do that. So I need you now, Johann."

"I'm sorry, Father, I think you're missing the point. The new order you referred to will see the Schettler Line nationalised for the German people. I'll fully support that move. Therefore, I'll not be joining the company. And I won't be returning to Germany until my job here is finished. I'm on the Executive of the Soldiers' Council looking after this part of the German Fleet."

"I believe this revolution is foolish and won't work, Johann." His father's voice had risen. "It's every man's dream to better themselves and capitalism is the tried and tested way to do it."

Johann took another fortifying gulp of brandy. The war had changed his views forever, and the old order his father was part of, repelled him.

"No, Father," he said. "I see capitalism as the exploitation of the masses to create larger markets to give the richest few more profit. Do you think this war with Britain would have started if capitalists in both countries had not been striving to dominate more of the world's markets?"

Johann got to his feet as if to reinforce what he was saying.

"And when the war began – was it the capitalists who were fighting each other? No, it was the common man who had to die. If we in the navy hadn't refused to fight, the conflict would still be raging today. But we did refuse and it's finished. Now we have a responsibility to remove the means of production from the capitalists and hand it over to the people. That way we can all benefit. We don't need to create profit to exist. We need to create an advanced means of production so that we can have a higher standard of living for everyone."

His father sighed and put his glass down. "I won't argue with you, Johann. I can see your mind's made up. But I'm afraid to say your order will be defeated. I think the SPD will win the struggle for the new Germany and they have room for capitalist companies like the Schettler Line to continue. To me, that can only be a good thing."

His words riled Schettler. "If what you say is true, we'll be fighting another war before long. I can guarantee that."

"I strenuously hope you're wrong. Anyway, after reading your letters, your mother was sure you would refuse to join the company and she made me promise not to fall out about it. We've lost one son and we don't want to lose another. I hope we can have lunch and you'll give me the pleasure of being with my son."

Johann heard the heartfelt plea in his words and he embraced his father.

The rest of the day was spent pleasantly, although it was marred by Heinrich's death. His father told him that Andreas had returned home from France and had immediately introduced the family to Erika Jäger, whom it turned out he had known since his school days. They were getting engaged to be married.

Johann remembered Erika. She had been the cause of him being teased relentlessly by Andreas's friends for an entire summer. As he looked different from his brothers, she had asserted that he must be a gypsy who had been bought as a servant and he had been continually taunted over this. Once, Andreas had given him a bloody nose for calling her a fat cow.

At quarter past eight, there was a knock at the cabin door. It was a member of the crew to say that the last of the officers and sailors were now on board and that Herr Schettler had to go immediately to the British barge as it would leave in five minutes.

Heinrich had just enough time to hand Johann a letter and a parcel from his mother, before they had to make their hurried goodbyes. A protracted goodbye would have been painful. He was glad he had to hurry away.

The short voyage to the Friedrich der Grosse was unpleasant. A strong wind was blowing from the north turning the heavy rain to sleet. Huddled against the bulwark with the barge being pitched and tossed across the bay, cold and soaked almost to the skin, Johann wished he was still on board the Norderney and about to head back to Germany. What was he really doing here, he thought. At that moment he couldn't answer the question. Loneliness swamped him.

Reaching his cabin, he found that a scribbled note that had been put under his door. The English text was written in pencil and the handwriting was difficult to read. It was from Charlie. He said he had made a chance visit to see him but he couldn't be found. There was likely to be another visit on Saturday and he would try to come then. The boat should be there by seven o'clock at the latest so Schettler was to wait for him on the quarter deck, as usual. The note surprised him and pleased him too. Perhaps the British wanted brandy for Christmas.

Once he had changed out of his wet clothes, he settled down on his bunk to read his mother's letter.

My Dear Son,

This letter will have to be short because your father is sailing to Orkney later today.

We are devastated by Heinrich's death. It's truly a terrible thing for a parent to outlive their child. I know you and your father will have talked about it at great length when you met. All I will say is that he will be missed always.

I'm sure you will not accompany your father home nor will you accept his plea to join the company. I am very proud of what you have done to help end this terrible war but I'm not sure that being governed by a Revolutionary Council is the best way for the German people to gain better lives. Your father is certain that the SPD will eventually take control of the entire country, and he is convinced that is for the best. I'm not sure, but I realise I don't know enough about what is right and wrong these days. Everything is so confusing. Anyway, we shall just have to see how things work out.

We miss you terribly and hope your time in Scapa Flow will not be long.

The Northern Isles of Scotland are particularly cold and wet at this time of year, so if you have already opened the parcel you will have seen I have sent you warm underwear. I went to see Herr Fisher in Schmidtborn's department store and he assures me that this new mix of cashmere and silk will be very warm but won't be uncomfortable to wear next to your skin. I have also included some soap, toothpaste and a nice bottle of Kölnisch Wasser. If there are any other things you want just write and tell me.

Andreas has recently returned home and, although he is very thin, he seems no worse for his long ordeal. We're very glad to have him back and no doubt your father has told you about his engagement to Erika Jäger. I'm sure we will all grow to love her in time and I'm so glad he has found a good woman.

If I am to give this letter to your father, I will have to end now. Take good care of yourself, son. We all love you very much. Please write back to us soon.

Your loving mother

How stoic she was about Heinrich's death. The comments about Erika Jäger had made him smile too.

He opened his parcel and went off to the toilet with his new soap and toothpaste, feeling a little happier.

Chapter 12

It was Saturday evening and Schettler had just arrived on the quarter deck, when several ratings appeared, carrying crates of Asbach Uralt and Schnapps which they reverently stacked on the deck next to the port side gunwale. In the dark they hadn't noticed him, as he stood in the most sheltered corner to escape the wind. It blew puffy clouds fast across the sky, passing under an almost full moon – alternately lighting and darkening the berthed ships and the land behind, in its silvery light.

Standing there he felt a shiver run down his back but it wasn't from the cold. Phantoms of the past kept breaking into mind, demanding attention – faces of his parents, Andreas, his first girlfriend, Kerstin, who didn't survive him joining the navy, and Elke the girl he met in Hamburg, who was so much fun and taught him everything about the wonders of sex. But he couldn't picture his dead brother.

As he changed position, one man noticed him and called out. "Who's there? Who is that?"

"It's Councillor Schettler," he replied stepping out from the gloom. The rating looked perturbed. "Oh it's you, Councillor. We're just—"

"I know what you're doing and under the circumstances, a small piece of private enterprise won't do much harm, although if we start running out of brandy, I might feel differently," he said, smiling. "Are you working for yourselves or Heini?"

"Everyone works for Heini. He negotiates with the English."

Schettler winked. "You tell that swindler that since he's stealing the brandy, I want some of whatever he's getting in return and I don't expect to pay for it." A shout came from off the ship and one of the ratings lowered a rope ladder over the side. Stepping back, he could hear the familiar bump as the wooden boat gently struck the side.

The first man to clamber up the rope ladder was Charlie Tennant, carrying a brown paper parcel, followed by two men with large hessian bags strapped to their backs.

Schettler asked how long Tennant could stay. The answer "half an hour" disappointed him.

When they sat down in the cabin, Tennant opened the parcel and brought out two large bottles of beer. "I want you to taste some Scottish beer, Johann."

"Listen, Charlie, my mother always called me Ian. Why don't you?"

"Aye I'll do that, Ian."

"I'll have to get a bottle opener. Won't it be warm?"

"We don't need one. They're screw tops, and that's the way we drink it," Tennant said, turning one with a hiss of gas. "This is McEwan's India Pale Ale." He handed the open bottle to Schettler.

Schettler took a drink. "Ja, it's different from ours but I think I could get used to it."

"I've just found out my brother Heinrich died in this flu epidemic," Schettler blurted out.

Tennant grasped his forearm in sympathy. "I'm sorry, Ian, that's very cruel, especially after he managed to survive the war. You must all be devastated."

"My parents are, but I can't seem to feel anything."

"Don't worry, it's the war. When you have time, grief will come."

"None of us are right these days."

Schettler put his empty beer bottle on his bunk. "Charlie, I'm afraid it's time you went."

He reached into his pocket and brought out a letter. "Can you post this to Margaret for me, without passing the censor?"

"Yes. Our mail isn't censored now."

"You're lucky. After only two weeks, the British have reintroduced censorship of our mail. I don't know why. I wish they'd stop trying to make things more difficult for us. I told Margaret not to write to me directly but do it through you. Is that all right?"

Tennant nodded and they left for the deck.

When they emerged onto the quarter deck, everyone was standing silently in small groups looking north. Following their gaze, Schettler and Tennant saw the sky was green, blue and purple as lights cascaded and billowed across the sky, like rippling waves across the sea, lighting up the land and bathing the ships in spectacular swathes of colour. Schettler had never seen the Aurora Borealis before and his body tingled with the thrill of its magnificence. He and Tennant stood there gaping in silence for more than twenty minutes until the spectacle subsided. When Tennant turned to say goodbye, Schettler could see tears in his eyes. "I hope you can visit again soon, Charlie." He wanted to say more, but that was all he could manage.

"When I bring Margaret's reply, we can try some German beer," he said and shook Schettler's hand.

Schettler found himself alone again. In the stillness, he felt it had all been a dream except he still tasted the beer. He stood looking north for another hour, hoping the northern lights would return. They never did.

*

In the next few weeks, conditions aboard the ships became intolerable. In the absence of Reuter, the officers became more dictatorial, causing increased conflict between them and the men. As Schettler predicted, the Red Guard re-emerged even stronger, as they gathered new recruits. On board some of the capital ships, the moderate ombudsmen were being ousted in favour of the Red Guard who often rejected the orders issued by the joint officers and SC Executive and went to great lengths to carry the, often justifiable, elements of discontent to an exaggerated level.

Meanwhile on the squadron of destroyers, a different regime developed. Their ombudsmen were ousted by crew members still loyal to the officers and imperial naval tradition, who left the running of the daily business entirely to their officers. In this milieu the executive tried to tread a line which was to the benefit of the men, but found it increasingly difficult.

In this atmosphere of boredom and discontent, men tried to find alternative sources of entertainment to keep their mind off their problems and clubs were set up, from choirs to bird watching. Many men played a diverse array of musical instruments and bands were formed on most ships, using the abundant time on their hands for practice. Within a relatively short period, some became very good and began to perform in concerts which were well attended.

Christmas came and went in a frenzy of drinking and gambling. The men had, at least, been paid regularly. The only solace was the lighting of the candles on the makeshift Christmas trees on Christmas Eve, a tradition which was respected by almost everyone throughout the fleet.

New Year was different. A few days before the end of the year, Heini and his team had let it be known to their most frequent black market colleagues on the Empress of India and Revenge that the German non-commissioned men were having a New Year party on the 'Dicke Fritz'. Turning an almost complete blind eye to the Royal Navy's total embargo on fraternisation, three boat loads numbering thirty one men turned up on the German ship, on what the Scots referred to as Hogmanay.

Boats started to arrive at nine o'clock. Heini had posted two ratings on the quarter deck to direct everyone, regardless of rank, to the petty officers' mess, a privilege which went down well with the British ratings.

The band was accomplished and by ten o'clock they were playing a medley of the most modern Al Jolson songs, but it was when they began to play 'Darktown Strutters' Ball,' that the party came to life.

Schettler was sitting with Karl Brand, Axel Kegel, Dieter Meyer, and Harald Herzmann who were into their third beer, when he noticed the first batch of British sailors arriving in the mess. He was pleased to see Charlie Tennant was one of them. He rose and made his way towards them, as they stood at the door not quite knowing what to expect. Their hosts were crowding around them in welcome and guiding them to the bar, and Schettler had to grab hold of Tennant's arm to get his attention. When he saw his friend, Tennant smiled and shouted at two others to stop. He introduced them as Stuart Campbell and Gordon Carmichael who, as he put it, were another two good Glaswegians.

Schettler guided the three to his table and introduced them to his four friends. He would act as translator, though Brand could also speak a little English, while Herzmann went off to get drinks for the Scots.

It was immediately apparent that almost everyone was hitting it off. The only one who seemed rather uncomfortable was Kegel, who sat drinking in silence.

Schettler translated the wise cracks which came thick and fast from both sides as beer and then whisky was consumed. He excused himself and went off around other groups containing British and German sailors to translate and was surprised to find that they were doing pretty well without his help, with a combination of facial expressions, sign language and some words that were common in both languages.

As midnight approached, Brand decided to make a speech and asked Schettler to translate. He welcomed the British comrades to a ship which he said was controlled by the Soldiers' Council and then went on to say that it was the end of 1918, a year in which the German Navy had proudly brought an end to the war which caused carnage on all sides. If there was any point to these brutal years, it was surely that henceforth they could never let themselves be ruled by a small minority who would exploit them in their millions for their own ends. As Germany had now risen against them, he hoped the English, which Schettler translated as the British, would now follow suit and set up their own socialist state. Widespread applause broke out and as the clock moved to midnight, he went on to ask them to raise their glasses to 1919 and the foundation of a new socialist order in Europe. The men began to cheer and shake hands, wishing each other a socialist new year. Schettler called for a rousing chorus of the International which was sung with great gusto in two languages by the majority.

As the song came to an end, a lone voice emerged out of the din from the place where most of Schettler's comrades were sitting. Kegel had stood up. "Fuck your socialist revolution. I didn't get half killed at Jutland for this. God save the Kaiser!"

Two of Penzberg's Red Guard rushed forward and grabbed him. As he resisted, Tennant and his two friends, not understanding what he had said, intervened and in a few seconds a fight broke out. Brand and Schettler ran forward and tried to break it up. Schettler concentrated on the Scots as he grabbed Tennant's arm and shouted, "Axel said something really stupid, Charlie."

Tennant half turned to look at Schettler. "Why, what did he—"

But one of the Red Guard aimed a punch at his stomach winding him and causing him to double over in pain and surprise. Schettler turned to the man and punched him full in the face. As he reeled back and started falling, Stuart Campbell punched him on the side of the head and the man went sprawling over the table, sending glasses crashing to the floor. Brand and Meyer now had the other Red Guard under control and Schettler was able to help Tennant to a seat. At that moment, a voice boomed from the other side of the room. "Oh, so this is how it is, is it? We invite the British here to share our New Year celebrations and the Soldiers'

Council protect a man who still stands for the Kaiser and Imperial Germany."

Schettler knew who it was. Even if he hadn't recognised Penzberg's voice, the sentiment was unmistakable. Schettler felt his temper rise, no doubt fuelled by the unusual combination of German beer and Scotch whisky. He took to his heels, sprinting across the room, grabbed Penzberg by the tunic, and powered a backhand punch into the side of his face.

Penzberg was a big man. He merely shook his head, snorted and came back at Schettler, driving his fist into his ribs while trying to force his knee up between his legs. Luckily for Schettler, he missed the target though he knocked him to the floor. Penzberg was just about to place his steel toe capped boot into Schettler's face, when a shout came from behind. A huge, British seaman grabbed Penzberg and threw him down shouting, "We'll have none of that dirty stuff here, matey."

Seeing the size of the intervening sailor, Penzberg decided to stay motionless on the floor, giving Schettler time to get to his feet and with the adrenaline still surging through his veins, he began to address the assembled group.

"Every time something happens, this idiot Penzberg uses it to try to bring the executive into disrepute..." But as he spoke he could see that no one was paying attention. They were back in their groups, once again, enjoying the festivities. The band who had taken the disturbance as a suitable point for a short break, started again and Schettler abandoned all hope of conveying any message to anyone. As he made his way across the room towards his own crowd, he was jostled from behind by four members of the Red

Guard who were supporting Penzberg slumped between two of them in an exaggerated posture of a man who had been seriously injured. As the group shuffled towards the door, one of them made it plain that Schettler should expect retribution for what had just happened to Penzberg. Schettler sneered.

When he reached his table, everyone was enjoying the celebrations and he quickly joined in. They sat singing along with the band and cracking jokes which Schettler translated, often badly, misinterpreting the point of the joke and causing much light-hearted derision by which ever nationality was receiving the translation.

After some time had elapsed, Schettler realised that Kegel had disappeared. He turned to Brand. "Where's Axel, Karl?"

"Oh him, the bastard staggered out during the fighting."

"I better go and see if he's all right. He was pretty drunk."

"Don't bother, he's likely to have puked up in the Schei haus and then gone off to get his head down. After the trouble he caused, I hope he has a monumental hangover when he wakes."

The explanation seemed fair enough, but something nagged at Schettler.

Soon after one o' clock, a Royal Naval chief petty officer stood up and drunkenly suggested that it was time for the British to leave. His words were greeted with much derision and back chat but nevertheless he lurched towards the door, loudly expressing his gratitude in slurred, newly-taught German. "Danke Kameraden für eh einen schönen Abend eh eh and ah eh froh-es neues eh Jahr." He turned to the group of Germans he had been with. "Was that right?"

When they cheered their support, he burst into infectious guffaws of laughter, which affected everyone in the mess. The rest of the British fell in behind him, loudly shouting their goodbyes, some in newly learned German and others in many different dialects of English and, as the happy band filed out of the mess, they once again began to sing the International, mostly out of tune.

Tennant stood up. "I guess if big Charlie thinks it's time to go then we better be off. Are you two coming?" he asked Cameron and Carmichael. "Or are ye going to do the rest of your military service in the German Navy?"

The two Scotsmen got to their feet – Cameron, rather unsteadily. He embraced every one of his new friends in turn, finishing up with Schettler. "It's been a great night. It's nice to be in the company of men who haven't allowed the war to blunt their fight for social justice. All power to the revolution comrades! I just hope we can soon do the same. All power to a socialist Scotland!"

After Carmichael had enthusiastically shaken everyone's hand, Charlie Tennant also embraced everyone saying, "I agree with Stuart. It may not be long till we join you."

Schettler's interest was piqued. "What have you heard, Charlie?"

"Just wait, Ian. Margaret will be writing to you soon to tell you what's going on. That's all I can say right now."

A young stoker came running back into the mess in an agitated state and yelled, "Chairman Brand and Councillor Schettler! I've been sent to get you. You must come immediately."

"What's the matter, Comrade?" Brand answered his plea.

"It's the other Bootsmann. I think he's dead. We found him in the Scheißhaus. You'd better come."

Schettler turned to Tennant. "You see. We're never finished here. Something's happened and we have to sort it out. Take care of yourself, my friend."

As Schettler, Brand and the young stoker hurried along the corridor, Brand asked, "What Bootsmann did you mean?"

"I don't know his name – the one who started the fight."

At this Schettler stiffened. "You mean Bootsmann Kegel."

"Yes, I think so – the one who shouted, 'God save the Kaiser.'"

Schettler knew he should have heeded his instinct and gone to look for his friend earlier. When they arrived at the toilet, they had to push their way through a crowd who had also just left the party and were now clustered around the door. When they got inside they found Kegel wasn't dead but was lying on the floor in a pool of blood and vomit. Oberstabsbootsmann Dieter Müller and two ratings were tending him. As non-drinkers, they had volunteered to be the master-at-arms team for the New Year celebrations.

"What's happened, Dieter?" asked Brand.

The other shook his head. "I don't know, but he's been pretty badly beaten. He's got severe injuries to his head and face, so I've sent a rating along to the wardroom to fish the doctor out of their party. God knows what state he'll be in when he gets here. But until he comes, I don't think he should be moved."

Schettler knelt beside his friend. It seemed clear that this was the work of Penzberg and his cronies. Kegel was going in and out of consciousness and when his eyes flickered open, straining against the electric light on the ceiling, Schettler said, "Did Penzberg do this to you, Axel?" But the other closed his eyes, unable to fight against the brightness and quickly lost consciousness again.

The doctor arrived and contrary to Müller's prediction, was sober enough to take control of the situation, dispersing the crowd of drunken seamen at the door. As Kegel was lying in a confined space, it was going to be difficult to do anything but a cursory examination, so he sent two ratings to the infirmary to fetch a stretcher. While they were gone, he made his initial assessment, concluding that the damage caused by the beating, though severe, seemed to be confined to the head and face. When the stretcher arrived, he ordered Schettler, Brand and Müller and one of the returning ratings to lift Kegel as straight as possible, while the other was instructed to insert the stretcher under him before he could be lowered onto it and strapped in for his precarious journey to the infirmary. When they made to follow the stretcher, the doctor instructed Schettler, Brand and Müller that he would need time alone with Kegel to make a proper assessment of his injuries and that they should not come to the infirmary for at least twenty four hours. Müller went about his business and Brand and Schettler returned to the mess.

There were still a few stragglers around but they soon dispersed, leaving the two men alone with their thoughts. The silence was broken by Schettler exclaiming, "I'm sure that was Penzberg and his cronies who beat Axel up."

"Yes, I heard you ask him that." Brand shook his head. "You don't know that for sure and we mustn't jump to conclusions."

"You were the one jumping to conclusions, Karl, when you castigated Axel for having a different opinion to the rest of us. It's unthinkable that someone should be beaten up for having a different opinion. If we start that, then the revolution will be still born and the old order will, through our intolerance, re-take control."

"You're misinterpreting a statement of frustration for an attitude of mind and that's unfair of you, Johann. All I said was that I hoped he would suffer from a hangover. I never wanted him to get beaten up. Whatever he believes, the old order's dead and the Kaiser isn't coming back. That's all I meant."

"Fine, but you must agree he was probably beaten up by the Red Guard because of what he said earlier."

Brand frowned. "Listen, if he was beaten up by the Red Guard, it was as a scapegoat for the embarrassment you caused to Penzberg. So get off my back."

Schettler nodded. "Fair enough, Karl, I'm sorry."

On a visit to the infirmary later that day, Schettler discovered that Kegel's jaw had been fractured and was now wired up. He had bad bruising all over his body, consistent with a widespread beating and he was sleeping. The doctor, who looked tired, told him that it would be several days before he would be in any condition to be questioned, advice he had already conveyed to Müller earlier.

In the days that followed, Müller questioned Kegel but he claimed that his attackers came from behind and he never saw their faces. Müller and Schettler believed he was scared to tell the real story. When Penzberg and his cronies were questioned, they denied having anything to do with the beating and as no other witnesses came forward, Müller had to drop his investigation through lack of evidence.

Chapter 13

Although Gerry O'Brien had been working in Parkhead Forge for only six weeks, this was the second time he had been summoned to a meeting with Dick Bradshaw. At their first meeting O'Brien had explained there had been no meetings since he had joined the BSP two weeks previously and, as far as him joining the shop stewards committee was concerned, even if there had been a vacancy, they were hardly likely to accept someone who had been employed with the company for such a short time. Bradshaw hadn't taken the news well, storming out of the pub without bothering to say goodbye.

It was with a heavy heart O'Brien returned to the Alexandra Bar in Duke Street on that rainy January evening. He was ten minutes early when he sat down with his beer at the same table as before and rolled a cigarette which when lit, immediately burned down half way.

At the specified time, Bradshaw entered the half empty pub. He ordered a drink for himself, then sat down opposite O'Brien and without a word of greeting, lit a cigarette and took a pull on his pint. "Well, get on with it." His clipped tones accentuated the London accent.

"They're calling an all-out strike beginning on January 27th. They're..." O'Brien began, his voice as low as possible.

"Who the fuck, are they? Gerry. Be more specific," snapped Bradshaw.

"The strike committee."

"Names, Gerry, names."

"The chairman's Emmanuel Shinwell and the other leaders are Willie Gallacher and George Kerr. That's all I know."

"Shinwell, the chairman of Glasgow Trades Council?"

"Yes."

"I know Gallacher's a communist bastard but where does this Kerr fellow stand?"

It was common knowledge what role Kerr held, so why was Bradshaw asking this?

"He's the secretary of the Scottish TUC, the Trades Union Congress."

"Don't be fucking cheeky," Bradshaw snapped. "I know what the TUC is. I want to know the bastard's politics."

"I don't know."

"Find out then! Right, is this strike going to be solid?"

"Oh aye, one hundred per cent."

"Do you think the leaders are trying to make it more than a strike?"

"What do you mean by that?"

"Don't be stupid – you know fine what I mean. Are they out to start political trouble."

O'Brien exhaled loudly and shrugged. "I've not heard anything about that, but I guess it could escalate."

"Will your pal, John Maclean, be involved?"

"No, I've heard he's doing a tour around England."

"Will the miners come out in support?"

"I haven't heard, but I wouldn't be surprised. Everybody supports it."

"Right, Gerry, don't think you've given me anything I don't know, but at least you've clarified a few things. So keep your ears pinned back, I'll be in touch."

He quaffed his pint, rose from the table, and was gone.

Fucking right, bastard! O'Brien thought as he tried to make sense of what had just taken place. He had only told Bradshaw what everyone knew. For a member of the security services, he seemed to lack the basic knowledge of the trade union movement.

Maybe this wouldn't be so compromising after all. Perhaps in the future he could even stick in a few pieces of misinformation.

*

In January, the news getting to the ships from Germany was erratic. In many cities civil war, was raging between the right-wing Freikorps and forces loyal to the revolution, and the indication was that the left was being heavily defeated.

Brand received a letter from Artelt which made grim reading, at least what could be read, for it had been heavily censored by the British. From what he and Schettler could glean, Artelt was unhappy with the way SPD, and in particular Noske, had been going along with the revolution in public, while secretly gathering forces to oppose it. In consequence, Artelt had resigned as chairman of Kiel WSC and returned to his home in Magdeburg. This was a shock. Brand and Schettler knew him as a fighter. If he felt it was necessary to resign, then the revolution must be as good as over, particularly as Karl Liebknecht and Rosa Luxemburg had been arrested in Berlin by a unit of the Freikorps, tortured and put to death.

The results of the election for the National Assembly held on the nineteenth were equally dire. The KPD, the newly formed German Communist Party, boycotted it, and so the working classes were forced to vote for the SPD, who won the largest number of seats in the Reichstag. They formed a government with the parties of the centre right.

The situation within the fleet was equally grim. Brand was accused of being too close to the officers on the joint committee and was deposed as chairman of the Soldiers' Council in favour of leading stoker Schröder, who then persuaded the majority that the Red Guard should be represented on the council and nominated Penzberg for the post. He went even further by proposing that Penzberg should replace Schettler as the councillor of the Friedrich der Grosse. Only this final proposal was defeated and the six councillors became seven.

The addition of Penzberg to the council gave the Red Guard a new legitimacy. They threatened to expel the officers who, it was true, had taken a hard line against the men after Reuter had gone on leave. In this situation there was no cooperation between enlisted men and officers, and work to maintain the ships almost ground to a halt.

At a meeting of the joint council during this time, Commodore Dominik reported that if the situation between the crew and officers didn't improve, the British would take control of the German ships by declaring martial law. Schettler and Brand argued that the Soldiers' Council had to step back from their current, aggressive position. If the British declared martial law, the men would become prisoners and not be eligible for repatriation. The council seemed to take no notice. This was the situation Admiral von Reuter would inherit when he arrived back on the ship the next day.

Schettler left the meeting, a feeling of panic rising up within him. It was the feeling one got when witnessing something so dire and yet being unable to do anything to stop it. When he reached the deck, his thoughts were incoherent and he stared out at the darkening sky towards the other ships and the bleak, mountainous outline of the island of Hoy beyond.

He stood on deck for some time, before he became conscious of how cold he was and returned stiffly to his cabin.

A note had been pushed under his door.

I've been told that your friend, Charlie, will be over to see you tonight. The boat will arrive at 19.00 so be there to meet him. Also, if you need soap, I've got some nice English bars at a knock down price of 1 mark a bar. Special to you!
Regards, Heini

Schettler smiled at Heini's complete opportunism. The thought of Charlie's visit lifted his spirits. He checked his watch. He had time to tidy his cabin, freshen up, go for something to eat and collect half a dozen bottles of Becks from the mess before heading aft to meet his friend.

The boats arrived promptly and, as usual, Charlie was first up the ladder. They shook hands and Tennant said, "I don't know what's going on tonight, Ian, but it must be big business, because I'm told we have two hours."

When they closed the cabin door, Tennant asked, "What's the matter, my friend? You look fed up." As Schettler poured them each a beer, he told the story of what had been going on since last they met. After he had finished, Tennant went into the pocket of his tunic and brought out a few pages of writing paper. "Perhaps this will cheer you up."

Schettler could see it was Margaret's writing and the letter had been written for both of them.

Dear Charlie and Johann,

Let me begin by wishing you both a Happy New Year and I hope that the bad circumstances you both find yourselves in at Scapa don't drag on too long. New Year, for us, turned out better than we expected as my dear brother, Bob, was demobbed in time to get home for Hogmanay. I haven't seen my mother so happy for a long time. On the first, Bob and I went to a party at the Trades Council which we both enjoyed very much. The mood here is of cautious optimism. The talk among the labour movement is of change. The influence of the Russian Revolution has shown what working-class power really means and it is fast taking hold. There is now talk of forming a communist party. Many of our unions are amalgamating to increase their strength and there are rumours of a national miners' strike to demand that coal mines should remain nationalised and not be returned to the old mine owners now the war it over. However, the overriding problem here is unemployment, which is growing all the time with the men returning from the war. The twelve hour, seven day, working week must now be reduced and I have heard that negotiations are taking place between the Clyde Workers Council, Glasgow Trades Council and the Amalgamated Society of Engineers to launch a campaign for a forty-hour week. This will bring better conditions to those in employment and create new jobs to reduce unemployment, if it's successful.

The letter ended abruptly at the bottom of the second page. "The rest was personal to me but she did send her love to you," Tennant said. "She also mentioned that since you're so close, it would be great for you to visit Glasgow."

"Yes, right now it would be wonderful," Schettler said, "if we could only devise a way for me to get there."

"I have a way – and it's not only clever, it's undetectable. How would you like to go to Glasgow for a week, Johann?"

Schettler looked at his friend in disbelief. "Yes, I'd like that very much but how do you propose I get there?"

"Ah well," the other said with a sly smile. "You remember my pal, Gordon Carmichael?"

"Yes I do. He's a good fellow!"

"He's an even better fellow now! He and I have just been granted a pass for seven days leave, starting on January 29 and yesterday he had to be taken to hospital in Wick to deal with a recurring foot problem. So, as they don't cross check, the pass is going spare. He said you could have it if you wanted."

"They don't check their leave passes?" Schettler asked in astonishment.

"That's right. The leave passes are issued from another ship and they don't cross check up here any more. I know it sounds bizarre, particularly to a German, but it's true. Anyway what do we care? It happens. The only thing is, you'll have to wear a British uniform for the journeys. Once we reach Glasgow we wear civvies."

"What's civvies?"

"Civilian clothes."

"I didn't bring any civilian clothes here. There was no call for them and how do I get my hands on a British uniform?"

"I can take Gordon's for you. He's about your size anyway and as far as civvies are concerned, between your cousin Bob and me, we can kit you out for a week."

"What if we're stopped by the shore patrol during our journey? What do I do?"

"The Royal Navy Police you mean? I've never seen them between here and Glasgow, but if they did turn up, you'd show them your pass and if they ask you your name and number you say you're Gordon Carmichael and you're going home to Glasgow. I've got his details, which I'll give you before I go, and all you do is memorise them. It's easy! God, even if you forgot part of it, they'd just think you're drunk. And what's more, I'll be there as well, remember."

"What about my accent?"

"I've heard you speak like a native. I admit you wouldn't get away with a detailed conversation, but a few words and they'll never know. Anyway practice makes perfect. What do you say?"

Schettler smiled. "As long as I can think of a way to cover my tracks here, it should be okay. Given the circumstances, it shouldn't be too difficult, but I'll have to tell Brand and Herzmann the truth, so they can cover for me."

"So you'll come then?"

"I don't see why not. But how will I get ashore?"

"Oh, I've thought of that too. I'll be on the boat that comes here and when it leaves it will take us to Stromness before it returns to the The Emperor of India. We'll take the night ferry from Kirkwall to Aberdeen and then catch the train to Glasgow. We'll both have to pay a 2/6d supplement to take the ferry, but the rest of the travel we get free through our passes."

"How do we get from Stromness to Kirkwall?"

"Bus."

"Right, that's fine then, but what about money?"

"That's easy. Just ask your friend, Heini. He'll sell it to you."

Tennant looked thoughtful. "The only part of the uniform that must be perfect is the hat. You can't have one that's either too big or too wee. What hat size are you?"

"Fifty seven centimetres."

"I don't know what that means. You better try my cap on." He passed it to Schettler. "How is it?"

"It's fine, it fits."

Tennant took a piece of paper out of his pocket on which he had written, 'Chief Petty Officer Gordon Carmichael, number 3496394 The Emperor of India. '867 Paisley Road West Glasgow SW3' and handed it to Schettler.

"That's who you are – memorise it. You have twenty four hours before I come over tomorrow night to pick you up. Just remember to pronounce the letter W properly – don't say, vest for west. Other than that they'll never know."

"Don't be cheeky, you know I don't do that."

"Well then, what are you worried about? The boat will be here at seven o'clock and as there's only a quick delivery to be made, we'll be on our way by seven thirty. I'll bring a duffle bag with Gordon's uniform inside and my spare cap and you can change here before we leave."

Later, when Schettler left Tennant to climb down to the boat, he had a lot to think about and prepare before his strange journey though Scotland began. Already, he felt his stomach churning in anticipation.

PART 2

Chapter 14

It was ten past seven and the boat ferrying Tennant over to the Dicke Fritz hadn't appeared. It was never late. Schettler paced nervously up and down the after deck. Two unfamiliar ratings there to take delivery of whatever was being bartered that evening, watched this representative of the revolution with apprehension. They didn't know how he would react to the nefarious business about to be carried out.

By quarter past seven Schettler was frantic, imagining all manner of irrational reasons for the boat's non-appearance. It was almost twenty past when he heard the sound of a motor heading towards them, followed by the bump of the boat against the side of the ship.

He waited for the familiar sight of Tennant coming on board, but he didn't appear. He could hear someone shouting and much huffing and puffing going on below. When he looked over the side, he saw two British sailors trying to manhandle a large, awkward package up the rope ladder with Tony Chummily, Heini's British counterpart, directing operations from the boat. To Schettler's relief, Tennant was standing next to him.

At that moment, Heini appeared by his side and when he saw the package, he clapped his hands together. "Gott sei Dank es ist angekommen!"

"What the hell is it, Heini?" Schettler said, puzzled.

"It's a picture of a large stag."

"A what?"

"A stag, a bloody stag, you know, a big, boy deer."

"Yes, I know what a stag is." Schettler glared at him. "Who the hell is it for?"

"Would you believe Commodore Dominik wants it for Reuter's birthday?"

"Jesus Christ! Where the hell did they get hold of that?"

"I don't ask questions and I get told no lies. That's the safest way to do business here."

It was the second time Schettler had dealings with Heini that day. He had dropped in to see if he could buy pounds for marks and, sure enough, the man was prepared to do business. Schettler was able to buy five large, white five-pound notes with 'The British Linen Bank' ornately printed on one side, for 250 marks – money he had been saving for some time.

To Schettler, the one-sided bank notes didn't look real, but Heini assured him they were. It was unlikely he'd received a good rate of exchange, but beggars couldn't be choosers and at least Heini didn't enquire why he wanted the money. This should be more than enough for his week in Glasgow but, as he didn't know how much things cost there, he didn't want to be left short.

When the parcel reached the deck, it was uplifted by the two ratings and, directed by Heini, they disappeared through the bulkhead door. The deck was empty again until Tennant appeared with the duffle bag.

He handed it to Schettler. "Hurry up and change and put something in there because you'll have to take it with you. No one travels without a bag. I'll stay here till you get back."

When Schettler returned to the deck, Tennant looked him up and down. "You look the part all right. Does the uniform fit?"

"Yes, it's not bad for length, the jacket and overcoat are a bit loose but not enough to look stupid. The hat's fine."

"Good, here's Gordon's travel pass and pay book. Don't lose them and don't produce the pay book unless absolutely necessary. Have you memorised the information you'll need?"

Schettler recited the name, number and address from memory making an exaggerated W sound at 'West' before putting the pass into his inside jacket pocket.

"Alright, funny man, let's get going," Tennant said and the two of them climbed down to the motor boat and sat at the rear.

They soon left the lights of the German fleet behind and headed east into open water. The two ratings on board chatted with Chummily and, according to the scraps of conversation they could hear over the noise of the engine, all three men seemed to come from the Portsmouth area. Schettler and Tennant sat in silence until Chummily shouted over, "So, you're off on leave?"

"Aye, thank God," Tennant answered. "A week away from this god-forsaken place. It'll be good to get back to Glasgow, won't it, Gordon?"

Schettler realised that these men thought he was Carmichael. "Aye, Charlie, it will," he said in his broadest Scottish accent, while wondering what Tennant had said about him being on the Dicke Fritz.

As silence fell again, Schettler thought about the recent developments on board the German ships. Since Reuter had returned from Germany, any idea of the Soldiers' Council keeping meaningful power was inconceivable and there was an increased likelihood of its members being sent home. He had wanted to stay with the men to protect their interests but increasingly this task was being made impossible by the hysterical actions of the Red Guard and High Command's hardening attitude towards them. Recently he had realised how futile his position was and, although this visit to Glasgow was ill conceived, he had consented to go because he felt so useless.

His thoughts were interrupted by the rumble of a ship's engine which seemed to be getting closer and he saw lights coming towards them out of the darkness. A search light was trained on their boat. When the ship was about 100 metres away, a voice with a heavy, Orkney accent boomed over a loudspeaker. "This is His Majesty's armed trawler, Chirsin. Please identify yourselves."

Chummily shouted out, while cutting the engine, "This is motorboat number eleven, attached to HMS Emperor of India. We're ferrying two CPOs to Stromness to go on leave."

Schettler felt his heart begin to race.

"Identify the CPOs please."

Tennant shouted out his name, rank and number. When he finished, he dug Schettler in the ribs indicating he should do likewise. Schettler swallowed his nerves and managed to shout out in a clear voice Carmichael's name, rank and number.

"Alright, where are you going on leave?"

"We're taking the bus to Kirkwall and then catching the night ferry to Aberdeen for a week's leave in Glasgow," Tennant replied and gave his address there. As Schettler began to do the same, the voice came back. "Aye, that'll do. Just you be waitin' a few minutes now."

As the search light continued to light up the motorboat bobbing around in the swell, there was only the muffled sound of the trawler's idling engine and the occasional raised voice echoing in the breeze.

The minutes passed slowly, endlessly, until Tennant whispered, "What do you think's going on, Tony?"

"They'll be checking back by radio to see if you're legit."

By this time, Schettler was almost beside himself as the silence continued.

The voice boomed out, making Schettler jump. "Aye, you're all right boys. You have a nice leave and don't be getting drunk and causing trouble in that nice, peaceful Glasgow. Oh, by the way, when you get to Kirkwall, just tell the Master-at-Arms there that ah've already checked you out."

"Will do, Chirsin," Tennant shouted. "What's all the security for anyway?"

"Ach, it's two boys off the Revenge who've gone AWOL. Unless they catch them you'll probably get checked a lot before you get home. Hard luck, boys!"

Schettler stared at Tennant who just shrugged as Chummily re-engaged the engine and they chugged off in the direction of Stromness.

When the boat entered the harbour, it was busy with drifters and boats of all shapes and sizes and they ended up tying off against an inshore fishing boat. Scrambling over its deck with ropes and nets strewn everywhere, they reached the metal ladder to take them up to the harbour. They were surprised to see Chummily and the two ratings following behind, each lugging a case of brandy and, as the five men reached the harbour entrance, the three walked off in the direction of the local bars while Tennant directed Schettler to where he thought the bus would be.

As they hurried along, Schettler asked, "What did you tell—"

Tennant shook his head. "Keep your questions for later, Ian. We're in a hurry. According to my watch, the bus leaves in less than ten minutes."

They arrived just in time and as soon as they had shown their warrants to the driver, the bus moved off. It was less than quarter full, with seven people on board. The two of them made their way to the back seat where they were able to lay their duffle bags on one side while sitting on the other, well away from the other passengers.

Schettler couldn't contain himself any longer and whispered, "What reason did you give Chummily, for me being on board the Dicke Fritz?"

"The what?" said Tennant.

"The Fredrick der Grosse. Dicke Fritz is our nickname for it."

"Ah! That's funny – ours is Freddy the Grocer."

Schettler found that amusing. "Anyway, what did you tell them?"

"I said you wanted something German to take home to Glasgow and you asked the boys going to the Moltke to take you to the Freddy first so that you could carry out your business in time for us to pick you up for Stromness."

Schettler nodded. "Clever. I was right then. They thought I was Gordon. But wouldn't they have known him?"

"Maybe, but the Emperor has a crew of 1,450 so it's highly unlikely – wouldn't you say? You're a naval man,

Ian. Do you *know* your entire ship's company?" Schettler shrugged. "No, I suppose you're right."

"Anyway, it was almost completely dark. They probably didn't see your face."

"Not until the Chirsin's searchlight was on us."

Tennant shook his head. "They had their backs to us then. Look, will you stop worrying. It'll be fine."

The bus entered Kirkwall sometime later and drove through its narrow, deserted streets towards the harbour. When they stepped down from the bus, Schettler and Tennant could see the St Ola enter the harbour having completed the first leg of its voyage from Shetland. They were immediately approached by a Chief Petty Officer and an able seaman both wearing Master-at-Arms insignia.

Schettler's heart sank. Christ not again, he thought.

Tennant smiled. "Look here, Chiefy, we know all about the two who are AWAL. The armed trawler Chirsin already checked us out…"

*

Once in Glasgow, Schettler and Tennant bundled their duffle bags into the first taxi in the rank at Buchanan Street Station. Tennant leaned over towards the driver's cab. "Dennistoun, driver – 8 Seton Terrace."

"Very good sur, but you'll have to understand, there's been demonstrations today. I don't know what roads are open, so it might take a while."

"Aye, that'll be fine, ma friend. As long as we get there."

It was a dark, dreary January evening and the city was unrecognisable to Schettler. What struck him was how drab the place was, and how downtrodden and sad the people looked as they trudged along. This must be what four years of war does to people. When they passed through George Square, which Schettler did recognise, there were still traces of the earlier demonstration with pockets of men and police still milling around and placards and home-made banners strewn over the ground. The taxi headed east to Duke Street. Schettler recognised the stark, black, stone edifice of the building his mother had told him was Duke Street Prison. Like the last time he had seen it, the place sent a shiver down his spine.

When the taxi drew up midway along a grey, sandstone terrace, with houses on one side and a garden running along its length on the other, Schettler clearly remembered the house.

They paid the driver and approached the front door. Schettler felt a buzz of anticipation.

The door was opened by a man who looked the same age as them. He registered no surprise at seeing the sailors.

"Hello, Charlie! Come away in. Margaret's had to attend a meeting after school that seems to have dragged on a bit, but she shouldn't be long."

As the two men stepped through the door removing their caps, a voice came from the back of house. "Who is it, Bob?"

"It's Charlie, Mother and he's brought a friend."

"She's not in, Charlie, she's at a meeting…" The voice grew louder as Schettler's Aunt Nell entered the hall.

"Show them through to the parlour, Bob," she said. "Hello, Charlie. Is this you home on leave, again? You're certainly getting a lot of leave these days. And who might this nice chap be?" She looked Schettler up and down.

They turned into the parlour, and although Schettler recognised it, it was now decorated differently.

"This is my friend from the ship, Chief Petty Officer Carmichael," Tennant replied and winked at Schettler.

Understanding the ploy, Schettler said, "How do you do? Charlie's told me such a lot about you all."

"I hope they were nice things, Mr Carmichael."

"They certainly were, Mrs Nairn." Schettler thought his aunt looked much older than he had expected, but he realised that it had been twelve years since he'd seen her and then it was through the eyes of a boy.

Nell began to fuss around them nervously. "Please take a seat. I'm sure Margaret won't be too much longer. Have you eaten, or would you like something? I haven't got much prepared, but I could make you a sandwich." And this was how Schettler remembered her.

As the mariners sat down on the settee, Schettler noticed Bob studying him.

Tennant held up his hand. "Don't worry, Mrs Nairn, we had something on the train."

"Well, you must have a cup of tea, at least."

They heard the outside door open and close, and a woman's voice came from the hall. "That dammed meeting went on and on. Harkness is getting worse, and then I had to walk from George Square. The trams aren't working properly because of the demonstration. Where are you both?"

Tennant realised that their taxi had probably passed her en route.

"We're in the parlour, dear," her mother replied. "Charlie's arrived, and he's brought a friend."

Margaret stuck her head round the door, walked over to Tennant and kissed him on the cheek. "Why didn't you tell me you were coming? I would have made an excuse and been here when you arrived."

Tennant smiled. "Oh well, it was really a last-minute thing. We just got the passes a few days ago and there wasn't time to write. And you know how you don't like me phoning the school. Anyway, I could only have done that today, which wouldn't have made much difference, would it?"

"I suppose not. It'll be alright from now on, though. Did you not notice we have our own telephone now? They installed it yesterday. Mother thought we should have one now that Bob's home. I'll write down the number for you later. Anyway, aren't you going to introduce me to your friend?"

Nell butted in before Tennant could reply. "This is Chief Petty Officer Carmichael, Margaret."

Schettler rose from the settee and Margaret came to shake his hand. As she looked into his face she retorted in surprise, "I don't think it is, Mother. I think you've been the victim of a joke!"

Her mother gazed at her in surprise. "What do you mean?"

"I think I'm looking at my cousin, Johann Schettler."

"Bloody hell, I knew it," Bob cried, as he got to his feet.

Margaret embraced her cousin. "Oh Johann, it's wonderful to see you. What a lovely surprise."

Bob came across and shook his hand saying how happy he was to see him again. Nell had burst into floods of tears.

Johann put his arm around his aunt. "Surely my visit has not made you unhappy, Aunt Nell?"

"Oh, no, Johann." Her voice cracked. "I'm so glad to see you. I just wish I could talk to my sister. It's been so long and so many appalling things have happened since we spoke last. Charles and Heinrich are dead..." Unable to speak further, she sobbed uncontrollably. Margaret too had tears in her eyes. She took her mother in her arms and they stood there for some time.

Tennant eventually broke the silence. "Look, I better get home if I want to see my parents before they go to bed. They seem to be going earlier and earlier these days."

Nell looked up and smiled as Margaret released her. "Why don't you just stay here tonight, Charlie? There's plenty of room."

Her mother's change of attitude towards Charlie surprised Margaret, and as she glanced at Tennant, it was clear he was also surprised.

"Thanks, Mrs Nairn, but I better get home. My parents are expecting me. You all have a lot of catching up to do."

"If you're sure, but you know the invitation's always there."

Margaret took Charlie to the door, passing the new telephone on the occasional table.

Tennant raised his eyebrows. "We're getting really posh now, with a new phone and all. La de da."

Margaret disappeared into the kitchen and returned with a piece of paper with BRI 1641 scribbled on it. "There's the number, put it somewhere safe." She pressed the note into his hand. "What a surprise you gave us. I should be angry with you for not giving us warning. Clearly you could have, since your parents *are* expecting you." Tennant made to protest but she put her hand up to his mouth.

"What I was going to say is, Charlie Tennant, I love you! What a wonderful thing you've done. We're all so excited to see Johann." She kissed him and whispered in his ear, "We'll have to get some time alone, won't we?"

Then, in a louder voice, "How long are you both here?"

"This is the first day of a seven-day leave, so we have five more days in Glasgow."

"That's good. There's a lot happening this week, though. The Unions have called a general strike in Glasgow in support of a forty-hour week."

Tennant nodded. "Yes, we read about that in the paper."

Margaret continued, "Everyone except the tramway workers have heeded the call."

Tennant smiled. "Although I'm in full support of the strike, I'm more interested in time alone with you, Margaret Nairn." And he kissed her back.

"Get out of here, you're up to no good."

Back in the kitchen Nell prepared a meal, while asking questions about how her nephew had got there.

When the meal was served, his aunt kept apologising for its lack of quality, but Schettler thought it was the best he had eaten since his last home leave, more than two years ago.

The conversation turned to politics and Margaret told him all about the strike. "There was a mass meeting in the St Andrew's Halls on Monday, then a march to George Square to demonstrate solidarity. Today the strikers marched from all sides of the city to George Square again. Bob was there. Tell us what happened," Margaret said excitedly.

"The strike was so solid there must have been 30,000 there. Members of the strike committee took their proposals to the Lord Provost to gain support from Glasgow Corporation. A couple of strikers somehow got on to the roof of the City Chambers and hoisted a red flag on the main flag pole. It could be seen all over George Square and the crowds began to sing the International. It fairly set the heart thumping!"

Her mother interrupted. "That's terrible, flying a red flag over the City Chambers."

Margaret exclaimed, "My mother cast her first ever vote in the General Election last month and would you believe it, Johann? She voted Tory."

"What is Tory?" Schettler looked puzzled. "And look, my mother always called me Ian. So you should too."

"Yes, I do remember that," Margaret replied, "but I didn't like to assume. You were just a wee boy then. And as for the Tories, it's what we call the Conservative Party. They represent the ruling class, don't they, Mother?"

Nell just shook her head. "They represent business and your father always voted for them. Ian, according to this family, I never do anything right. I should just rub myself out."

Margaret gave her mother a hug and winked at Johann over her shoulder. "Blessed are the constantly misunderstood!" They all laughed.

"Why did the strike committee think they could trust, what was it, Glasgow Corporation? Is that the city council?" Johann asked.

"Yes, that's what I was thinking," Margaret said, with feeling. "They're also Tories. To me, it was naïve of the committee."

"When the strike committee returned to address the workers, they said that as well as asking for support for a forty-hour week they requested that the trams be taken off the streets as long as the strike is on," Bob said. "But according to Shinwell, the Lord Provost would have to telephone the Prime Minister. When the provost returned, he said that the Cabinet needed time to discuss their proposals and the committee should return on Friday."

Schettler looked quizzical. "I think your strike committee was wrong to have accepted this. It gives the government time to manoeuvre against the strike, surely?"

Margaret nodded. "Yes, I agree."

Nell suddenly snapped. "Oh, for goodness sake! Haven't we spoken enough about politics, Margaret?"

Margaret looked suitably chastened and talk returned to the family and old times.

Johann told them about his father's visit to Scapa Flow, the circumstances of Heinrich's death and his mother's influenza.

Nell's eyes widened in shock at the thought of her sister's illness and Johann had to assure her several times that her sister had now fully recovered.

Sometime later, Margaret noticed Johann could barely keep his eyes open and suggested he should go to bed.

*

The next morning Schettler was wakened by his cousin, Bob, knocking.

"Good morning, Ian, I'm sorry to disturb you but Charlie's just arrived to see you."

Johann sat up in bed and looked at his watch, discovering it was a few minutes after eleven o'clock. He had slept badly, his night troubled by dreams of being arrested by the British Naval Police. It must have been almost his normal waking time before he had fallen into a deep and dreamless sleep.

"Come in, Bob. I'm sorry I slept so late. I don't usually."

Bob entered the room carrying a large pile of assorted clothes.

"You must have needed it," he said, as he laid the clothes at the bottom of the bed. "I thought you could choose a few things and if you need any more, you can have a look in my closet. Charlie's not in a hurry and I said you might want to take a bath before coming down. There's also a dressing gown and some shaving kit there."

"Thanks, Bob. I'll try not to be long but it's been a few months since I've had a bath. When I get in, it'll be hard to get back out."

"That's fine, but be a bit sparing with the water. When I mentioned a bath, Charlie looked so envious that I offered him one too. His folks don't have a bath or even an inside toilet in their tenement."

"I'll do that," said Johann. He already knew about Charlie's living arrangements in a small Glasgow tenement.

Johann appeared in the kitchen, slightly abashed, wearing a green, Harris Tweed suit, a white shirt and bottle green tie looking every bit the Scottish gentleman which both his aunt and cousin commented on. It was fully an hour later before Charlie came down wearing a dark blue suit and a pale blue shirt with rounded collar and tie. The two men stared at each other incredulously, for neither had seen the other out of uniform.

Charlie was first to break the silence with a huge guffaw. "My God, Ian, what do you look like?"

Nell gasped, no doubt worrying her nephew might be offended, but he spluttered, "Well, you look very strange yourself. What is it you're selling, Charlie?"

The joke was kept up as Johann tried on a couple of hats Charlie had brought and they all sat around the kitchen table eating bacon rolls and drinking tea.

Later, Charlie and Bob took Johann on a short tour to re-acquaint him with the city. He was surprised at how different everything looked compared with his memories of years ago. He wanted to see Glasgow School of Art since Margaret had mentioned it in her letter and was in awe of its innovation and beauty.

*

After the evening meal, as Charlie and the family sat around the kitchen table, Bob asked his cousin to explain what had happened in Germany.

Oh, not more politics, Nell thought. She rose, making an excuse that she needed to do some sewing, and left the room, feeling somewhat disgruntled.

Bob grimaced, knowing that his mother wasn't pleased, before he shrugged and continued, "What I really want to know, is, in the light of the mass demonstration tomorrow, is there any comparisons that can be made?"

Johann couldn't really understand what Bob was driving at.

"In Kiel, the navy took power because the men had access to weapons and were able to defeat any reactionary forces being used against them," Johann explained. "As the mass of the people were in agreement with a movement to defeat the government, it spread fast across many cities and towns throughout the country.

How can there be comparisons, Bob? Tomorrow in Glasgow they're having a demonstration. There's no means to take power. Is there?"

Margaret cut in, "What Bob means is, could a mass strike, like that happening here in Glasgow, turn into a movement to bring down the government and establish a socialist state?" Bob nodded in agreement.

Johann pondered the point. "In my experience, the rank and file of the army must be in support of the strikers and be prepared to defy orders to force a change of power. But no such support exists here. Is that not right?"

"Partly, Ian," Charlie said. "Although the army is kept under tight control here, many militant ex-servicemen's organisations that have been set up are prepared to fight in support of the strikers and there are some in Glasgow."

"But will they be armed?" asked Johann.

Charlie shook his head. "No, I doubt it." He turned to Bob. "Have you got a gun?"

"No."

Johann looked grim. "As long as the forces are loyal to the Government, it's almost impossible, but I'm no expert on what happens in this country. The only way forward is for the trade unions to encourage the left-wing parties to fight for social justice. That's a long and protracted process. Given the German experience, this hasn't worked. The SPD sided with the Government in 1914 to start the war. They were voted into power at the general election two weeks ago and they are using reactionary forces to fight against the revolution."

"I know exactly what you mean, Ian," Margaret said emphatically. "The labour party has been ill serving the workers almost since its inception. Now its support for the forty-hour working week is, at best, unenthusiastic."

Charlie said he thought the only way forward was for the working class of Scotland to take power themselves, as

Maclean had advocated. "We'll have to see what tomorrow brings," said Bob, leaning back in his chair and yawning.

Margaret reminded Bob she wouldn't take a day off school for the demonstration but Kate A'Herne would be waiting for him at the corner of George Street and High Street at ten o'clock.

Charlie winked at Johann. "Well, it looks like we should go to the demonstration tomorrow, Ian."

At this Margaret gave him a withering look and retorted, "Well, of course, what else would you do?"

Chapter 15

It had rained heavily overnight and the streets were still wet when Nairn, Tennant and Schettler left Seton Terrace to rendezvous with Kate. As they reached Duke Street, they came upon a large group of demonstrators marching in regimented rows of eight abreast, accompanied by their district band playing a medley of Harry Lauder songs. The three men strode along the pavement, keeping time with the music and listening to the light-hearted banter from the marching men. They could see from the banners they were a contingent from Beardmore's Foundry in Parkhead.

Suddenly, a small man came running up to Tennant, breathing heavily and grabbed his arm. Tennant recoiled in surprise. It was Gerry O'Brien. The two stared at each other for some time before O'Brien blurted out between gasps. "I saw you comin' down that road. I knew it was you, even a distance away. How are you doin', Charlie?"

Tennant stayed silent, staring at O'Brien. There were many issues going through his mind. What could he say to him after the years the man had spent in prison? How should he introduce Schettler? Carmichael he supposed – they should have discussed this yesterday. He should have known that they were bound to meet someone. Wasn't Glasgow, even with a population of over a million, known as the biggest village in the world?

"What's wrong, man? Do you no ken me?" O'Brien asked.

"Of course I know you, Gerry," said Tennant. "You're looking well. I'm just surprised to see you, that's all. Do you work at Beardmore's now?" Before O'Brien had time to answer, he turned to the others. "Just walk on you two, I'll catch you up in a minute."

O'Brien's breathing had eased. "Aye, I started there before Christmas and here we are out on strike already. But it's right that we are. It's good to be fighting for a just cause. Mind you, I could have done with earning a bit more money before I went on strike. What are you doing with yourself, Charlie?"

"I'm still in the Navy for the time being, but I don't think it'll be long before I'm demobbed. Look, Gerry, I'm a bit pushed for time. We're just off to meet someone before we head to George Square, so how about meeting in Lang's in Queen Street at about half past one and we can catch up on everything then?"

"Aye, alright, that'll be fine. See you later then." O'Brien re-joined the marchers.

"Who was that, Charlie?" Nairn said as Tennant caught up with the other two.

"He's just a lad I used to know in Fairfield's before the war. I said I'd meet him in Lang's bar in Queen Street later." He had to think fast because he had never told the Nairns about being arrested back in 1914. But that wasn't so important now. He knew Margaret wouldn't be at all bothered once she understood the circumstances. On the other hand, the less they knew the better.

*

Thomas Sinclair arrived at the John Street entrance of Glasgow City Chambers at ten minutes to ten and was immediately escorted to the office of the Lord Provost, Sir James Watson Stewart. When he was shown into the sumptuous room with its golden, embossed wall covering and ornate, crystal chandeliers, he could see five men sitting around the large, conference table. The imposing figure of Stewart with his large moustache, sat at their head.

Without looking up, Stewart said, "Sit down please. Is there anyone here you haven't met?"

Sinclair scanned the faces, seeing James Stevenson, the city's chief constable, Colonel Anthony Stephens who wore the uniform of the Scots Guards, Sheriff Mackenzie, Charles Hungerford, Stewart's personal assistant in his capacity as Lord Lieutenant of the County of the City of Glasgow, and one other man he hadn't met before.

"Only this gentleman here, Lord Provost," Sinclair said, pointing to the man.

"This is Mr Hugh Macmillan, one of my senior officers in charge of coordinating all ancillary services – Ambulance and Fire and also support services such as keeping the police personnel fed and watered. A very important job wouldn't you say?"

The provost turned to Macmillan. "This gentleman – you don't need to know his name – is in charge of security services. If you happen to meet him throughout this time, you don't know him. Is that clear, Macmillan?"

Macmillan nodded. "Crystal clear, Lord Provost."

"Let's get on, then. We're in the process of assessing the situation and judging from the numbers of these infernal strikers already in George Square, we feel it's essential to call in the army which is currently waiting in London Road for their instructions. Are you in agreement?"

Sinclair said with a cold smile, "I am indeed, Lord Provost."

"Good. Then get on with it, Colonel." As Stephens rose, Stewart said, "Are you also clear about your duties, Macmillan?"

"I am, sir," the other said emphatically.

"Good, then you can leave with the Colonel."

When both men had left the room, Stewart went on, "The strike leaders are due to meet me at eleven o'clock but I don't want to meet them, so can you arrange this, Stevenson?"

"Yes, I can, sir," Stevenson said, in his strong Irish brogue, "as soon as they're inside this building. Is it Shinwell and Gallacher you're supposed to be meeting?"

"Yes, but Kirkwood could be there. Must they get into the building?"

Sinclair butted in, exasperated, "Yes, of course they do, sir. We must give the impression that we're co-operating with them."

"Very well," Stewart said waving his hand. "But I won't see them."

"That's fine, sir," Stevenson said. "As soon as they arrive inside, I'll give the signal to commence the action and a few minutes later Sheriff Mackenzie will read the Riot Act to give us the powers we need to deal with the situation." He smiled and nodded conspiratorially at Sinclair.

Sinclair nodded back. "I have men strategically placed to stir up trouble and also find the ring leaders. We need scapegoats. We must demonstrate to the country that this is not just a strike but the start of a revolution and be seen to snuff it out immediately and decisively. That is the message

I've been given by the Secretary of State for War, Mr Churchill. As he says, we don't want this to spread to English cities, so we better nip it in the bud here and now."

*

As Nairn, Tennant and Schettler continued alongside Duke Street Prison, the rows of marching men were swallowed up by the street-wide crowds of demonstrators moving relentlessly towards George Square, passing on all sides of two rows of stationary trams that the crowd had rendered immobile earlier that morning, by unhooking their trolleys from the overhead wires and cutting the trolley ropes. The vast crowd of men, with a scattering of women, waving red flags or carrying banners were in jubilant mood. Obviously, they expected to hear good news from the Lord Provost.

The three men reached High Street where they were to meet Kate A'Herne but in the unrelenting moving crowd, Tennant realised that Kate's diminutive height would make her hard to find. As they began their search of the street corners, he was stopped in his tracks by a shout from behind. "Is that you, Charlie Tennant?" By the Irish brogue, he knew it was Kate. He stopped the other two and they turned in the direction of the voice. When they saw her pushing her way through the crowd, the two sailors couldn't hide their surprise.

Seeing this, Bob chuckled. "Haven't you two ever seen a lady in trousers before? You better get used to it, Charlie. Margaret's wearing them a lot these days."

As Kate drew level, the three men smiled. She looked beautiful in her light green, tweed jacket and bottle green trousers, brown brogue shoes, white shirt, green tie and a long, green, woollen scarf loosely wound several times around her neck. The outfit perfectly matched her rich, auburn hair which was swept back and held in a bun. The overall effect could have made her look masculine, but it didn't. In fact, it seemed to accentuate her femininity.

Once Charlie had introduced Kate to his friend Carmichael, the four tried to continue along George Street to Glasgow's main square but the crowd soon ground to a stop. Kate pressed on doggedly, pushing and shoving and shouting for the men to make way and, sure enough, the crowd parted enough to allow them to squeeze through the gap to the beginning of George Square. It had taken half an hour to penetrate the crowd. When they got closer to their destination, they noticed large contingents of police with batons already drawn waiting in every side street. Five lines of police had also formed outside the City Chambers and senior officers were patrolling up and down, keeping a clear area of half the width of the street between the police and the demonstrators.

Once they arrived in George Square, they worked their way along to the statue of Prince Albert which was closest to the City Chambers and would be a good viewing platform for anyone being hoisted on to the plinth. Kate talked loudly and excitedly about the demonstration and how the hordes of people should turn and march west to Maryhill Barracks to persuade the soldiers from Glasgow's regiment, the Highland Light Infantry, to join their struggle. Schettler thought this was the right move, if the leaders of the strike wanted to begin the process of taking power for the people. He looked at the waiting police. The demonstration was only about a forty-hour working week, so why were there so many officers on the streets?

Kate's suggestion caused a buzz of agreement from the men around them. One shouted that he had heard the HLI were locked into Maryhill Barracks so that they couldn't come out in support of the strike. But another, an older man, shouted, "What's this got to dae wi' you, hen? Does yer man know yer oot in his clothes? What the hell is a lassie doin' here anyway?"

Some men around him laughed but others grinned in anticipation of what the woman would say in reply. Tennant was about to intervene on Kate's behalf, when she spoke up. "If you think the class struggle only affects men, then you're sadly out of touch, my friend. Who was it who organised the Rent Strikes in 1915 but women headed by Mary Barbour, and didn't that succeed in getting legislation to curtail the callous, money grabbing landlords – and allowed you to keep a roof over the head for your family? I've been sacked because I wouldn't accept increased working hours for the pittance they gave me at the end of the week and I tried to mobilise my work mates against the employers. And you think I shouldn't be here? If we are to fight for social justice we're going to need support from the other fifty per cent of the population – us. WOMEN. Have you ever asked your wife what she thinks? If you haven't, it's time you did."

The man's face had turned puce with anger. "Ma wife does whit she's fuckin' telt and if that's yer man wi' ye, then he should be telling ye tae get hame and look after the weans. Where ye fuckin' belong."

Both Schettler and Tennant made to step forward, but Kate stopped them.

"Is that where your wife is, lookin' after the weans?" She wore a wry smile.

"Aye, it fuckin' well is."

"It's a wonder she let you close enough to have weans with an attitude like that."

The men around him began to snigger and laugh, which made the man angrier. He moved as if to strike her and Schettler quickly jumped in to block his path.

The two men eye balled each other, till a cry went up from the tightly packed crowd. "Here's Gallacher, Kirkwood and Shinwell coming now."

The crowd started cheering and waving their flags as everyone turned towards the City Chambers. Charlie began to climb on to the plinth of the statue to get a better view and was offered a hand up by one of the young men already there. The plinth was more than half full by the time he made it to the top but there was still space and he shouted down to the others for one more to come up.

Nairn suggested that since Kate wouldn't see anything, she should take advantage of the lofty viewpoint. Nairn lifted her light frame up enough for Tennant to grab her hands and pull her up to join him. As they looked towards Glasgow's town house, they could see the three strike leaders walking along the space in front of the building. When they drew level with the front entrance, they stopped and exchanged a few words. Kirkwood and Shinwell entered the building while Gallacher crossed the street, protected by the police cordon and walked into the crowd, who gave him enough room to reach the statue.

As Gallacher prepared to climb up to the plinth, the city's Chief Constable walked briskly out of the City Chambers and began speaking to his senior officers. One walked off to Cochrane Street, where a large force was gathered in readiness and at a signal they started forward en masse towards the people on the south side of the square. They moved slowly but their pace quickened and soon they fell upon the unsuspecting hordes, kicking and punching with their truncheons flailing. The people who had chosen to stay on the outer edges of the crowd had, in many cases, done so to allow them a quick escape if trouble did break out and many of them were women with children. As the police rampaged through, many protesters were left lying on the ground bleeding and crying for help, some with serious injuries.

The police moved relentlessly on, now joined by other units from the side streets. The vast crowd was either constricted in George Square or were escaping through the side streets with the police chasing at their heels. Gallacher quickly dropped to the ground, evading the approaching police, and ran towards the entrance of the City Chambers where the Chief Constable was standing, directing operations with his senior officers. He landed on the group with flaying fists, trying to contact Stevenson. He managed to land a glancing blow to the side of the Chief's jaw, before the group of senior officers managed to restrain him with many blows to his head and body.

By now, the crowd had managed to regroup and a pitched battle between them and the police began. Accompanied by six policemen, the Sheriff came out from the City Chambers and began to read the riot act, but the police were quickly beaten back. The exposed Sheriff had the Act physically torn from his hands, before he turned tail and ran quickly back though the door.

Kirkwood and Shinwell, who had not yet met the Lord Provost, ran to the anteroom of the banqueting hall on the building's first floor, where a large French window led to a balcony above George Square. From here, they appealed for calm and told the demonstrators to march to Glasgow Green. The noise and fighting prevented all but a few from hearing their message.

The fighting continued, the mass of bodies moving towards the statue of Prince Albert, so Schettler and Nairn made to help the other two down before the attacking police engulfed it. As they did so, they saw the man who had earlier harangued Kate stretch his arm up towards the top of the statue's plinth and grab her ankle, causing her to overbalance. Schettler rushed forward and struck the man in the face with his fist, causing him to hit his head on the side of the plinth. As Kate fell, screaming in surprise, Schettler managed to turn and catch hold of her, breaking her fall. The pair fell into the crowd and slithered to the ground. Nairn tried to pursue the man as he made his escape through the crowd. Some, having seen what he had done, aimed kicks and punches at him.

As the men round about helped the pair to their feet, one man asked Schettler, "What was that you were shouting there, pal? It sounded like German to me." But he was gone before Schettler had time to reply.

What had he said? He had no remembrance of saying anything, but if he had shouted something in German that was foolish. He would have to be more careful.

It was imperative that the police shouldn't apprehend him, both for his sake and that of Carmichael. He looked around for Charlie. It was a serious matter for naval personnel to be involved in civil strife. He was nowhere to be seen.

The fighting had almost reached the statue and the police were gaining ground. Schettler quickly grabbed hold of Kate's arm. "Are you hurt, Miss A'Herne?" When she shook her head, they began jostling and pushing their way through the crowd, away from the fighting. After a few minutes, they had managed to move to an area at the south side of the square close to Hanover Street. Schettler felt Kate crumple by his side. He still held her arm and he increased his grip to prevent her falling. When he turned her to face him, he could see blood from the right side of her head, staining her white shirt as it trickled down her neck.

Schettler held her up by one hand and was relieved to see she had begun to revive a little, although her pale complexion was now a ghostly white. He fished out a neatly-folded handkerchief from his jacket pocket. It hadn't been used but it was a little grubby at the folds. He put it on the gash on the far side of her ear. "Can you hold that there while we find a cab to take you to hospital?"

"I'm not going to hospital, Mr Carmichael. This is nothing. I'll be as right as rain soon. I just need to sit down for a couple of minutes."

"Where will we find a seat?" Schettler asked.

"We'll go to 'The Cranstons' in Renfield Street."

"Is that a pub, Miss A'Herne?"

A'Herne looked at him, bemused. "For a Glaswegian, Mr Carmichael, you don't seem know much about your native city. 'The Cranstons' is a tearoom and cinema here in the city centre. Surely you must have been there? It's very popular. It's also a great meeting place for many of our comrades on the left. Are you sure you've never been there?"

*

By the time Nairn had pushed his way back to the statue from his unsuccessful pursuit of the fleeing man, there had been a counter attack by the demonstrators which had pushed the police back towards the City Chambers. There was no trace of his three compatriots.

Many men who were not actively fighting the police were now being organised by an ex-serviceman's group. Some of them were to form a rear-guard action if the police charged again and to follow Kirkwood and Shinwell's earlier instructions, many were being formed up to march to Glasgow Green. Thinking it was likely that his three friends had already obeyed the instructions to go there, Nairn joined the group who soon began marching off six abreast, leaving the mayhem in George Square behind them. He'd no sooner started marching, when he began to hear loud shouting from around the corner ahead of him. When the marchers reached Glassford Street, they found a large contingent of police waiting in readiness but so far not deployed. As they passed the waiting lines of police, they jeered and shouted obscenities, but this time they were allowed to pass un-impeded. However, as they continued to march east through Glasgow's Merchant City, they could see men running down towards them from George Street to the north. As these men reached the marchers, they shouted that tanks and trucks loaded with armed troops, were heading along Duke Street towards George Square. At this a young man, wearing a red arm band, lithely suspended himself from a street light and bellowed, "We must return to George Square immediately to help our comrades who are being attacked by forces of this reactionary government. Go now, Comrades. There's not a moment to lose."

At this the men turned and bolted back in the direction they had come. But the cordon of waiting police had moved in to block their way and an almighty battle began. Many of the unarmed strikers were seriously injured by callous officers, wielding their lead cored truncheons in all directions. Seeing this, the group Nairn was in turned quickly into Brunswick Street to circumvent the police and as they ran south towards the River Clyde, they pulled up timber and iron palings and some took metal refuse bin lids to act as shields.

Chapter 16

When Kate had fallen from the statue, the crowd had surged – some forward, some backwards, causing a vortex effect. Tennant, who had jumped from the plinth, was pushed around and propelled towards the north side of the City Chambers. The movement was so violent he thought he would lose his balance. Knowing that as a serving sailor he couldn't afford to be picked up by the police, he headed for safer ground which put him at least fifty yards from the statue.

It was imperative to get back there to find Schettler, because he was in even greater trouble if caught by the authorities. In this mayhem, it would take a while – time he didn't have. Panic welled up inside him and he could feel his legs shaking violently. As he stood there trying to get a grip of himself, he felt a slap on his back. He swung round ready to defend himself, but found he was looking at the top of a man's head. Gerry O'Brien smiled up at him.

"Oh Christ. It's you again, Gerry."

"Are you all right, Charlie? You look like you've seen a ghost, man."

"I've lost my friends," Tennant blurted out, "and one is also in the navy. If we get picked up by the police, we're fucked. I'll have to find him."

"Where did ye get separated?" Gerry asked.

"Over there at Prince Albert's statue."

"Aye, right then, we'll push our way through and if they're still there we'll find them. Mind you, if they're not, you've got no chance of finding them in this crowd. They could be anywhere."

The two men pushed and jostled their way towards the statue as the crowd continued to surge and writhe. Tennant's heart was pounding all the while.

God, he could be arrested as a German spy and I could be accused of treason.

He shook himself, trying to clear his mind of the terrible consequences that would result. *For Christ's sake, pull yourself together, man.*

It took the two over ten minutes to get back to the statue. There was no sign of Schettler, Nairn or A'Herne.

"Listen, my friend," O'Brien said, nudging Tennant, "there's nothing you can do about it. Did you not nominate a place to meet up if you got separated?"

Tennant shook his head.

"Then I suggest we head off to Lang's and have a drink and a chat. After all, the police canny do anything to you there, can they? You'll just have to hope your friend has the gumption to keep out of trouble."

Tennant brightened at this suggestion. "Aye, that's right. I told Ian that I had made the arrangement with you to meet at Lang's, so they'll likely go there."

O'Brien smiled. "There you go. What were you worrying about?"

Standing in the shelter of the statue, they heard the loud drone of engines and a voice coming from a loudspeaker somewhere at the east side of the square. At first, it wasn't clear what the voice was saying, but soon the engines began to drown out the noise of the crowd. As the crowd at the centre of the square began to move quickly in two directions, a tank appeared above them. It moved slowly through the crowd and the loudspeaker mounted on it told people to disperse. The tank, followed by an army lorry, moved through from north to south with people scrambling to get out of the way.

When the two vehicles got to the south side of George Square outside the General Post Office, they swung round behind a tram car which had been marooned there. Troops, armed with rifles, jumped out of the truck. Eight soldiers, two carrying a machine gun, disappeared into the Post Office and the rest formed a guard outside its two front doors while others ran to the sides and rear of the building. The crowd began to disperse, and Tennant and O'Brien could see that a similar action was taking place outside the City Chambers, where two tanks and four trucks had drawn up, one towing a howitzer. The crowds were moving to the surrounding streets, particularly North Hanover Street, where a pitched battle with the police was now in full swing.

Because of the tanks, the south side of the square soon became almost clear of demonstrators and before the police could move in to fill the void, Tennant and O'Brien took the opportunity to make a run for Queen Street and the safety of Lang's. O'Brien found running difficult and when they reached the pub, he had to lean bent double against the wall outside for some time to get his breath back. The pub was packed, but instead of a hostile and intimidating atmosphere, it was positively vibrant. It was like entering a different world. There was a man playing popular tunes on a piano accordion and the local bylaw which banned singing in pubs was being breached without objection from the management. The two men managed to work their way towards the bar, although it took several minutes to penetrate the crowd.

"What do you fancy, Gerry?" Tennant bellowed over the top of the noise.

"I'll have an India Pale Ale, Charlie. I'm not a great drinker these days."

Once Tennant managed to catch the eye of a barman, he ordered two bottles of IPA and a whisky to settle his own nerves. As soon as it was poured, he knocked the amber liquid back in one gulp before he paid for the drinks. He and O'Brien worked their way towards a corner which had a shelf for glasses and a place to lean.

O'Brien looked decidedly pale and was still finding it hard to breathe. "Jesus Christ, I never expected that they would set the army on a legitimate strike. The bastards! They must be frightened."

Tennant, whose concern for Schettler was still forefront in his mind, just nodded and they sipped their beer in silence.

After a while O'Brien said, "This place brings back memories, Charlie. The last time I was here, I was getting a parcel with a gun in it." Tennant recoiled, gesturing with his hand that O'Brien should be quiet.

O'Brien just laughed. "Nobody will be able to hear much above this din." Tennant had to admit this was true. As they relaxed, they began to talk about why O'Brien had ended up getting four years in prison.

"I didn't pass the medical for the navy. They took me back to Glasgow and gave me a medical for the army, but they wouldn't have me either. They said there was something wrong with my lungs and as you've seen, they were right.

Do you remember that guy, Sinclair? He said since I couldn't join the forces they had to charge me with treason, but he hoped when I was found guilty, I wouldn't get a death sentence." He raised his eyebrows. "That's what happened to Charlie Hood and Peter Heaney. I was lucky. I got four years for a reduced charge of illegal possession of a firearm. But it's a lot to get for having a bad chest, eh?"

Tennant was staring at the pub door.

"Were you not listening to me, Charlie? If it's your friend you're looking for, he'll not be in for a couple of hours yet, so it's no use staring at the door."

"Aye, I suppose you're right. Anyway, I *was* listening. I think your treatment was diabolical."

O'Brien nodded. "Aye well, I suppose prison wasn't all bad. In my last two years, I got a job in the library, which was good. Last May, I met John Maclean in there and when I told him we used to go to his lectures in Glasgow, he took me under his wing and taught me a lot about Marxist economics. He even said I had a great understanding of it and when I was released, I should go to night school to get the qualifications to go to university."

"That's great. Are you doing that?"

"Not yet, Charlie, but I will. John and I were even released on the same day, you know."

That reminded Tennant that he had seen him. "That's right. I saw you that day in Jamaica Street. You had a case and the police set upon you and marched you away. I tried to catch up to see if I could help but the crowd was too thick. I just couldn't get near. Why did they want you anyway?"

At that moment, someone in the bar started singing the International and in only a few seconds everyone had joined in.

When the singing stopped, Tennant said, "I didn't hear you, Gerry. What did you say?"

"I said they got the wrong man. It wasn't me they wanted."

"Did they say what they wanted the other guy for?"

"No, of course they didn't."

"Well it's just—"

"Just leave it. It wasn't me they wanted, all right. Do you want another beer?"

As the time passed, they were drawn into conversations with those around them, all of whom had been involved in the events in George Square. Some men were clearly injured. Everyone had been extremely surprised and disheartened that the authorities had reacted in such a violent manner. When the army had arrived, the feeling was that this was the last straw and it was now not just a strike for a forty-hour working week. The working class had to make a challenge for power, just as people had done in Russia and Germany.

One man, who was holding a blood-stained cloth against his head, arrived with the news that the strike leaders Kirkwood, Shinwell and Gallacher had been arrested and the fighting had now spread to Glasgow Green, as well as the area around George Square. Suddenly, Bob Nairn appeared by Tennant's side.

"Hello, Charlie, I thought you might be here." Glancing at his watch, Tennant was surprised to see it was twenty-five past two and he could hear the staff calling time.

"Am I glad to see you, Bob! But where are Ian and Kate?"

*

Cranstons' was almost empty and Kate went to the toilet to clean herself up while Schettler sat down at a table

173

set for four. The waitress arrived almost immediately and pompously told him that he should have waited at the door to be seated.

Schettler looked abashed. "I'm sorry. There are two of us. The lady has just gone to the toilet, but if you want us to move?"

"No, no, since it's quiet, it won't make any difference, this time. Would you like to see a menu, sir?"

He pored over the menu for fifteen minutes until the waitress returned to ask if he was ready to order. Schettler smiled tentatively. "No, I'm still waiting for my companion to return."

She looked annoyed and walked away but just then Kate re-entered the tearoom. The waitress waved and quickly intercepted her before she had a chance to reach the table. He watched the two women engage in a lively conversation for some time, before Kate came across and stood before him. "Sorry I was so long, Mr Carmichael. Agnes lives up the next close to me and as I come here a lot we know each other very well..."

What the hell's a close? Schettler thought. But knowing this would point to another instance of him not understanding Glaswegian things, he decided not to ask.

"...Once she starts to speak, it's hard to get away," she went on with a laugh. "Anyway, when I told her about my cut, she went to get a bandage from their first aid kit so – if you don't mind, I'll go back to the toilet for her to help me. I won't be long."

It struck him how vulnerable he was impersonating a Glaswegian. How would he cope with the questions Kate would ask him over lunch, if that was what they would be having? Should he get up and leave right now? No, he couldn't. She was Margaret's friend. And anyway, he liked her. Actually, he liked her very much. But that was no reason for putting himself at risk.

Where were Charlie and Bob for that matter? Had they been picked up by the police? Should he go back to look for them?

Before he could decide what to do, Kate and Agnes were standing before him. A few more tables were now occupied, and other waitresses were busying themselves around the tearoom. Kate was smiling at him. "You looked deep in thought, Mr Carmichael."

Schettler got to his feet.

"This is my friend, Agnes Cairns," Kate said.

"How do you do, Miss Cairns."

The waitress was dressed in the standard, black dress with a white apron which she smoothed down. "How do you do, Mr Carmichael. It's very nice to meet you. You should have told me you were with Miss A'Herne."

All traces of the earlier brusqueness were gone. "I hear you live close to Miss A'Herne," Schettler said.

"Yes, just up the next close."

That word again. Schettler just nodded.

"Miss A'Herne tells me you're in the navy."

"Yes, I am, at the moment at least." Trying to paraphrase what he'd heard Tennant say, he went on. "I expect many of us will be demobbed once our ship is finished in Scapa."

Agnes nodded. "I hope when you are demobbed you can find a job. It's not easy, and there's so much unrest these days, but of course you know that only too well. You've seen it for yourself."

Not wishing to prolong this conversation in case he was asked a question he would find difficult to answer, he said, "Yes, I hope I can, Miss Cairns. I think we better have a look at the menu, I don't know about Miss A'Herne, but all this fighting has given me an appetite."

"That's fine. I'll come back in a few minutes and take your order."

When she had gone Schettler said, "Do you think that sounded a bit cheeky, me saying we wanted to look at the menu?"

Kate shrugged. "No, she'd talk all day if she thought she could get away with it. Anyway, I only want a cup of tea."

"Aren't you hungry?"

"It costs money to eat here – money I don't have."

"Please allow me to buy you lunch."

"Oh no, I couldn't do that."

"I want to have lunch and I would be honoured if you'll join me."

"If you put it like that, then, thank you very much".

After lunch was cleared away, Schettler decided to tell her the truth about his identity. After what she said to that man in George Square, she was certainly no friend of the authorities and unlikely to reveal his identity to them.

He started hesitantly to tell his story, bending over the table. "I have to tell you something, Miss A'Herne. My real name isn't Carmichael, it's—"

The young woman started to laugh. "No, it's Schettler, I'll bet," she whispered.

He looked bewildered. "How did you know?"

"I didn't know. I just guessed. Mags talks a lot about you and when I met you, you just didn't seem like a typical

Glasgow man and not knowing 'the Cranstons' – well, that really seemed odd. So, I just put two and two together. I also knew Charlie had contacted you in Scapa, so it wasn't beyond the bounds of possibility that you could be here."

She bent towards him, her eyes dancing. "But, how *did* you get here?"

Once Schettler explained, they chatted for some time.

Since the General Election in December, she told him, the Irish people except for the six counties of Ulster, had voted overwhelming to elect Sinn Féin. Instead of taking their seats in Westminster, Sinn Féin had set up their own Parliament called the Dáil Eireann, and its first meeting had just taken place on the twenty first of January when an Independent Irish Republic had been declared. This unilateral declaration of independence, however, didn't mean the British would allow it, so she felt her place was back in Ireland once again to fight for an Independent Socialist Irish Republic.

Now that she was unemployed there was nothing to stop her going. She talked too about how she had come to live in Glasgow in 1916 to escape the brutal recriminations after the Easter Rising, particularly when her brother, Liam, had been taken prisoner and the leader of the socialist movement, James Connelly, had been executed.

"As a Lieutenant in the Citizens Army, Liam was sentenced to ten years and is still in Lincoln jail in England."

Her tale enthralled Schettler. "I'm sorry about your brother. Although we're from different countries, Miss A'Herne, we're certainly fellow travellers."

A waitress clearing the surrounding tables, prompted Schettler to look at his watch and he realised it was just before two o'clock.

"We might be able to meet up with Charlie and Bob if we go soon. Charlie met a friend this morning and arranged to meet him in a pub at one thirty. I think he said in Queen Street, something like Ling's. Could that be right?" he said.

A'Herne nodded. "There's a pub in Queen Street called Lang's."

"Yes, that's the one. We should go and see if they're there."

"We better hurry because they close at half past two."

Kate waved at Agnes and mouthed, "Bill, please." She came straight over and presented it folded on a saucer.

"Did you enjoy your lunch? I thought the liver looked particularly nice today."

The bill was two shillings and eight pence. He fished in his pocket and, to his horror, realised he had left his change in Carmichael's uniform. The only money he possessed was the four five-pound notes in his wallet. When he extracted one and handed it to Agnes, her eyes bulged in disbelief. "A fiver, Mr Carmichael! Haven't you got anything smaller?"

"No, I'm sorry, I haven't."

Turning to Kate, she giggled. "You better hold on to this one, Miss A'Herne! He's obviously made of money. I'll just go and get your change, Mr Carmichael. I won't be a minute."

When she left, Schettler asked, "How much should I give her for herself?"

"If you mean a tip then fourpence will be plenty."

"What did you call it, a tip? I didn't know that."

When Agnes returned with four pound notes, a ten-shilling note, two half crowns, two sixpenny pieces and four pennies on the plate, he gathered up everything except one sixpence and the four pennies. At this, the waitress said,

"Thank you very, much Mr Carmichael. Are you two going to do something nice?"

Kate looked annoyed. "Listen, Agnes, we're in a hurry. I'll likely see you soon. If you're ready, Mr Carmichael, I think we should go." With that, she walked off briskly.

Leaving the building, Kate said, "That was far too big a tip to give her."

As they crossed Renfield Street into Drury Street, they noticed there was now a cordon across the other end of the street and two armed soldiers stood guard. When they got there, A'Herne walked up to one of the soldiers. "We need to get into Queen Street, ma man, can we pass through here?" The soldier, who seemed to be English, shook his head. "No, me duck, no one gets in here until all the demonstrators are out of the area. There's still fighting going on. Martial law's been declared, and this area is closed."

She saw there was no point arguing with him. "When do you think it'll open again?"

"I couldn't say, but it won't be today I'll tell you that and I doubt it'll be this week either."

"Are all the streets blocked off?"

"They certainly are, me duck."

"What about the people in there. Are you letting them out?"

"Yes, as long as the police aren't looking for them they're free to go."

"How do they know who's who?"

"Believe me, dear, there's a lot of police and soldiers in there sorting things out. Are you Irish? I hope you're not here to cause trouble."

The soldier sounded threatening.

179

"Me? Not at all. Glasgow's my home now. Thanks for the information."

"That's fine, dear." As Schettler and A'Herne turned, he retorted, "I've never seen a woman in trousers before. Are you one of these lesbians?"

She chose to ignore the remark and they walked away.

"What a detestable man!" A'Herne said once they were out of earshot. "I hate being called dear and worse still duck. I'm not a lesbian, but I'll defend any woman's right to be one."

Schettler looked puzzled. "What's a lesbian?"

"It's a woman who prefers other woman."

"Ah, Lesbisch. I see."

"Yes. Since the suffragette movement started, any woman who wants self- determination in any way is branded a lesbian."

"That's ridiculous," Schettler said. "I've heard dear before but never duck. What does it mean?"

"God knows. Just another way of demeaning women."

As they continued walking, Schettler mused over the issue of his missing friends. "If they pick Charlie up he could be in a lot of trouble. Do you think he'll manage to get out of there?"

They reached St Vincent Street in time to see a tram appear to pass seemingly un-heeded through the military cordon. As A'Herne watched its progress into the sealed area, she said, "I don't know if he will or not, but I think we have just found a way in."

Schettler asked what she meant.

"The tram just entered the area we can't enter. If we go back a stop and get on the next tram, it will take us to

George Square and maybe we'll still be in time to meet up with Charlie and Bob in Lang's. We'll have to hurry."

They walked along St Vincent Street to the next stop and in less than two minutes a tram appeared. It was very busy, and they had to go upstairs to find the only available seat together. When it reached the cordon, the tram stopped, and two armed soldiers got on, one at the front platform beside the driver and the other on the platform at the rear. The tram moved off and the conductor shouted, "This tram won't be stopping until it gets to High Street." Many of the passengers voiced their complaints in no uncertain terms, as the majority of them had wanted off in the city centre. One man, who was sitting close to them, ran down stairs to the rear platform but was prevented from jumping off by the soldier who threatened him with the butt of his rifle.

Frustrated, A'Herne turned to Schettler. "Did you understand what the conductor said?"

"Yes, they won't let anyone off the tram until it's out of the restricted area. So we won't get to Lang's after all."

When the tram reached the grey, rain-soaked George Square, the sight that met their eyes was like something out of a war zone. There were tanks and a howitzer outside the City Chambers and more tanks outside the GPO with soldiers guarding the entrances to the public buildings. Half a dozen army trucks stood in the centre of the square, some still full of soldiers and on the roof of many buildings, soldiers were manning machine guns pointing downwards to the square below.

In one corner men were corralled inside a cordon of soldiers and police and from there a procession of men were being escorted or frogmarched towards a line of Black Marias awaiting their reluctant passengers on the south side of the square. There were other men, clearly very injured, lying on blankets on the wet ground either waiting for treatment or ambulances to take them to hospital while next to them soldiers and police officers stood around a trailer smoking and drinking tea, some in jovial mood.

As the tram turned onto the north side of the square, the police stopped it to allow a large contingent of mounted police with their long batons to set off in three broad lines first at a canter which increased to a gallop as they crossed the tram's path and into North Hanover Street. There, a large group of demonstrators armed with, for the most part, iron palings, stood their ground at the top of the hill awaiting the attack.

As soon as the mounted police had passed into the embattled street, the tram was quickly waved on, perhaps to prevent the passengers from witnessing the carnage which was about to take place.

A'Herne put her head in her hands. It was a sickening sight. It was clear to her that the strike, which had been so solid, would once again be crushed by the power of reactionary forces. For the rest of the short tram ride they rode in silence.

When the tram approached High Street, A'Herne prodded Schettler and told him it was time to get off. "Look, there really isn't any point getting off here," Schettler said. We can't get back into the city centre, so what can we do? We'd be better off going to Seton Terrace and waiting for everyone there. My Aunt Nell can fix up that cut of yours a bit better. She was a nurse. What do you say? We can also see Margaret when she returns from school." Kate nodded in agreement.

As the tram continued along Duke Street, its progress was once more impeded by hordes of dejected strikers leaving the restricted area. Along much of the opposite side of the street there were rows of army trucks filled with troops waiting to be deployed. Some strikers were gathering around the trucks to try to dissuade the soldiers from being strike breakers, but it was obvious they were getting short shrift. Some soldiers had even climbed down from the trucks and were pushing the strikers around, until inevitably scuffles broke out.

When they arrived at Seton Terrace, Nell was alone, although she was clearly expecting a crowd from the size of the evening meal she was preparing. She cleaned and sorted Kate's wound, while lecturing them both on their foolishness in getting involved in the demonstration and wondering what had happened to Bob and Charlie.

Margaret was next to arrive home, later than usual. She had experienced a similar situation while travelling through the city and was beside herself with rage at what she had witnessed. She was glad to see Johann and Kate but when they described their experiences, together with the outrageous treatment meted out to the strikers, she clearly became worried about her brother and fiancé and when her mother started to voice the same worries, through frustration, an argument began between them.

In an effort to calm the situation, Johann said, "I was fascinated by the School of Art when Bob and Charlie took me round it yesterday. I didn't get a chance to talk to you about it, Margaret."

Margaret said nothing, but fortunately Kate joined in. "Yes, isn't it wonderful? Margaret and I both love the Art Nouveau movement."

"Do you?" Schettler said. "I think it's decadent and belongs to another age."

That remark brought Margaret's attention into focus.

"What on earth do you mean, Ian? You can't be serious!"

And so began a wild debate, which went on right through their meal, about the merits of the various schools. The women cited people such Gustav Klimt or Koloman Moser as great examples of the Art Nouveau school, while Schettler argued there was no such thing, as they were both from the Pre-Raphaelite school and, anyway, if they wanted to talk about the Vienna secessionists they should only consider the radical wing artists like Max Liebermann who was so disenchanted with the decadence of the movement, he left to form the Berlin secessionists.

He had been talking tongue in cheek but now he became serious. "Art Nouveau is a beautiful idea but it's out of touch. I admit that the architects such as Mackintosh here in Glasgow, Victor Horta in Brussels or Antoní Gaudí in Barcelona got it right because they designed public buildings that the masses of people could enjoy but for the most part the concept of décor and art are beyond all but the very rich and can't be seen by the people. We have just fought a war which hopefully has changed the world, so we have to look at new ways to express this new world in art."

There was a brief silence, until Kate said, "That says it all. I agree, so when do we begin?"

Margaret said, "I agree too. Did you know Kate is also an artist, Ian?"

But before he could reply there was a knock at the front door.

Chapter 17

At twenty past two the bar staff of Lang's began their daily ritual of calling time. As usual, this had no effect on the clientele who remained there resolutely drinking. At the stroke of half past two, the doors burst open and a police sergeant and three constables accompanied by two armed soldiers walked through, causing even more crush in the pub as people edged away from them, taken aback by their arrival.

The sergeant's voice boomed over the top of the noise. "Right, put your drinks down and start moving outside, NOW."

This had little effect at first, until two constables grabbed a man, forced the beer out of his hand and pushed him out of the open doors. The second man they tried to manhandle, side stepped and threw a punch at one of the policemen. At this, the third constable pulled out his truncheon, jumped forward and hit the man hard on the shoulder. Simultaneously, six more police came through the door with their truncheons at the ready. "There's no point causing trouble," the police sergeant shouted. "There's twenty more of us outside so just do as you're told, and nobody'll get hurt."

As the hapless man, whose shoulder was undoubtedly broken, was dragged outside, the clientele began grudgingly to obey, putting down their drinks and making for the door. The police now formed two lines, only wide enough for one person to pass between them, so progress towards the door was slow. O'Brien, who had been in deep conversation with another striker, was well behind Tennant in the line. When he reached this phalanx of police, he saw that some men ahead of them, including Tennant and the man who was with him, were being pointed to by a group of civilians, removed from the line and marched away. O'Brien felt a shiver run down his back. Dick Bradshaw was among the group of civilians and was already pointing at him, so he knew he too would be dragged from the line. The police took hold of him and marched him across the road, pushing him inside a cordon of police and soldiers on the other side. As he walked past Tennant, he whispered, "Charlie, don't let on you know me," and went to stand as far away from his friend as he could.

Tennant turned away.

"My God, Charlie, did you see who pointed us out?" Nairn asked. He was agitated. "It was that bastard that pulled Kate off the statue."

They stood there watching, while ten more men were added to their ranks and the rest of the pub's clientele were let loose in the direction of Argyle Street and out of the secured area.

Eventually an army truck drew up. When the tailgate was lowered, they were made to climb into the back and soon they were being driven away under armed guard. As the truck reached George Square, it was already getting dark and many of the twenty-seven men in it were firing questions at their two guards to find out where they were being taken. No answer was forthcoming. Tennant and Nairn had been first on to the truck and were jammed up against the driver's cabin.

After about twenty minutes it came to a stop. The two guards jumped out, opened the tailgate and told the prisoners to get out. As the men started jumping to the ground from the truck's dark interior, Tennant whispered to Nairn, "Don't move, stay completely still."

When all the men were on the ground, one of the guards shouted, "Billy, jump up and check that none of these bastards are still inside." To Tennant and Nairn's relief, the soldier answered, "No need, Bert, I counted them when they got in and they're all here." He replaced the tailgate without bothering to glance inside.

"Very good. Let's get this lot inside then. Right you lot, start walkin'."

Edging forward to the tailgate, Tennant peered around the side of the truck and saw the men and the guards disappear though the entrance of what he thought must be Barlinnie Prison.

"Right, Bob, now's our chance." The two men climbed over the tailgate and jumped to the ground, but the driver and the other soldier in the cab felt the movement and as the two started running down the road, the soldiers jumped from the cab and gave chase. Tennant and Nairn had a good start and were heading for a wooded area about one hundred yards away when Nairn tripped and fell. Tennant stopped to help him, but Nairn shouted, "Don't stop, keep running." Tennant turned and continued towards the wood.

Reaching the trees, Tennant glanced back to see both soldiers, each holding one of Nairn's arms, marching back towards the prison gate. He used the protection of the trees as a hiding place to see if the soldiers would take the truck to continue their search for him, but they didn't.

As he waited in the shadows, he realised this road through the countryside only serviced what he now understood was Barlinnie Prison. If he was caught, his reason for being there would be questioned. He started running. Soon, some distance away, he saw a set of headlights turn into the road and he looked for a place to hide from the approaching vehicle. There was nothing but a post and wire fence which separated the adjacent field from the road, so he jumped over and sat against the post with his head between his knees.

The vehicle took forever to reach him. Just as it drew level, the noise of the engine changed, and it sounded like it was about to stop. He tried to sit stock still, but he was shaking uncontrollably. He heard the driver change gear and the vehicle continued on. Tennant turned his head to get a glimpse of it, and realised it was another army truck full of prisoners heading for the prison.

He reached the public road, which he thought must be Cumbernauld Road, and turned to head in the direction of the city. The road was busier with traffic now and many vehicles passed him. Soon he was back in a lit-up area of city tenements. As he walked along the pavement, he looked down at his feet and was horrified to see that the bottom of his trousers and his shoes were covered in mud from the field. When he felt his backside, it was the same – a sure giveaway for anyone looking for him. In a waste bin mounted on a lamppost, he found a discarded copy of the Daily Record, which he took into a close and cleaned the dirt off as best he could, before returning to the street.

He crossed into Alexandra Parade. To his horror, he realised the army truck that had taken them to prison was now driving parallel to him. Neither the driver nor the guard, who had chased him earlier noticed him, but when the truck passed by, the two soldiers who were standing up against the tailgate, recognised him. One shouted, "Hey, you there," and the other ran inside to get the truck to stop.

Tennant turned quickly, ran up a close and into the back yard. He scaled a wall which took him to a lane between the blocks of tenements and sprinted to the end of it. The lane finished at a side street which he crossed and entered another close. He hid inside the brick shed that housed the dustbins in the back yard. A shape darted past his feet, followed by another, hissing loudly and he jumped in fright. His heart pounding, he realised it had only been two cats, but fear kept him in this dark and smelly place for half an hour before returning to the street. From there, he knew it was only ten minutes' walk to the safety of Margaret's house in Seton Terrace.

Margaret opened the door to a wet, cold and frightened Tennant just after half past seven. "It's you, Charlie. You look dreadful. Are you all right?" But not waiting for a reply she gasped, "Where's Bob? I thought he was with you?" She glanced behind her, not wanting her mother to overhear.

Tennant hung his head. "Margaret, I need to talk to you alone." Margaret, who looked shaken, took him by the forearm and led him into the parlour, closing the door behind them. "What's happened to Bob, Charlie?"

"There's no easy way to tell you this—" Tennant sounded sepulchral.

"Charlie, for God sake! Will you just tell me," Margaret cried.

"He's been detained by the police and he's in Barlinnie." Tennant could see the panic spread over her face.

"Barlinnie! Is he alright?"

"Yes, I think so, although he tripped and fell when we ran away, but I don't think he's hurt"

"What do you mean we ran away? Were you there too?"

He nodded. "Yes, look let me tell you the whole story."

There was a tap on the door. "Is everything all right, dear?" Nell asked.

"Yes, Mother, it's just Charlie. We'll be out in five minutes. He's telling me something at the moment."

"Oh, right you are, dear."

Margaret shook her head. "My God, I don't know what I should tell her. She'll be frantic when she hears. Anyway, you better start at the beginning."

When he had finished, she looked bewildered. "I wonder what they can charge him with? It can't be a crime to run after someone, especially if you don't catch them. I'll go down to Police Headquarters in Turnbull Street tomorrow morning early to see if I can find out anything. Isn't that the O'Brien fellow in the newspaper cutting I sent you when you were stationed in Portsmouth? The one who went to prison?"

Tennant looked concerned. "Yes, it is. Listen, Mags. There's something else you need to know about Gerry..." and he started to explain that they had both been arrested in 1914.

"So, there might be more to why they picked us up," Tennant continued. "I just don't know. They may also be looking for Ian. He struck the man who pulled Kate off the statue and I'm worried about where he is."

"He's here, Charlie. He and Kate are both here. They arrived before I got home from school."

Tennant sighed in relief. "Thank God for that. Now it's just Bob we have to worry about."

"Right then," Margaret said. She sounded resolute. "Let's go through to the kitchen and I'll try to pack Mother off to bed. Then we can have a discussion about what we should do."

As Tennant entered the warm kitchen, fatigue washed over him. He also realised he was desperately hungry. It was good to see Johann and Kate. He had spent a lot of time worrying about them and he greeted them warmly.

Margaret came straight to the point. "Mother, Bob was in a group of men who have been detained by the police today, but I don't want you to worry. They'll have to release him since he didn't do anything wrong. But Charlie said hundreds were picked up, so it might be a while before he's set free."

Nell's reaction was predictable – somewhere between panic and bewilderment – and both Margaret and Charlie had to reassure her several times. She started fussing around trying to keep herself busy by feeding Charlie. She was both concerned and angry with her son, wondering what the neighbours would say if they found out.

"How will we live this down?" she asked, followed by, "Oh my, I hope he'll be alright. He will be all right won't he, Charlie?"

Tennant reassured her again, although he wasn't at all certain himself. The authorities had used disproportionate force against them. He could never have imagined the government would send in the military with tanks to quell a strike. But as they had done so, Tennant was pretty sure they would use every legal avenue possible to throw the book at the arrested demonstrators. And he had more than Bob to worry about. Between Bob and Gerry, they could identify him and Johann, depending on how much pressure they were put under while being questioned. Thinking back to 1914, this alarmed him. If their true identities were known, the authorities would stop at nothing to apprehend them. After all, one was a German revolutionary and the other had previously taken up arms against the state.

It took an hour for Margaret to persuade her mother to go to bed, but the clever girl had whispered to Tennant that he use the time to take a bath. He did so willingly.

It was almost nine o'clock before the four were able to sit around the kitchen table with a cup of tea to discuss the day's events and the consequences that would stem from them.

"I presume you really know who this man is, Kate?" Charlie said.

Johann butted in. "Whatever do you mean, Charlie? Miss A'Herne knows I'm Chief Petty Officer Gordon Carmichael from His Majesty's Ship Emperor of India stationed at Scapa Flow guarding the Hun fleet."

Margaret intervened, shaking her head. "Yes, Charlie, Kate does know who Ian is."

Charlie nodded. "Good. At least we can now dispense with that charade. Listen, Ian, the way I see it, we could be in a lot of trouble…"

He told them the whole story about his and Bob's arrest, how he had evaded the army on two occasions to escape from custody and how the man who had pulled Kate from the statue must have been an agent provocateur. He went on to explain his links with O'Brien before the war and, given that both Bob and Gerry knew his identity, and Bob knew Johann's, they should get out of Glasgow and return to Scapa as fast as possible.

Schettler looked thoughtful. "If Bob or your friend Gerry identifies either or both of us, won't the police look for us on the ships anyway?"

Tennant frowned. "Perhaps they will, but if we're both on board our ships you at least will find it easier to deny you were ever in Glasgow and I feel I might be treated better by my own people. We can also keep Carmichael out of trouble. We owe him that, after all."

Tennant and Schettler came to the conclusion that they would leave Glasgow on the first train to Thurso, in the morning. Margaret phoned the station and was told that the first train left at six thirty-five, changing at Inverness. She asked if Charlie wanted to stay in Seton Terrace overnight.

"I'd love to, Margaret, but I'll need to collect my uniform and kit, so I better go home and meet Ian at Buchanan Street Station at six o'clock tomorrow." He sighed, looked at his watch and began to rise from the table.

Kate also stood up. "I better get home too. It's been a long and eventful day. I hope Bob's released soon, Mags. I think you're right – they haven't got any reason to hold him."

They all looked at each other questioningly as they heard the front door opening and closing. The kitchen door opened wide and Bob stood there, framed in the hall light, holding a dirty cloth to his bleeding face.

He began to totter. Margaret and Tennant rushed forward and supported him to a chair at the table.

"What on earth's happened to you, Bob?" Margaret asked.

Bob's voice was slurred, and they could see he found it difficult to speak. "Give me a drink of water, will you, Mags?"

Margaret filled a tumbler from the tap. Her brother's hands were shaking and blood-stained.

"You better give him a glass of whisky, Mags." Tennant said. "Is it still kept in the press next door?"

"Yes, it is. Get it will you, Charlie."

Margaret boiled the kettle, filled a bowl of water and started bathing Bob's face, while he sat sipping tea with a large tot of whisky in it. It was only when Kate said again she had better go, that Bob broke his silence.

"Don't go yet, Kate, I need to tell you something. I need to tell you all something."

But he fell silent, once more.

After a couple of minutes, Kate asked, "What was it you wanted to tell us, Bob?" He stared at her questioningly and she mouthed the word "concussed" to the others.

Johann put his hand on Bob's arm. "Do you remember what you were going to tell us, Bob?" Even this gentle touch made him flinch with pain which brought him to his senses.

"Yes, I do. It affects you as well, Ian. They're looking for an Irish woman dressed in trousers and a German man."

Margaret lifted his cup. "In your condition, Bob, it's only tea you're getting." She emptied the contents down the sink, refilled the cup and placed it in front of her brother.

Tennant took his chance. "Did you tell them who we were, Bob?"

He shook his head vigorously and shouted which made him slur even more. "No! That's how I got this." He pointed to his face.

"Who beat you, Bob? Was it the soldiers?" Tennant asked.

"No, it was civilians. I kept telling them I didn't know who you were. I was just standing beside you in the crowd. They must have believed me eventually, because they took me back to the truck with a few others and drove us into Glasgow. We had all been beaten. When the truck was in Duke Street, I asked the guard if I could get off. He got the driver to stop. They dropped me at the bottom of Craigpark."

He was beginning to drift off again. "They were really quite nice these Highland soldiers – it was good of them to…"

"Right, I want you to tell me everything," Margaret said. "I think you have concussion, Bob, so you mustn't go to sleep. Do you hear?" She raised her voice. "Bob, do you understand me?"

"Yes, Mags, I do."

"Start talking then, and every time you stop, I'll give you a shake. You don't want that because it'll be painful."

She took charge. "First, Kate, go to my room and choose a skirt, blouse, coat and shoes. Mind and choose an old pair of my shoes and not my good ones. Change and leave your clothes here for the time being."

She turned to the rest of them. "Ian, take your uniform and whatever else you have and go with Charlie to his parents' house and stay until it's time to get the train. You must all leave by the back door in case they're watching the front of the house. I guess that's unlikely so soon, but I don't trust the army. It seems suspiciously kind of them to have let Bob out at Craigpark."

Johann made to speak but she stopped him. "Go now, Ian." She pointed to the door leading to the garden. "You'll have to leave by that door, so you can say goodbye on your way out, dear. Right, Bob. Get on with your story. I'm listening." And she began to bathe his head with the wet cloth she had used to clean his face.

"Look, Mags, my parents' place is only a room and kitchen. Are you sure Ian wouldn't be better off here?" Charlie said after Johann and Kate had gone upstairs.

"Well, what do you think, Charlie? Surely you must realise since they're likely to know where Bob lives, this house must be a target – especially if they believe he knows Kate and Ian."

Charlie turned to Bob. "Did they ask you your address?"

Bob sounded more lucid. "Yes, they did and I told them."

"The authorities don't arrest you and not ask your name and address!" Margaret protested.

"It's just that they didn't ask us before they took us to Barlinnie."

"That was very lucky for you, Charlie. If they had, you would be in a lot of trouble by now. When the others come down, you'll have to go straight away." She rose and kissed him. "Take care of yourself. I love you very much, you know."

"I love you too, Mags. I just hope all this stupidity blows over quickly. The only thing I don't understand is how they knew to look for a German."

Margaret nodded. "Yes, I don't understand that either." Turning to Bob, she said, "You didn't say anything about Ian, did you?"

"No, I didn't, Margaret. I denied knowing anyone and that was my line until they finally released me."

Johann appeared first with his duffle bag. As he was saying goodbye to Margaret and Bob, Kate appeared. She looked very different in Margaret's clothes.

"Right then, Mags," Kate said, as she opened the back door, "I'll get these clothes back to you before I leave for Ireland. They fit fine except for the shoes. I just got my feet into them and they're pinching like hell. I didn't realise you had such small feet. Bye then, Bob, I hope you feel better soon. Well done for standing up to those bastards."

"Kate, if you can't get the clothes back to me, it's not the end of the world but it'll be good to see you one last time before you go – if that's possible!"

A'Herne, Schettler and Tennant walked through the back garden. Just before they opened the door to the service lane, Tennant said, "Look, Ian, my parents' place is very small. I don't think it's going to be a very comfortable night for either of us. We'll have to share my single bed, or one of us will have to sleep on a chair or on the floor."

Schettler was about to say that it was alright, he would take the chair, when A'Herne spoke up. "Mr Carmichael, you can stay the night at my place, if you want? I've got a settee. You can sleep on that. The place is in a mess, but if you want…?"

Schettler nodded enthusiastically. "Yes, that would be good, if you don't mind, Charlie?"

"No, I don't mind at all."

"Thanks, Miss A'Herne, that's very nice of you."

"For God sake," said Tennant, "don't you think since you two are going to share a flat, you should be on first name terms?"

They looked at each other.

"That's fine," she said, her eyes narrowing, "but don't get any ideas, Ian."

Tennant's demeanour changed. "When you two were upstairs, I said I don't know why they're looking for a

German and Bob assured us he said nothing about you in Barlinnie."

Johann bit his lip. "I'm afraid I do. When I was trying to stop Kate landing on the ground this morning, I think I shouted something in German and I guess the man who toppled her must have heard me and reported it."

"That explains it, then. Look, I'll go first and walk to the right. You two give me a couple of minutes and when you leave, turn left. I'll see you at Buchanan Street Station at six o'clock, Ian."

He bent over and kissed Kate on the cheek. "Cheerio then, Kate. Take care of yourself in Ireland. We'll miss you here, you know."

He opened the door and was gone.

Chapter 18

It was the first of February, a dark and gloomy day. The rain was teeming down when Schettler's taxi drew up outside Buchanan Street Station in the early morning. On the way through the city, Schettler had been surprised to see how many armed soldiers were hanging around in groups or riding in army trucks. Martial law was very evident. He paid the driver, this time with change, so he didn't have to suffer the barrage of abuse when producing a banknote. When he opened the taxi door, the cold, damp atmosphere immediately hit him, and he felt that long shiver that emanates from the bottom of the spine and immediately fires its tentacles to every extremity of the body. He was very tired, for he and Kate had talked well into the wee, sma' hours.

She had given him a couple of whiskies, so he was also slightly hung over as well. Their conversation had progressed from earlier in the day and she gave him a potted history of the Irish situation over the last hundred or so years. It was then his turn to explain the current, political situation in Germany and they went on to discuss the likelihood of the revolutionary movements in both countries winning over. Kate had high hopes for Ireland while Johann was less confident about Germany. They discussed Britain but decided, at least in the short term, there was little chance of a revolutionary movement succeeding here.

They had moved to personal stories, the two of them describing their lives and it was after three o'clock when

Kate retired to her room and Johann lay down on the couch.

When he had woken, he put on the naval uniform and packed Bob's clothes into the kit bag as silently as possible. Kate hadn't slept well. The alcohol hadn't prevented her mind racing and when she heard him moving about, she came to say goodbye. When he was ready to go, he bent to kiss her on the cheek, but she turned towards him and they shared a lingering kiss.

"It was nice to meet you, Ian, or Gordon, whatever your name is. I hope our paths will cross again one day."

"I hope so too, soon, perhaps in better times." And then he had smiled. "Yes, I have more names and identities than I can handle these days. My real name is Johann, but my mother always called me Ian. Now you know the whole truth."

These thoughts had accompanied him into the station and as he stood daydreaming on the concourse till Tennant appeared.

They went to the booking office, showed their warrants and received their tickets without fuss. It was too early to board the train, so they headed to the buffet for a quick cup of tea and perhaps, if they were lucky, a bacon roll. Unfortunately, the buffet didn't open till seven o'clock. There was nothing else to do, but hang around the concourse watching the station's busy, early morning routine of papers and food being delivered to various establishments.

As the time to board the train approached, a small detachment of troops consisting of a young lieutenant, a corporal and three private soldiers arrived. When the first passengers got to the barrier, their tickets were checked, and each person was questioned.

Tennant watched the proceedings with alarm. He nudged Schettler. "Let's wait until the train is about to leave."

When they reached the barrier, the corporal greeted them. He seemed friendly enough. "Where are you two off to then?"

"We're going back to our ship in Scapa, Corporal, where else eh?" Tennant replied.

The corporal nodded in commiseration. "Can I see your tickets and travel warrants please."

Both men offered the corporal their documents and he inspected them one after the other. Then he excused himself and took them over to the young lieutenant, who also had a good look. The officer came across and said, "Which one of you is Carmichael?"

Schettler's groin tightened in fright as he acknowledged it was he.

The lieutenant looked him up and down. "Why are you leaving Glasgow when your leave isn't finished for another two days, Mr Carmichael? This isn't behaviour we're used to."

The statement confused Schettler. "What do you mean, sir?" he said in his strongest Glasgow accent.

"Well, sir, we're thoroughly browned off, you see." Tennant butted in. "Who would want to stay here when there's so much trouble going on? You know we can't even get a drink in peace without these bloody strikers causing bother. So, we've decided to pack it in and go north. We might stay in Perth or Inverness until it's time to go back to our ship. We haven't made up our minds yet."

The lieutenant looked at Schettler. "Is that right, Mr Carmichael?"

"Aye, it is, sir."

"You don't approve of this strike then?" The lieutenant nodded thoughtfully.

"No, I don't," Schettler said emphatically.

Just then the guard blew the whistle and the lieutenant waved them through. "You better run if you want to catch your train."

They ran on to the platform and had to throw their duffle bags through the door of the last carriage before they both jumped on to the moving train.

The train wasn't busy and as they moved down the corridor, it wasn't long before they found an empty compartment. The two of them planted their bags on the rack and sat at either side of the window. Within minutes, both were asleep.

*

It was very early on Saturday morning when the cell door was opened by a prison warder, accompanied by two soldiers. They called Gerry O'Brien's name and he was led away. It was a relief to leave the stinking cell which had been designed for two prisoners, but now held four. He had a good idea who he would meet and, over his eighteen-hour incarceration, he had prepared what he would say. He knew it probably wouldn't be enough and he would have to spoon feed further information, trying to keep it to a minimum. Self-preservation was necessary.

He was escorted through three, separate confinement areas which had to be unlocked and relocked by warders, then up two flights of narrow, iron stairs and along a dimly-lit corridor. It struck him that Barlinnie wasn't much different from Peterhead. One of the soldiers knocked on a door and there was a muffled sound from the other side. Opening the door, the soldier pushed O'Brien inside.

As he'd suspected, Dick Bradshaw sat at a desk in the small room, which was dingy, with a single, dim electric bulb suspended from a wire in the centre of the ceiling. The room had no windows. O'Brien could smell a strange smell, partly of sweat but something else too. Rubber, perhaps. Two other men sat on chairs next to the wall by Bradshaw's right side. The only other piece of furniture in the room was a small cupboard and there was a black iron sink with a bucket in it, at one corner of the room.

"Come and sit down, Gerry," Bradshaw said with a smile, as he pointed to the empty, wooden arm chair opposite the desk. "Make yourself comfortable."

O'Brien moved into the seat. Bradshaw continued. "This is Gerry O'Brien, gentlemen. He works for us, but you wouldn't know it. He gives us a very a bad return for our investment. He only tells us what we already know."

He shook his head as he turned back to face O'Brien. "I'm sorry you had to wait so long in that cell, Gerry, but you were so far down our list it's taken us till now to get to you."

He turned to the men. "Of course, Gerry's used to cells because he's not long out of Peterhead. Isn't that right, Gerry?"

O'Brien nodded.

"He got four years for treason. Treason, mind you – he had a gun and a German gun at that. What kind of gun was it, Gerry?"

"A Mauser, Dick."

"That's right, a Mauser. Four years for that is very lenient wouldn't you say, gentlemen? Two of his pals were executed.

I think if he continues to give us as little as he's done so far, we'll just have to pin something on him and see that he dangles from a rope this time."

O'Brien had learned by now that this was how Bradshaw always talked, but nevertheless it did frighten him and panic welled up within him.

Bradshaw paused, before continuing. "Gerry, when we talked in early January you made the excuse that you were so new in Beardmore's that you hadn't had time to learn who was who and I, very kindly..." he turned and nodded towards the other two, "...accepted that." Bradshaw leant forward. "Look what's just happened in Glasgow. Did we get any prior warning from you? We knew about it, of course but it would have been nice and friendly, if you had warned us."

O'Brien answered defensively. "I told you when the strike would start, who the leaders were and when you asked if it would be solid I said it would. It was you who told me you already knew that, but I cannie just take information out of thin air – can I?"

Bradshaw gestured to the others. "See what I have to contend with, gentlemen?"

One of the men walked over to O'Brien and smacked him hard on the back of his head.

O'Brien's head was knocked forward and his chin hit the top of his ribs, rattling his teeth. He had to put his foot out to stop himself falling off the seat. He saw stars. "Look, Dick, I don't want all this. I'll tell you all you want to know. You know that."

"Good. We'll get started then. Who are the political activists in Beardmore's, Gerry?"

O'Brien was ready for this and he recited names, together with the political parties or organisations of which they were members. The man who hadn't hit him had taken a notebook and pencil from his pocket and was taking notes.

"Have any of these men talked about bringing down the Government, Gerry?"

"Only in as much as they were sorry to see the Tories winning the General Election, back in December."

Bradshaw nodded. "Have any of these men ever talked to you about the German revolutionary situation? Or have they any links with Ireland?"

"Not to me but that's not to say they don't talk about these things amongst themselves. They still don't talk to me much at all, although I'm never done trying to talk politics with them. Even saying that I ken John Maclean hasn't broken the ice. I don't think they trust me. I think they know I'm a plant."

"Why, have you told them? You wouldn't be working on both sides of the fence would you, Gerry?"

O'Brien felt sick. "No, I'd never do that, Dick. I know what side my bread's buttered."

"I'm pleased to hear it, Gerry. What were you doing in Lang's when we picked you up on Friday?"

"I was just having a drink, Dick."

"What, alone?"

"Aye."

Bradshaw shook his head. "That's the thing about you, Gerry. You want me to be fair with you and you start telling me lies. I was told you came in with another man who stayed with you all the time you were in there."

O'Brien put his hand up. "Alright, I'm sorry, Dick, his name is Charlie Tennant and I knew him before the war."

Bradshaw raised his eyes with renewed interest. "Is that the Charlie Tennant you were involved with in the Citizens Army, Gerry?"

O'Brien nodded.

Bradshaw turned to his colleagues. "Is Tennant's name on the list?"

The two men looked at each other and then one shook his head. "No, it's not."

"You're sure?"

"Of course, I'm sure," snarled the other.

"But we picked up the man Gerry was speaking to in Lang's, so where is he?"

The other man's expression had darkened. "How would I know? If he managed to escape, no one's reported it."

Bradshaw slammed his fist on the desk, and growled. "You don't know anything about where your friend went Gerry?"

"No, I don't know. I was here sitting in a smelly cell."

Bradshaw lowered his voice. "Gerry, who was the man Tennant was talking to just before closing time? My contact tells me they knew each other."

"I don't know, Charlie never introduced us. I was talking to another man at the time and the pub was busy."

"Gerry, this just won't do." Bradshaw signalled to the two men.

Both of them jumped up. One lifted O'Brien out of the chair, and the other aimed several punches at his stomach and chest. They let him fall to the ground, winded and in pain. As O'Brien lay there, one of the men filled the bucket half-full of water and threw it over him, while the other forced him back on the chair.

He sat there breathing heavily for two or three minutes.

"Tell me the whole story in your own time, Gerry." Bradshaw said in a low voice.

Barely audible, O'Brien related the whole story about his meetings with Tennant in Duke Street and George Square, and that Tennant had told him he was still in the navy. He was in Glasgow for a few days leave and had referred to his friend as Ian.

"So, was it this Ian who came into Lang's then, Gerry?" asked Bradshaw.

O'Brien leaned forward. His chest was still very painful, but he managed to shout, "I fuckin' told you, Dick, I was never introduced to him. Do you no understand what I'm saying to you?"

Bradshaw rose. "It's time we showed this little shit that we really mean business." He went over to the cupboard and brought out a two-foot length of thick, rubber hose as the other two lifted O'Brien out of his seat and laid him face down over the desk. As one held him by the neck, so he couldn't move, the other pulled his shirt up and Bradshaw began striking him with the hose. He had struck him five times when they heard a loud intake of breath. O'Brien's body went into a spasm and then was still. When they turned him over and checked, he had no pulse. They tried to revive him, but it was too late. He was dead.

"Oh fuck," said Bradshaw. "The little cretin's died on me."

The note-taker blurted out, "You're a fucking, sadistic bastard, Bradshaw. That man was telling you the truth. You could see that a mile off. He didn't know the man with Tennant."

"That's enough Willis. *We'll* go and speak to Sinclair."

"*We'll* go and speak to Sinclair – my arse! You'll go and speak to Sinclair yourself and if you try to pin any of this on me and Andrews here, we'll squeal so loudly, you'll be up shit creek. Got that? You're still in the army and even in military intelligence, there are rules and you've broken a few today."

Bradshaw glared at him. "It was Sinclair who told us to put the fear of God into these bastards in the first place and it wasn't just me who was doing that."

This time Andrews spoke up. "Willis is right – we put the fear of God into that little man half an hour before you beat the life out of him. It's you that's the cretin, Bradshaw."

Bradshaw tried to get control of the situation. "We need to calm down. I'll go and see Sinclair now. You arrange to get him out of here. Then find out how Tennant escaped and what his address is."

He stopped and thought for a moment. "Wait. He told O'Brien he was on a few days leave, so go round the railway stations first and tell the uniforms to look out for him and hold him for us. I'll see you later, back at Turnbull Street."

*

The soldiers had already checked three trains when Willis and Andrews walked up to the lieutenant and one addressed him. "Are you checking the identities of the passengers travelling on the trains this morning, Lieutenant?"

"Yes, sir, we are."

"If you come across a sailor by the name of Charles Tennant, we want you to hold on to him and contact the person named on this card or the telephone number shown there too."

"Who are you gentlemen?" the young lieutenant said haughtily, not at all happy at being given orders by civilians.

"Never you mind who we are, Lieutenant. All you need to know is we're official and not complying with our instructions will be viewed very seriously. Got that?"

The lieutenant looked uncomfortable. "That sailor is actually a CPO and he boarded the first train for Inverness this morning. There were two of them and they said they were going back to their ship, HMS Emperor of India stationed at Scapa Flow."

"Can you describe the other man, Lieutenant?"

The lieutenant shrugged. "He was also a CPO, about the same height as Tennant. His name was Gordon Carmichael. As a matter of fact, I questioned them as to why they were returning to their ship with two days of their leave still to go, and he said he didn't want to stay in Glasgow while all the trouble was going on. I asked if he approved of the strike and he said he didn't."

"What kind of accent did he have, Lieutenant?"

"I'm no expert but it sounded Scottish to me." He shouted the corporal over.

"Corporal Wright, do you remember these two CPOs I questioned this morning? What accent did Carmichael have?"

"Glaswegian. They were both Glaswegians, sir."

"Are you sure, Corporal?"

"I'm perfectly sure, sir."

Andrews broke in. "Carmichael couldn't have been German, could he, Corporal?"

"German? No, sir." The reply was emphatic. "He spoke with a broad, Glasgow accent."

The lieutenant was asked where and when the train would stop en route. Andrews addressed his colleague. "We've missed Tennant in Perth. We'll have him picked up in Inverness." Without another word to the soldiers, the two men turned on their heels and hurried out of the station.

When they were out of earshot, the corporal commented, "Tennant said they might get off at Perth, sir."

The lieutenant nodded. "Yes, he did, but that's none of our business is it?"

The corporal smiled. "No, sir."

Chapter 19

Twenty minutes out of Glasgow, Tennant woke up in a cold sweat – the result of a dream where he was tied to a chair. A man, who had his face only inches from his, was shouting at him and when he caught a glimpse of his arms, they were bleeding.

He shook off the remnants of the dream and sat watching the smoke from the engine billowing around the window, thinking about what happened the previous day. Memories of his experience in 1914, were also on his mind. The dream, though. It wasn't his experiences his subconscious had dredged up, but those O'Brien had described to him.

When Schettler awoke, he found his friend in an agitated state. "What's wrong, Charlie? You look troubled."

"That guy, Gerry, knows all about me and he's not long out of jail after serving four years. They beat the crap out of him in 'fourteen, and I don't know how much it would take for him to tell them about me. Do you still have Bob's clothes you were wearing yesterday?"

Schettler nodded and Tennant continued, "We have our tickets all the way to Thurso, so we shouldn't need to identify ourselves as naval personnel. I think we should get off this train in Perth and either find somewhere to stay the night or at least change trains and continue our journey in mufti."

"In what?" Schettler said, his forehead creased.

"In our civilian clothes."

"I thought that was civvies."

Tennant gestured with his hand, "Same thing."

"That's fine, Charlie, but they'll recognise us whatever we're wearing, carrying these naval kit bags. I was waiting to be stopped by the police last night as I walked to Kate's place with it."

"Aye, you're right, but if we get off at Perth we could buy a couple of cheap suitcases in Woolworths, or somewhere like that."

Schettler stared at him.

"Look, I'm sorry," Tennant said, "but I've just got a premonition that they'll be after us, that's all."

"What if they're waiting for us in Perth?"

"In that case, they'll get us, but the quicker we react, the better chance we'll have. What do you say?"

Schettler pursed his lips. "Very well. Let's do as you say, Charlie."

*

Bradshaw arrived at Glasgow Police Headquarters in Turnbull Street, Military Intelligence's temporarily operational headquarters, to find that Sinclair was at high level meetings in the City Chambers and would be there for at least two hours. The chief's personal assistant, Miss Teal, a brusque woman at the best of times, complained that this was a bad time and it was unlikely Sinclair would see him at all that day. When Bradshaw stressed that the matter was of the utmost importance, she reluctantly agreed to phone him in his office when he returned, stressing that he couldn't have long.

As he was moving to the door of the outer office, she quipped, "I hope you're not the bringer of bad tidings, Mr

Bradshaw. I can tell you, when he went out this morning he was in a foul mood." This information dismayed Bradshaw and he walked to the office he shared with Willis and Andrews, to wait for their return from the railway stations and Miss Teal's eventual call.

He wasn't going to take the blame for O'Brien's death, although he had been his case officer. The other two had been totally involved throughout. He had gone too far when interrogating O'Brien, but he had taken such a dislike to him that he deserved all he got – the ignorant little Scotch git.

He didn't have to wait long for his colleagues to return and when they settled themselves at their desks, they explained how they had been lucky. Buchanan Street Station, only the second they had been to, had rendered an immediate result. The army there had told them that Tennant and another Scots petty officer boarded the early train to Inverness to get a connection to Thurso to join their ship.

With this information, Bradshaw had a call sent out to the police stations where the train was scheduled to stop, to find Tennant, have him arrested and returned to Glasgow, immediately.

The train had departed from Perth well before the local police received the call. But a phone call by the desk sergeant ascertained that the railway staff had seen two petty officers get off the early Inverness train, leaving the station in the taxi belonging to Willie McDougal. So later, when the back shift came on duty, they were sent to find McDougal and apprehend Tennant.

Bradshaw sat at his desk for another hour and a half before Miss Teal's call came through, telling him Sinclair would see him now. He was nervous. Sinclair was not a man to be trifled with. When he entered Miss Teal's office, she told him to sit down.

She smiled imperiously. "I'm afraid his mood hasn't changed for the better, Mr Bradshaw." He grunted and shifted uncomfortably in his seat. It was a further half hour before the door opened and Sinclair gestured for him to come in.

Sinclair listened to Bradshaw's explanation of the morning's events and the circumstances surrounding Tennant, in silence.

When Bradshaw had finished, he said, "Remind me when we picked O'Brien up to offer him the job in Beardmore's Foundry, Dick?"

"The beginning of December, sir."

"And he started, a week or so later, about the middle of December. Is that right? Then he had two days off on the first and second of January."

Bradshaw nodded. "Yes, that's about right, sir."

"How many times did you meet with him?"

"Twice, sir."

"What, once in December and once in January?"

"Almost. It was more like twice in January."

Sinclair seemed calm and Bradshaw began to relax.

"Was it? And during these meetings what did you ask O'Brien to do?"

"I told him to join the shop stewards' committee and get as much information as he could about the political activists there."

"I see. You thought this was enough time for him to be elected as a shop steward. Six weeks." Sinclair raised his eyebrows. "What did O'Brien tell you at the meetings?"

"First, he told me there weren't any vacancies for a shop steward, then he said that the other stewards wouldn't talk to him."

"And did you believe him?"

"No."

"I see. Do you consider yourself an expert on industrial relations then, Dick?"

"No, sir."

"And did it ever occur to you that O'Brien might be telling you the truth?"

Sinclair's tone had changed and Bradshaw found himself starting to sweat.

"I found him devious, so no, I thought he was lying."

"I get the feeling you didn't like him, is that right?"

"I wasn't too fond of him, I suppose."

"You disliked him sufficiently to beat him to death?" Sinclair snarled.

Bradshaw's hands were clammy. "I wouldn't put it like that, sir."

"Well, how would you put it?"

"There were three of us in the room and I only administered the last punishment."

"Was that not the punishment that killed him?"

"I don't know. Perhaps he had an underlying medical problem."

Sinclair laughed. "Oh I see, you want us to organise a post-mortem?"

"No, sir."

"How many punishments, to use your expression, were 'administered'?"

"Three, sir."

"Three punishments for someone who's supposed to be working for you!" Sinclair sounded furious.

Bradshaw made to answer, but the other man put his hand up to stop him. "Let's leave O'Brien aside for the moment, Bradshaw, but we will come back to him."

His tone was measured once more. "Why are you so keen to pick up Charlie Tennant? It is Charlie, isn't it?"

"Yes, it is, sir. You want scapegoats and after what he was involved in, at the start of the war, I thought he would be just right. I know he took the Inverness train this morning, so we've asked the police there and in all the intermediate stops to find him."

"What was Tennant convicted of in nineteen fourteen, Dick?"

"Nothing, sir."

"That's right, nothing. Since then, and to this day, he is a serving seaman who I understand has climbed to the highest rank as a non-commissioned officer. We can conclude from that he's got a good service record." Sinclair raised his eyes.

"What then are we to feed to the press about him? We can't say he's stirring up trouble in Glasgow, whatever his political allegiances are, because he's not bloody been here until a few days ago. Has he? The thing about finding scapegoats, is we have to have evidence against them or at least they have to be vulnerable enough for us to fabricate some, isn't that right? So as soon as you leave this office, you'll call off this bloody manhunt and hope the police haven't managed to locate him. Do you understand?"

"Yes, sir." Bradshaw's answer was barely audible.

"Now, tell me about your man who says he heard someone shouting in German on the demonstration."

Bradshaw related the story about his agent and a haughty, Irish woman in the vicinity of Prince Albert's statue during the height of the trouble.

"The man who rushed forward to strike my agent and break her fall shouted something in a foreign language, which my agent thought was German, sir."

Sinclair thought for a minute before saying, "How dependable is this man and would he know what German sounds like?"

"He's one of the Orangemen. They're fanatical about King and country but not very dependable. I don't know if this one would know if the man was speaking German. These men did a good job, though."

"Yes, it seems so. Alright, you can leave that one with me."

Bradshaw looked surprised. "Don't you want me to carry on with that investigation, sir?"

Sinclair pointed his finger at him. "Bradshaw, the only place I want you is back in London, as of immediate effect, and when everything has blown over here in Glasgow, I'll decide what I'm going to do with you. You're a fucking liability. When I gave O'Brien that job it was for the long term. I didn't expect him to get results this quickly. How the fuck could he! These things take time. Get out of my sight!"

When Bradshaw returned to his office, Willis looked up from his desk. "Oh, you're back then? You'll be happy to know that the Perth Police have located Tennant and as soon as they apprehend him, they'll telephone us again. What did the chief say then, Dick?"

*

When the train had pulled into Perth Station, Tennant and Schettler waited by the inside of the carriage door until the guard had blown his whistle, before they stepped down on to the empty platform. They hung around for five minutes before making their way over the footbridge which lead to the station building.

As they walked through the building towards the door a railway porter was deep in conversation with the booking clerk and they didn't even look up as the two sailors passed. They went to the timetable on the station wall and checked the times of the trains the next day. It was Sunday, so there weren't many to Inverness. The first one was six twenty, changing in Dundee. They boarded a taxi and asked the driver to take them to a cheap boarding house, via Woolworths.

The small, boarding house was located in a terrace of four identical houses with large, front gardens, but still close to the centre of Perth. They persuaded the landlady that their financial situation was such that they would have to share a room but not a bed and she let them have her family room which contained a double and single bed, for 4/9d including breakfast and an evening meal. The room's furniture was old fashioned – barely making it into the second half of the nineteenth century, but the beds were comfortable.

Once they had eaten the typical Scottish dinner of broth, mince with tatties, neeps and dough-balls, apple tart and custard washed down with as much tea as they could drink, they went out to find a pub.

As they walked through the town streets, the peace and quiet of Perth compared with Glasgow was palpable, even on a Saturday night.

They chose a traditional pub, with high, frosted glass windows, a semi-circular bar, with a large gantry in the centre, mostly full of whiskies. It had bench seating along the walls with fixed tables and wooden chairs on the outside.

Schettler had been very quiet during their meal and, once they had settled themselves with their pints of heavy beer close to the coal fire, he continued to be monosyllabic. Midway through their second pint, Tennant said, "I've never seen you so quiet, Ian. A penny for your thoughts?"

Schettler was forthright. "I'm having a lot of problems with the prospect of going back to the ship, Charlie. I think I'll be sent home very soon. High Command is doing all they can to take power away from the Soldiers' Council and the idiots in the Red Guard are only making things worse by their extreme behaviour. At home the SPD are gaining power in Berlin. Liebknecht and Luxemburg have been murdered and the SPD supported their murderers. As I understand it, the Peoples' Republics are all but finished. And, I just know that the armistice, when it's signed, will be brutal for Germany. It will be the people who will have to pay the price. We didn't fight battles on the streets of Berlin, Kiel and Wilhelmshaven, just ten weeks ago, for that to happen. I don't want to go home to watch the people being ground into the dirt, once again."

Tennant looked at him across the table, incredulous. "What'll you do?"

"I'll go to Ireland, may be. I was talking to Kate about the situation there and she reckons the British will soon cave in and give the Irish their independence. I might go there to help them fight for a socialist government when independence comes. How do I get to Dublin from here?"

His last remark sounded so flippant that Tennant laughed out loud. "That beer must be stronger than I thought. Are you kidding me?"

Schettler glared at him. "No, I'm deadly serious, Charlie."

Tennant shrugged. "In that case, Ian, you go back to Glasgow and get the night steamer from Broomielaw. It's really easy."

Schettler saw the other man's concern. "Look at it from my point of view, Charlie. If the British find out that I left my ship, I'll be arrested, and I'll spend time in jail here before I get sent back to Germany. God knows what will happen to me then."

Tennant retorted, "If you don't go back, wouldn't your High Command report your absence to the British and then you'll become a hunted man?"

"I might be a hunted man already but – no, our High Command doesn't really have a clue who's on board and who has already gone home. But to make sure, before I left I asked my friend Karl Brand, to attach my name to a list of men being returned home, if I didn't return from Glasgow. So, I've nothing to fear there. But if I went back to the ship, I'll get sent home anyway, so what have I to lose? The other thing is if you travel back alone in munty—"

Tennant grinned. "It's mufti, Ian"

"Whatever. You'll stand a far better chance of making it if I'm not with you, whether it's in mufti or in uniform."

"If you do make it to Dublin, how will you live?" asked Tennant. "You're not going after Kate, are you? God! That's what it is. You're going there because of Kate. Go on, admit it, Ian"

"That's not the reason, although I'll admit that I do like her, but we don't know each other. I have a bit more than twenty pounds left. That should last me a bit of time until I can find a job."

Tennant sighed and nodded. "I guess so, if you're sure. Let's celebrate with another drink. What would you like?"

"Anything except whisky, Charlie."

They left the pub at nine o'clock and headed back to the boarding house. When the landlady answered the door, she looked surprised. "Oh, it's you, gentlemen. I expected you to be out much longer. Would you like some supper?"

Just then the bell rang and when the landlady opened the door again, two policemen were standing there. "That's Mr Tennant there, officer," said the landlady pointing to him.

"Are you Chief Petty Officer Charles Tennant?" When he answered that he was, one of them said, "You'll have to accompany us to the station, sir."

"What on earth for, officer?" Tennant sounded calm.

The policeman shook his head. "I have no idea, sir."

Schettler said, "Do you want me to come too?"

"No, sir. We just want Mr Tennant."

As the door closed, Tennant shouted, "I'll probably see you back on the ship, Gordon."

The landlady looked embarrassed. "I'm sorry, the police came while you were away. They must have waited for your friend out on the street. There was nothing I could do. I hope it's nothing serious."

Schettler nodded. "I'm sure it's nothing at all."

The landlady went on, "I'm sorry, Mr Carmichael, but I'll still have to charge you the 4/9d as Mr Tennant has had his tea."

"That'll be alright," Schettler said as he mounted the stairs to his room. As the landlady turned to walk away, she said, "And he looked such a nice man too."

Schettler sat on the edge of the bed, wondering what the hell to do. The single gas mantle hissed loudly but the meagre light gave the room a depressing feel, which accentuated his current mood. Issues crowded his mind. Would they take Charlie to Glasgow? What would they, whoever they were, do with him when they got him there? His uniform, kit bag, and new suitcase were still here. Would the police come to pick them up? Should he get away from here before they came back for him? But the police had said they only wanted Charlie.

The doorbell startled him. He looked at his watch. It was late, he thought, so this time it must be the police for him. He went over to the window and glanced out, but could see nothing. He tried to open it, but it was stuck.

He could hear a man's voice speaking to the landlady. After a few minutes, there was the sound of footsteps coming up stairs and the door handle turned. When the door wouldn't open, there was a loud knock.

"Who is it?" Schettler shouted.

"It's me – Charlie. Open the door."

He was relieved to see his friend, who seemed to be unaffected by his visit to the police station.

When Tennant closed the door behind him, Schettler said, "What on earth's going on, Charlie?"

"I'm buggered if I know, Ian. As soon as I got to the bar—"

"What, they took you to a pub?"

"No, that's what they call the counter in a police station where the criminals are processed."

Tennant sounded relieved. "Anyway, as soon as I got there, the duty sergeant apologised to me and said the people from Glasgow who had asked them to apprehend me, phoned back later to say they had been given wrong information and I was no longer wanted. So, I was free to go. I asked what it was all about, but the sergeant didn't know. I was out of there by five past ten."

They looked at each other, hardly able to believe what had just happened.

"It looks like we don't have to worry about being arrested, so why don't you just come back to Scapa with me tomorrow?" Tennant said.

Schettler shook his head. "No, Charlie, I've made up my mind, I'm not going back to the ship."

*

There were snippets of conversations, the echo of footsteps and the ghostly outline of people, as Schettler walked along George Street with his suitcase towards Kate A'Herne's flat in Bathgate Street in the east end of Glasgow. If there were still soldiers on the streets, he couldn't see them. All public transport had been suspended because of the dense fog which had covered the city in a toxic blanket. From time to time, he caught a glimmer of eerie light emanating from a stranded tram before the fog swirled thickly to obscure it again.

It was twenty minutes to five, and after saying goodbye to Charlie Tennant at Perth Station that morning, he had spent most of the day on trains. The journey from Edinburgh took almost three hours as the fog came down quickly after the train left Falkirk and it was too dense to continue at more than a snail's pace. Tennant had advised him to take the train to Edinburgh and then change for Glasgow. His logic was that the Edinburgh train terminated at Queen Street Station and if there were still troops checking people getting on and off trains, they would be different to the ones they had encountered in Buchanan Street Station and he wouldn't be recognised. As it happened, although there was a military presence in the station, they seemed less interested in people arriving from Edinburgh and let them through the barrier without being challenged.

As he walked in this relative peace, it seemed strange to think of this street packed with throngs of jubilant people walking towards George Square last Friday like lambs to the slaughter. It was another example of how little the working class were respected by those in authority – all right when they were fighting wars for them or manufacturing the means for them to make vast profits, but if they wanted social justice, they were beaten down with a very heavy hand. He thought of how many poor souls had been killed or seriously injured at the hands of the police and the army that day. How many families' lives had been wrecked?

As he passed the bottom of Westercraigs, he wondered if Bob had recovered from his severe beating.

When Kate answered her door, and found Schettler there she smiled, walked forward and kissed him.

"Somehow, I thought you might be back."

PART 3

Chapter 20

When Kate A'Herne reached the door of Tullamore Station, in Ireland's County Offaly, Johann Schettler was still struggling behind her with their heavy cases. As he drew level, he dumped them down by his side with a clatter and wiped the sweat from his brow. She caught sight of her brother, waved and shouted, "You're here right enough, Michael. So, you got my note."

Michael A'Herne, Kate's oldest brother, was waiting in the old model T truck and as he stepped down from the open cab, Kate grabbed Johann's hand and pulled him forward. "This is my friend, Johann Schettler. He's come to help us fight for a Socialist Republic. This is my brother, Michael."

The men shook hands and Michael embraced his sister.

"You're just as beautiful as ever, Kaitlin A'Herne, so Glasgow couldn't have done you much harm, after all."

"Sure, and you're still using that silver tongue of yours," she said with a chuckle. "By the way, we don't want anyone, not even the family, to know Johann's German, so you should call him Ian Nairn – Ian because that's what his Scottish mother calls him and Nairn because that's the name of his relatives in Glasgow."

Her brother stared at her, finding it difficult to understand what she was on about.

She shook her head. "Never mind, we'll explain later."

Schettler smiled. "I can understand your confusion. Sometimes, I find it difficult knowing who I am myself."

"Nothing surprises me when she's involved – but we better make a move. The farm's an hour away, Mr Nairn."

"Fine, but call me Ian."

Michael walked forward and picked up the couple's suitcases. "For the love of God! What are ye carrying – scrap iron?"

They turned right and headed away from Tullamore and soon the truck was chugging through the flat, Offaly countryside, struggling to reach thirty miles an hour. It was difficult for Schettler to imagine, on such a monochrome day, what the scenery really looked like. There seemed to be enormous, black patches on the land – some large enough to accommodate a small village. When he asked what they were, Kate said it was peat and had to explain what that was. Torf, Schettler thought.

"Sure, you're truly in the land of the bog now, Ian," she shouted over the loud rattling of the engine.

As the cold began to bite, Schettler noticed Kate shivering and he took off Bob's Harris Tweed overcoat and wrapped it around them both. She snuggled herself down into it while he supported her head with his arm. She smiled up at him and at that moment he thought she was the most beautiful woman he had ever seen.

Feeling calm for the first time in ages, his thoughts drifted through the events of the last three months.

He realised he'd dealt with the political events with single-mindedness. But things were different now. He had more people to care about – meeting his mother's family, cementing his friendship with them and Charlie Tennant, and finally these feelings he had for Kate. He didn't know what Kate felt for him, if anything, and it was too early to ask her. He had been very happy to accept her invitation to stay with her in her uncle's cottage while they assessed what was happening in Ireland and how they could get involved. The Irish wanted independence from Britain but was a socialist government possible? What could he do here? He certainly wouldn't join the ranks of the rebels to get involved in killing people with whom he had no fight…

As the truck drew level with a cottage, Michael applied the brakes and it came to a grinding halt, interrupting Schettler's thoughts. As suddenly as the truck stopped, two men appeared from the door. Greeting Michael and his companions with only a muffled grunt, they jumped on to the back, removed two, large wooden boxes from under a tarpaulin and together manhandled them inside the cottage. Without saying a word, Michael engaged the gears and the truck trundled on its way. They continued until Kate broke the silence, as she leaned over Schettler. "Who was that with Eamonn Duffy at Cairn Cottage?"

"I don't know much about him. His name's Kiernan and he has recently arrived from Dublin." Michael broke into Gaelic, but Kate stopped him.

"Don't speak in Gaelic, Michael, there's nothing we need to keep from Ian," she shouted over the noise of the engine. "After all, as a German he's an illegal alien, so they'll be nothing he'll be passing on to the RIC, will there?"

Michael nodded. "He's an IRB man, sent from Michael Collins and while we're on about the RIC, did you hear about Suichóid Bheag?"

"No, what happened?"

"The day Sinn Féin declared Independence, about three weeks ago, a party of Tipperary volunteers led by Dan Breen decided to raid the quarry and steal a consignment of gelignite being delivered. They ambushed the explosives wagon that was being guarded by RIC constables and two of them were shot dead at point black range in the scuffle."

He shrugged. "So, we're now at war a little earlier than we thought we'd be. The stuff we just dropped off at Cairn Cottage, was part of that consignment."

A shiver ran down Schettler's back and Kate cried out, "Oh, for the love of God! What are you going to blow up?"

"Nothing at all. It's how we transport the stuff. We use local vehicles for short journeys. That way the police don't suspect what we're doing. Someone else will pick it up and take on its next stage, later on today."

"You better be careful," Kate scolded. "If they catch you, they'll lock you up and throw away the key."

After a pause she continued. "Is Rose Cottage still empty since Uncle Darragh died?"

Michael nodded. "Yes. Why? Do you want to stay there?"

"Of course we do. You don't expect us to stay in the house with you lot, do you?"

Since their parents died, Michael had taken over the family farm and lived in the house with his wife and their four children.

Michael shook his head. "Well, you'll have to, for a couple of days at least. The place needs a damned good clean." He sniggered. "What will we tell Father Boyle since you're not married?"

"You can tell him what you bloody like."

They crossed a bridge over a canal, climbed a hill and turned left into a large, square farm yard where a substantial, stone-built, two-storey house faced them, flanked on either end by two large barns.

"Welcome to Teach Feirme Baile," Michael said.

"That's the name of the place. It means Home Farm House," Kate piped up.

As the truck drew to a stop, two collies ran from one of the barns barking and the front door of the house opened. Two small, red haired girls ran down the steps towards the truck shouting excitedly.

Kate unwound herself from Schettler's coat and holding up the skirt of her own coat, jumped deftly from the running board to the ground, bending down in time to receive their embraces. They talked excitedly until Kate said, "Now, talk in English you two! I know you can. There's someone here who doesn't understand Gaelic and you wouldn't want him not to understand you, would you?"

"No, Auntie Kate."

Kate turned them towards Schettler, who was still standing on the truck. "This is Mr Nairn, a good friend of mine from Glasgow. These are Michael's two youngest, Ailish and Claire."

The two girls chorused, "How do you do, Mr Nairn."

Schettler smiled. "How do you do, girls. It's very nice to meet you."

As Michael was making a fuss of the dogs, a female voice shouted from the house, "Are you going to stand out there in the cold all day?" When Schettler looked up, a small, portly woman in her late thirties, also with flaming red hair, was standing on the stoop.

"This is my wife, Lucy. This is Kate's friend, Ian—"

Kate interrupted. "It's Ian Nairn, Lucy. He's my friend from Glasgow."

"I didn't realise you were bringing a friend, Kate. How do you do, Mr Nairn. Welcome to our humble abode. Come into the warm. It's cold out there."

"No, Lucy," Kate cried. "I want to take Ian to see Rose Cottage before it gets dark. Can you give me the keys? We won't be long."

As the two walked back to the road, Kate pointed to a ruined tower on the opposite side. "That's Clonony Castle. I don't suppose you know much about British history? It's a ruin now but it used to belong to the Boleyn family. Anne Boleyn was the second wife of the English King, Henry VIII. She came to a sticky end. He had her head chopped off. There's a great view from the top. We'll go up there some time if the stairs are still safe."

They walked on for less than two hundred yards to a white, single-storey cottage with a well-kept front garden full of rose bushes. Kate opened the door and they walked through a small hall into a parlour of modest proportions. Although dusty, it was tidy with old but perfectly serviceable furniture.

The kitchen was altogether different. It was dark, mainly because a tree had grown over the outside of the rear window. Kate had to open the back door to allow in more light. The walls had been cream at one time but now they were more of a dingy brown. A peat burning range was set into one wall, surrounded by a wooden mantelpiece, painted dark brown, and a black, iron sink sat in a wooden surround under the window – all of which were painted in the same hideous colour. The only furniture in the room was an old table and four wooden chairs that didn't match. Another small door in the wall opposite the range, housed a small pantry. When Kate opened the door, they could hear the rustling noise of mice, so she quickly closed it again.

Kate was first to comment. "I was encouraged when we went into the parlour but Michael's right. The place will need a lot of work if we're going to live here. My Uncle Darragh was a bachelor who lived alone, and I don't think it's had a lick of paint in all the time he was here."

Schettler nodded. "I'll go outside and try to clear the tree away from the kitchen window."

"Right then. I'll inspect the rest of the place."

They stayed there till darkness began to fall. As they walked back uphill to the house, Schettler asked about the canal they had crossed earlier, and she told him it was An Chanáil Mhor.

"That's the Grand Canal in English. But I don't want you thinking it's as grand as the one in Venice! It connects Dublin with the River Shannon just down the road at Shannon Harbour." Then she returned to the subject of her family. "There's two of Michael and Lucy's children you haven't met. They're Seán and Cathleen. Seán's now working on the farm. He's a bit sullen, like most fourteen-year-old boys, unless he's changed since I saw him last – so you won't get much out of him. Cathleen, she's different altogether. She's eleven and never stops talking. She'll ask you questions all the time."

As Clonony Castle came back into view, Schettler thought it looked somewhat foreboding in the moon-light.

*

They spent a week in Teach Feirme Baile while they cleaned the cottage from top to bottom. They painted the kitchen with paint that Michael had left over from his renovation of the family house. Lucy had some spare fabric and because the windows were small, there was enough for Kate to sew up some curtains for the parlour and bedroom.

There were some colours of paint left over from the redecoration and Kate suggested they try to create a French café scene on one of the parlour walls. Johann thought it would take a bit of imagination to get round the obvious colour deficiencies but it would be fun to try. The mural took two days of intense mixing and painting with each of them concentrating on different aspects of the scene, trying to invent colours that would work and the time flew by in a blur of enjoyment.

When they reviewed the finished composition, Kate declared that it was rubbish, but Johann could see she possessed considerable flair and although the work had its deficiencies, mainly due to the lack of colour, their styles had married well together. This prompted him to suggest that they find a source of paint and canvas and start painting in earnest.

Kate asked Lucy if there was anywhere in either Tullamore or Birr that would provide art materials. Lucy thought it was highly unlikely but suggested they use her J.D. Williams catalogue which supplied any unusual items which couldn't be bought locally.

The day Kate and Johann moved into the cottage, Michael delivered peat to the small barn behind the house and while Johann lit fires in the hearth in the parlour and the kitchen range, Kate primed the oil lamps ready for the evening.

They cooked a meal of mutton stew, potatoes and cabbage in the range together and after it was eaten, washed up and cleared away.

Johann was about to retire to the parlour when Kate took his arm and drew him close to her. "It looks like we're living like a married couple, you and I. So, if we're going to do that, I think we'd better do it properly," and she stretched up and kissed him on the mouth.

Johann was surprised, though he'd been wondering how to broach that subject since he had walked into her flat in Glasgow. He took her in his arms and returned her kiss passionately and they stood there for several minutes locked in each other's embrace until Kate broke free and led him to the bedroom.

Schettler nervously fumbled his way out of his clothes and quickly jumped under the blankets to Kate's amusement. She had no such inhibitions and removed her clothes slowly, as he watched her reveal her beauty, with his heart beating ever quicker.

Naked, she got into bed beside him and feeling the softness of her body next to his, against all his basic instincts he asked her what they would do about contraception. "I'm glad you asked that, Ian, but don't worry, I've taken care of it," she said smiling up at him.

Caressing her cheek, he said, "You're so beautiful, Kate."

When their first sexual encounter was over, and they lay there dreamily in each other's arms, Schettler thought how wonderful it had been. He had reached a climax, almost as soon as he had entered her, but he managed to keep going. His thoughts drifted through the last few days in her company. He realised they had been the happiest of his adult life and he knew he loved her. He had never met anyone with such an outgoing personality. She was able to reason everything out in the most logical and uncomplicated way. He thought back to her encounter with the lout in George Square and how she had taken him down and ridiculed him so completely in only a few sentences. She was also a talented artist and beautiful – everything he had ever dreamed of and he felt he wanted to be with her always.

Kate, however, was thinking that his sexual prowess left a lot to be desired – probably because of his inexperience, or at least not having done it for a while. Not that she had a lot of experience herself – a fumble in the barn with Eamonn Duffy when they were sixteen. It was strange seeing him the other day. Once with Brendan, her bother Liam's friend, up against the wall of a small room in the GPO in Dublin during the Easter rising, but he had smelt bad. Then there was Charlie Forsyth, the local trade union official at her work in Glasgow, last year. She had invited him to her flat, but he was all talk and no substance. It wasn't much experience really, she thought.

Sex with him would improve with time. He was a gentle and caring man and she was aware that he was probably in love with her. She was very attracted to him and the chemistry was definitely right.

She admired him for his politics and prowess as an artist and the last few days had been fun. They got on so well and had so much in common – but love wasn't what she wanted at the moment.

Kate knew she shouldn't have invited Johann to Rose Cottage – at least not so quickly. His presence might get in the way of what she had to do.

It was warm and comfortable lying in this man's arms and as she listened to his steady breathing, her personal critique soon gave way to sleep.

Chapter 21

It was Saturday morning and the first, heavy snow of the year had fallen over night. Schettler was clearing a path between the back door and the barn to make it easier to collect the peat for the fire, when he heard a voice from inside the cottage shouting, "It's all come, Auntie Kate – three big boxes. It's so exciting you'll have to come up to the house quickly. I'm dying to see what's inside."

He walked back to see what the commotion was and found Cathleen standing next to Kate. As he appeared, Cathleen blurted out, "It all came this morning. The post van just delivered it to the house." Then she paused, looking perplexed. "If you're staying with my Auntie Kate, should I call you Uncle? My mother says I have to be respectful and call you Mr Nairn, but I don't feel that's right. What should I do?"

Schettler smiled. "You can't call me uncle. But we're friends, aren't we?"

"Oh yes, of course we are."

"Just call me Ian, then."

She shook her head. "I don't know, I don't think mother would think that was respectful."

Kate declared, "If it makes her feel better, you'll just have to become her honorary uncle."

"That's fine, but what's just arrived?"

"The art materials," they both chorused.

Schettler nodded. "Very good! I wasn't expecting them yet."

Just then, Michael and Seán walked in each holding a large cardboard box.

"Where do you want this lot?" asked Michael.

"Just put it in the parlour for the moment," Kate said, kissing her brother on the cheek. When she turned to her nephew, he recoiled and quickly shuffled into the parlour.

"There's still one at the house. Seán'll bring it down later but right now we've got to check on the sheep and it'll take some time to find them in the snow."

Ian offered to lend a hand, but Michael looked reluctant to accept. Kate said, "Go on, Michael, I know you could use the help and if Ian goes with you, Cathleen can stay here and help me unpack the boxes." Cathleen gave a hoot of joy.

It took three hours to check that all the sheep were safe and when they began to walk back towards the house, Michael told Seán to run home and deliver the last box to Kate.

When the boy had gone, Michael said, "Kate tells me you're from Bremen, but you have family in Glasgow. I must admit I don't really understand that."

Schettler told him his story. When he finished, they had reached the road and as Michael closed the gate from the field, he leant on it. "Look, Ian, sure, I'm a broad-minded man. God knows I have to be with a brother and sister like Liam and Kaitlin. You do know me brother's in jail in England, don't you?" Schettler nodded. "Anyway, that's not the point. It's Kate I'm worried about. I know she doesn't care what people around here think of her, but we live in a small community and there'll be a lot of tongues wagging. I've heard a few things already. But we can cope with that."

He paused. "Look, what I really want to know is, what are your intentions? I'll be blunt. I don't want you to be waltzin' off leavin' her with a bun in the oven."

Schettler squinted at him. "A what?"

"You know, pregnant and all."

Schettler nodded. "Oh, I see. No, I won't do that. She's not likely to get pregnant anyway but I'm sure you don't want me to go into that," Schettler said, feeling himself flush.

Michael cleared his throat. "Aye, well no."

"I've never met anyone as wonderful as Kate and I don't intend to be waltzing off anywhere unless we're going together. I know we haven't known each other long but I have strong feelings towards her, Michael."

Michael shook his head. "Aye, she's a terrible one for doin' things on the spur of the moment."

He looked at Schettler quizzically. "So why don't you just get married then?"

"That's a decision we'll both have to make and neither of us are anywhere near contemplating that yet. Perhaps when the troubles are over we will. Personally, I hope so."

There was a long silence before Michael said, "How are you two thinking of keeping yourselves, Ian? You can't live on thin air."

"Kate says they're always looking for men to labour – digging the peat and I was thinking I would apply there for a job."

"Right then." Michael looked quizzical. "Just one more thing. Kate said you wanted to help us fight for a socialist republic?"

"Yes, I do. I can see most of the Irish people want independence from the British but what I gather from Kate is the leadership is far from socialist and since James Connelly was murdered by the British, the socialist movement is a minority and the Irish Citizens Army has now been merged into the IRB."

"You're right. It's very unlikely they'll be a socialist government. I have to admit that although Liam, and through his influence, Kate, are both socialists, I can't say I'm one myself. As a member of the IRB, I certainly want independence and I'll fight to the death to get it, but I'm even in two minds about setting up a republic. But anyway, are you prepared to help us?"

"Look, Michael, I'm prepared to help the cause of independence, but I'm not prepared to kill people. I'll help you as much as I can. I'll carry information and I'll help you carry armaments, and if you teach me how, I'll drive the truck – in fact I'll do anything short of killing people."

Michael nodded slowly. "Well, I suppose I couldn't really expect any more, given your circumstances."

Then he smiled. "When I took over the farm, I got the chance of acquiring more land and till now, I've just been using it for grazing. If I got some help, I could plough it and sow in a good crop of wheat. If you wanted to help me instead of extracting the peat and having to walk five miles to your work and back each day, I'll pay you. Not much, you understand but enough for you both to live on. What do you say?"

"I'll have to discuss it with Kate of course, but I can't really see why not." Schettler extended his hand. "Thank you very much, Michael."

When Johann discussed Michael's proposal that evening, Kate seemed to be in favour. She took exception however, to Michael's assessment of the strength of the socialist movement and that her principals had been influenced by Liam. She was adamant they would have to go to Dublin to help the cause, but he understood by the way she posed it, that there was no urgency.

The days turned to weeks and the weeks to months, with Schettler working with Michael and Seán on the farm – work, which although hard and physical, he took to extremely well. Kate spent her time painting and, since he was bringing in the money to support them, they agreed she should to take care of the domestic chores. When he wasn't toiling in the fields, he too painted and they began to use each other as models with each one posing nude for the other to paint. Invariably, these sessions were interrupted by sex as that aspect of their relationship had blossomed.

Spring became summer. It was clear that there wasn't much being asked of the local IRB units and all was quiet, with Schettler and Michael making only a couple of trips to transfer arms and ammunition along the line. Michael had heard that in Dublin, Cathal Brugha and Michael Collins were planning to spring the leading Sinn Fein members of the Dail, who had been languishing in English jails since they were elected as MPs in the general election. This news caused heightened anticipation between Michael and Kate that their brother Liam would be included, though he wasn't an MP.

*

Early on the morning of Monday the twenty third of June, Michael and Johann loaded ten sheep on board the truck to take them to the abattoir in Tullamore. Johann had been driving under instruction for the last six weeks and Michael thought he was now a good enough to drive alone.

He suggested that, as it was mid-summer, Johann should drive the truck to Tullamore and take Kate with him for the day, to enjoy themselves.

Johann set off feeling on top of the world. The weather was warm, and the sun shone in an almost cloudless sky, promising that it would get even warmer as the day progressed. When he got to Rose Cottage, Kate happily agreed to join him.

"You'll have to hurry, though. You know how long it takes the truck to get to Tullamore and I have to deliver these sheep before midday."

But she had already disappeared into the bedroom. "You'll have to give me five minutes. I can't go looking like this."

When she appeared fifteen minutes later, she was wearing a new dress she had ordered from Lucy's catalogue which had the new shorter mid-calf length skirt. She had also applied some make-up. Johann was captivated and went to embrace her, but she pushed him away. "I thought you said we were in a hurry, so we better get going?"

The sheep were bleating under the tarpaulin and the truck seemed to be going faster than usual. The couple were in high spirits and after a while Kate started singing a happy, traditional Irish song. When she finished he shouted, "Hurrah, sing another."

"Oh no, it's your turn. Sing one in German."

"Me, I can't sing a note, I'm unmusikalisch. What is it you call it when you can't keep a tune?"

"Tone deaf."

"Right then, Ah'm tone deaf."

Kate howled with laughter.

241

"Do you realise you just said that in a broad Irish accent?"

He started to sing 'O Tannenbaum,' which was the only song he could think of.

She continued to laugh. "That's a Christmas song. Is that all you know? Anyway, you can stop. You're right. You are tone deaf."

But he went on singing louder and louder while Kate put her hands over her ears.

Shortly after passing the small village of Clochan, the road turned on an almost ninety-degree bend. Ahead of them they could see an army truck blocking the way with four soldiers standing with rifles over their shoulders. As they approached, a corporal signalled for them to stop.

"The top of the morning to you, Corporal. Isn't it a beautiful day?" Kate shouted.

He ignored her and ordered Schettler to switch off the engine and step out of the vehicle.

He began questioning him about their identity, where they had come from – where they were going and why. Then he asked to see what was in the truck. He climbed in beside the sheep to check there was nothing else being transported, banging the floor with his foot to hear if there were any hollow places in which to hide things.

Jumping out of the truck, he said, "You're not Irish, are you mate? Where are you from?"

"Glasgow."

The corporal looked puzzled. "Oh, I thought I heard a foreign accent in there somewhere."

Schettler looked him straight in the eye. "Ah don't know where ye get that idea pal, but ah'm just an ordinary Glaswegian, right?"

"All right, mate, keep your hair on."

When Schettler and the corporal returned to the cab, the soldiers were crowded round Kate, laughing and joking. One of them shouted over to Schettler, "You're a lucky bastard. How did you manage to get such a beautiful wife, mate?"

"Just lucky right enough, pal."

"You'll never guess, boys," said the corporal. "This bloke's from Glasgow." Then he chuckled. "We were in Glasgow in January and February – posted there to keep all your commie pals from causin' a revolution. We kicked the shit out of them. Were you there?"

Schettler answered dryly. "No, we were here."

"We'll kick the shit out of these Republican bastards too, won't we boys?" And the other three shouted, "Too right, Corporal Dixon."

"Look, Corporal Dixon," Kate said, "we need to get these sheep to the abattoir in Tullamore by noon. If you're finished with us, can we go, please?"

The corporal made an exaggerated bow. "Certainly, madam, you're both free to go"

But as Schettler walked passed him to get to the starting handle he whispered, "I don't know what a fine girl like that is doing with a piece of Glasgow shit, like you."

Schettler ignored him as he turned the starting handle, jumped into the cab and navigated his way around the army truck.

As they drove on, he looked at Kate and sighed loudly. She burst out laughing.

Schettler looked thoughtful. "Did you ask them where they were from?"

"They said they're from the Middlesex Yeomanry. They just arrived in Ireland last month and they're stationed in Birr."

He told her what the corporal had whispered to him just as they left.

"The others were telling me," she chuckled, "that I should dump you and go off with them and they'd show me a good time."

Schettler thumped his hand on the steering wheel. "The bastards!"

"Don't worry about them, Ian, they're just stupid boys. They were telling me that they only joined up a couple of months before the end of the war. Prior to being posted here, Glasgow was the only place they'd been. Even the corporal had never fought in France."

Schettler felt the anger welling up within him. "They may just be boys, Kate, but they're still dangerous. I should have—"

"Shush, Ian, nothing's going to get in the way of us enjoying ourselves today. Now, sing me that nice Christmas carol again, I so enjoyed it."

They soon reached Cairn Cottage where another army truck was parked off the road. When they had put a bit of distance between the house and themselves, Kate said, "That place isn't due for a drop, is it?"

Schettler shook his head. "I don't think so. Michael hasn't said anything, but we better get a warning out."

Kate nodded. "Yes, we'll tell Quigley."

They arrived at the abattoir on the edge of Tullamore and deposited the sheep with Brendan Quigley. Knowing him to be an IRB man, Kate told him about the army's activity, but he seemed unconcerned.

Johann and Kate drove into town, parked the truck in St Patrick Street and headed off to Mullin, the painters, to see if he could order painting materials cheaper than it had cost through Lucy's catalogue. They were getting short of canvas for stretching over frames – the construction and process of which they were becoming highly proficient.

Mullin's shop itself, was badly in need of a lick of paint. The old man greeted Kate like a long lost relative. He had been a close friend of her father and they had to listen to him drone on for half an hour about how much he missed him. When the conversation eventually turned to what they had come for, surprisingly, he was much more helpful. He explained that he could order anything they liked, because he had an account with O'Leary's, the main art store in Dublin.

The old man went on, "I've had the account for years, so I have. I used to order art materials for old William Bury, you know, the Earl of Charleville? He did a bit of painting himself, although he wasn't much good. Well, I didn't think so, anyway. That was just before the family abandoned Charleville House in nineteen twelve and disappeared back to England, I wouldn't be surprised. It's a dammed shame that place is just lying there derelict. I have a whole forty-inch-wide roll of canvas I ordered just before they went and the old bugger left me with the lot. You can have it for five bob."

The old man led them into an area at the back of the shop and showed them the large roll of canvas. Although seven years old and a bit dusty, the material was still in good order and they took it. After ordering oil paints of various colours, turpentine and varnish, Schettler lugged the heavy roll of canvas back to the truck while Kate paid the old man and tried to extricate herself from the shop.

Later, Schettler managed to buy some badly needed summer clothes and, flushed with their successes, they went for lunch at Flynn's restaurant and tearoom on Kilbride Street.

They were midway through their lunch, when Schettler noticed a well-dressed man at an adjacent table reading the Irish Times and as he folded the paper over to read an internal page, Schettler could see a headline midway down, 'GERMAN FLEET SUNK.' Anxious to find out what this was about, Schettler rose, quickly excused himself and rushed out the restaurant. He returned five minutes later with a copy of the Irish Times and began to thumb through it.

"What are you looking for, Ian?"

"Just give me a minute, will you," he mumbled.

The short and rather sketchy article was on page five and after reading it Schettler turned the paper over and showed it to Kate.

Kate glanced at the article and then to Schettler. He looked devastated.

She took hold of his hand. "What does this mean, my love? "

He spoke hesitantly. "It would seem Reuter has ordered the fleet to be scuttled. That was always the Soldiers' Council's worst nightmare."

"Who's Reuter?"

"He's the Admiral in charge of the interned fleet."

"I don't really understand what this is all about, Ian. You'll have to explain it to me."

"I don't have the heart to explain anything at the moment, Kate." He hesitated for a few seconds then it all poured out.

"All I can say is, as long as we held on to these ships there was hope, something to negotiate against the harshness of the Allies retribution and now we have nothing." He hung his head. "I've always said the German people would have to answer for the sins of the ruling class and now the old military order has sabotaged our only bargaining tool in the name of misplaced military heroism. My heart's telling me I should have stayed with the fleet, but I could never have changed the outcome. Anyway, it's likely that I would have been forcibly repatriated – but right now I feel incredibly guilty."

She pressed his hand and whispered, "You know, I love you, Ian." As he stared at her in surprise, tears rolled down his cheeks.

After lunch, as circumstances dictated that their day out in Tullamore had come to a premature end they headed back to Clonony. The journey was completed in silence and thankfully, as far as Kate was concerned, without further contact with the British Army, for she didn't know how he would have reacted, if subjected to more intimidation.

The truck pulled into the deserted yard of Teach Feirme Baile just after four o'clock and not wanting to have to answer questions about their day from interested relatives, Kate quickly shoved the truck key through the letterbox and the couple made a break for the road before anyone could get to the door – the purchases could be picked up later.

Earlier Kate had suggested that rather than hurrying home on such a beautiful day, she would take Johann to the top of Clonony Castle to see the beautiful views from there. They walked across the grass to the open gate within the ten feet high, outer wall with its square, saw tooth top and across a grassy knoll to another gate which led into a small, inner courtyard – now completely overgrown with wild brambles. They carefully edged their way between these lethal bushes to the entrance of the tower which was now without its door and stepped into a small hallway, where a circular staircase spiralled up to the top of the ancient building. With Kate leading the way, they walked up three flights of rough stone stairs passing the entrance to each floor, but the timber floors were missing. Reaching the top, the stair ended at a narrow opening which led them to a stone allure around the four sides of the battlements. The view through the embrasures allowed them to see for miles in every direction and in the afternoon sunshine the scenes were breathtaking. They stood with arms around each other for some time, until Johann broke it by kissing Kate's cheek. "I've never known happiness like this, Kate. Even the news of the scuttled fleet today couldn't really move me to sadness and when you told me you loved me, I experienced such joy. I just don't want this to ever end, mein schöner Liebling."

Kate turned to face him. Her expression was serious. "I do love you so very much, Ian. At the beginning, I thought I'd acted impulsively inviting you here. I'm often impetuous and I was frightened things would turn sour, but this time it's worked out right and I also don't want it to end. I guess it will have to sometime because we have things we must attend to – but we can attend to them together, can't we?"

Schettler nodded. "Yes, we can," and he held her tight.

Later, when they were about to leave, Kate said, "They say a ghost of a tall, thin man haunts the top of the tower wearing old fashioned clothes and he's supposed to be surrounded by a halo of mist."

Schettler shrugged. "Yes, I see that."

Kate looked bemused. "What do you mean?"

"He's right behind you."

She laughed and slapped his shoulder.

Chapter 22

"Ian, Ian!" When Seán saw he had attracted Schettler's attention, he brandished something white above his head and shouted something else which was swallowed up in the breeze.

When the boy arrived at Schettler's side, he was out of breath. "Me father's takin' me mother to Birr to do some shoppin', so he said I've to help you mend the fence." He wheezed and patted the satchel at his waist. "Mother's given us some lunch."

"Great, I'm feeling tired in this heat and hungry too, so let's eat now."

The boy put down the satchel and pulled out the contents. There was bread, cheese, two home-made pork pies, a bottle of Guinness and one of lemonade.

Schettler noticed Seán eyeing up the porter. "We'll keep the lemonade for later and share the Guinness now, shall we?"

Seán smiled broadly. It had taken Schettler a while to befriend him but in the last few months he had lost his inhibitions and had even begun to use Schettler as a confidant.

As they settled down on the grass in the bright, midday sunshine, Seán said, "I think the Guinness was meant for you, the lemonade was mine."

Schettler smiled as he cut some cheese with his knife. "Well, I won't tell, if you don't."

As they ate and passed the Guinness between them, Seán talked animatedly about his friends and what they got up to on Sunday afternoons. "Sometimes we cycle up to Clara to meet some girls from the convent school. Peter and I might get a trial for the Rugby Club up there. They're looking for strong, young lads – the man there, you know the trainer, said it doesn't matter that we don't know how to play the game because they'll teach us."

Schettler had never heard of rugby before coming to Ireland and he had never seen it played. All he knew was that it was a rough game. "I don't know much about it myself, I've never played it but that's great, Seán, I'm sure you'll do well."

"Don't they play rugby in Glasgow, Ian?"

Schettler didn't know the answer to that. "Not very much."

Seán's expression lightened. "Of course, it's soccer you play there isn't it, with your Celtic and Rangers and all."

Schettler felt uneasy. What the hell was soccer? He'd better ask Kate later. "Yes, that's right. What was that white thing you were waving earlier?"

Seán looked puzzled. "Oh, you mean this," he said, pulling an envelope from his pocket. "It's a letter for Kate and you from Glasgow. It came in the post this morning." He handed the thick envelope to Schettler.

Schettler opened it to find six small pages written on both sides by his cousin Margaret and with them, another thick sealed envelope, with his name written on the front in a different hand.

He began to read Margaret's letter.

10th July 1919

Dear Ian and Kate,

I hope this letter finds you both well. We're certainly all in fine fettle here although Mother constantly complains of being tired and invariably goes off to bed at eight o'clock.

Our recent correspondence to each other has been justifiably guarded and superficial in its content but we've come to the conclusion that the unpleasant happenings surrounding the events in January are well behind us now and we are satisfied that our letters aren't being intercepted and read, so as you can see from the thickness of the envelope, I have decided to bring you up to date with what's going on here. Not that I have anything to write that's remotely interesting to the authorities. Charlie has also contributed and that's what's inside the other envelope.

Bob, who sends his kindest regards and best wishes to you both, has taken on a position of under manager in our family business, junior to Mr Rowantree. Since Father and Charles died, our solicitor has employed him to look after the business on our behalf. It's time the family took a greater interest in our own affairs and Bob's position as under manager will allow him to learn the business. He is also determined to take a course in accountancy at night school and there's one held in our local secondary school, Whitehill.

I was sorry to hear about the scuttling of the German Fleet at Scapa, Ian. I know, from talking to Charlie that was precisely what you didn't want, as it would weaken the bargaining position at Versailles and of course you

252

were proved right in your prediction. When the treaty was signed on the June 28, I was sickened to hear the extent of Article 231 – that Germany has to take total responsibility for all loss and damage caused by the war and pay vast financial reparations to the Allies. Of course it will now fall on the German people to account for the sins of the ruling classes. The fact that Germany has to disarm and lose many of its peripheral territories is less of a shock, since most were gained through earlier wars. However, I really cannot be the judge of that and would value your opinion.

Here in Glasgow, the troops have all gone. Most of them left during February but some were stationed around Glasgow till fairly recently. The strike was officially called off on Monday, February 10 but it wasn't a total failure. Although it didn't achieve its goal of a forty-hour week, a national agreement was reached with the Federation of Employers for a forty-seven hour week with no reduction of wages. That's a great step forward. No more do workers have to start work at six o'clock in the morning. I'm still outraged that almost two hundred activists and strikers ended up serving time in prison because they wanted a reduction in working hours and troops and tanks had to be used against them.

The forty-hour strike, while not a revolution, was the first rank and file agitation to be led by socialists since the war. This is just the beginning! There's a lot more to come. We've seen what lengths Churchill and his cronies will go to defeat us but next time we'll be better prepared.

Since then, there's been an unprecedented level of political discussion throughout the British Socialist

Movement with many advocating the formation of a revolutionary Leninist party, so we'll see what transpires. The next few months will be very exciting.

Leaving politics aside, I must say we loved your visit, Ian, as short as it was. There's seldom an evening goes by without the three of us discussing it. They were indeed exciting times.

I miss you very much, Kate, as our meetings are dull affairs without you there to wind them all up, although I do my best.

I have left out any reference to Charlie as he has written himself.

Lastly, we are going to write to your mother, Ian. Now that hostilities are finally over there can be no problem in doing so. We will let her know that you are well and in good spirits. I know she'll be very worried about you. I don't think it's wise for you to write from Ireland. Since the Casement affair, the British may still be interfering with letters for, so called, security reasons. If you disagree with my logic feel free to write to her yourself. Please write back to us soon and let us know that you are both well and what you're doing, if you can.

Your loving cousin, and friend.

Margaret

When he'd finished reading he thought he'd better get back to work, so he shoved the unopened envelope in his pocket. He would read it later.

After work was over for the day Schettler headed back to Rose Cottage, with a spring in his step. He was excited to let Kate see Margaret's letter.

When Johann had closed the front door of the cottage, he called out. "Guess what, Kate? We got a letter from Margaret. Seán delivered it this morning."

As he walked into the parlour, Kate, who was painting, just grunted and carried on. He waved the letter in front of her, but it was met with sullen indifference.

"What for dinner?" he asked cheerily.

She snapped. "All I've had time to prepare is soup. It needs to be heated up."

He nodded. "Soup's fine, I ate a substantial lunch courtesy of Lucy."

Kate exploded. "Well that's just bloody great for you, then, Ian, isn't it? As for me, I've had bugger all since breakfast."

This was only the second time Johann had seen her like this and remembering what she had been like the first time, he decided not to question the reason for her mood. "You carry on with your painting and I'll heat up the soup and then I'll make us some Speck und Spiegeleier. Gute deutsche Küche"

She glared at him. "What the hell does that mean?"

"Bacon and eggs, good German food."

"Oh, whatever you want," she said and turned back to her painting.

She had been at this painting for a week. It was a large canvas, five feet tall by three wide, and was the biggest they had made themselves. They were very proud of it. It was her first attempt at defining her thoughts straight on to canvas and it was a scene in George Square during the strike. The painting was dark and moody, almost abstract and Johann wondered if it had been getting under her skin.

He went to the kitchen and prepared the meal. When he called her through, she came quietly and kissed him before they sat down to eat, but still said nothing. After they had finished, she brightened a little and they discussed the painting, which she admitted was causing her difficulty. Somehow, he felt this wasn't the only reason for her mood.

He rose, walked around the table and put his arm around her shoulders. "What else is wrong, Liebling?" He could see a tear fall down her cheek – this was the first time he had seen her cry.

He bent over her. "What is it, Kate, what's happened?

"Remember the corporal we saw on the road to Tullamore? Well, he was here today," she sobbed and nestled her head in his arm. "I wasn't going to tell you, but he frightened me."

Schettler felt the sweat break out on his forehead and when he spoke it came out as a high-pitched squeak. "Did he do anything to you – did he hurt you?"

She shook her head and they stayed like that until she seemed to pull herself together. He sat down next to her at the table and said gently, "Tell me what happened."

She took a hanky, blew her nose and smiled. "Look I don't know why, I'm just being stupid about this. It wasn't much really."

"Just tell me what happened, Kate, I need to know," he said firmly.

"It was about half past ten and I had just finished making the soup when there was a loud knock on the door and it was that corporal. What was his name? I've been trying to remember all day."

"Dixon," Johann replied sharply.

"Ah yes, so Corporal Dixon was standing there and the truck with the same three soldiers was parked on the road. He asked if you were in and when I told you weren't, he smiled and asked if he could come in, calling me darlin'. When I said no, he started touching my face – oh – he was horrible, creepy," Kate said, with a shiver.

"I got angry and asked him what the hell he wanted, and he tried to force his way in. I was really worried. It was only when one of his men shouted that there was somebody coming, that he stopped and walked away. When he reached the gate, he shouted back that he knew where we lived."

Then she mimicked what he had said. "That fucking Glaswegian husband of yours better watch himself. We'll get the commie bastard. You just see if we don't." Then he jumped into the truck and they drove away. Less than a minute later, Charlie Leamas from up the road passed in his truck. They must have seen him coming and thank God, they did. I don't know what would have happened if they hadn't. Oh, Ian, he frightened me. How did he know where we lived?"

Johann bit his lip. "Because when they stopped us, he asked me where we were from and I had to tell him."

Kate nodded. "Oh of course, but how does he know your politics?"

Johann shook his head. "He doesn't – I think I was just an excuse to get to you. Remember what he said to me the last time."

"I suppose you're right, but what should we do?"

"The first thing we'll do is talk to Michael about it. See what he thinks."

Kate brightened. "Yes, he'll know what to do, right enough. He's coming round when he and Lucy get back from Birr. They stopped in at lunch time to see if they could pick up anything for us and I asked them to get a few things. You better show me the letter you got. I suppose it was from Mags?"

Johann fished the wad of paper from his pocket and handed it to her. Once she had found the order of pages she started reading, but she was interrupted by the arrival of Michael.

He walked into the kitchen carrying a box, which he deposited on the table and kissed his sister.

Kate asked him to sit down but he refused, saying Lucy was making supper and he'd have to get back. But Johann insisted. "Look, Michael, we need to talk. Something's happened today, and you need to know about it."

Michael eyes widened, as he sat down at the table and Kate began to tell her story.

When she had finished, she could see he was angry. "Bejesus, we'll not have that," he hissed.

"Shouldn't we inform the police?" said Schettler.

"Don't be naïve, Ian," Michael said contemptuously. "Where the British Army's concerned, the police will do nothing. They're on the same side, after all. No, we'll have to deal with it ourselves."

He thought for a moment, then said, "We'll get the boys in Birr to identify them – where they go – when there're off duty – and then we might show them that behaviour like that won't be tolerated. You two just leave this to me. In the meantime, Ian, Seán and I will keep an eye on the comings and goings around here and if we see anything, we'll be here in a jiffy."

He bent over and kissed Kate on the forehead. "Don't you worry about this now, me darlin'. Right then I better go. I'll see you tomorrow, Ian."

When Michael had gone, Johann and Kate sat looking at each other not knowing what to say, until Kate lifted the letter and started reading again. This reminded Schettler that he hadn't read Charlie's so he pulled the envelope from his pocket, tore it open and began to read.

10th July 1919

Dear Ian,

As Margaret's mother would say, I'm on leave again! This time it's because the Emperor of India is pulling out of Scapa next week and sailing to Malta. I'm sure you must know that your Admiral Reuter had your entire fleet scuttled. What you probably don't know, as it's not been made public and I regret to be the one to tell you, is that nine unarmed German sailors died of gunshot wounds and sixteen more were wounded, shot in their lifeboats as they tried to escape from their sinking ships. The only tangible reason for this happening was panic on behalf of our navy. Another 1,774 officers and men are now being held throughout the country as prisoners of war, and yet Britain is not at war with Germany. I know you were always against this action being taken by your High Command. You made that plain to me many times. I believe that there was a proposal at Versailles that the High Seas Fleet should be split amongst the Allies, to set against the cost of reparations, but I am led to believe this was vetoed by the British.

Three months ago, I re-enlisted for two years and I know

you're aware of the reasons why I felt this was the right thing to do. However, after this event, I feel no pride in being a serving Senior Warrant Officer in the Royal Navy.

I've never been one to believe in conspiracies, Ian, but I have to admit it seems highly suspicious to me that our whole fleet, battleships, cruisers and destroyers stationed to guard the High Seas Fleet, left their post early on the morning of the 21st June, to carry out an exercise, leaving only a few armed trawlers and drifters on guard duty. Rumours had been circulating within both navies for a week or so, and as you know only too well being carried back and forward between us, that Reuter was planning to scuttle sometime soon. Some of my shipmates were making bets that when we returned to Scapa it would be empty. How right they were, even although we had to turn back after only a few hours at sea.

Going back now to our escapade in January. As we expected, I completed my journey from Perth to the Emperor without further incident. When I arrived on board, I managed to replace Gordon's uniform and pay book in his locker without any trouble. The next day his locker was searched because it's next to my own, but nothing was found to be missing. That leads me to believe someone had enquired about his whereabouts and circumstances. I was never asked any questions about it, so that's how things were left. After Gordon was released from hospital, he was also asked to re-enlist which he did. It seems they're short of Warrant Officers.

A couple of weeks later, I received a message through the black-market boys that your friend, Karl Brand, wanted to see me urgently on board the Freddy, so I went across there in the usual way. When I met him, he told me your name was down on the roster for immediate repatriation along with himself and all the members of the executive of your Soldiers' Council. He said this had been forced upon them. He also told me Reuter had moved his flag ship to the Cruiser, Emden, and because the Red Guard had taken control on board the Freddy, a state of anarchy now existed. He assured me that everything was so chaotic that no one will be aware that you had disappeared, and he said he was glad you got out when you had the opportunity.

You have a very good friend there, Ian. He was anxious to know you were safe and well. We went to the mess and over a good bottle of German brandy, I told him what had happened in Glasgow. I didn't realise he spoke a little English, but he told me he had learned it in America before the war.

Talking of friends, I was shocked to learn that my friend Gerry O'Brien had been knocked over and killed after running into the path of an army truck that fateful Friday. Margaret told me she'd read about it in the papers. This was nonsense of course, because he had been taken to Barlinnie with me and Bob. We can only speculate what really happened to him.

I'm going to miss Margaret very much. I'll be away a lot, I fear, but at least it gives me some more time in employment to amass some money. When I finally leave the Navy, I want us to live together. We can't get married without her having to leave teaching and she wouldn't want that. Alas, unless the law is changed, we're caught in this trap. I'm sorry to sound so glum but when I leave here next week, it's likely I won't see her again for almost a year and that's going to be difficult.

Finally, I must say that I hold our friendship in very high regard. It was a pleasure knowing you, Ian, and I hope we will meet again someday, perhaps in happier times.

My kindest regards to you and Kate.

Yours sincerely

Charlie Tennant

When Schettler had finished reading, he went through to the parlour. It was strewn with paints and paintings in various states of completion and he too, attempted to paint. His theme was Ireland, colourful and vibrant, but in his present melancholy frame of mind, he couldn't face it, so he asked Kate if she wanted to go for a walk in the evening sunshine and was glad when she said she would.

The next morning as the three men continued to work on the fencing, Michael sent Seán back to the barn for some more nails. When the lad had gone, Michael handed a heavy brown paper bag to Schettler. "You better take that and carry it around with you, from now on."

Inside there was a Smith and Wesson service revolver and a box of cartridges. Schettler looked at Michael.

"Don't stare at me like that, Ian," Michael said, "you don't know when these bastards will be back or what they'll do if they come back. I know you said you wouldn't kill people you have no fight with, but they look like they want a fight with you, don't they?"

"I think this corporal was trying to have his way with Kate."

"You better hold on to that gun then, for I sure as hell don't want anything happening to my sister, and I hope you don't either?"

"Of course, I don't." He put the package in his jacket pocket.

"I suppose you know how to use and maintain it."

Schettler nodded.

Throughout the next few weeks a careful watch was kept on Kate, with Schettler even going back to the cottage at lunch time, while in Birr, the local IRB had done their homework. They had identified the soldiers and now had a complete picture of what they did while off duty, which was usually drinking in Nolan's Bar along with a number of their comrades. This practice was not discouraged by Nolan, a staunch republican. It was a good source of intelligence about the army and what they were doing in the area. The IRB had asked what Michael wanted done about Corporal Dixon and his men, but he had decided since no other incident had taken place and as they hadn't even been seen in the area, they should be left alone, at least for the time being.

Chapter 23

August was almost over. More than a month had elapsed since the incident at Rose Cottage and they all began to drop their guard.

When Michael proposed a repeat trip to deliver sheep to the abattoir in Tullamore, Johann and Kate jumped at it. They set off before nine o'clock and reached Quigley's by ten twenty, offloaded their cargo and got to the town centre in plenty time for shopping before lunch, although as with the previous visit to Mullins, it took some time to pick up the art materials they had ordered.

Unusually, the sun had shone for almost two months and there was no sign of a change in the weather, so Kate bought a wide-brimmed hat. They both had Guinness with lunch, a half pint for her, but as he had become rather partial to this drink, he had two pints. In consequence, he felt a little tipsy, so he suggested a walk along the Grand Canal, to clear his head.

They ambled along the flat tow path out of town and passed one set of locks with only the sound of the birds to break the silence. It was pleasant and as they watched swans, ducks and coots gliding through the water. Johann talked to Kate about their paintings. He was excited that he could complete some pictures with the new colours. After they had walked a couple of miles, they saw a stone bridge which crossed the canal and when they got closer they could see two men swimming close by. Schettler looked at his watch and found it was twenty past three, so they turned and started back towards town.

A voice rang out behind them. "Oi! You there, stop, stop right now."

As the couple turned to look, two soldiers were running towards them, holding their rifles. As the men caught up with Johann and Kate, one shouted, "Look who we've got here, Bert. It's the fucking Glaswegian communist and his beautiful wife." They pointed their rifles at the couple, and forced them to turn and walk towards the bridge.

"Where the hell are you taking us?" Kate shouted angrily.

"We're taking you to see Corporal Dixon. He's going to be very happy to see you darlin'. He really fancies you – he just can't stop talking about ya."

Kate quickly turned and tried to run but one of the soldiers grabbed her. As he did so, Schettler aimed a punch to the side of his face, knocking him to the ground and almost into the canal. However, the other soldier hit him hard on the neck with the butt of his rifle knocking him flat on his back, where he lay with his head swimming until he was yanked to his feet.

Seeing the commotion, the corporal and the other soldier came running up wearing only their dripping shorts. Dixon grinned. "If it isn't our friendly Glaswegian and his lovely wife. Aren't we glad to see them, boys?" They manhandled the couple back to their truck, parked by the side of a ruined canal building opposite the bridge.

Dixon spat out, "You take that bastard and show him what we think of Glaswegians and after that show him what we think of fucking communists." Then in a quieter tone, that was no less threatening, "And when you're doin' that, me and Alf here'll have a nice, friendly chat with his missus."

The two soldiers dragged Schettler, still groggy, into the bushes beside the tow path and the others, still only in their wet shorts, dragged Kate kicking and screaming into the ruined building.

They took it in turns to hold Schettler, while the other aimed well placed punches at his face and body. He could hear Kate screaming from the building – a sound which became less audible as he began to lose consciousness.

They finally let him go and as he fell to the ground, in his mind he saw the face of Kalb shouting, "Sie sind ein kommunistischer Bastard, Schettler." The soldiers continued to aim kicks at his body. When his assailants had finished with him and walked off, he heard one say, "I thought that cunt was mumblin' in a foreign language just there, Frank."

"That'll have been Gaelic, Bert. They speak it here as well as there you know."

"Where's there?"

"Where he comes from, Scotland, you fucking plonker."

"Oh. It sounds like German, then."

"Yeah, prob-ly does."

When Schettler came too, he crawled over to the base of a tree, pulled himself up on his feet and leant there while he tried to focus his brain. Once again, it was his stomach that hurt the most but when he looked down he saw spots of blood hit the ground. Touching his face, he could feel blood trickling from his nose and mouth. He checked his teeth. They seemed intact but as his hand moved to his chin, the pain was intense. He tried to look at his watch, but his left eye had almost completely closed, and he couldn't focus.

The memory of Kate's screams came flooding back and he thrust himself forward and staggered towards the canal. He got there in time to see the truck turning the corner beyond the bridge and disappearing through the trees, its retreat punctuated by the sound of laughter. He tried to shout Kate's name, but all that came out was a squeak, barely audible. He staggered to the building and looked through the gap that had once been the door and saw her sitting flat on the ground up against the far wall. Her legs were splayed out in front of her, her clothes ripped, and her knickers torn and still at her knees. All he could hear was her sobbing.

He lunged towards her. "Aw Kate, what have they done to you?" and touched her shoulder. She looked up and screamed, "Take your fuckin' hands off me." He yanked his hand away in fright, turned and heaved himself down beside her. He burst into tears, not for himself, but for what they had done to her.

They sat saying nothing for some time until Kate moved and began to sort herself. Finally, she stood up, looked at him and gasped. "Oh my God, what have they done to you?" She bent down and gently touched his face, but he winced, so she withdrew her hand.

"Can you walk?" We need to get out of here." He nodded and pulled himself up with the support of the wall.

Schettler tried to wash his face in the canal but his legs were too sore to kneel, so they started walking. It took them two hours to get back to the truck. As they walked through the streets of Tullamore, some people asked if they needed help and others just stared at them in horror, but they just walked on saying nothing.

The drive back to Clonony took four hours because Schettler could barely see and the pain he was suffering meant he had to stop the truck many times to rest and stretch.

It was fortunate it was still a bright, sunny evening. Kate kept talking to him, to try to lift his spirits, mostly about painting and how happy they'd been and how this incident would make no difference to that. Inside though, she felt sick and dirty and she knew all too well that life wouldn't be the same, at least not for some time. They abandoned the truck at Rose Cottage and Kate helped Schettler inside and sat him down. Then she changed her dress quickly and walked up to Teach Feirme Baile to fetch Michael.

Sitting at the kitchen table alone, Schettler's mind raced. He had left the revolver at home that morning in case the truck was searched either by the police or the army. If it had been found, they would have been arrested. But what if he had taken it? Under the circumstances he couldn't have carried it without it being seen, in Tullamore or on their walk, because all he was wearing was a shirt and trousers. Even if he had been able to devise some hiding place, he knew it would have been of little use against the soldiers' rifles. He still felt terrible guilt at his inability to protect the woman he loved. Fury swept over him. He needed to avenge this unspeakable barbarism and he needed to do it quickly. In the half-dark stillness, he roared and his eyes filled with tears.

Michael came back with Kate immediately, but as they walked to Rose Cottage, she refused to tell him what had happened, preferring that he should see the results for himself.

It was dark and still, and all Michael could see in the gloom of the kitchen was Schettler's dark figure sitting at the table. Kate went to light the lamp and Michael shouted, "Bejesus, will one of yees tell me what the hell's goin' on?" Kate turned up the light, illuminating the room and Michael stared, in horror, at Schettler's face.

Schettler mumbled, "Don't bother about me. Your sister's been raped. It was that bastard, Dixon. We'll have to get him. I want to go to Birr tonight."

Michael could have happily conformed to Schettler's desire to go straight to Birr. Inside, every sinew was shaking but he knew he had to keep himself calm. "You're in no condition to go anywhere tonight. We'll get the bastards alright but right now the two of you will have to come to the house. You can't stay here. Kate ma darling, you should have told me sooner. Are you all right for God sake? You need Lucy's help and I need to fetch Doctor Murray for you both."

As Michael helped the two out to the truck and drove them up the road to the house, Schettler was still declaring, somewhat feverishly, that now he was involved, he needed to get to Birr.

Michael returned with the doctor later that night. He found that Kate had no lasting internal damage, but there was bruising around the top of her legs and genitals which made it uncomfortable to walk. He fully expected this to subside in a week or so. The psychological effect of this brutal attack, however, would take much longer to heal – if ever. Schettler, on the other hand, had three broken ribs, a broken nose and two black eyes, a distended stomach and bruising to more than half of his body. How he managed to drive the truck earlier that evening was a matter of wonderment to the people around him. The doctor said as he was young he would heal quickly.

*

Schettler was laid up in Teach Feirme Baile for three days, following the attack. On the second evening, he asked to see Michael and Kate together. When they entered his room, he got straight to the point. "I told you before, Michael, I want to be the one to deal with these bastards, and I mean it. As soon as I'm fit, I want to go to Birr to take care of it."

Michael shook his head. "That's not possible, Ian. I shouldn't really be telling you this but the only reason the IRB have sanctioned these assassinations is that there's been a directive from the National Executive, or perhaps Collins himself. We must embark on a campaign to create a general state of disorder around the country. If we target these four soldiers, I've argued we're sticking to that directive and that allows us to get justifiable revenge for what they did to you two. But it will have to be done efficiently and certainly not by you, Ian. You're far too emotionally involved and would probably make mistakes."

Schettler was undaunted. "What you're saying makes sense, Michael, but there's no way to avoid the conclusion that I was responsible, and I failed in my duty. I need to make up for that."

Kate looked horrified. "Are you trying to say you think you have a duty of responsibility for me, Ian?"

"Yes, of course I have. I love you and I let you down."

Kate's face flushed. She spoke through gritted teeth. "Well, you're about as bad as that bastard Dixon and his thugs, for it's your masculinity that's been dented for not being able to protect your property against other men. Well,

I'm no body's feckin' property, nor am I an object that you need to protect. I'm a free-thinking human being and if there's any avengin' needin' to be carried out, then it's me that should do it."

Schettler was livid. "That's ridiculous, I don't think of you either as my property or an object, but surely it's natural to want to protect the person you love? Anyway, you've never shot anyone in your life – you need training to use a gun. I've used one, so it makes sense that I should be the one to do it."

Kate spat out, "Don't be stupid—"

Michael held up his hand. "Shut up. Enough's enough. I just told you there's no way either of you is getting involved in this. Everything of this nature has to go through our local executive and there's no way that would be sanctioned, so forget it. Just cool off and let us deal with it and be happy when it's done. Then you'll have your revenge." He turned and made for the door. "But don't expect it to happen for a while yet, mind."

Kate remained sitting on Schettler's bed and when they were alone she spoke once again in a matter of fact tone, "I'm getting out of here, Ian. I've had enough of this inactivity. I'm off to Dublin where I should have been months ago."

"When you say you, Kate, does that mean you alone, or am I included?" Schettler tried to stop himself sounding fractious.

"You can do what you like. If you want to come, come, if you don't you can always stay here."

And with that she rose and walked out the room.

A week later Johann and Kate were driven to Tullamore station to catch the ten nineteen train to Dublin. Each had packed a suitcase – essentials for life for an, as yet, unspecified length of stay in the city.

Michael wished the still battered and bruised couple a safe journey. "Now you've got the papers I gave you for the big fellah in a safe place? After you've seen him, perhaps you'll be able to let me know who's running things over there, him, de Valera or Cathal Brugha. It would be good to know who's handin' out the orders these days."

Chapter 24

Sinn Fein's office at 76, Harcourt Street, was locked when Kate and Schettler arrived, although it was a normal working day and they stood around on the front steps wondering what they should do. Eventually, a young man opened the door and, Kate confronted him. "Is this the offices of Sinn Fein?"

The young man looked suspicious. "Who wants to know?"

"My name's Kate A'Herne from County Offaly and this is my friend, Ian. We would like a word with the big fellah."

"I don't know who you mean," the young man said and made to move on.

"Sure you do. It's Michael Collins I'm talking about. My brother gave me some papers to deliver to him."

The man's gaze fell on Schettler and he looked him up and down. "It looks like you've been in a fight, my friend."

Before Schettler could answer, Kate said, "Sure, he just had a wee altercation with the British Army."

The young man nodded. "I'll take the papers and see to it that they're delivered."

"You'll do nothing of the sort. I've been told to deliver them personally by my brother Michael and that's what I intend to do."

"Tell me again, who your brother is?"

"Michael A'Herne of Home Farm, Clonony in County Offaly. The big fellah knows him fine."

The man weighed up the couple. "All right, go round the corner to Connelly's Bar and wait a bit," he said, pointing to the adjacent street. "I'll get back to you as soon as I can." And he turned and walked off towards the city.

They sat in the bar for over an hour toying with two half pints of Guinness, while Schettler looked at his watch every few minutes. He was concerned that they still had to find a place to stay for the short term, until they found jobs and somewhere permanent to live.

Eventually, the young man came into the bar and invited them to come with him immediately. Entering the fine, Georgian building, he said that Collins could see them for fifteen minutes if they allowed their cases to be searched.

When they were shown into Collins's office, the 'big fellah' jumped to his feet and walked round his desk beaming. Schettler was surprised to see a man not much older than himself and although they were roughly the same height, Collins looked taller and certainly broader. He was good looking with a full head of brown hair on top of a round face with a strong jaw, but his strongest feature was his piercing blue eyes.

He took Kate's hand. "How is me old friend, Michael, these days, Kate? I'll have to go up that way soon. It's been too long since I've seen these fine fellows, good comrades all of them." Without waiting for a reply, he went on, "Now who's your friend? You'll introduce me to this hooligan who goes brawling with the British Army."

Unfazed, Kate replied, "This is Johann Schettler, Mr Collins, who till last January was a member of the Soldiers' Council of the German High Seas Fleet stationed at Scapa

Flow in Orkney. Why he's here is a long story, but we have the time to tell it, if you have the time to listen."

"Just call me Michael. How do you do, Johann. I must say, I'm taken aback." He pointed to the young man still with them in the room. "Pat here, told me your name was Ian."

"Yes, it's both." Schettler gave Collins a reassuring smile. "I suppose that's part of the story."

Collins cried, "Bejesus, now you're sounding more Scottish than German. Sure you've got me so intrigued, I'll have to listen to your story. Give Pat the papers your brother sent me, Kate, and we'll settle down over a cup a tea."

Over the next half hour Collins listened to their story – sometimes interrupting to ask questions, particularly about their ties with Glasgow and why Schettler had come to Ireland and not back to Germany to fight for socialism, and finally about the brutal attack on the couple by the British soldiers.

When they had finished he said, "You're both here to work for the cause then. Well, that's very providential. Your identities aren't known around here, so you'll be mighty useful in gaining intelligence from the British, although, the fact that you're German, Johann, is something we'll keep to ourselves. Just keep using Ian Nairn, from Glasgow."

Collins stood up. "Right then, I suggest you meet with Pat two days from now. He'll arrange the time and place with you and by then we'll have worked out something for you to do. It's no good coming here because it's often watched, although it's not today. Lucky that, isn't it, given how you tried to get in." Collin's winked at his guests.

Kate shrugged, then went on to say they were looking for jobs and somewhere to stay, and was told that they would probably be fixed up with both, when they met Pat.

On their way out, not only did Pat give them a time and location for their meeting but also the address of a good, cheap boarding house, belonging to a sympathiser, where they could stay in the mean-time.

When they arrived at their digs, a terraced, town house in Herbert Place, the landlady, Mrs Duffy, seemed to be expecting them. When she showed them to their room, she made a quip, "I'm presuming you're married, so I'm putting you in a double room. Will that be acceptable?"

"Yes, quite acceptable," Schettler answered. Kate stared at him in silence.

When they were alone in the room, Schettler said, "I couldn't help seeing your look of disgust, when I said that a double room was fine."

Kate shook her head. "It wasn't disgust, Ian. It's just that I'm not ready to have sex with you yet. I hope you understand that."

"Of course, I understand," Schettler said. "You know you can take as long as you like."

He put his arms around her. "I love you, you know," but she pushed him away. "Yes, I know that, but you'll have to give me some space for now. Every time you come near, I feel I can't breathe. I know it's not your fault and I feel so guilty about that, too. Perhaps it would have been better if I had come to Dublin on my own – oh. I don't know. I'm just completely confused. In my mind I keep seeing that man leering at me as he deliberately hurt me. I'm sorry." Her voice broke and the tears stung her eyes.

Schettler sat on the bed and tried to deal with how he felt. Inside him, anger mounted – anger at not being able to prevent the soldiers from raping her, anger that he couldn't neutralise her fears, anger that she seemed to lump him in with the rest of mankind and guilt that he harboured such selfish feelings.

"Take all the time you need, Kate. We'll get through this together." He forced himself to smile. "Anyway, it looks like Mr Collins wants to keep us busy, so there probably won't be much time to think about ourselves."

They had a free day before they were due to meet the young Sinn Fein man, so Kate gave Schettler a tour of the city. This also served to remind her of its layout and the location of the places of importance. The weather was overcast but it was still warm, with no sign of rain so they were able to relax and enjoy the experience and not allow the recent incident to dominate their thoughts.

*

When Johann and Kate walked through the door of McCrea's Bar, a dingy, old pub in Forbes Street close to the docks, they were hit by a haze of pipe smoke. Little light was able to penetrate the dirty windows, even on such a bright day. The stark walls were yellow caused by the constant level of tarry smoke and the only decoration was a series of dirty mirrors advertising beer, whiskey and tobacco. The occupants, who propped up the dark brown counter, turned and stared at them. As soon as the barman noticed their arrival, he immediately shouted belligerently in Gaelic. Kate guided Johann into a small, six feet high, partitioned area built around the end of the bar. The barman glared at them and Kate asked for a pint and a half of Guinness, and he turned grumbling, towards the beer taps. While the porter was being poured, Johann asked her what was going on.

"He doesn't like women in his bar and it looks like none of the regulars do either, so we can only sit in here – it's called the snug. He was talking to you and he said I'd better not want to use the toilet because they don't have one for women."

The barman planted the two drinks heavily on the counter.

"Is that pint for me?" Johann asked. "I didn't want that much, so early in the day."

"In a pub like this," Kate said, "if you want a half pint you have to have a whiskey with it, so just pay the man, Ian. That's your prerogative."

They had just settled themselves when Pat appeared with a pint already in his hand. He sat down beside them and whispered he was going to speak in Gaelic and Kate could translate their conversation to Schettler later.

An intense discussion followed in low voices which became heated at times. Schettler could see that Kate didn't always agree with everything Pat proposed. In the end Pat handed her a sheet of typed paper, drained his pint, shook their hands and left.

Schettler opened his mouth to ask what had been said, but Kate shushed him, stood up and started out the bar, with him having to scramble behind her. On the street, she turned back in the direction of the boarding house and, after a couple of minutes, she explained what had been said.

Pat had told her to answer an advert in the Irish Independent for vacancies for clerical staff in the Lord Lieutenant's office in Dublin Castle. He gave her the text of a letter, including the pseudonym she should use for the application, which she should copy out in her own hand. He told her that she would get the job if she got to the stage of an interview and the letter was worded in a way that would get her to that stage, as Mr Ronald Burgess, the civil servant who carried out the interviews, was partial to young women.

When she started work, she should expect to have her bottom pinched daily, but she should ignore this, work hard and try to ingratiate herself, particularly with the male staff. He also explained after six months or so she would be transferred into the section that dealt with the translation of coded messages sent from London for the British Secret Service working in Ireland. If they were lucky, she would be transferred to the British Army Intelligence Centre in Benburb Street, or if not, it would be the GPO in Sackville Street. When Kate asked why he was so confident that this transfer would take place, Pat told her they already had contacts there with significant influence in these matters, but were not in the position to do the job themselves. She asked how she would pass the information on and was told that she would find that out in good time.

Kate became silent for some time while they continued walking. Finally, she spoke again hesitantly. "Look, Ian, the truth is, I'm not sure you're going to like what they've got lined up for you. All they can offer is a job driving a truck for a company called Murphy and Sons, a wholesale greengrocer in Cork Street. The Murphys are activists and you wouldn't just be delivering vegetables around the greengrocers of Dublin but moving arms, passing on confidential messages and anything else that might be required. There's no doubt that it's potentially a dangerous job."

She stopped again not quite sure how he would take what she next had to tell him. "The other thing he told me is that they don't want us to live together until I've been doing the job for at least a couple of months. See, my application will say that I'm single and unattached. That's their preference."

Schettler couldn't hide his surprise. "What the hell's that about?"

She shook her head. "Look, I don't like it either. That was what we were arguing about in the pub – but he said if we were together, it could jeopardise my security in the office. They sometimes watch new employees very closely for a while and I suppose he's right. Don't take it personally."

"I'm going to be stuck in a city I don't know, and I'll not even be able to see you!" Schettler looked devastated. "What's going to happen to us? Oh, for God sake, how do you expect me to take it?"

They were back at the digs and the conversation had to stop until they reached their room. Kate put her arms around him. "Nothing's going to happen to us, Ian. We love each other, don't we?"

He nodded.

"Well then, everything will be fine. It won't be long until the security around my job is over and we can find a place together." She reached up and kissed him. "What do you say?"

How quickly Kate had given in to Collins' demands! Why was he in Ireland at all? Schettler tried to stifle his unworthy thoughts.

Kate pushed him down on the bed and allowed him to make love to her, even if her recent ordeal still made it difficult.

The next week, Schettler started work driving for Murphy and moved to another digs in Ivy Terrace, not far from his work in Cork Street. His landlady, Mrs Reilly, was a widow, who in the best local tradition, provided rooms with bed, breakfast and evening meal for young working men, mostly from out of town.

Kate stayed where she was in Herbert Place. She meticulously wrote out the letter to the Lord Lieutenant's Department and delivered it personally to Dublin Castle. A week later, she received a reply asking her to attend an interview. As Pat predicted, it was successful and two weeks later she started working in Dublin Castle in the name of Elizabeth McDonnagh.

*

"Oh thank you, Mr Burgess,"

Burgess had delivered some papers for processing and was now bent over Elizabeth, rubbing his left hand up and down the back of her blouse, while leering at her, his face only inches away from hers. As she had been warned, she was subjected to frequent encounters of this kind, each making her skin crawl. Sometimes, she was hard pressed to prevent herself from screaming. What she hadn't been warned about was his bad breath, which made her feel sick.

"You're a lovely girl, Elizabeth. I wish you'd change your mind about coming for a drink with me," Burgess said, in his broad Ulster accent.

"I couldn't do that, Mr Burgess. The nuns at my convent school always told me the pub was no place for God-fearing women, and in any case if I went for a drink with you, what would your wife say?"

Burgess jerked his body upright. "You just suit yourself then." He stomped off. After he had disappeared into his office, she wondered if her forthrightness could land her in trouble, but she had to do something to try to discourage him.

She left work as usual that evening at five thirty, with the throng of many other Castle employees. It was cold but dry and as she walked down the busy pavement towards her tram stop in Dame Street, she heard a female voice behind her calling, "Coo-ee!" As she turned she saw a young woman, caught in the light of the street lamp, waving as she ran towards her. She was someone who also worked in one of the adjacent rooms in the Castle. When the woman caught up, she greeted Kate with a bright smile. "Hello, I'm glad I caught you. I'm Kitty O'Connell. I work just down the corridor from you. You're quite new, aren't you? I've been meaning to introduce myself for a while."

Kate put out her hand. "How do you do, I'm Elizabeth McDonnagh."

They shook hands. "Yes, I know who you are. If you're not in a hurry, we could go round to Brown Thomas in Grafton Street for a cup of tea and a chat? Please say you will, Elizabeth."

Kate wasn't in a hurry to get back to her digs so she agreed and the young women changed course towards Grafton Street.

As they walked on, the crowd of office workers began to thin out. Looking behind her, Kitty checked that no one was within earshot. "Listen, Elizabeth, I'm really here to pass you a message from Frank Thornton. He gathers the information we pick up for the intelligence operation. He needs to speak to you tonight. He'll be calling in to my place in Meath Place at eight o'clock, so that still gives time for that cup of tea and a chat."

The two young women had talked animatedly throughout their tea at Brown Thomas's department store, both realising that they had much in common beyond the politics of an independent Ireland.

Back at Meath Place, the women sat in the small kitchen on old leather chairs, at either end of the large, black, iron range which dominated the room making it look dark, even although Kitty had tried to brighten it up by painting the walls with a light cream distemper.

At three minutes past eight, there was a loud knock on the outside door which led straight into the kitchen. Kitty opened the door to a small, thin man who looked in his early thirties, with a shock of bright, red hair. He brushed past her without a word of greeting and sat down on one of the four chairs which surrounded the rather dilapidated, oak table, the only other furniture in the room.

He didn't look at either of them. "Kitty, me darlin', it would be better if you didn't hear what I need to say to Elizabeth, so why don't you go up to your room and I'll give you a shout when we're finished? It won't take long and then we can all have a nice cup of tea."

Kitty nodded. "Right you are then, Frank." She walked across to the narrow stair, situated at the far end of the kitchen.

Thornton didn't speak until he heard Kitty's bedroom door close above them.

"Elizabeth, I'm handling any information you come across in the next few weeks. It won't be much until you're transferred to somewhere where there's access to sensitive material. In the short term, though, there may be jobs we ask you to do for us. That's why I would like you to move in here with Kitty."

Kate nodded. "That suits me fine, Frank. It's pretty lonely sitting night after night on my own and Kitty and I seem to have hit it off pretty well."

"That's great then, me darlin'."

Kate bristled. "Look, Frank, let's get one thing straight. I'm nobody's darlin' and you won't get anywhere trying to patronise me. Just treat me like any other soldier fighting for the cause and we'll get along fine, understand?"

"Fine by me!" Thornton said sullenly. "Let me explain a few ground rules. I call in here every night to check whether you, or Kitty, have information for me. This is better than having to meet somewhere else and needlessly draw attention to us together. There are other people too who'll come with information from time to time but Kitty can give you the low down on them. Is that all right with you?" Kate nodded.

"If anyone asks you about me, just tell them Kitty and I are walking out together. You and Kitty won't discuss anything to do with the information you're gathering as a matter of security. The less you know, the less you can tell the Brits if you are picked up. Is that all clear?"

Kate nodded again.

"The last thing I have to tell you is that we've had word from your brother, Michael that the four soldiers have now been taken care of. I suppose that will be a relief to you."

Kate was shocked to hear this news and surprised at how much Thornton obviously knew about her. She pulled herself together.

"So, *are* you?"

Thornton looked puzzled. "So am I, what?

"Walkin' out together?"

"No, we're not."

"She's not your darlin' either, then." She allowed herself to smile. "Listen, Frank, now that we understand each other, we can surely be friends?"

Thornton lowered his head and smiled. "Ah, sure we can. Oh, I was asked to give you this." He pulled a blank, manila envelope from his coat pocket and handed it to her before shouting in the direction of the staircase, "Kitty, we're finished here. You can come down now."

Later that evening when she had returned to her digs in Herbert Place, Kate opened the envelope to find a letter from her brother.

Mo deirfiúr daor

Tá mé ag scríobh chugat...

My dear sister,

I'm writing to you in a mood of elation because I'm no longer encarserated in His Majesty's Prison. How I got out is too long a story for this letter. I'm lying low at the moment until the IRA decides it's safe for me to emerge once again. Be reassured, I'm still contributing to the cause in a clandestine way, as I know you are yourself. I hope to be able to visit you soon and I'm just waiting for a suitable opportunity to do so. I am longing to see you again and hopefully hear news of Michael and the rest of the family who, alas, know nothing of my whereabouts.

For the sake of security, please destroy this letter as soon as you've read it.

Your loving brother

Liam

She placed the letter in the hearth, struck a match and set it on fire. Tears rolled down her cheeks. She was happy to hear from Liam and she hoped he would visit soon but that feeling contrasted and jarred with the news of the soldiers. The thoughts of the rape and the state of Ian's face in its aftermath, dominated her thoughts and she ran over to the sideboard and vomited into her washing bowl.

Chapter 25

Schettler hated the six-day grind imposed by his job driving for Murphy and Sons. He had to be up and dressed by four o'clock, prepare his own breakfast and walk to the depot for four forty five.

After their visit to the fruit market, the day's orders of fruit and vegetables had to be sorted out and loaded up. Then he set off with Tim Murphy, to make the deliveries around the city's greengrocers. As this was being done, the consignments of arms and ammunition arrived by various means and after lunch the truck was used, while collecting vegetables from farms surrounding the city, to deliver them wherever they were required. Stores of arms were never left in the depot overnight in case the G men raided the premises.

On the Saturday at the end of his second week, the Murphy boys told Schettler they had some news for him but jibed that they would only pass it on, if he joined them on their night's drinking.

Anxious to find out what they had to tell him and for something to do to break the monotony and loneliness, he agreed to join them.

The first pub they visited was Mulligan's in Poolbeg Street. They ordered Guinness and went over to stand at the fire burning in the hearth opposite, warming their backsides. None of them were wearing overcoats to protect against the evening's inclement weather.

"Right, I'm out with you. Tell me the news," Schettler said, as he rubbed his hands together. He wondered if it was a message from Kate.

"Ach, sure, we'll tell you later. It's time to get a few Guinness's down your neck and enjoy yourself," Alex said, slapping him hard on the back.

Rather than spoil the evening with an argument so early on, Schettler decided to go along with it.

The boys were in good form and in the mood for drinking. They managed to put away two pints for every one Schettler drank and soon their loud banter was spilling over to others around as their repertoire of jokes came thick and fast and laughter now pervaded the area.

Alex, the older of the two, was the most prolific and he held his audience spell bound with his stories.

"Did you hear about me Cousin Michael Murphy..."and when he delivered the punch line the whole bar went into an uproar. During the next hour, the jokes came hurtling back and forward across the room. While Schettler was consuming his third pint, Alex said, "Let's get out of here. I want to listen to a bit of music." They downed their beer and headed to Ruggy O'Donohoe's in Wicklow Street.

The pub they entered was called the International Bar. "I thought you said we were going to somewhere called Ruggy O'Donohoe's?" Schettler said.

"Well, this is Ruggy's," shouted Pat, as the full sound of an Irish jig blared out at them.

"But it's called the International Bar," Schettler shouted back.

"Sure, but we know it as Ruggy's. Ruggy O'Donohoe used to own it."

It was Schettler's round and he delivered more pints of Guinness to the boys who ridiculed him for his lack of stamina as he had bought nothing for himself, preferring not to spend his Sunday off with a hangover.

Eventually, the band stopped for a break and Alex decided to sing a song, choosing the Foggy Dew which had been banned by the British.

As down the glen one Easter morn to a city fair rode I... and slowly people began to join in until by the second verse the entire clientele were singing their hearts out.

When it finished, the bar returned to normal and the buzz of conversation started again. A posse of barmen descended on Schettler and the Murphys and ordered them to leave. The two brothers attempted to defend themselves but as they were outnumbered two to one, all three found themselves on the street.

"Right then," said Alex undaunted, "let's go down to Davy Byrne's in Duke Street." He made to walk down Wicklow Street but Schettler stopped him. "No, I've had enough, I'm going home."

"What!" Alex peered at his watch. "The night's still young. We've got a bit to go yet."

Schettler shook his head. "Not me, you two go if you like. But before you go, I'd appreciate if you'd tell me my news."

Alex sulked. "Well, since you're clearin' off – I suppose I had better tell you. You'll be delighted to hear that your four soldiers have been taken care of," he said, drawing his fore finger along his neck, from right to left. "The news just came in from the big man today."

The news surprised Schettler. He hadn't expected to hear it from that source, which as he now reflected, lacked any form of privacy or security. What if the Murphys had bawled it out in the pub?

A few weeks had elapsed since the attack and Schettler's feelings had mellowed. However much those soldiers deserved it, the thought of them being executed on behalf of him and Kate was upsetting. The realisation that he once wanted to do it himself made him feel sick, although that was probably compounded by the Guinness.

He had just passed St Stephens Green when he heard the engine of a vehicle behind him. It overtook him on the road and stopped ahead of him. It was Dublin Metropolitan Police. Two constables jumped out, walked across the deserted street and as one grabbed his arm, the other gruffly asked him if he had been in the International Bar with two other men a while back. Schettler didn't know whether to say yes or no, but when he heard the brothers singing inside, he said he had, so he too was taken to the van.

At the station, the three men were escorted to a holding cell which was already occupied by two equally drunken individuals. Schettler stood looking on, as the four continued to sing.

They had only been there for a few minutes when a constable came and took away the first two drunks and twenty-five minutes later came back and took Schettler but left the brothers in the cell.

He was taken to the bar room. The sergeant looked him up and down then asked for his name and address. Schettler reeled off the number and street, accentuating his Glasgow accent. His confidence in his accent had increased enormously since his arrival in Ireland. If he made small mistakes here, it was less likely to be noticed.

The sergeant asked him where he came from and when told Glasgow, asked how long he'd been in Ireland. Schettler replied that he had come eight months ago to look for work after leaving the navy. This answer seemed to impress the sergeant. He nodded thoughtfully.

"Do you know why you were picked up, son?"

"No, I don't."

"You instigated the singing of a banned song,"

Schettler shook his head. "I did nothing of the sort, Sergeant. I don't even know the song."

The sergeant changed tack. "You seem to be a lot more sober than your friends and therefore more in control of your actions. That's why I'm holding you responsible for starting the singing."

"You can't hold me responsible for the actions of a couple of drunks, Sergeant. I'm telling you I never opened my mouth in that pub."

"How do you know these men anyway?"

"I work with them and since I'm here on my own, they asked me to join them for a drink, that's all."

The sergeant nodded. "Alright, I'm inclined to believe you, so this time I'm going to let you go. I'm going to let your pals off with a caution too, but they'll have to sleep off the Guinness first."

"Thanks Sergeant, but what if I managed to get them home without causing any more trouble?"

"Look, lad, don't push your luck. Just be happy you're not joining them in the cells. What ship were you on anyway."

"HMS Emperor of India."

"Stationed where?"

"Scapa Flow."

"That'll have been handy for you, then! You'd better get out of here before I change me mind."

When Schettler left the station, he hadn't a clue where he was, so he turned right and began to walk taking over two hours to get back to his digs.

In the morning, he awoke with a slight hangover. How must Alex and Pat feel? With that thought, he realised he better walk along to the Murphy house after breakfast, to let their parents know where the brothers were.

Chapter 26

Thomas Sinclair left Glasgow at the end of June 1919, to return to London. He was glad to move back to the seedy building belonging to the Super Clean Laundry Company in Tunstall Road, Brixton. There would be no more dealings with troublesome Glaswegians who were fine when being used as cannon fodder – very good troops actually, that's where their natural aggression served them best – but since the war ended, they had reverted to the pains in the arse they had been before, with their appetite for creating industrial unrest and the re-establishment of the fight for socialism.

The situation had improved since the strike for a forty-hour week had been defeated and the ring leaders were now languishing in jail where they belonged, although it pained Sinclair to see the employers cave in by acquiescing to a national agreement for a forty-seven-hour week, at no reduction in pay. In his eyes, the country was clearly going soft. He had left a network of informants, recruited mainly from the Orange Order, together with three of his best operatives led by Willis, in readiness for the next flare up.

Overall, he had been happy with his unit's performance in Glasgow. He had concluded that they had identified the ringleaders – not always the most prominent activists – and with the cooperation of the police and the army, had dealt with them decisively. After they served their jail sentences, it would be easy to keep tabs on most of them. The difficulty was the rank and file who had been politicised by their experiences and who would look to intellectuals like John Maclean to further a political momentum beyond the Labour Party.

He had been particularly angry about Gerry O'Brien's death at the hands of his own people. O'Brien had a great understanding of revolutionary socialism and in time could have moved easily around the more clandestine political movements, as long as he was skilfully manipulated. He would have been a first-rate informant. It satisfied him that Dick Bradshaw was now working out his army service peeling potatoes in Aldershot Barracks.

Shortly after his arrival in London, Sinclair received a report from the German Admiralty, in a bid to build cooperation between the two countries. A senior petty officer by the name of Johann Schettler had not arrived in Germany. This was despite him being on the list of personnel being repatriated from the High Seas Fleet in Scapa Flow. Subsequent enquiries had shown he wasn't on board his ship, Friedrich der Grosse, and therefore was now listed as missing and likely to be in England. The report did point out that record keeping procedures were not, as yet, reliable.

Sinclair remembered the rumour that there had been a German in George Square on January 29th. At the time he hadn't made much of it. It was unlikely that one German would have any effect on the outcome of the strike and Sinclair knew he'd been right to treat it as a low priority. Nevertheless, this further development intrigued him. Was this Schettler the one who had turned up in Glasgow? If so, how the hell did he get there and more importantly, where was he now? Sinclair wrote back to the Germans asking them to provide any background information they had on Schettler.

In The Shadow of the Gathering Storm

A week later, an envelope with Sinclair's name in small, neat handwriting, landed on his desk, unopened. This was almost unheard of. He opened it, pulling out the single sheet of paper. The first thing he noticed was the heading of the Ministry of War and Air, and when he glanced at the bottom of the page, he saw the signature of Winston Churchill.

Dear Sinclair,

I am writing to you to thank you personally for a job well done in providing the intelligence necessary to break the strike for a forty-hour week in Glasgow and in so doing preventing it from spreading into England, which of course, would have had a devastating effect on the economy of the country. Sir James Watson Stewart has written to me in glowing terms, of your expanse of ideas, diligence and attention to detail in routing out the ringleaders and fellow travellers hell bent on the eventual overthrow of our very system of government. I therefore wish you to be in no doubt that I value your work very highly.

At this time, we are involved in three main theatres of conflict; the third Anglo/Afghan war, which I'm glad to say is almost won, the overthrow of the Red Army in Russia, although I fear this will not ultimately be successful, and finally the worsening situation in Ireland, with Sinn Fein having recently declared independence illegally. The first two are relatively straight forward, especially as I have given permission for a newly developed secret weapon to be used, which will have a devastating effect on our enemies, in both conflicts. Ireland is altogether different. We are trying to fight against this

newly formed Irish Republican Army whose use
of guerrilla tactics is much more difficult and
dangerous to combat. Our agents tell us that
Michael Collins is directing these units and
therefore, I need someone with considerable
experience in this type of intelligence work to
rout him out, find the identities of the senior
officers and finally have them dealt with. I need
you, Sinclair, and therefore I am putting the
necessary arrangements together to have you and
a team of your choice transferred to Dublin
forthwith.
Yours sincerely
Winston Churchill.

Sinclair had mixed feelings about this letter. It was a
great honour to receive a thank you from Winston Churchill
personally, although he felt that Churchill seemed to be
particularly frank about what must be sensitive, military
information even if he was writing to a member of the secret
service. He knew that the job he'd just been given would be
extremely difficult.

Despite the urgent tone of the letter, it took two weeks
for Sinclair's superiors to give him the go ahead to put a
team together. By the beginning of September, he and his
six men were offered space in the British Army Intelligence
Centre in Benburb Street Dublin, adjacent to the Royal
Barracks. Sinclair turned this offer down. He was determined
that knowledge of their presence in Dublin should only
be known to the fewest number of people and he realised
that BAI HQ was likely to be watched by his republican
counterparts. He insisted he find his own accommodation,
so he and David Andrews, with whom he had already worked

in several locations including Glasgow, went to Dublin. They rented rooms in a run-down building, using an importer of bananas, as a front.

The first task was to go back over all previous background reports from the BAI and the various police departments, to form a profile of the men and women thought to be agents or activists in the Irish Independence movement. As the security team worked through this mountain of information, they realised there was no cohesive pattern. Although the names of the leaders were known, in most cases, that was where the intelligence ended, with no knowledge of what they looked like or where they lived. This was particularly true of Michael Collins. It was claimed he worked out of Sinn Féin's headquarters at 76, Harcourt Street, but any time this or the previous HQ at 6, Harcourt Street had been raided, no sign of him had ever been found. This pointed to a sophisticated, intelligence network, working inside the agencies of the state, that was able to alert these people, when a raid was to take place. Indeed, where Collins was concerned there was no record of his movements anywhere, although rumours abounded that he enjoyed an expansive lifestyle. Sinclair concluded that they would have to recruit a new team of local agents. The problem was how to do this.

Reading through a series of boring police reports, Andrews came across one that caught his eye – a group of three young men had been apprehended for instigating the singing of a banned song in a pub. The police had insufficient evidence to prove they started the singing and, although two of them were held in the cells from Saturday to Monday for drunkenness, no further action was taken against them. The third, a Glaswegian whose name was Ian Nairn, was let go on the Saturday because he wasn't considered to be drunk and he claimed he had nothing to do with the singing that evening, insisting he didn't even know the song. When interrogated by the Duty Sergeant, Nairn claimed to have come to Dublin to find work after being demobbed from the Royal Navy Battleship, Emperor of India, stationed in Scapa Flow.

Andrews remembered there had been a Robert Nairn picked up in the raid on Lang's bar in Queen Street in Glasgow on January 29th. Nairn had been subjected to a robust interrogation as he was thought to have been connected with the man who was overheard, by an agent in George Square, shouting in German. He had vigorously denied this and had been released that evening. Andrews thought this was a coincidence worth further investigation, particularly when compared with the information sent to Sinclair by the German Authorities about this man, Schettler.

When Andrews contacted the Admiralty, he was told that no one called Ian Nairn had been demobbed from the Navy. He reported his findings to Sinclair, who agreed that further investigations were needed.

*

The rain poured down and the gas mantles cast intermittent veins of light against the houses then died away, almost to complete darkness, before the next lamp took up the impossible challenge of spreading light along the length of the street. As Schettler walked home from his work at Murphy's depot, his sense of futility deepened. He was lonely and missed Kate enormously. He was worried too. The truck had been stopped by the police three times in the last week and he felt the searches were becoming more thorough. It was only a matter of time before their hiding place for the arms, under the chassis, would be found and they arrested.

A few days earlier, he'd received a short letter from his mother, inside an equally short letter from Margaret. She had written of her happiness that he was safe but there was a reference to men who had been stationed at Scapa, who were now safely with their families. She had also made derogatory references to Ireland indicating that she didn't understand what he was doing there. She had given him some good news, however. Since the war had ended, the Schettler Shipping Line had recommenced a regular freight service to Dublin and mail could be delivered to her by this means. He had written a reply which awaited an opportunity to go to the docks on the off chance there was a ship berthed there.

The rain dripped down his back as he walked, making him shiver. The thought of another dinner dominated by potatoes, followed by an evening sitting alone in his room up against the small gas fire, reading another boring western while trying to keep warm, made him feel acutely sorry for himself. Instead of delivering the letter, perhaps he should deliver himself back to Bremen.

In his misery, he failed to notice a man sheltering in a doorway. As he passed, he heard a voice whisper, "Ian – Johann Schettler."

Startled, he swung round in the direction of the voice and found himself looking into the eyes of Charlie Tennant.

Schettler stared at him in disbelief. "My God, it's you, Charlie. Why on earth are you here?"

Tennant shivered. "Look, Ian, I need to get out of this rain. Is there a pub we can go to? I could do with a drink."

"The only pub around here's the Grapes. I hope it's warm."

To the relief of both men, there was a fire burning in the hearth and they were early enough to get a seat next to it.

"What will you drink, Charlie?"

"Whisky,"

Tennant had said nothing on their way to the pub.

Studying his friend in the light, Schettler could see he was pale and drawn and he had marks and bruises on his face. He looked as though he hadn't slept for days.

"I don't think they'll have Scotch here. Will Irish do?"

"Aye, whatever you like."

Charlie downed the double Schettler brought back in one gulp. Returning his glass to the table he said, "We're in trouble, Ian – I'm on the run. They know all about how we got to Glasgow. They know you're German and you're Margaret's cousin and you came with Kate to Ireland. Christ, Ian, they know everything. I had to warn you."

Schettler felt his stomach knot, particularly when Charlie mentioned Kate and Ireland, but he tried to stay calm. "I'll get us another drink and then you tell me everything, right?"

Tennant nodded.

When Schettler returned with the drinks, Tennant explained that when the Emperor of India had finally docked in Portsmouth a week ago, he'd been arrested and taken to an old, rambling house somewhere in the countryside. He had been subjected to a brutal interrogation over three days.

"Who interrogated you, Charlie?"

Tennant took a long draw on his whiskey. He began to sound more like himself. "This Irish stuff isn't half bad," he said with a smile. "Well, it's funny you should ask that. They

300

were men who worked for the guy who nailed me and Gerry O'Brien back in fourteen – a man called Sinclair who had a side kick called Andrews back then. The guys who did this," he pointed to his face, "knocked me out cold but as I was beginning to come round I heard them talking outside the door and they mentioned Sinclair and Andrews. One told the other they had been sent here to Dublin – they said something about getting some guy called Collins. Anyway, they knew all about you talking in German in George Square. They even knew Bob and I had been arrested in Lang's and I had escaped on my way into Barlinnie."

"How on earth did they know all that?" Schettler asked, puzzled.

Tennant knocked back the rest of his whiskey. "Because I fuckin' told them, Ian," he growled. "When they keep beating the shit out of you and stopping you sleeping, after a while you'll tell the bastards anything they want to know."

Schettler stared at Tennant not knowing what to say.

Tennant continued. "I didn't have to tell them you were German, though. They knew that already and I don't know how."

"How much do they know about Kate?"

"Everything I knew, but that wasn't much, thank God."

"Do they know where she lives in Ireland? After all, you wrote to me there, through Margaret."

"No. Margaret never told me your address in case something like this happened. She's a clever girl, your cousin."

"Have these people been to see the Nairns?"

"Yes, the police came to see them, but Margaret claimed Kate was only a passing political acquaintance who she hardly knew. Both she and Bob insisted they didn't know Kate or your whereabouts. Fortunately, Margaret had already burned all your letters, so when the police searched the house they found nothing."

"How did you find out where I lived here in Dublin?"

"I'll get to all that."

Thanks to the whiskey, the roles had now reversed. Tennant sounded relaxed while Schettler was boiling over inside.

"But how did you escape then, Charlie?"

"Just listen will you. After I told them everything I knew about you and the political situation in Glasgow, they suddenly changed their tune – all friendly like. I was allowed to have a bath and given a good meal and a comfortable bed for the night." Tennant took another sip of whiskey.

"When I was taken to see them the next morning, they proposed that I should leave the Navy. They would see to it. I should return to Glasgow and they would get me a job in Beardmore's and from then on, I was to get involved politically and report back to them about what was being discussed and who was involved. Margaret was to know nothing of this, so I could also tell them about her political associations. If I refused, I would be imprisoned for helping an enemy of the state. That's you, Ian. They would see to it I never worked again. So I said yes to them, Ian. What else could I do?"

Schettler could hardly believe what he had been told. "I'm so sorry, Charlie. What happened then?"

"I was returned to the Emperor to wait for them to put my demob papers through. They told me it was likely to take a couple of weeks. What they obviously didn't understand, was that because the ship was in dock, I was entitled to shore leave, which I took immediately. As soon as I left the ship, I phoned Mags, got your address and here I am. That's also how I know about the police questioning her and Bob. But look Ian, they must be looking for you and Kate here right now. My guess is there going to try to use you and Kate to find this guy Collins. Who is he anyway?"

Schettler shrugged. "You'll find that out in time but right now, we'll have to move fast."

He needed to get this information to someone close to Collins and the only way this could be done was to go back to Murphy's. "Look, Charlie, you need to stay here while I go to make some arrangements about us. I'll try to be back before closing time but if I'm not, just hang around outside till I get back. Keep out of sight as much as possible. I'll be as quick as I can. Are you hungry?"

"Yes, ravenous. The last food I ate was on the ship over here."

"I'll see if they have food here, but I wouldn't hold out much hope."

Schettler went back to the bar and asked if they served food.

"Listen, me friend, this is a pub not a feckin' restaurant," the barman said. "We serve some food for the regulars at twelve o'clock."

Schettler nodded. "It's just that my friend has come over from Glasgow and he hasn't eaten."

"Ah sure, you should have said that! I'm a great Celtic man, so I am, and I've still got a nice bit of coddle left over. I'll heat it up and bring it over when it's ready. Will that do?"

"Yes, that'll be fine."

Schettler went back through the dingy bar to where Tennant was sitting trying to dry his coat by the fire. "You've got something called coddle coming when the barman heats it up."

"What the hell's that?"

"I've no idea but you're only getting it because he's a Celtic supporter. Don't get drunk, whatever you do. We'll have to move fast when I get back. Stay where I can find you."

Schettler decided to go back to his digs and quickly pack up his things before he went to Murphys'.

He was about to turn into the small entrance lane to the houses at Ivy Terrace, when two men appeared from a parked car in front of him.

One of them said, "Ian Nairn". It was more of a statement than a question. "We'd like you to come with us."

"Who might you be?"

The man took a card from his trench coat pocket and flashed it in front of Schettler's nose but withdrew it before he had time to see it. In the darkness, it would have been impossible to read anyway. As it was, he could barely see their faces under their hats.

"We're from Dublin Metropolitan Police, Mr Nairn, and we would like a word with you, sir. It might take a little time, so we'd prefer to do it somewhere warm and dry."

Schettler smiled to hide the fear that ran through his body. "Well you could always come to my digs we could talk there. What's it about anyway?"

"We'll tell you that when we get to where we're going. Let's just get on our way," the man said as he took Schettler by the arm.

Schettler let himself be led to the car and the two pushed him into the centre of the back seat while they sat one on each side of him. With its plush leather upholstery, it was clear this was no police car. Two more men got in the front, half a minute later.

As the car made a three-point turn, one of the men grabbed Schettler's arms to restrain him while the other quickly thrust a black cloth bag over his head. The man to his left drawled, "Don't get yourself distressed, Mr Nairn, we're not out to hurt you as long as you don't do anything stupid. Do you understand?"

Schettler stayed silent, until he felt a dig in the ribs. "I said, do you understand?"

"Yes," Schettler shouted and his voice seemed to resonate inside the bag.

He felt the car turn left at the end of the road, heading towards the city centre. They drove for about ten minutes at what seemed to be a sedate speed before coming to a halt. He heard the muffled sound of voices and what he took to be a gate being opened before the car started again, only to come to a stop a few seconds later. He was dragged out roughly by the man on his right and as they stood there, another man grabbed his left arm and he was frog marched between them into a building. They continued along what seemed like a corridor with a stone floor and their footsteps echoed in the cavernous space.

One of the men snapped, "Stairs down, Nairn," and they pulled him to one side. The three of them descended a narrow, circular staircase almost in single file. The man who was on the step below him had to take Schettler's full weight, as he twice lost his footing, making his heart beat faster. At the bottom, he was pushed along a corridor. After a few twists and turns, he was forced into a chair and his forearms were manacled to its wooden arms.

Once he was secured, he got the impression that the men left the room closing the door behind them, leaving him in a black silence. He knew that these people were likely to be the same ones as Charlie had described earlier and he tried to control his panic. Where was this place they had taken him? He desperately needed to piss. At one point, he thought he heard the sound of someone breathing shallowly, but when he shouted out, asking if anyone was there, he received no reply. More time passed until a voice boomed out, breaking the silence and making him jump. He felt the trickle of urine running down his leg before constricting his muscles to make it stop.

"So, you claim to be Ian Nairn from Glasgow, but I don't think you are. I think you're Johann Schettler from Bremen."

The blunt remark further increased Schettler's anxiety.

"Who are you? I want to know why I've been brought here," he shouted.

"There's so much we want to know about you, Schettler. Isn't that right, Mr Black?"

"We certainly do, Mr White."

Schettler was surprised to hear the other voice in the room. There must have been two of them all this time, observing him as he sat attached to the chair.

"Look, whoever you are. I need to get to a toilet urgently."

"Is that right? Well, we don't want to make your stay with us more uncomfortable than it needs to be!"

Schettler felt the manacles being removed from his forearms. He was dragged to his feet and marched out the room. The short break gave him time to think. What methods would they use to extract information from him? Would there be physical abuse as with Charlie? That was a possibility.

When he was returned to the room and manacled to his chair, the voice of the man called Mr White started again.

"We're not going to beat about the bush, Schettler. I'll tell you what we know about you and you're going to fill in the gaps."

He went on to say that they knew he had escaped from the Friedrich der Grosse in January, helped by Charles Tennant, a Senior Petty Officer in the Royal Navy, who was the fiancée of Margaret Nairn, his cousin from Glasgow. They also knew that both he and Tennant had turned up in Glasgow on or before January 30th.

Mr Black broke in. "Who taught you to speak English with such a pronounced Scottish accent?"

"My mother's Scottish and I was brought up bilingual."

"I see." said Black. "And your aunt Helen Nairn is your mother's sister?"

"Yes."

The voice of White came back at him. "Are you a communist?"

"I believe that power should be in hands of the majority, if that's what you mean."

"Don't be obtuse, just answer the question."

"I don't really understand you, but if you mean am I a socialist, the answer's yes."

Black again interjected. "I find that difficult to understand, Schettler. After all, your father owns the Schettler shipping line in Bremen and you were brought up in an upper-class environment."

This sounded particularly naive to Schettler. "That's true but it was my mother who taught me my socialist principals."

White continued to explore the subject. "Is that right? What was her background?"

"My mother was from a poor, Glaswegian family."

Schettler could hear White's scepticism. "Oh, why did your father choose a woman like that to marry? How could they have met?"

Schettler found himself bristling at the inference that his mother was inferior. When he answered, his voice gave him away. "You'd have to ask my father that, but they met in America."

White said, "Yes, it's one thing to marry a person beneath your social status, but a Glaswegian – that's really scraping the bottom of the barrel. How on earth did he converse with her? They can't speak English, far less German."

Schettler took a deep breath to calm himself. "Meine Mutter sprich sehr gut Deutsch."

"What did you say?"

"I said my mother speaks German very well, which I see is more than you–"

He didn't get a chance to finish the sentence. The chair was almost tipped over by the force of the blow he received to the side of his head making him gasp for breath, more from the shock than pain. White must have been standing right next to him.

White's voice boomed. "The last thing we need from you, Schettler, is smart talk."

Black spoke again. "Now, gentlemen, let's not fall out. Why did you go to Glasgow, Schettler?"

As he fought to gather his wits again, his voice sounded breathless. "To see my Scottish relatives."

"You didn't go to help fuel the flames of revolution, then?"

"There was no revolution, just a strike for a forty-hour week which I didn't know anything about until we got to Glasgow."

"And to get there you impersonated a senior petty officer of his Majesty's Navy – a certain Mr Carmichael, who was at the time, ill in hospital. Is that not right?"

"Yes."

"And when did you leave Glasgow again?"

"Tuesday, the fourth of February."

"And you travelled directly here to Dublin?"

"Yes."

"That's not what we understood you did. We've been told you travelled north with Tennant on Saturday the 1st of February. Is that information wrong?"

"No, it's right. I travelled with Charlie as far as Perth, where we stayed the night. It was at that time I decided not to return to my ship, so the next day I travelled back to Glasgow while he went on to Scapa."

"So why did you lie?"

"I didn't lie. I just missed a bit out, because it didn't seem important."

White exclaimed, "Don't do that again. Is that clear? We need to know everything. Did you meet an Irish woman called Kate A'Herne when you were in Glasgow, Schettler?"

He realised this was the time to tell as much of the truth as possible. He explained how he and Kate had met, what had happened at the statue in the Square and their lunch at The Cranstons, where she had told him she was returning to Ireland the following Tuesday. He also told them about their tram ride back to Dennistoun together but missed out the part that they had both gone to Seton Terrace and instead told them he had seen her back to her flat in Bathgate Street.

Black spoke now. "Were you attracted to Miss A'Herne?"

"Yes, I was. She's a very attractive lady."

"How well did your cousin Margaret know her?"

"I don't really know. All I know is they knew each other through some political organisation. I don't think they were friends, if that's what you mean."

This seemed to satisfy them. White moved on. "We know you stayed at your relative's house until you took the train to Perth but where did you stay between Sunday and Tuesday?"

Schettler hadn't pre-empted this question and it slightly panicked him, until he remembered on the way along Duke Street one time, Bob had pointed out a building opposite the prison – a place for down and outs. The name came back to him.

"The Great Eastern Hotel, in Duke Street," he said, laughing nervously.

"Was it a funny place, Schettler?"

"It was for down and outs, so it wasn't a nice place, but it was cheap. Right now, it's full of demobbed soldiers who can't get jobs, so from that point it's serving a necessary purpose."

He cursed himself. Now he was embellishing the story and that could be dangerous.

"When did you tell Miss A'Herne you would accompany her to Dublin?" White asked.

"I called on her on Monday evening because she had complained that her case was so heavy she wouldn't be able to carry it, so as I decided to go to Dublin myself. I volunteered to help her carry it. She was very grateful."

White continued. "When you and Miss A'Herne arrived in Dublin, what did you do then?"

"She was going to the station to get a train home and I was going into Dublin to find somewhere cheap to stay till I found a job, so she took a taxi and told me to get the tram, which I did."

"Did she tell you where she lived?"

"No."

"What station did she go to?"

Schettler shrugged, "She just said the station and at that time I didn't know there was more than one station in Dublin."

"I presume you and she didn't hit it off romantically then," Black said with a laugh.

"No, but we got on very well."

"And have you ever seen her again."

"No." Schettler closed his eyes. If they knew he was lying, he could be beaten, and he was glad they couldn't see his face.

But they seemed to accept it.

White said, "You mentioned cheap accommodation. Did you have money, and if so where did you get it?"

"There was a thriving black market in Scapa, so I changed my marks for twenty five pounds which lasted me until I found a job."

"Why did you come to Dublin, Schettler?" White continued.

"I came to look for a job."

"Yes, that's what you told the police, wasn't it? What's your attitude to Irish Independence?"

"I don't have any strong views one way or another."

"I must say, I find it difficult to believe that after escaping from an interned ship in Scapa Flow you turn up in Glasgow during a state of political unrest, then travel to Dublin which is in an even greater state of unrest and you claim to be either ignorant of the situation or indifferent to it. I think you must be a communist agent provocateur. I think we should take you to Kilmainham Jail and string you up like a turkey. What do you say to that?"

Schettler was thankful that the bag over his head prevented his captors from seeing the fear in his eyes.

"Look, we were bored to distraction being stuck on a ship in Scapa Flow for three months and when I got the opportunity to visit my family in Glasgow, I jumped at it. When I left, I fully intended going back but when it came to it I just couldn't, so I thought it was better not to stay in Scotland. I came here to look for a job on the spur of the moment. Had I known what things were like, I wouldn't have come."

Schettler was surprised that this explanation was accepted. White asked for more details. "So where did you stay when you came to Dublin?"

This was where his experience driving Murphy's truck became useful. He had noticed a small place that had a bed and breakfast sign close to the fruit market called the Bellaire. "The Bellaire Bed and Breakfast in Mary Street," he said clearly and without hesitation. If they checked up, he would be in more trouble.

White continued, "So you're now working for Murphy and Sons delivering fruit and vegetables around Dublin. Is that all you do, Schettler?"

Schettler still spoke clearly and confidently, "Yes, it is."

"I see. I thought you also delivered guns and ammunition to those who would wish to pick a fight with us Brits and force us out of Ireland."

Schettler broke into a cold sweat. The remark had taken him completely by surprise – they had backed him into corner. He could say nothing.

Black now spoke. "We'll take your silence to mean you realise what we're saying is true, which of course it is. The authorities have known about the Murphys' activities for some time but it has suited their purpose to do nothing about them. What is going to happen now, Schettler, is you'll be working for us. You will work for us because we have at least three reasons to take you out and hang you. One, for impersonating a member of the British Armed forces, two, incitement to cause civil war and supplying weapons to an enemy of the state is the third. We could even just hang you as a foreign spy. Just in case you have a complete disregard for your own life, you better think of your family and friends. They harboured an enemy of the state. Last January, our countries were technically still at war. They could all be hanged for that alone. But if you co-operate with us, we'll allow your Glasgow family to live in peace and your cousin Margaret to keep her job as a teacher and you know how precious she thinks that is. I hope you'll see all this in black and white and understand you don't have a lot of room to manoeuvre."

Schettler nodded, unable to say anything.

"Good, we'll now release you. We want you to live a normal life working while gathering information for us. We'll wish you goodbye for the time being."

He could hear the two men laughing as they left the room and walked down the corridor. No wonder their interrogation had been so accommodating. They knew they had him where they wanted him.

Half an hour later he was standing on the street close to his digs, where he had been picked up earlier. The rain poured down once more.

When he looked at his watch, it was eleven thirty. He thought of Tennant standing freezing outside the Grapes, but he had to work fast. He needed to speak to one of Collins men quickly. His first thought was to ask them to spirit Tennant and himself away to a safe house, while they tracked down this new British Intelligence Unit under the leadership of Sinclair and Andrews. But he realised if he stayed where he was, at least until someone in the unit contacted him, he might have a face, as well as names to go on.

Right now, he would have to get to Murphys' place. What if he was being watched? Under the circumstances it seemed likely. He entered his digs but instead of going to his room, he went through the kitchen to the back-court area and climbed over the wall to the house next door. He repeated this process until he reached the end of the block of houses. He made his way through back lanes and over walls, stopping from time to time to see if he was being followed. If he was, he couldn't see anyone. When he was almost there, his next thought was that they might be watching the place, so he circumnavigated the area and entered the yard through a hole in the fence at the rear of the compound. Once inside the office, he hammered on the locked door which led to the house above.

It wasn't long before he heard the unmistakable voice of Alex, swearing as he descended the stairs. The door opened, and he stood before him, carrying a lighted candle in a holder and wearing an old-fashioned, striped night-shirt which ended just below his knees exposing a large pair of green socks. In different circumstances, Schettler would have burst out laughing.

As young Murphy peered at him, he snarled, "What do you want, Nairn? Do you not know what the fuckin' time is?"

Schettler nodded unable to control a smirk.

"What do ye think is funny, you eejit."

"Alex, I need to speak to the three of you. It's an emergency."

"You better come in," Murphy said and turned quickly to climb the stair, but the candle fell out of its holder and he made a grab for it. It burned his hand and that made him fall forward. He landed on his face on the stair, the nightshirt gathered up around his torso exposing a large bare arse, while he uttered another string of oaths. Schettler burst into a fit of uncontrollable laughter and leant against the wall, unable to move.

Suddenly a voice exploded from above. "What the fuck's goin' on down there – is that you Alex?"

"Aye, it is. Ian's here and he needs to talk to us, urgent like."

"Right, then. The two of you get your arses up here and stop fuckin' about."

The reference to arses set Schettler off again and Alex had to grab hold of him to push him up the stairs. "Are you drunk or something, you fuckin' eejit?"

When Schettler got to the lobby at the top of the stairs, the other two Murphys were standing there equally ridiculously dressed. Any mirth left in the situation evaporated. The old man was pointing a Mauser semi-automatic pistol at him.

Nervous tension was Schettler's driving force again. All he could think to say was, "Sorry, I didn't think you'd be in bed yet." All three men showered him with expletives.

"I'm sorry. I've got a lot to tell you. Can we sit down somewhere?"

He was led into an old-fashioned parlour and told to sit on a couch.

"You'll have to bear with me because I'm going have to tell you about this evening's happenings in order because it's the only way it'll make sense." And over the next half hour he told them the story.

"So, first we need to get Charlie Tennant to safety and secondly, I need to talk to one of the big man's men."

Chapter 27

A week elapsed before Schettler, again, found himself in the hands of the British Secret Service. As he walked home from work, he was confronted by two men who appeared from a doorway and invited him into the car parked close by. The same sequence of events took place and he was blindfolded.

Remembering the previous journey, this time he felt he was being driven to a different location which was confirmed when the car arrived at its destination and he was marched up a stair rather than down. He was pushed into a chair where he was manacled and then left alone. After five minutes, he heard the door opening and closing. The blindfold was removed from his eyes and, as he blinked to regain focus, a tall young man was standing before him. The room they occupied was small, less than three metres square with a window and the only furniture was a desk and four chairs.

The man grabbed him by the lapels of his coat, peering straight into his eyes. "When were you in contact with Charlie Tennant?" His accent was different to that of Schettler's previous interrogators.

The question lacked conviction and the show of force seemed like a bluff. Schettler pushed his luck to see where it might lead. "I received a letter over three months ago."

The other shook his head. "Don't be stupid. We know you've seen Tennant."

The man seemed to hesitate as he was saying this, making Schettler press a little further. "And when was I supposed to have met him? Firstly, I can't see why he would be in Ireland and secondly he doesn't know where I live."

Releasing him the man continued, "Oh, he's in Ireland all right."

So, while they knew Tennant was in Ireland, they were guessing he had met Schettler and they certainly didn't know he was now being held in an IRA safe house.

"If you're lying, Schettler, we'll soon find out and it will be the worse for you. Do you hear?"

Schettler was surprised at how easily the man had acquiesced to his assertion, so he chanced another question. "Why is Charlie in Ireland anyway? According to his letter he should be on his ship steaming off to Malta by this time."

The man looked back at Schettler blankly, before mumbling that he didn't know. He had to be a junior member of Sinclair's team and Schettler thought he could use this to his advantage.

"Are you going to be my liaison officer?" Schettler said. "I thought it would be either Mr Black or Mr White."

Again, the man looked blank.

Schettler pressed on. "Is that not their names? What are their names then?"

"Yes, I'm your liaison officer and that's all you need to know."

"What do I call you and how do I get in touch with you when I have information? I hope I don't have to go through this stupid situation of being blindfolded every time you want to speak to me."

"I was just coming to that. My name is George McBride and I'll meet you every Tuesday on the second floor of Café Cairo at 59, Grafton Street at seven o'clock."

"What if I need to contact you at another time? How do I do that?" Schettler asked.

"You can find me most nights either in the Café or in Davy Byrnes pub just round the corner in Duke Street. That should do you."

Schettler nodded.

McBride continued. "Have you got any information for me?"

Schettler shrugged, emboldened by McBride's amateurish performance. "I don't know what you want, George, do I? Until I know that, all I can tell you is the Murphys are still distributing armaments around the area, but you know that already."

"Well, you can start by giving me the names and addresses of the people receiving these armaments. What kind are they anyway?" McBride blustered.

Schettler shrugged again. "Usually small arms – Brownings, Smith and Wesson. Mostly ex- British service revolvers but there are some German guns too, Mausers and Lugers – that kind of thing. Surely you don't want to go raiding that ragtag group? That will do more harm than good, and it will certainly blow my cover."

"No, we just want to know who and where they are," McBride retorted with a smile.

Was it possible that the man thought he had established a bond with him?

"You can also try to find out the names of Collins' intelligence network and where Tennant is."

Schettler laughed. "You're not asking for much. But for you, George, I'll certainly try. Have you worked in Dublin long?" Schettler changed tack.

"No, I've just been transferred here from Belfast a couple of weeks ago."

That explained the accent.

"Is Belfast your home town?"

"Yes, it is, and I believe you're German."

"I'm sure you know all about me."

"I suppose I do. I think that's all we need to discuss for now. But you better have these names and addresses for me next Tuesday. I'm afraid you're going to have the blindfold put on again one last time."

As the blindfold was slipped over Schettler's eyes, he said, "You'd better not call me Schettler in public. The name's Ian Nairn, remember."

*

When Thornton appeared at the little house in Meath Place, Kate thought he looked excited. In an unusually matter of fact manner he asked Kitty to go to her room while he talked to Kate. "Things have changed, and we need you to do something quite different now and if it all works out after tomorrow, you won't need to worry about being molested by Burgess ever again. Your boy Nairn has been picked up by the Brits and forced to work for them."

Kate eyes widened. "What? Is he alright?"

Thornton nodded. "He's fine. They didn't hurt him, and he was sensible enough to get right back to us about it. Our intelligence is telling us that this is a new group who have been sent over to hunt down our leadership, particularly the big fellah. They seem to be more careful than usual. We haven't been able to find out where they're working from.

But now Nairn's been allotted a minder and a meeting place, so that gives us an opportunity to find out. The

320

minder's a young, Belfast man called George McBride and Nairn has a meeting with him tomorrow at seven o'clock in the Café Cairo in Grafton Street. We want you and Kitty to go there at the same time and after Nairn leaves, if everything goes to plan, McBride should be buzzing around you like a bee lookin' for pollen. Strike up a bit of a rapport with him."

"Why is McBride going to be so interested in me?"

When Thornton told her, she was shocked. They talked on for another half an hour before Kitty was called back to join them and, as she walked downstairs, Thornton said, "By the way, I forgot to say they're meeting in the second-floor café."

"What's all this about then?" Kitty asked.

Kate laughed, "Ah, you'll find out soon enough, girl."

Chapter 28

The girls pushed the door of Café Cairo open and the wind blew the leaves of the palm tree in the vestibule, causing it to rustle loudly. They shook the excess water from their umbrellas and put them in one of the trays provided.

When they arrived at the second floor, they were met by a waiter dressed in a white, loose fitting shirt, a broad red belt with a fez to match and black baggy linen trousers. He looked around the crowded room before inviting them to follow him to a table situated close to the bar. It was Kate's first visit to the famous Dublin Café and she was intrigued by the décor which was dominated by a continuous mural around the walls depicting scenes of ancient Egypt complete with sphinxes, pyramids and camels with more palm trees located around the long room. The ceiling too, depicted similar scenes in stained-glass panels. In the corner, a band which included two black musicians, played jazz. She thought it was amazing, so different from the drab and troubled world she had just left outside.

As they sat down at the table set for two, Kate caught the first sight of Schettler who was propped up at the end of the bar talking to another man who was obviously McBride. Seeing him was upsetting. He looked thin and drawn. But she knew she had to keep her mind on her task. The two men were so intent in their conversation that they weren't aware of what was going on around them and she was convinced they hadn't noticed them arrive.

"Right Kitty, see the two fellahs there at the end of the bar? The one with his back to us is McBride. You'll have to go over there and ask him for a light…"

At that point the waiter placed an open menu in front of her and as she turned to look at him, he gave her a knowing smile. She returned the smile and raised her eyebrows. He laughed, laid a menu in front of Kitty, and walked quickly away.

As soon as he was gone, Kate said, "How much did that waiter hear? Did he hear me saying McBride's name?"

Kitty shook her head. "For God's sake, stop panicking. He got here when you told me to ask him for a light."

"Very good. You see we'll need to do something to attract McBride's attention in case he leaves with our man."

Kitty bent forward and whispered, "You know the other one don't you, Elizabeth?"

"What makes you think that, Kitty?" Kate tried to look bemused.

"It was the expression on your face when you saw him. You know him all right."

"We'll talk about that later. Just go before they decide to leave."

"Why don't you go yourself?" Kitty giggled.

"This is no time for teasing. You know I don't smoke. Just get your cigarettes out and go, Kitty."

When Kitty had gone, Kate wondered how she had been perceptive enough to recognise what must have been the slightest reaction. She wasn't even aware of it herself. How she wished she and Ian could be back at Rose Cottage together instead of living this life of boredom tinged with mortal fear. Perhaps it would be over soon.

She watched Kitty get a light from McBride and talk animatedly with him and Ian. Kitty threw her head back and laughed before she turned and pointed at Kate. Kate smiled and gave a coy wave in the direction of the men, before all three turned and began to talk amongst themselves for a further couple of minutes. Cigarette in hand, Kitty returned to the table.

They watched the two men as they talked intently to each other. From time to time Schettler nodded his head in Kate's direction while McBride furtively looked over. After ten minutes, Schettler made his way out of the room. McBride continued standing at the bar before walking over to the telephone cubicle situated close to the door. He was on the phone for some time. Then he walked over to their table and Kate felt a pang of fear as she watched him approach.

McBride reached their table, a smile on his face. "Would you mind if I joined you, ladies?"

The women agreed he could and introductions were made. The astute waiter appeared, carrying a chair and another menu. Giving Kate another knowing smile, he said, "Will you people be eating with us tonight?"

McBride rubbed his hands. "I'm sure we will."

"Right then, I'll come back to take your order when you've had a chance to study the menu. Our special this evening is lemon sole served with French fries and garden peas. Would you care for an aperitif while you choose?"

"Yes, we will. What do you suggest?" McBride said.

Two Gin Rickeys – gin with lime and club soda – which the waiter insisted was straight from America for the girls and Irish and soda for McBride were ordered.

Kitty blurted out, "Can we afford all this, Elizabeth?"

McBride laughed. "Don't worry, girls, this is all on me."

He cupped his hand around his mouth and whispered, "I've just had a bit of a success on the nags today. That's why I had to make a telephone call just there."

They talked animatedly until the waiter returned to take their food order. All three ordered the sole.

The chatter continued throughout the meal. McBride was quite good company, but it was clear his interest lay with Kate. At a pre-arranged signal, Kitty made an excuse that she needed to go, and a debate started between the girls about Kate going with her for safety reasons but eventually Kitty left on her own.

The couple sat on while the waiter brought coffee and strange, almond biscuits Kate had never tasted before, while the band played 'Jelly Roll Blues'. The conversation turned more serious and McBride talked about the war and his time in France with the 16th Ulster Volunteers.

When Kate asked him what a good Belfast boy was doing in Dublin, he told her he was in the fruit import business.

"And what do you do, Miss McDonnagh?"

"I'm with the civil service, Mr McBride," and when he pressed her, she told him where she worked.

At ten o'clock Kate said she had to go and he asked if he could see her home. She agreed.

The bill for the meal came to 8/9d, a horrific sum to Kate. It was half a week's wages.

When they reached Grafton Street, the rain had stopped, and she and McBride turned in the direction of Dame Street, where they could catch a tram car. Suddenly, Kate remembered she had left her umbrella in the café's vestibule and ran back, leaving McBride standing on the pavement. When she returned umbrella in hand, he was standing beside a large motor car which had just stopped beside him. The rear door opened, and McBride grabbed her and bundled her into the back seat, while the umbrella fell to the ground. He pushed her towards a woman who was sitting on the far side, before jumping quickly in after her. It happened so quickly Kate had no time to react and she was about to shout out, when the man thrust a bag over her head as the car drove off. She started screaming but a heavy blow to her head stopped her and she struggled with dizziness.

McBride began talking to her. His mouth was close to her right ear. "You thought you could trust your ex-boyfriend, Kate A'Herne, but all the time he was betraying you to British Intelligence. It just proves you can't go trusting the Germans. They'll always stick the knife in your back, eh, Kate?" McBride laughed cynically.

She felt his hand push hard down through the folds of her skirt between her legs, groping her. As she tried to pull his hand away, the woman sitting on her left shouted. This time the accent was local. "They'll be none of that kind of stuff while I'm here, you dirty bastard."

"Sure, I just wanted something for the 8/9d that I had to spend on these Republican bitches," McBride said through gritted teeth.

There was silence for a few minutes then McBride started again. "You know, Kate, Schettler told me all about what you were doing during the Easter rising. What you did in Glasgow and what happened to four poor British soldiers because of you in County Offaly. That's what you get for throwing him over for that bastard Collins."

Kate squirmed beside him.

"When he saw you in Café Cairo tonight he was so mad he just had to tell me everything. He said you were have'n a bit on the side with big Michael. That's why he hates you so much and if anyone knows where Collins is hiding out, it's you. We're going to have to find out everything you know. I'd advise you to co-operate with us. The team you're going to see can lack subtlety and we don't want you to endure needless pain now, do we? After spendin' the last few months spyin' on us, we would have every right to take you off and hang you."

The car came to a grinding halt and the driver shouted, "Will you shut up McBride and let us get the bitch inside."

She heard the door open and the woman on her left dragged her out of the car. The other doors opened and closed again. She was grabbed, and her wrists were tied tightly together. Both her arms were grasped, and she was lifted up what she realised were two flights of stairs and along a corridor and thrown into a room, landing heavily on the floor. The door closed, and a key turned locking it from the outside.

She lay there in silence, panic welling up inside her. She fought to try to keep her emotions in check. Thornton had told her that something like this might happen and she should view it as an indication that the plan was working. That was easier said than done. She lifted herself into a sitting position and sat there for half an hour, trying not to speculate on what might happen to her in the next few hours.

The key turned in the lock once again. She was lifted to her feet by her upper arms and dragged down a set of stairs screaming at the top of her voice. This seemed to counter her feeling of fear.

She thought they were at a door and, as it was opened, she could hear voices coming from inside the room. A man's voice barked, "Put her down there." And she was prised into a chair. The man spoke again, in a softer tone. "Let me introduce ourselves, Miss A'Herne. I'm Mr Black and my friend here is Mr White." Then he laughed, "Of course, you can't see us. But you can be assured we are here, aren't we, Mr White?"

"Yes, we are, Mr Black."

Black started again. "I'm told George McBride's had a good talk to you already, so I hope when we start asking you questions, you'll be wise enough to cooperate. We don't want to hurt such a pretty young lady. Of course, as your face is covered up, we'll just have to take McBride's word for that won't we?" There was laughter throughout the room.

Kate shouted out, "For God sake, surely I don't need my hands tied? It's very painful. I'm not going anywhere, am I?" To her relief she heard Black's voice give the order for her hands to be released.

As she sat there feeling the blood flow back, Black continued. "I believe you were in Glasgow during these terrible disturbances at the end of January and it was there you met Mr Schettler before you and he came across to Ireland. We've brought Schettler here, so perhaps if you're good, we'll reunite you later." The sniggering started again.

"As a matter of fact, Mr White and I were also in Glasgow at that time, but that's in the past. I'm much more interested in what you're doing now. I hear you're having quite a cosy relationship with Michael Collins in the evenings while you're trying to spy on us during the day. I'm very interested in meeting Mr Collins. Perhaps you'll be good enough to introduce us?"

Suddenly, there were loud noises from outside the room. Black barked an order to McBride to see what was going on. She heard running feet, then a shot rang out.

At the sound of the gun shot, Kate launched herself sideways off the chair. On the way down, she struck her right temple on something which made her see stars and she lay on the floor trying not to pass out from the pain. She pulled at the ties of the hood, tearing it off. As her eyes adjusted to the light, she saw two men had risen from behind a desk and were reaching for their weapons. Her brother, Liam, arrived at the door and shot one of them. As he slumped over the desk, the other who had managed to draw his gun, turned towards Kate on the floor. He was about to fire when Liam shouted, "No you don't, ye bastard," and shot him repeatedly until the man fell over face down on the desk joining his compatriot.

All this happened in seconds, then, just as suddenly, there was silence. Everything stopped. Nothing moved, and nothing was said. The suspension of time seemed to last forever while Kate tried to rationalise what had just happened.

The silence was broken by Liam shouting, "Come in here, Charlie, and identify these bastards."

To her amazement, Charlie Tennant walked through the door, looked at the men and said, "Yes, that's the two who interrogated me and Gerry in nineteen fourteen – that one's Sinclair."

As he made to turn, the man Liam had shot first, pulled himself up. Kate screamed, "He still has a gun." The man shot Tennant below his left shoulder sending him hurtling backwards. Liam fired several shots into the man, propelling him back to the chair he had been sitting on, upending it. He and the chair went crashing to the floor.

"Charlie," Kate cried and stood up. She ran to him as he lay propped up against the office wall. His right hand was pressed against his upper chest. His face was ghostly pale and when she touched him, he slumped over, moaning.

"Help me," she shouted, and Liam rushed forward. Between them they raised Tennant back into a sitting position.

"That looks bad." Kate gasped. "We'll have to get him to a doctor, fast."

Liam jumped up and tore the shirt from one of the dead men, folded it and put it under what remained of Tennant's shirt to try to stem the bleeding. "We'll get him out as quickly as we can, but we're not finished yet."

"What's going on, Liam? Why is Charlie here?" Liam pulled her up and guided her outside and brother and sister embraced for the first time since the spring of 1916. Filled with shock and emotion, she sobbed on his shoulder. She heard the sound of more gun shots coming from another part of the building. Again, they lasted just a few seconds before silence prevailed. Then a single shot rang out, followed a few seconds later by another.

Liam gently pushed her away and she became aware of her surroundings. She was in a large, store room with boxes piled up against the walls. It was dank and dimly lit. An open door led to the small office where the shootings had taken place. In the gloom she noticed a man standing holding a pistol by his side while another lay dead on the ground. The man walked across to her and gently pulled her away from her brother's side. "Come on, Kate, we'll try to find a place to sit while Liam finds out whether it's all over. But I think it is now." She realised it was Pat, the young man who had taken her and Schettler to see Michael Collins several weeks ago.

"I have to go back to Charlie, he needs help."

"You can't do anything for him at the moment," Pat said as he led her away. "We'll get him to a doctor as soon as we can."

Just then they heard someone running down the stairs. Liam lifted his gun in readiness towards the staircase, but when the man appeared, it was Schettler. Kate screamed, "Liam, don't shoot him. After everything he's being saying about me I want to shoot the bastard myself." Liam lowered the gun and smiled at her. "I see you haven't changed anyway, Kaitlin A'Herne, but I think you'll find it wasn't his fault. We told him what to say about you. We had to be sure they'd take the bait."

Schettler rushed past him and took her in his arms. "Thank God, Kate. Are you all right?"

"Yes, I am – I think," she said as they clung on to each other.

Frank Thornton came through the open door, accompanied by two other men, neither of whom was known to Kate.

"I think you'll find all this was his idea, Kate," Liam continued, pointing to Thornton.

Thornton wore his usual grin. "My idea, what do you mean, my idea?"

"It's fine, Liam. Frank explained the danger I might be in last night," Kate said.

Pat piped up. "If the job's done, I suggest we get out of here before the G men show up and it all starts again."

Kate looked at her brother. "Where are we going?"

"I'll explain that later. Pat's right, we have to get out of here fast."

He looked at the two men standing next to Thornton. "Right, John and Dan, can you go into that room and take Charlie out to the van, and be careful. He's badly hurt."

As the two men walked off Schettler turned in surprise. "What – do you mean Charlie Tennant?"

Liam nodded. "Sure I do, Ian. I'm afraid he's been shot. Let's get moving right now."

When they got to the street, Liam took his sister and Schettler to the car that had been used earlier to tail the Military Intelligence vehicle to their secret headquarters in the fruit warehouse. The others, including Tennant, went with Thornton in what turned out to be Murphy's van.

When the three got to the car, Schettler walked round and slipped into the back seat beside Kate. Looking at her in the faint light of the street outside, he could see she was crying. He took hold of her hand.

"I'm heart sore about Charlie. Why was he here?" Kate sobbed.

"He was in Ireland to warn me that Sinclair and his team were after me and we managed to get him to a safe house. But I don't understand why he was here tonight."

Liam spoke out from the driver's seat. "He was the only one who could identify Sinclair and Andrews. We needed to know it was them. If not, we might have been dealing with more than one group."

Schettler turned to look at Kate. His eyes were full of

emotion, boring into hers. He spoke urgently. "Listen, Kate, the reason this operation had to be done tonight is because one of my father's ships, the SS Norderney, is loading a cargo in Dublin docks. She sails tomorrow morning at five o'clock and I'm leaving with her. I want you to come with me and I want us to get married. What do you say?"

Kate made no reply until Liam retorted from the front seat, "Bejeesus, the man's just asked you to marry him. Are you not going to give him an answer?"

"Liam, the man asked me two questions. Am I going with him to Germany and the answer to that one is 'yes' because I'm not hiding out in some Dublin hovel on my own, waiting till it's safe to surface again. I'm thinking about the second question and for that one, I'll need time. If it's the docks you're taking us to, Liam, I suggest you better get going."

Schettler put his arms around her and he felt her snuggle into him. As Liam got out to start the car, she whispered, "Ach, I might just marry you, right enough, you eejit."

Schettler squeezed her tight. "Good. Perhaps we can get on with some painting then."

"I hope I've got the brains to learn to speak German." She sounded doubtful.

"If my mother could do it, so can you."

Liam parked the car at the bottom of the ship's gangway. They were getting cases, which had been packed for them earlier, out of the boot when another car's headlights came into view. Liam reached into his pocket, covering his gun. But when the car stopped, Michael Collins got out.

He walked across and shook Schettler's hand, then picked Kate up and kissed her on the cheek. "Ah, you two have done a fine job tonight. Frank Thornton's just phoned me to say it all went according to plan. Well, almost. I'm sorry your friend, Charlie, was shot. He's a brave man."

Schettler butted in, "Yes, Liam explained why but it's terrible he had to get shot in the process."

"I know you're probably not feelin' that good about what happened this night but all of you can be sure that you have done the cause of Irish Independence a great service. The British come here to destroy us and we have no alternative but to destroy them and we'll have to go on like this till they stop and give us what the Irish people want. I'm afraid things will get much worse before they finally get the message. Be happy in the knowledge that you have been part of this noble struggle."

He paused and sighed. "We'll get Charlie the best medical attention. There is no shortage of good doctors sympathetic to the cause."

Schettler nodded and Kate spoke up. "Listen, Michael, Charlie's engaged to Ian's cousin, Margaret. He has a phone number for her in Glasgow. Will you telephone her with the news and tell her we'll write to her soon from Germany."

Collins nodded. "That, I can do. We also have lots of loyal operatives in the post office telephones and I'd be honoured to do it." He took a notebook out of his pocket and Schettler recited the number.

Kate went over to Liam. "I'm glad to see you, Liam, even if it is for such a short time. Will you try to visit Michael some time? He worries about you."

She hugged and kissed him. A tear ran down his cheek.

"Oh God, Liam, don't. You'll get me started too." She turned and picked up her case from the wet cobbles and made for the gangway.

Schettler shook hands with the two men, lifted his case and followed Kate up the gangway. He got half way up when he heard Liam shout, "Just you see that you take care of me sister."

Reaching the top of the gangway the couple waved and Schettler shouted, "I'll make it my life's work, Liam."

"You'll do no such thing, Ian." Kate said, as walked away from the rail.

*

Six months later, a letter landed on the desk of the head of British Military intelligence in Ireland addressed to Thomas Sinclair now crossed out. It was from the German Admiralty saying that further to his last letter asking for information on Petty Officer Johann Schettler, he had been located in Bremen and had since been demobilised.

German revolution

Artelt, Karl – and Lothar Popp became the leaders of the sailors' mutiny in Kiel in November 1918. Artelt was the first to raise political demands and founded the first soldiers' council on 4 November 1918. As a representative of that council, he was asked by governor Souchon to meet him for negotiations. Artelt personally confronted those troops who came to quell the uprising and convinced them to either move back or to support the mutineers.

Hipper, Franz Ritter von – Rear Admiral –The Imperial German Navy. Appointed commander of the High Seas Fleet in 1918.

Liebknecht, Karl and Luxemburg, Rosa – were German socialists and co-founders of the Spartacus League and the Communist Party of Germany. Both were murdered by the Frei Corps in Berlin in January 1919.

Noske, Gustav – A politician of the SPD - served as the first Minister of Defence of the Weimar Republic between 1919 and 1920; mainly responsible for the military crushing of workers' uprisings at that time.

Popp, Lothar – Chairman of the Kiel USPD in 1918.

Souchon, Wilhelm Anton – Rear Admiral – Military Commander of Kiel in 1918.

Final Voyage and Internment
German

Dominik – Commodore – took charge of the interned fleet while Reuter was on home leave between December 1918 and January 1919.

Lessel, Johann von – Kapitän zur See – Commander of the **Friedrich der Grosse** until December 1918.

Reuter, Ludvig von – Rear-Admiral – Commander of the 74 ships of the High Seas Fleet interned at Scapa Flow between 26th November 1918 to 21st June 1919 when he gave the order for them to be scuttled.

Wachter von – Korvettenkapitän – First Officer then after December 1918, Commander of the Friedrich der Grosse.

British
Beatty, Sir David – Admiral – Commander-in-chief of the Grand Fleet in 1918.

Hodges, Michael – Commodore – Admiral Madden's Chief of Staff. He was the highest-ranking officer to board the Friedrich der Grosse in the Firth of Forth.

Scotland
Churchill, Winston – Secretary of State for War and Air in 1919.

Gallacher, Willie – Scottish trade unionist, activist and communist. He was one of the leading figures of the Shop Stewards' Movement in wartime Glasgow and a founding member of the Communist Party of Great Britain.

Kirkwood, David – a leading figure of Red Clydeside. However, his leadership was questioned by many of the activists of the time, especially those not members of the Labour Party.

McShane, Harry – a Scottish Socialist and a close colleague of John Maclean.

Maclean, John – notable for his outspoken opposition to the First World War, which caused his arrest under the Defence of the Realm Act and loss of his teaching post, after which he became a full-time Marxist lecturer and organiser. In April 1918 he was arrested for sedition. He was sentenced to five years' penal servitude, but was released after the November armistice. In captivity, Maclean had been on hunger strike, and prolonged force-feeding had permanently affected his health. He collapsed during a speech and died of pneumonia in November 1923, aged forty-four.

Maxton, Jimmy – a Scottish far-left politician, and leader of the Independent Labour Party. He was a pacifist who opposed both world wars.

Montefiore, Mrs Dorothy – leading suffragette and campaigner for womens' rights. Friend of John Maclean.

Shinwell, Emanuel – a British trade union official, Labour politician and one of the leading figures of Red Clydeside.

Stevenson, James Verdier – Chief Constable of the City of Glasgow Police during the strike for a 40-hour working week on 31th January 1919.

Stewart, Sir James Watson – Lord Provost of the City of Glasgow and Lord Lieutenant of the County of the City of Glasgow during the strike for a 40-hour working week on 31th January 1919.

Ireland

Collins, Michael – At the time of this story Collins had been appointed Minister of Finance and Director of Intelligence in the First Dáil Éireann.

Skinnider, Margaret – a revolutionary and feminist born in Coatbridge, Scotland. She fought during the 1916 Easter Rising in Dublin.

Molony, Helena – fought beside the men who attacked

Dublin Castle, during the Easter Rising. Later she became the second president of the Irish Trade Union Congress.

Markievicz, Constance – known as Countess Markievicz was an Irish Sinn Féin and Fianna Fáil politician, revolutionary nationalist, suffragette and socialist. She shot a policeman near St Stephen's Green during the Easter Rising.

BSP – British Socialist Party. Later it was absorbed into the Communist Party of Great Britain.

Chirsin – captured German trawler. It was armed by the British and used for guarding interned fleet at Scapa Flow.

Cumann na mBan – an Irish republican women's paramilitary organisation formed in Dublin on 2 April 1914. In 1916 it became an auxiliary of the Irish Volunteers. Many of its members fought valiantly during the Easter Rising.

Freikorps – was the name adopted by some right-wing nationalists who took up arms to fight against Socialism from the end of WW1 until 1923. Later many joined the Nazi Party.

G men – men of G division (Special Branch) of Dublin Metropolitan Police. Known for their ruthlessness against republicans.

German High Seas fleet – was the battle fleet of the Imperial German Navy and saw action during the First World War.

Germany's Economic situation during WW1 – Almost from the beginning of the war in 1914 Germany and Austria-Hungary had been cut off from crucial supplies of food from Eastern Europe by the hostilities with Russia and since 1916 this was exacerbated by the Allied naval blockade in the North Sea, which made it impossible to get ships carrying essential supplies into the country's northern ports. During 1917, it was estimated that 250,000 people had died of hunger in Germany and there were many strikes throughout the country. In January 1918 a coordinated General Strike was called. Fearful of this leading to revolution, the Government brutally crushed the strike, sentencing some of the ringleaders to death and others to long prison sentences or to fight on the western front and as 1918 continued nothing improved, for workers were still being underfed, underpaid and overworked.

Irish Citizens' Army – was a group of trained trade union volunteers from the Irish Transport and General Workers Union established in Dublin for the defence of worker's demonstrations from the police. It was formed by James Larkin, James Connolly and Jack White on 23 November 1913. In 1916 it took part in the Easter Rising - an armed insurrection aimed at ending British rule in Ireland.

IRA – Irish Republican Army. Formed in 1919. Paramilitary organisation.

IRB – Irish Republican Brotherhood. - Paramilitary organisation.

Jellicoe Express – The train from Inverness to Thurso which conveyed sailors to and from Scapa Flow - called after Admiral of the Fleet John Rushworth Jellicoe.

Kaiser Café – Café and bar in Kiel where forty five dead and wounded demonstrators were taken after they were sprayed by machine gun fire by troops loyal to the Keiser on Sunday 3rd November 1918.

KPD – German Communist party.

Maryhill Barracks – The Headquarters and barracks of Glasgow's own regiment the Highland Light Infantry (HLI).

Ombudsmen – a trade union representative of the Non-commissioned Officers and men of the Imperial German Navy. Although these representatives were unofficial they were tolerated on most ships during WW1. They ultimately became official.

Pinnace – a small boat forming part of the equipment of a warship.

RIC – Royal Irish Constabulary.

Red Clydeside – Is a generic term which covers the class struggle and political radicalisation in Glasgow and the surrounding areas on the River Clyde such as Clydebank, Greenock and Paisley from the Singer strike in 1911 to the General strike in 1926 and it covers famous occurrences such as the Rent Strike led by Mary Balfour in 1915 and the strike for a 40-hour week in January 1919, when the army was called in by the government to break the strike. This is known as the battle of George Square and is the incident covered in this book.

SPD – German Social Democratic Party.

Schillig Roads – The name given to the mouth of the bay of the river Jade leading to the city of Wilhelmshaven harbour.

Schillig Roads episode – took place on the 29th October 1918. As 27 capital ships of the Imperial German Navy's High Seas fleet gathered to await orders from their commander Admiral Franz von Hipper to sail to engage the British Grand fleet in battle for a final time. The high command's strategy was that as the German fleet was intact having never been beaten in battle a major engagement at this late stage of the war would add to the bargaining power of the Germans to seek better conditions for the forthcoming armistice regardless of its outcome. However, many of the ships' crews staged a mutiny against this course of action and although the mutiny was quickly crushed the action was cancelled. This had the effect of spreading the discontent more widely throughout the navy and in the next few days it would be the catalyst for the revolution and the setting up of many German Socialist Republics under Workers' and Soldiers' Councils. So although the mutiny had initially been brought under control, it had achieved its primary goal to foil High Command's plans to engage the enemy.

SC – Soldiers' Council.

Statue of Prince Albert – this statue was located across from the front entrance to the city chambers in Glasgow until it was moved in 1924, to make way for the cenotaph.

USPD – German Independent Socialist Party.

Vogeleiland – A small Island in the Werdersee.

Werdersee – Part of the river Weser in Bremen.

WSC – Workers' and Soldiers' Council.

GERMAN TRANSLATION

Bootsmann – Petty Officer

Glasgower Straße – Glaswegian Street in Berlin's Wedding district.

Glasgower – Glaswegian.

Hochschule für bildende Künste – The Hamburg University of Fine Arts.

Kapitän zur See – Naval Captain.

Korvettenkapitän – Lieutenant Commander.

Oberstabsbootsmannn – Chief Petty Officer.

Reichs Kriegshafen – Kiel Military Harbour.

Scheißhaus – Shit House.

Sophienblatt – Square outside the Station in Kiel circa 1918.

Staatsbahnhof – Central Station.

Unteroffizier – Non-Commissioned Officer.

BIBLIOGRAPHY

The author wishes to acknowledge the following books as the primary sources of historical reference used in writing this book.

All Power to the Councils. Edited and Translated by Gabriel Kuhn, The Merlin Press, 2012.
John Maclean, by Nan Milton, Pluto Press, 1973.
Michael Collins – A Life, by James Mackay, Mainstream Publishing, 1996.
No Mean Fighter by Harry McShane and Joan Smith – Pluto Press, 1978.
Scapa Flow – Vice-Admiral von Reuter – Hurst and Blackett, 1940.
The Lost Revolution, by Chris Harman, Bookmark Publications, 1982.
The Grand Scuttle, by Dan Van der Vat, Waterfront Communications, 1986.
The Mitchell Library Glasgow.

ACKNOWLEDGEMENTS

Many thanks must go to my wife, Anne, and good friends Dave Terrey, Penny Cole, Donald Christie, Emma Baird, and Ingo and Irma Schmidtborn, for their help and encouragement.
I would also like to thank Gordon Lawrie for his useful advice.